Main Chara

* Denotes real people.

*Maria Volkonsky. Daughter of war hero General Raevsky and most famous of the Decembrist wives.

*Prince Sergei Volkonsky. A member of one of the most illustrious families in Russia who became a Decembrist.

*Alexander Pushkin, the celebrated Russian poet. Sympathetic to the cause although he did not take part in the insurgency.

Anna Ivanova Brianski.; in love with Peter Dashkovy.

Alexander (Sasha) Ivanich Brianski, Anna's brother. A cavalry officer and Decembrist.

Sofia Yurievna Pavel, Anna's best friend, who marries Sasha Brianski.

Peter Igorovich Dashkovy. Sasha's senior officer and a leading figure in the revolution.

Michael Yurievich Pavel. Sofia's brother. A member of the Imperial Guard loyal to the tsar.

Count Nicholas Petrovich Bulgarin. Guardian to his sister, Olga.

Olga Petrovna Bulgarin. Anna's rival for Peter Dashkovy's love.

Boris Renin. Officer in the tsar's Imperial Guard.

The Rebel Daughters

Also by Cecil Cameron

An Italian Scandal

The Rebel Daughters

CECIL CAMERON

Harper North

HarperNorth
Windmill Green
24 Mount Street
Manchester M2 3NX

A division of
HarperCollins*Publishers*
1 London Bridge Street
London SE1 9GF

www.harpercollins.co.uk

HarperCollins*Publishers*
Macken House
39/40 Mayor Street Upper
Dublin 1
D01 C9W8

First published by HarperNorth in 2025

1 3 5 7 9 10 8 6 4 2

A catalogue record for this book
is available from the British Library

HB ISBN: 978-0-00-854090-6
Printed and bound in the UK using 100%
renewable electricity at CPI Group (UK) Ltd, Croydon

This novel is a work of fiction.
Some of the names, characters and incidents portrayed in
it are the work of the author's imagination.

This book contains FSC™ certified paper and other controlled
sources to ensure responsible forest management.

For more information visit: www.harpercollins.co.uk/green

"Twas all mere idle chatter
'Twixt Chateau Lafite and Veuve Clicquot,
Friendly disputes, epigrams,
Penetrating none too deep,
This science of sedition
– the fruit of boredom, of idleness,
The pranks of grown up naughty boys.'

Alexander Pushkin
1799–1837

'The human spirit shines brightest in
the darkest of times.'

Alexei Navalny 1976–2024

Part One

Chapter One

Russia, June 1823

It was the season of the *Beliye Nochi* when the sun never set and days slipped effortlessly into pearlescent nights. Water lapped the shore and the breeze stirred with excitement and promise. No one could sleep on a night like this. Tiny stars appeared, clusters of yellow in a paper sky. When you looked again, they were gone. The fleeting northern summer was a time of magic when the world was young. Anything was possible, every dream within reach, and in the summerhouse of Madame Davydov's garden, four young women were playing a game.

Anna Brianski was the youngest. She was slender and pretty, her face dominated by large dark eyes flecked with amber. A pair of arched eyebrows accented her sweeping dark eyelashes. She was fair-skinned with lips that curved upwards at the ends. It was an arresting face, a face open to the world, her thoughts and emotions playing over its delicate features. Her posture was demure but her eyes gave her away. They were eager, rebellious and passionate. For all her mother's training, Anna Brianski had reached the age of sixteen with the wilder side of her nature untamed.

A mane of tawny hair, arranged so carefully earlier, had escaped its pins and now fell untidily over her shoulders. Anna twisted a stray lock around her fingers. She had never played this game before. Would she win the knave of hearts? A small frown creased her forehead. Pray God the cards would be true to her tonight!

Into her mind crept the memory of last summer. Anna had been sitting on the front veranda reading a novel when Captain Dashkovy and her brother rode up to the house. She could see every detail as if it were yesterday. How handsome the men looked in their white uniforms and shining helmets, her dress with green ribbons and the book falling from her hands as the captain smiled at her. Anna had fallen in love with Peter Dashkovy before he dismounted from his horse. When he lifted her hand to his lips, she gazed into his blue eyes, speechless.

'The Second Life Guards are stationed at Strevinka, Anna.' Her brother Sasha, affectionate and teasing. 'Captain Dashkovy's billeted in our home. Please can you inform our parents that we've arrived?'

Anna had run so fast down the passage she tripped and bruised her knees. Picking herself up, she burst through the doors of the salon and startled her parents out of their chairs.

At dinner that night, Captain Dashkovy had remarked to Sasha in a voice loud enough for all to hear. 'Your sister's so pretty, I swear I'll marry her when she grows up.' Her parents laughed but Anna kept his words locked in her mind. Peter Dashkovy had stayed with them for a week, and in that time her life changed. Why he had captivated her so entirely, she did not know, but she had loved him ever since with all the violent passion in her young heart.

Beside Anna, her friend, Sofia Pavel, now reclined in a rocking chair. Everything about Sofia was delicate, from the bones of her wrists to her heart-shaped face and cloud of fair hair. There was shyness to her, a softness in her voice that belied the strength of her character. She had a habit of looking dreamily at the world through her grey eyes, but tonight her gaze was alert. Anna knew Sofia was fond of her brother. If Sofia's dreams came true, she would claim Sasha for her own.

Music for a polonaise floated down from the house and Maria Raevsky whispered, 'Before we begin, let me remind you of the rules.'

Maria was Madame Davydov's granddaughter. Unlike other members of her family, she was dark-haired with olive skin. Vivacious and beautiful, she was everyone's favourite. Last night, in a birthday concert for her grandmother, Maria had played a piece by Mozart on the piano.

As her small, strong fingers moved over the keys with hypnotic grace, both men and women in the audience raised handkerchiefs to their eyes.

'We'll each be dealt seven cards.' Maria spoke slowly. 'We then take turns to pick a card from the pile and discard one. Whoever has a queen wins the knave of that suit. If anyone claims the same knave three times, the man he represents will be her husband. Nine rounds will complete tonight's game. Do you all understand?'

A mist, fine as gauze, rose from the lake and the three girls nodded in silence.

'Then we shall begin.' Maria removed the knaves, cut the pack and gave it to Olga Bulgarin.

Olga had lost her parents to cholera as a child and was Maria's best friend. She was a rare beauty, with creamy white skin and ebony hair coiled in plaits around her head. A nosegay of jasmine was pinned to her bodice. Anna inhaled its sweet, heady fragrance. Olga was a year older and, along with Maria, would be presented at court next season. It was said she would conquer every heart with a single glance from her emerald-green eyes. Anna didn't care if every man in St. Petersburg fell in love with her – apart from one.

Olga shuffled the cards and glanced over her shoulder. Who was she looking for, Anna wondered? Guests were assembled at the dacha for the ball in honour of Madame Davydov's birthday. The girls were too young to attend, but Olga could have stayed up at the house. Why join in their game – unless she had a favourite among the knaves? Could it be Prince Sergei Volkonsky? He was a younger son of one of the most illustrious families in Russia. Had Olga set her cap at him? Volkonsky's name had been mentioned in connection with Maria, but that wouldn't deter her. Beneath the sensuous languor, the fighting blood of the Tatars ran in her veins and Olga was ambitious.

The cards were passed round for inspection and Anna's heart missed a beat as she touched the knave of hearts. She closed her eyes a moment before she passed him on. The next card was the knave of clubs for Prince Volkonsky, then black spades for Nicholas Bulgarin. She had met Olga's brother once and quickly handed the card to Sofia. Smiling, she looked down at Sasha in his suit of diamonds.

The knaves were put to one side and Olga dealt the cards, placing the remaining pack face down on the table. Maria took the top card. She deliberated a moment and then rejected it. Anna followed and collected an ace. A tiny sigh escaped her lips. She held the queen of spades and needed a king to discard her. Every card she picked up, she was disappointed.

As they finished the fourth round, Olga held up her hand. 'I have the queen of hearts and claim my knave.'

She spoke softly, her heavy-lidded eyes half closed, and Anna felt her mouth turn dry. Surely, she was mistaken? Olga needed clubs for Prince Volkonsky – not hearts for Peter! Without bothering to pick up her knave, she tossed the black queen onto the table.

Daylight still glowed through the trees and the game continued. Once more, Olga claimed hearts; once again, Anna won spades, while Maria took clubs. Sofia hadn't won a single knave, but Anna was too flustered to notice. No one must suspect that she cared and she smiled rigidly until her jaw ached with the effort. When they came to the last round she could hardly bear to look. Olga won the knave of hearts outright and glanced at Anna.

'The cards say Captain Dashkovy will be mine.' A smile curved her velvety lips. 'The perfect match, wouldn't you agree?'

Anna swallowed her breath and choked. She fumbled in her sleeve for a handkerchief and held it over her mouth. A nightingale began its plaintive song as Maria gathered up the cards.

'So, who do you want as a husband, Maria?' Olga stood up, scooping her bag off the table. 'Will you marry a poet or a prince?'

'I want to marry a man who is faithful. A poet's obliged to fall in love with every pretty woman he meets.'

The older girls linked arms as they walked ahead to the house, Maria's inky hair cascading down her back and Olga with the sinuous movement of a gypsy. Anna felt her corset chafing at her ribs and her shoes pinching her feet. Olga was as unfathomable as the universe. What was her purpose this evening? She didn't even know Peter Dashkovy! Why make a song and dance about someone she'd never met? Has she found out that I love him, she wondered? Did she deliberately want to upset me? How could she be so cruel?

Her hands felt cold as Anna stopped to wait for Sofia. Her friend had suffered rheumatic fever as a child, causing weakness in her lungs, and she walked slowly.

When she caught up, Anna's lip trembled and Sofia asked, 'What's the matter with you tonight?'

'Olga fixed the cards! I know she did.'

'Don't be silly. Why should she do such a thing?'

'Because she always has to win.'

Sofia shrugged and walked on past the cascade of fountains that divided the garden. How had Olga arranged it, Anna wondered? Her bag had been lying on the table. She must have come down earlier and hidden extra queens beneath it. Sofia's too kind, she thought. It's unwise always to think the best of people.

'I bet you'd be suspicious if she'd won the knave of diamonds,' Anna said.

'I wouldn't mind. Lucky in cards, unlucky in love, you know what they say, Anna. It's only a game. You shouldn't take it so seriously.'

Plumes of lilac shivered in the breeze, their scent cloaking the air as the girls climbed the steps to the house. Anna drew her shawl about her shoulders. She always felt better when she was with Sofia. Playing cards couldn't predict the future and Russians were too superstitious. You couldn't move without breaking some taboo that had been drummed into you since birth. If your right eye itched, then good luck was on the way – if the left, misfortune awaited. Never break bread with your hands – use a knife or ruin the rest of your life. And pray no black bird lands on your windowsill. God forbid it taps on the glass with its beak! If you boast of future happiness, your dreams will turn to dust...

Why hadn't she thought of the last one before? The tender blue sky and peaceful night quietened Anna's heart. Sofia was right. Lucky in cards, unlucky in love. It was silly to have been upset, for she had nothing to fear. Olga Bulgarin would never marry Peter Dashkovy.

Chapter Two

Kamenka, the country home of the Davydov family, was a sprawling dacha with a wide balcony and front door that opened onto a shadowy hall. The other girls had gone to bed but Anna was too wide-awake to sleep.

'Let's walk once around the house before we go up. Please, Sofia! It will only take ten minutes.'

Sofia hesitated but Anna took her hand, pulling her along towards the sound of the music. They stopped outside the ballroom where the windows were open and guests were lining up on the dance floor for a quadrille. Candles in sconces threw shimmering light onto dresses of floating silk, evening coats and military regimentals. Ladies who were sitting out fanned themselves while gentlemen conversed in small groups, occasionally glancing in the mirror and adjusting their cravats as they awaited their turn.

At the far end of the ballroom, Madame Davydov was seated on a throne-like chair. She was a tall, handsome woman with steel-grey hair pinned beneath a sapphire tiara. Attached to her voluminous robes was an enormous brooch bearing the initials of the former empress. Anna stared at her. To think she had once been lady-in-waiting to Catherine the Great! Surrounded by a court of friends and relatives, Madame Davydov looked grand enough to be an empress herself. She was a niece of General Potemkin and a woman of some importance. Anna knew Maria adored her warm-hearted *babushka*. She watched as a young man, presumably one of her relations, leant down to whisper in her ear. The lady burst into a peel of deep-throated laughter.

The orchestra began to play a waltz and Anna looked around the ballroom for Peter Dashkovy. He wasn't on the floor, but her brother, Sasha, was dancing with a raven-haired beauty. Sofia must have seen him too, for she lifted her skirt and walked on. Apart from the ballroom, the ground floor was in darkness until they came to the billiard room windows where oil lamps were burning. Anna peeped in past the shutters, then hastily drew back, pulling Sofia out of sight. She put a finger to her lips before she poked her head round again.

Peter Dashkovy and Nicholas Bulgarin were seated across an unlit hearth. Her gaze passed briefly over Bulgarin and settled on Peter Dashkovy. How many times had she drawn him from memory? Whole sketchbooks were filled with his image, but not one of them did him justice. Peter was even more handsome than she remembered. His wide-apart eyes and broad forehead reminded her of the classical statues she studied for her art. Lamplight shone on his blonde curls as he sat with elbows on his knees, the tips of his fingers brushing his clipped moustache. Peter had the strong hands of a soldier. Anna imagined them holding her face.

There was a knock at the door and a footman entered with a bottle and glasses on a tray. As he went out, Peter stood up and poured two shots of vodka. His back was turned and Anna glanced at Nicholas Bulgarin. With his jet-black hair and high cheekbones, he was as different from Peter as anyone could be. Thick lashes shaded his eyes so their colour was hard to define — they could be blue or green. He was clean-shaven and his mouth finely carved, the middle of his upper lip forming a wedge that closed firmly on the lower one. This, together with his drowsy eyes, gave an impression of sensuality that reminded Anna of his sister.

She knew Count Bulgarin had been one of the young men who'd accompanied the tsar to Paris after Napoleon's defeat. He had been rewarded with honours and a white imperial star was pinned to his dress coat. Half of St. Petersburg and Moscow were his relatives or friends, yet he gave the impression few people were worthy of his attention. He was undeniably good-looking, but his features were marred by an expression of bored condescension that annoyed Anna. Nicholas Bulgarin wasn't the only war hero staying at Kamenka. What made him think he was superior to everybody else?

Peter Dashkovy said something and Bulgarin leant forwards, listening attentively. Anna strained to hear what he was saying.

'Serfdom is Russia's national disgrace! When Napoleon was defeated, we believed that slavery would end in our country. How can we tolerate a society where our own people are bought and sold like cattle?'

'You may free all the serfs, but how will they live? What will they own?' Bulgarin replied. 'Russia needs a new economic system and a constitution before serfdom can be abolished.'

This was strange talk. Anna and her friends were not encouraged to involve themselves in politics, affairs of state were the preserve of gentlemen, but she was curious. Last week, when she went to look for Sasha in his room, she had spotted a manuscript on his desk. A sheet of paper lay across the page. Moving it aside, she'd bent to read the small print.

'A body flayed, an ankle chained,
The useless tears of slavery,
The law perverted and profaned—'

Sasha had interrupted her at that moment. He gave no explanation, picked up the book and put it in a drawer. Anna had resisted the temptation to question him, but she had not forgotten.

'We do not fear death on the battlefield — yet are unable to speak out in favour of justice.' Peter's voice broke into her thoughts. 'Tsar Alexander promised us a constitution. How much longer must we wait?'

'Peter Igorovich, you know that nothing changes in this vast empire except by slow and cautious steps. Habit is everything to a Russian—'

'Then habit must be broken! Did we free Europe from tyranny to be kept in chains ourselves? Did we gain pre-eminence among nations to be humiliated in our own country?'

Peter's face was taut, the anger in him palpable. Anna had never heard him sound so passionate and gazed at him in awe as he went on. 'We believed our tsar was an enlightened ruler – and we were wrong. Alexander has turned his back on freedom and equality. We have no alternative but to take action.'

'Listen to me, my friend.' Bulgarin's voice dropped low. 'I urge you to petition the tsar before embarking on any such adventure or your dreams will end in Siberia—'

He broke off as the door opened and Sasha Brianski walked in. Her brother was of medium height, her brother was five years older than Anna, tall with a springing step and muscular physique, fair hair and a drooping moustache. He made a fine figure of a soldier, she thought proudly, before her attention was diverted by the man who followed.

After the tsar, Alexander Pushkin was the most famous person in Russia. The poet was dressed in a tailored frock coat with a tartan sash draped over one shoulder, his cravat tied a la Byron. Anna was struck immediately by the piercing blue of his eyes and his impudent stare as he shook hands with the two other men.

Pushkin was not tall, barely shoulder height to the others and incapable of staying still. He seated himself, then almost at once stood up and began pacing up and down, talking and gesticulating with his hands. He had a wild reputation in St. Petersburg. There were stories of outbursts at the theatre, love affairs and duels, but Anna had read his poem 'Ruslan and Ludmila' and the beauty of his verse made her heart sing. The poet was a burning torch, aflame with so much creativity she felt he might set alight anything he touched. Her fingers itched for pen and paper. She must draw him! If she could just capture a small measure of his dazzling personality, she would be happy. I'll ask Maria to arrange a sitting, she thought. Was it true that Pushkin had declared love to her and she turned him down?

Anna felt Sofia touch her arm. The atmosphere in the room had changed and was crackling with animosity between Dashkovy and Pushkin. The two men were talking over each other so that it was impossible to hear what they were saying. Then Pushkin threw his arms in the air.

'I believed my existence had a high and noble purpose!' he exclaimed. 'Now I see it was nothing but a cruel and malicious joke. I've never been more humiliated, more unhappy in my life!'

There were tears in his eyes as he stormed out of the room. With a click of his heels and dip of his head to his senior officers, Sasha followed him.

Anna leant towards Sofia, confounded. 'What on earth was that about?'

'Pushkin's a friend of the Davydov family but some people here don't trust him. They call him an irresponsible, babbling youth.'

'But he's Russia's foremost genius—'

'A genius exiled from St. Petersburg for his incendiary verses. Madame Davydov may entertain whoever she wants — the tsar would never move against her — but it's different for other people.'

Nicholas Bulgarin closed the door and returned to his chair. Peter filled a Turkish pipe and bent his neck to light the tobacco. Captain Dashkovy had impeccable manners. Anna had never heard him be rude to anyone. What could he have said to so offend Pushkin? A curl of smoke escaped his handsome mouth and she cast the question aside. Peter was no more than four paces away. She could almost reach through the window and touch him. She longed to feel his arms round her and his lips on her mouth.

'We must go up now, Anna. It's past midnight.'

Sofia's voice floated across her consciousness. Anna wanted to stay but her friend was tugging at her sleeve. Reluctantly, she dragged her eyes away from Peter. As she did, she caught Nicholas Bulgarin looking at her through the open window. There was an ironic, inquisitive glint in his eyes, and she felt her cheeks turn crimson. How long had he been watching her? Could he tell from her expression what she was thinking?

A knowing smile played at the corners of his mouth and Anna's temper began to rise. Her love for Peter Dashkovy was the most beautiful thing in the world. A man like Nicholas Bulgarin could never understand such an emotion. How dare he assume he understood what was in her heart? A surge of dislike swept through her. For a long moment, she stared back at him, scowling. Then she stuck out her tongue and ducked beneath window ledge, before running after Sofia.

Chapter Three

Anna woke up late the next morning. Sofia had already gone from the bedroom, but she was in no hurry. Nicholas and Olga Bulgarin were leaving today and she wanted to make sure they had gone before she went down. What had possessed her last night? Not only had she accused Olga of cheating, she had then acted like a child eavesdropping on the gentlemen.

The memory made her cringe. Mama would be appalled. Thank heavens she wasn't here. Her mother despaired of her unruly behaviour. Too often her thoughts were elsewhere, deep in a book or contemplating a painting she had in mind. Papa loved her spontaneity, but Mama was more critical. She rebuked her for moving too fast, interrupting conversations and speaking without thinking. If Valentina Brianski ever heard what happened last night, Anna would never be allowed to go anywhere again.

But Count Bulgarin was older than her and it was unlikely she would run into him again. There was no point in worrying, Anna decided, her natural optimism asserting itself. Lila, the maid she shared with Sofia, had given up waiting, so she chose a simple muslin gown with a wide yellow ribbon. The dress slipped on easily but the buttons down the back were more difficult. Twisting and turning in front of the mirror and using a buttonhook, she'd managed to get most of them done up as the clock in the stable-yard chimed twelve.

It was later than she realised. Where had she left her new Moroccan slippers? After a frantic search, Anna found them at the back of the wardrobe. She ran a comb through her hair, tucked it loosely under a linen bonnet, then collected her parasol and hurried out to the main staircase.

'Good morning, Anna Ivanova. Or should I say good afternoon?'

Anna was halfway down the stairs and Peter Dashkovy was standing in the hallway. The light streamed through the doorway behind, skimming around him so that his body was outlined by a thread of darkness, and all she could see were rays of sunshine turning his hair gold. He was alone and she stared at him over the banisters, gripping the rail to steady herself.

'The houseguests have gone on ahead. I'm here to escort you to the picnic.'

Peter smiled, the lazy smile she loved, and Anna slowly let out her breath. Then, not taking her eyes off him, she continued on down. 'How kind of you, Captain Dashkovy. I'm sorry to have kept you waiting.'

As Peter led the way through the hall and down the steps to the garden, Anna rested the handle of her parasol on her shoulder. The lawns were scattered with buttercups and daises, but she barely noticed her surroundings. Her heart was fluttering wildly as thoughts dashed around her head. Peter had been waiting for her! He was worried that she was late. Everyone at the picnic would see them arrive together. What would they think?

'You've grown up this last year, dear Anna. Are you enjoying yourself?'

Anna nodded and touched the verbena sachet in her pocket. She wished she had done up her hair and chosen a prettier dress. This was the first time she had ever been alone with Peter. She mustn't spoil it by saying something stupid. They walked in silence until Peter remarked, 'Miss Bulgarin asked me to convey her best wishes to you and say goodbye. Her brother insisted they depart directly after breakfast. Poor Olga. It's a shame she had to miss the final celebrations.'

'Have you been acquainted with the Bulgarin family for long?' Anna tried to make her voice indifferent.

'Nicholas Bulgarin was a colonel when I joined the Hussars. I only met Miss Olga two days ago. And you?'

'I know her through my friendship with Maria. The two of them are inseparable.'

'Except when Monsieur Pushkin's paying court to one or the other,' Peter observed unemotionally. 'The young whippersnapper's incorrigible when it comes to the ladies.'

'Alexander Pushkin's a poet, sir. Women are his inspiration.' What did she know about a poet's inspiration? Anna could have bitten off her tongue. She sounded pretentious and wished Peter hadn't mentioned Olga. He was waiting for me — for *me* — she reminded herself and turned to him. 'I've always admired Pushkin's poetry.'

'He's talented but an excitable fellow. Have you met him or Count Bulgarin?'

'I'm going to ask Maria for an introduction to Monsieur Pushkin, but I've no desire to meet Count Bulgarin. I'm sure we have nothing in common. What's your opinion of him?'

'We don't always agree, but I admire him. He's an acquired taste — for some, too self-opinionated for their palates.'

'Indeed! I was impressed by his conceit.'

'Really? And when was that?'

Thankfully, there was no chance to answer for they had arrived at the picnic. A throng of people were gathered on the lawn where Madame Davydov was seated in an armchair brought down from the house. Catching sight of them, she called out,

'Where've you been all this time, Captain Dashkovy? I was afraid you'd fallen under the spell of those wicked Bulgarins and been spirited away.'

'Sasha Brianski asked me to escort his sister to the picnic. Prince Repnin insisted on taking him and Prince Volkonsky on a tour of the island.'

'Your chivalry is beyond reproach.' Madame Davydov favoured Peter with a smile before she screwed up her eyes and turned to Anna. 'Miss Brianski's beauty is fair recompense for your labour.' Her hostess extended a gloved hand and touched Anna's cheek. 'How are your parents? I'm sorry they were unable to accept my invitation.'

Anna wasn't sure how to answer. She didn't know why her parents disapproved of Madame Davydov, but it had taken a letter from Maria to persuade them to let her accept. As she hesitated, a stiff-looking young man, obviously irked by the delay, made a show of opening his fob watch.

'Do put that thing away, Gaston!' Madame Davydov scolded. 'Since when has punctuality been a prerequisite for a picnic? Everyone may start whenever they wish.'

Long trestle tables, draped in fine linen cloths, stood under the thick shade of trees with benches on either side and hampers of food unpacked onto plates. Footmen moved between the guests, carrying silver trays, bowing and smiling as they served champagne in long-stemmed glasses. Older women sat in chairs while others stood around or sat on cushions from the house scattered about on the grass.

Peter was taken aside by a stout gentleman and Anna looked around for her friends. It seemed the whole island had been invited to the picnic. Anna caught sight of the Lenkov brothers with their sister, Anastasia. The Lenkovs were all good-looking and fine horsemen. Anastasia was the eldest and famous for her dashing exploits but too charming for anyone to disapprove. Today her glossy red hair was hidden under a turban and she wore Turkish trousers rather than a dress.

Her brother, John, was the same age as Anna and usually timid with girls. He had sat next to her at the concert, and she was surprised when he moved his chair close to her own. She had felt his eyes on her throughout, but John Lenkov aroused none of the passion she felt for Peter. He was a sensible, pleasant young man but she avoided his gaze until Sofia came over and took her to where Maria was seated on a hassock surrounded by friends.

'Why didn't you wake me up?' Anna whispered. 'I'm mortified to be so late.'

'You're not ... mortified.' Sofia retorted with a mischievous grin.' You look like the cat that's licked the cream.'

'I gather Captain Dashkovy was only too happy to take Sasha's place,' Maria added. 'I don't know what happened last night but poor Monsieur Pushkin has taken to his bed. Babushka's sent him caviar and vodka to ensure he recovers in time for the fireworks. She wants this to be a day all of us will remember.'

And indeed, it was. Madame Davydov's hospitality was legendary. There were *zakuski* – bites of pickled salmon with truffles and wafer-thin *blini* pancakes piled high with caviar and served with different flavoured vodkas. Borsch soup was laced with soured cream and followed by sturgeon and cold meats accompanied by green vegetables and salad. In pride of place at the centre of the table stood an iced birthday cake three tiers high.

Guests began to help themselves, but Anna scarcely touched her food. She found a seat near Sofia and nibbled on a biscuit as her eyes wandered over the company. Stately matrons sat under an arbour, their heads close and voices hushed as they exchanged gossip. The day was melting with heat, and formal wear had been abandoned. Open-necked shirts replaced frock coats and cravats were loosened or discarded. Officers in uniform unbuttoned their tunics, and Peter was standing by the water's edge wearing a patterned waistcoat and ruffled shirt.

Light from the sea and sun made the colours dance with brilliance. Under a cloudless sky, the girls were bright as butterflies in summer dresses with open parasols fluttering in the breeze. It was a scene to be painted – but not today. Today Anna could think only of Peter. She imagined him close to her and repeated his name in her head. Peter Igorovich Dashkovy.

At that moment Peter looked round, his eyes roaming over the guests until he saw her. He smiled and Anna felt a jolt of lightning pass between them. Peter must have felt it too for he turned away quickly and began talking to one of his friends. He does love me, Anna thought excitedly. I haven't yet attended my first Bal Blanc – that's the only reason he's keeping his distance. It wouldn't do for him to appear over-attentive. When all the guests have gone and we're finally alone, he'll come and find me. We'll walk together in the cool of the evening. Will he make some kind of declaration? The thought made her feel giddy. It will be our secret — a sacred pact between us — until I'm old enough for him to propose. I won't tell a soul, not even Sofia.

Anna watched as Anastasia Lentov walked over and engaged Peter in conversation. She said something that made him laugh and a sliver of doubt pierced Anna. Two years was an eternity away. Oh, if only she were eighteen already! Peter might fall in love with someone like Anastasia in the meantime. What would she do then? Anna resolutely drove the idea from her mind. With the supreme confidence of youth, she told herself it would never happen. Their destiny was written in the stars and in two years' time she would be his bride.

Part Two

Chapter Four

Two years later. St. Petersburg, October 1825

'You must dance the waltz tonight, Papa! I am going to teach you the steps.' Anna held Mr Wilson's instruction book in one hand, the other stretched towards to her father. 'I'm informed the waltz is all the rage in England and France.'

'You're informed, are you? Well, may I remind you that we live in St. Petersburg and not London or Paris? I've no time for indecorous familiarity. You should be content with the polonaise and quadrille.'

'Are you going to spoil poor Sofia's party?' Anna pouted her pretty mouth. 'Oh, Papa, how can you be such a misery?'

'Please don't concern yourself on my behalf–'Sofia began before Count Brianski interrupted.

'My dear Sofia, you're now Sasha's responsibility, while Anna remains under my supervision. I shall decide with whom she may – and with whom she may not – perform the waltz'.

'So, you're going to be horribly strict and ruin my evening.'

A mischievous smile crossed Anna's face. She had a knack of manipulating her father and getting her way. Sofia and Sasha had been married a month ago and a reception was to be held in their honour this evening. Musicians were hired and Anna had already spoken to Monsieur Filot, manager of her father's affairs, and asked him to instruct them to play a waltz between every other dance.

'If you won't join in, Papa, then I'll have to be the man. Come on, Sofia! Put your hand on my shoulder. Take no notice of the old bear!'

Anna put the book down and placed her arm round Sofia's waist. 'One, two, three. One, two, three... Keep your arm straight. No dipping...'

The small salon was crammed with furniture and the two young women manoeuvred awkwardly between tables and chairs. When Count Brianski finally left the room, they collapsed on a sofa in giggles.

'Indecorous familiarity!' Anna said when she could speak at last. 'Isn't that the whole point of the dance?'

'My parents are more strait-laced than yours. Thank heavens they've returned to Moscow. Maman would have a fit!'

'Sasha will permit you to waltz, won't he?'

'I hope so – but he insists I dance with him and he's not fond of waltzing.'

'Lord above, I'm quite put off the idea of marriage.' Fresh laughter burst from Anna. 'I'll never marry, if waltzing is prohibited. Life wouldn't be worth living.'

Autumn had come early that year and the windows were sealed against the cold and damp. The scent of lilies was overpowering and when Sofia sneezed, not once but three times, Anna jumped up.

'I'll ask Mama to have the flowers taken downstairs. We can't have you sneezing and coughing all evening. I'll see to it at once.'

Anna hurried out of the room. Hearing her parents' voices, she stopped at the top of the staircase and saw them on the landing below.

'You spoil her, Vanya! You were far stricter with Sasha. Anna gets away with murder because she reminds you of your mother.'

'That's not true!'

'How else does she have the impertinence to give Filot instructions for the musicians? He came to see me and I put him right. Oh dear... why can't Anna be like other young women?'

'Because our daughter's an artist, and artists cannot be regimented. Her tutor says she has the talent to become an academician.'

'The only talent Anna needs is to be a good wife.'

Her mother's frustration puzzled Anna. Valentina Brianski belonged to a generation disciplined to always show restraint and ran the household with calm efficiency. She rarely showed emotion and only cried when she was happy. Why should such a trifling matter upset her? What harm could there be in a few extra waltzes? Anna was usually cheerful and wanted everyone around her to be the same. She was about to go down and apologise when the front doorbell rang and James, the footman, ushered an elderly couple into the vestibule. Anna recognised her grandmother's old friends. She would have to apologise later, she decided, and made her way to the basement by the back staircase.

The Brianski house, like all grand houses in the city, was a spacious building with a large front courtyard. Two elegant salons, a dining room, her father's library, and the orangery were on the first floor, with the morning room and bedrooms above. Situated close to the fashionable Nevsky Prospekt, the Brianskis entertained at least three days a week and the basement was a labyrinth of domestic activity. There were two kitchens, three pantries, a wine cellar, laundries and storerooms. Outside, in the large back courtyard, was situated the wooden *banya* for bathing. The stables were further away next to a small yard occupied by chickens and pigs.

Anna knew her way round every inch and walked quickly down the passage to the silver pantry where she found Josef, the head footman. She asked him to dispatch two pages to remove the lilies from the small salon. Please could they also take up a bowl of fruit for her painting? Then she hurried back, collecting her portfolio on the way.

But the time she arrived in the salon, the flowers had gone and Sofia was sitting by the window, working on her tapestry. Anna arranged the fruit in a bowl with a pineapple balanced on the top. She collected ink, water and paper, and sat down with her back to the light. As she leafed through her sketchbook, her eye fell on her studies of Alexander Pushkin.

She never did discover the cause of the argument at Kamenka. Pushkin had sat for her the day after the picnic and she had to draw fast so there was no time for conversation. The poet was restless, fidgeting in his chair, crossing and uncrossing his legs. When a new thought came to him, his expression altered dramatically so that it was impossible to get a true representation in a single study. In the end, Anna had decided to make a series of thumbnail sketches to work up later. In one, the poet was lost in thought, his brow furrowed as he chewed a blade of grass; in another, smiling as he related an amusing anecdote. Sometimes, he was lost in concentration, his eyes fixed on one point in a vacant stare, and in others, like a tormented soul, grimacing with his chin in his hands.

Anna studied his dark skin, his long nose and full lips. She drew the intensity of his blue eyes, his black hair and the claw-like nails of which he was so proud. Pushkin was in exile so she had sent a drawing to him at his mother's home in Pvosk. A reply was delivered within a fortnight. Pushkin wrote that he was devastated to learn that Maria Raevsky was engaged to Prince Volkonksy. He vowed he would never recover – but Alexander Pushkin was a poet with talent for exaggeration. Women all over Russia were in love with him and Anna suspected he wouldn't be heartbroken for long.

Maria Raevsky had been married the year before and returned to St. Petersburg with her son a month ago. She was living in the Volkonksy palace overlooking the Moika canal, and Anna and Sofia had called on her last week. Despite its grandeur, Anna found the house gloomy and ostentatious. Its atmosphere was so different from the Raevsky family home, she wondered how Maria could stand it.

The Volkonskys had been powerful boyars and every room was hung with family portraits. They were well-painted, proud aristocrats without a friendly face among them – and the coldest of them all was Sergeí's mother. The dowager princess had joined them for tea, dressed in a bulky kaftan over layers of goose down. As Maria poured tea from a steaming samovar, she beadily observed the young women over her lorgnettes.

'I hope you girls take plenty of exercise. I've no time for delicate creatures too feeble to endure our St. Petersburg climate.'

The old dragon went on to denounce open wood fires and pretty tiled stoves – the very same that kept the Brianski house cheerful and warm. Did they know that she had been First Lady of the Bedchamber to the dowager empress and was a close confidante of the present tsar? Of course they knew. How could they not, when all of St. Petersburg was constantly reminded of the fact?

Poor Mashenka... Anna sighed as she began the outline of her drawing. Maria had been the most exuberant of them all at Kamenka. Now, her wardrobe overflowed with furs and her jewellery box was crammed with gems but the laughter had gone from her eyes. Was she unhappy? Did she love her husband? Certainly not in the way Sofia was in love with Sasha – or how she loved Peter Dashkovy.

There had been no chance to speak to Peter after the picnic. Anna hadn't seen him again until after they returned to St. Petersburg and then not as often as she had hoped. When he visited, it was usually when Sasha was at home and she was able to study him from a distance. Everything about him was precious. She loved the way he moved and the sound of his voice. When he was near, she was enveloped in warm glowing happiness; without him, her world was dormant and cold.

Despite the devastating floods of last winter, her first season had been a success and Anna received two proposals of marriage. Both were summarily dismissed, for her mind was made up. Mama had sighed a great deal and Papa urged her to reconsider, but Anna took no heed. She would only marry the man she loved. There wasn't a ball last summer when Peter had not led her onto the dance floor, and she didn't understand his reticence to propose. Two years ago, she had been so sure of him. Still, he had hardly left her side during Sasha and Sofia's wedding. She was certain he would say something then, but he uttered not a word.

Did he still love her? Anna never saw in his eyes the hot, eager light she recognised in her other admirers. Peter was always courteous, and she wondered if his restraint was deliberate. He didn't openly flirt with her – though how could he when they were rarely left alone together? Peter was a mature man. He would have found a way, instinct told Anna, but he hadn't called at the house for weeks. Suppose – it was a terrible thought – suppose he had fallen in love with someone else?

Anna looked across the room to her sister-in-law, her slender neck bent as she threaded her needle. 'Has Captain Dashkovy spoken to Sasha recently?'

'They talk to each other all the time. Why?'

'I'm surprised we haven't seen him here lately.'

'Don't say you still carry a torch for him?'

The pitying look in Sofia's eyes made Anna lose concentration. A drop of ink slipped from her pen onto the paper and her drawing was ruined. She would have to cut out the page, but she didn't care. There's no such thing as still life anyway, she thought. Life is never still. It's always moving, changing from one minute to the next. To catch the essence of a fleeting moment — that's the skill of the artist.

'How did you make Sasha fall in love with you?' she asked as she reached for a paper knife.

'I didn't make him fall in love with me. It just happened.'

'But you loved him for ages before. You must have done something!'

'Darling Anna, are you so innocent of men?' Sofia drew her wool down through the canvas, studying the pattern. 'You must encourage them but not appear too eager. Respect is more important than coquetry.'

As Anna removed the ink-stained page and tossed it in the basket, a thought struck her so suddenly she gasped. Perhaps, Peter doesn't know that I love him? Since Kamenka, I've taken for granted he understands how I feel, but I've never said anything or had a chance to show him. He's afraid to ask me in case I refuse. That's why he hasn't proposed. He doesn't want to put me in a difficult position.

Anna was so absorbed, the thud of an explosion made her jump. The next moment the doors opened and Sasha walked in. Her brother was in his Hussars uniform and must have come straight from barracks.

'What was that noise? Is the city under attack?' Anna's heart was racing.

'There was a fire at headquarters. It's under control now, apart from a few barrels of gunpowder we didn't manage to salvage.' Sasha bent over Sofia and kissed the top of her head. 'I've come to take my darling wife for a drive.'

'How kind you are, dearest.' Sofia looked at her husband with a smile that lit up her face.

'Please be careful!' Anna interjected.' You could be blown to pieces.'

'Don't you trust me, Anna?' Sasha grinned and put his arm round Sofia's shoulders. 'You know I'd never put my beloved in harm's way.'

He's just like Mama, Anna thought. The roof could blow off and Sasha wouldn't turn a hair. He's always been the sensible, responsible one, helping me out of trouble and making excuses for me. She smiled and her voice softened. 'I hope you enjoy yourselves, but don't get cold.'

When Sofia and Sasha left, Anna stood up and walked over to the window. She loved this city with its wide avenues and bridges over misty canals. She loved its mystery and charm, the river Neva shining in the sun, its islands still clad in rippling green. Her gaze was familiar with the fine buildings on the waterside, the mansions belonging to nobility and the English Line where a colony of British merchants lived and worked. As her eye passed over familiar landmarks, she saw Peter's face everywhere, his eyes as blue as the summer sky.

I can only be myself, she thought. I'm no good at acting a part. Somehow, I must let Peter know I love him. If I don't, I might lose him. He's coming this evening. Shall I write to him like Tatyana in Pushkin's latest poem? He's a better man than Eugene Onegin. Peter will never break my heart.

Omelko, the head coachman, could take a letter to the regimental barracks that afternoon, Anna decided; then changed her mind. If Mama and Papa found out, they would be horrified. She must think of a way to speak with Peter in private. She racked her brains until an idea flashed into her head. She would ask him to sit for his portrait! No one was allowed to disturb her when she was working. It would give them a chance to be together without the family breathing down their necks.

A north-facing bedroom had been converted into a studio and Anna pictured the scene, Peter seated in the leather armchair as she stood at the easel. She imagined his expression when she confessed her love for him, his beautiful smile as he took her in his arms. What would it feel like when he kissed her? She thought of him pulling her up on tiptoes, pressing his lips to hers, and a shiver ran through her entire body. Be careful, warned a voice in her head. Let Peter speak first. But what if he doesn't declare himself? What do I do then? I'll tell him I envy Sasha and Sofia's happiness, Anna decided; that will give him the opening he needs.

Suddenly it was all so simple Anna couldn't think why the idea hadn't occurred to her before. She laughed aloud with happiness and then checked herself. Don't anticipate future contentment. Wait for good luck to tap you on the shoulder. The old taboos lingered. Only one person had refused to believe in them: Nan Maree, her Scottish grandmother. Despite being married to a Russian for fifty years, she insisted to the end that they were old wives' tales based on fear and ignorance.

'Your future lies in your own hands.' Anna remembered her lilting Highland accent. 'Depend on no one but yourself and ignore those superstitious old women.'

Nan Maree was born in Scotland and came to St. Petersburg with other exiled Jacobites at the time of Catherine the Great. She had been educated during the Scottish Enlightenment and was outspoken in her views. It was Nan Maree who introduced her to the novels of Sir Walter Scott and encouraged her to become an artist. She had died six years ago, and Anna still missed her

She told me to follow my heart and I won't let her down. I'll ask Peter to sit for his portrait as soon as he arrives. Anna hugged herself, closing her arms tight about her chest. In her mind, she was standing beside Peter in a chapel, wearing a red dress and her grandmother's long veil. Deep male voices were chanting, and candles lit up the darkness. The fragrance of incense filled the air as crowns were held over their heads. In a few days we could be betrothed, she thought. Happiness is within my grasp. By the grace of God, I'll be Anna Dashkovya before the year is out.

Chapter Five

Everything was ready for the reception. The dining room was laid out with long tables covered in damask cloths and laden with flowers. The best gold- and silverware was on display. The three magnificent candelabras had been lowered and lit with a hundred fresh candles and the house smelled like a tropical garden. Lilies, sent from the Crimea, welcomed guests and there were jardinières with cyclamen and magnolia in every room. The grand salons were heated by wood-burning stoves, their windows draped with heavy curtains, and all the servants dressed in their finest livery.

Upstairs in her bedroom, Anna was trying to decide what to wear. Mazra, her maid, suggested the green cuisse de nymphe but Anna had worn it twice before. She considered a dress of barège silk with rows of ruffles above the hem, but yellow didn't suit her complexion. Finally, she tried on a new creation of light gauze over pink silk with roses pinned to the corsage. Anna studied herself in the glass, twisting her neck to get a better view. A ribbon encircled her body above her waist, emphasising her slender figure and puff sleeves showed off her arms. Its deep flounces and low décolletage made it elegant yet simple. Yes, this was the one! She must be irresistible to Peter tonight.

The gown was spread out on the bed and Anna sat in her dressing coat in front of the glass. Her father's pet name for her was *Ivitsa*, little lioness, because she had inherited her grandmother's dark eyes and tawny auburn hair. Tonight, Mazra had arranged her hair à la grecque with a centre parting and ringlets on either side of her face. Her complexion was clear apart from summer freckles on her nose. Anna dabbed them with powder, hoping they wouldn't show in the candlelight, and then put a touch of Mazra's red pomade on her lips. A spray of scent behind her ears and she was done. She already had on her silk stockings and satin dancing shoes peeped from beneath her petticoats. Now for the dress!

As the gossamer and silk garment was lifted carefully over her head, there came a tap at the door. 'May I come in, my dear. It's nearly nine o'clock.' Her father's voice spoke from the passage.

'One moment – just wait a minute, Papa!'

Only when she was standing in the centre of the room, spreading out the floating skirt, was the door opened and her father let in. He held a necklace of pearls in his hand and Anna looked at him in surprise.

'Your mama and I want you to have these.' Count Brianski cleared his throat and handed the jewellery to Mazra. 'Please will you put it on? The fastening's at the back.'

A triple strand of perfectly matched *zhemchuzhina*, the rarest of pearls, was fastened round her throat, and Anna was lost for words. As the countess came in, she ran and flung her arms around her mother.

'I thought you were angry with me! What have I done to deserve such a gift?'

'Careful you don't ruin your dress. 'Valentina Brianski stood back to study her daughter.' You still have much to learn, Anna – not least the proper arrangements for a reception. However, your father and I are proud of you.'

Valentina Brianski was rarely effusive and a feeling of warmth spread through Anna. It was not the first time her parents had given her jewellery but why tonight when the reception was for Sofia and Sasha? Could Peter have spoken to Papa already, she wondered? The thought sent a tingling sensation down her arms and she blushed.

'Thank you, Mama and Papa. I'll treasure this forever. I'm sorry I spoke to Monsieur Filot without your permission.'

In a corner of her bedroom stood a prayer stool. Above it, a red candle illuminated a painted icon of Saint Anne. Once she was alone, Anna knelt down and pressed the palms of her hands together.

'Dear Saint Anne, please intercede with the Lord for me,' she prayed. 'May He guide Peter to my side tonight. I love him. Please pray to God and make sure that He brings him to me.'

Anna kissed the icon and came to her feet. She put on her white gloves and gathered up her fan before she hurried to join her family at the top of the stairs. Count Brianski was elegant in a blue swallowtail coat, breeches and white stockings, his receding hair pomaded and a good-natured expression on his face. His wife stood beside him in a burgundy-coloured dress that matched her toque and the rubies around her neck. They made a handsome couple, Anna thought affectionately. Sofia and Sasha, too. Sofia was dressed in blue jaconet, a treble ruff of lace at her throat framing her small face as she looked up at her husband.

The family walked down together and, while the others went into drawing room to receive their guests, Anna remained on the landing. The hall below was filling up. She could hear the murmur of voices, footsteps and greetings as carriages drove off and others arrived. Every time the door opened, a draught of cold wind swept in making the candles flicker. Footmen in capes stood outside, opening doors and letting down steps before guiding guests to the entrance where pages waited to take capes, furs and coats.

Anna's gaze searched the crowd for Peter. He would be wearing the same white uniform as Sasha and should be easy to pick out, but she couldn't see him anywhere. The musicians were tuning up in the gallery and a procession of guests began heading for the stairs. Gentlemen in uniforms decorated with stars and ribbons accompanied ladies whose sparkling, coloured gems caught the light as they made their way up. A few young men wore swallow-tailed evening coats, but most were in regimentals. A group of soldiers reached the first floor led by Michael Pavel, Sofia's brother.

'How are you, my beautiful sister-in-law?' He greeted her with a smile and kissed her hand.' I was afraid you might be snatched away by a prospective husband while I was out of town. '

Michael had curly brown hair and his eyes danced merrily as he introduced his companions. One of them, Major Renin, struck Anna as older than his companions. He was a short, wiry man with reddish hair, cut short and hard as bristles.

'I'm delighted to meet you, Miss Brianski.' The major's small blue eyes fixed on Anna's face.' Captain Pavel's told us of your beauty and charm, but his praise is wholly inadequate. I hope you will honour me with the first dance.'

'I'm sorry, but I my programme is full.' Anna lowered her gaze.

'Then I shall wait until the end of the evening.' Renin spoke with the confidence of a practised flirt. 'I shall claim you for a final waltz when your other admirers have gone home.'

Anna inclined her head but did not answer. She couldn't wait for Peter any longer and, taking Michael's arm, walked into the grand salon with the major close on their heels. Major Renin obviously considered himself a success with the ladies, but there was something sharp about him, she thought, noting how he surveyed the company in search of important guests.

Champagne was served and Anna moved on and laughed and chatted with her friends, casting occasional, quick glances towards the door. The reception was in full swing when she heard His Highness, Prince Gagarin, being announced. He was a distinguished gentleman with white hair and three imperial stars pinned to his coat. Her parents would be pleased he honoured them with his presence. But where was Peter? How could he be late, tonight of all nights? She couldn't still her fidgeting feet and tapped the floor with her slipper until she was distracted by the arrival of Prince and Princess Volkonsky.

Anna had yet to meet Maria's husband and observed him from a distance. He carried himself with the aristocratic bearing of his family. Maria looked ravishing this evening in a blue silk dress with a sapphire tiara gleaming in her hair. She seemed happier with her husband by her side and bestowed a dazzling smile on Count Brianski. Prince Volkonsky bowed low to her mother and Anna walked over to greet them.

'I believe you've known my darling wife longer than I have.' Sergei Volkonsky spoke softly. 'It was kind of you to call on Maria while I was away. I hope you'll come again now I've returned.'

A little grey touched his swept-up hair – he must be fifteen years older than Maria, Anna thought. He didn't strike her as an overbearing personality, and his courtesy and gentle manner appealed to her. She was about to answer when his eyes shifted over her shoulder.

'I certainly didn't expect to find you here, Renin. May I present you to my wife and our charming hostess?'

'Mademoiselle Anna and I are already acquainted,' the major answered, bowing to Maria before extending his hand to her husband. 'Good to have you in town, Monsieur Sergei.'

'I'm glad to be back with my family,' Sergei answered briskly. 'So, are you a friend of the bride or the groom?'

'I'm in the same regiment as the bride's brother, His Majesty's Imperial Guard. Tell me, do you have news of that rascal Pavel Pestel? I gather our beloved emperor has finally lost patience with him.'

'I haven't seen him in months. He could be anywhere in Russia as far as I know.'

It was strange that Sergei sounded defensive, Anna thought. The Volkonskys belonged to the highest society, while Renin was only a middle-ranking officer in the army.

'Are you referring to the officer who distinguished himself at Borodino?' Maria enquired coldly. 'Alexander Pushkin told me Pestel has the most brilliant mind of anyone he's ever met.'

'They're two of a kind, ma'am – and both subversive liberals.' Renin's teeth gleamed beneath his trimmed moustache. 'Fortunately for Russian literature, Pushkin's radical ideas are only in his head or on the page. Pavel Pestel indulges in more dangerous activities than writing verse.'

There followed a tense silence as Sergei stared at the ground and Maria's eyes darkened with anger. Anna was trying desperately to think of something to say to lighten the mood, when a voice spoke from behind her.

'Never trust a man born in the French year Thermidor. Their heat burns too fiercely for us ordinary mortals.'

Anna gave a start. No one had told her Nicholas Bulgarin was invited to the reception. She was sure she hadn't seen his name on the guest list. As far as she knew, he was neither a friend of Sofia nor Sasha. Someone must have dropped out, for he could only have been asked at the last minute.

'Pavel Pestel is a remarkable man — whether a force for good or bad only time will tell.' Count Bulgarin continued, holding out his hands to the Volkonskys. 'I'm delighted to see you both, dear friends. Your company has been sorely missed these last months.'

Would he remember her from the evening at Kamenka? As Anna curtsied, Nicholas Bulgarin's glance swept her face without a trace of recognition. Thank God, he has forgotten, she thought, and gave him a sideways look from beneath her lashes. Nicholas Bulgarin wore a blue tailcoat and pantaloons with polished Hessian boots. He was tall and strong, the muscles of his body visible beneath his well-tailored clothes. She had to admit he was handsome, with his high cheekbones and piercing blue eyes, but there was a cynical look about his mouth, and his air of self-assurance annoyed her as much as ever.

'Princess Galitzine caught me on the way in.' The count turned to Major Renin, indicating towards an alcove where two elderly ladies sat side by side. 'Her Highness is asking for you, Renin.'

'I spoke to her earlier. What does she want now?'

'I've no idea, sir. She simply asked me to tell you she requires your attendance.'

Major Renin's brow furrowed, and he shot a glance at Anna before he set off through the crush.

'I can't believe that awful man's a friend of yours?' Maria tapped Sergei's arm with her fan.

'He's an acquaintance from Moscow. I wouldn't call him a friend.'

'I should hope not,' Nicholas replied bluntly. 'He attempted to pay court to my sister, but she gave him short shrift.'

'And how is dear Olga?' asked Maria. 'I hoped she might be here this evening.'

'She arrived back from Moscow today,' Nicholas replied with a smile. 'She's exhausted and it's her own fault. I advised her to wait for the snow to arrive. It would have taken half the time – but you know what Olga's like. She'd rather risk the appalling condition of our roads than take my advice.'

Nicholas Bulgarin's voice was surprisingly playful. Through half-lowered eyelids, he scrutinised the room, his discerning gaze taking everything in. The drawing room was decorated with fashionable stripes and furnished in the French style. Did he appreciate her parents' good taste, Anna wondered? Was he impressed by the fine statues, malachite tables and collection of Old Master paintings?

It was the time when the hosts circulated through the room to spend a few minutes with each guest. Conversations were kept short and people gathered in small groups, no one wanting to appear impatient until the gong sounded, summoning them to the dining hall. Count Brianski led the way with Princess Galitzine, followed by her mother on Prince Gagarin's arm. As Sasha and Sofia stepped forwards, Anna's eyes went for a last time to the doorway. Peter should be here by now. Mama had placed him next to her and he was meant to lead her into dinner.

'May I have the honour?' Nicholas Bulgarin spoke beside her.

He offered his arm and after a short hesitation she laid her hand on it.

As they walked behind Maria and Sergei, Anna was acutely conscious of his easy grace and the light touch of his fingers. Nicholas Bulgarin was sleek as a panther and his physical aura made her self-conscious. She felt uncomfortable – as if her décolletage was too low and everyone in the room staring at her.

Embarrassed, she cast about for something trivial to say. 'Do you live in St. Petersburg all the year round?'

'I have homes here, in the country and in Moscow. I generally prefer Moscow in the winter, but the north has its own attractions. I gather you are sister to the bridegroom?'

Nicholas Bulgarin gave her a bold look. Anna had no experience of dealing with men like him and his seductive charm unnerved her. She lowered her eyelashes, looking straight ahead until they came to the anteroom where wedding presents were displayed on tables. There were gifts of every kind: bowls of alabaster and precious lazuli, decorated marble eggs, and a set of birch boxes, one nestling inside the other. Porcelain figurines were placed alongside a pile of books and in pride of place stood her two portraits in their oval frames.

She had painted Sasha with his head turned sideways to show off his profile while Sofia gazed out of the picture at the viewer. Her heart-shaped face and fair hair were delicately rendered and Sergei and Maria stopped to admire them.

'Why, they're wonderful, Anna!' Maria exclaimed. 'I had no idea you were so good.'

'Most accomplished.' Sergei bent down, removing his monocle. He tucked it into his breast pocket as he straightened up.' The happy couple are blessed to have such a good artist in the family.'

Now it was Nicholas Bulgarin's turn to inspect the pictures. He took so long that Anna braced herself for criticism. She tried to withdraw her hand and felt the pressure of his fingers tighten slightly.

'Have you been painting for long?'

'My parents say I was born with a paintbrush in my hand.'

'Many people believe themselves to be artists but very few have any talent.' He spoke in a slow drawl. 'You are the exception, Miss Brianski. I congratulate you.'

The praise was genuine and Anna was torn between pleasure and a desire not to appear flattered. Their eyes met and she saw a flicker of interest in their depths. Nicholas Bulgarin escorted her to her parents' table and she favoured him with a smile as he left to find his place.

Under the italianate carved ceiling, footmen moved quietly between tables. Anna's cousin, Andrei, was on her right and on the other side an empty chair for Peter Dashkovy. He was always so punctual. What could have happened to him? Might there have been an accident? Anna felt a knot tighten in her stomach. If something had occurred, surely they'd have heard by now? The idea that he might have forgotten the reception was inconceivable. Peter had been a witness at the wedding. He was one of Sasha's oldest friends.

The room felt hot and the sound of voices deafening, until a bell rang and the company fell silent. A swan carved of ice was carried in at shoulder height by four footmen and paraded between the tables before it was set down in front of Sasha and Sofia. Everyone clapped and Count Brianski stood up.

'Dearest friends and family, we're delighted to welcome you into our home this evening in honour of the bridal couple. I ask you to raise your glasses to Sasha and Sofia Brianski. May fortune bless them, heaven smile down on them, and health and happiness be with them always!'

The toast was given and Anna downed her vodka in one. Chairs scraped the marble floor and there was a clatter of knives and forks as the first course was served. At the head of her table, everyone seemed in fine spirits. Count Brianski was pouring wine into Princess Galitzine's glass, while Valentina was deep in conversation with a handsome officer of the Hussars. The noisiest group in the room was at Sasha and Sofia's table. Sofia sat beside her husband laughing as he recounted stories and Nicholas Bulgarin's dark head was bent as he spoke to his neighbour.

They were all enjoying themselves, the men's voices becoming louder each time their glasses were refilled. No one else seemed to have noticed Captain Dashkovy's absence. Fish followed soup, but Anna had no appetite. She pushed her food round the plate with a fork and craned her neck so she could see the door. Peter might have arrived and be downstairs, she thought. She imagined him running up the staircase and arriving breathless. He would go and apologise to her parents before he came to sit next to her. Surely, he would be coming through the door at any moment!

Hiding her agitation, Anna turned to Andrei and asked for the latest society gossip. Her cousin chatted away with Anna only half-listening. They were halfway through dinner and Peter's place was still unoccupied.

He'll think it impolite to come in now, she thought, and will be waiting in the salon. I'll find him when we go through. The idea soothed her and she drank more wine, laughing at Andrei's stories until dinner was over and the company rose.

They returned to the drawing room where rugs had been lifted for dancing, and Count Brianski gathered a small group of male friends and took them to the smoking room. Valentina and the other ladies sat down and couples formed two long lines for a polonaise. The musicians struck up and Sasha led Sofia onto the floor for the first dance. Major Renin was wandering around on his own and Anna moved to stand by the door. She waited until the dance began and then slipped out onto the landing.

Her fan dangled from her wrist as she peered over the balustrade. The hall below was silent and empty. Peter must be here somewhere, she thought and walked across the landing. In the red salon, tables had been set up for Boston. A few people were playing cards while others sat in low-backed chairs talking and drinking. No one noticed her as she passed through the room and headed to the conservatory. She could hear sounds of muffled laughter and pressed her face to the glass.

Younger children were playing hide and seek, flitting between flower tubs and greenery and Anna's lip trembled with disappointment. All her plans depended on talking to Peter this evening. She had counted on him, and he hadn't even bothered to turn up. She felt a lump in her throat, like a small stone, and swallowed hard. Peter's been delayed for good reason, she told herself. A member of his family must have fallen ill or his commanding officer needs him urgently. If he doesn't come tonight, he'll call tomorrow and explain everything. I will ask him to sit for his portrait then. I must talk to him alone.

The door to the conservatory opened and a young boy ran out. He waved to his friends before he headed down the corridor. Anna drew herself up. She couldn't stay away any longer. It was time to get back to the reception before she was missed.

Chapter Six

As Anna walked down the passage, she noticed the library door was open and looked in. The glow of oil lamps illuminated red leather-bound volumes of books on shelves that reached from floor to ceiling. The room was quiet, and Nicholas Bulgarin sat in an armchair, reading a book. As she took a step backwards, hoping to escape, he glanced up and saw her silhouetted in the doorway. Putting down the book, he came to his feet and strolled towards her.

'You must consider me very impolite, Miss Brianski. Have I missed a dance engagement?' The count took an enamel snuffbox from his waistcoat, flicked it open it with his forefinger and inhaled a pinch of snuff. 'Were you looking for me?'

Anna squeezed her fan between her fingers as she walked slowly forwards. She didn't want to get caught up, but Count Bulgarin was a friend of Peter Dashkovy's and it was worth a try.

'My brother sent me to find Captain Dashkovy of the Second Life Guards. Have you seen him, by any chance?'

'Peter Dashkovy?' The count's eyebrows lifted. 'I believe he's otherwise engaged this evening. I'm sure he will have sent his apologies.'

'He has not. My parents were expecting him for dinner and are most upset. When you next see him, you might tell him so.'

'Indeed, I will. It's a disgraceful way to behave – and I took him for a gentleman.'

There was laughter in his eyes and Anna flashed him an indignant look. Bulgarin's manners were hardly any better, she thought, sneaking off to the library when he should be dancing.

'If you were a gentleman, sir, you would be doing your duty on the dance floor.'

'You're right and I apologise. I've an irresistible fascination for other people's libraries. Count Brianski's is most impressive.'

'So, what were you reading when I came in?'

'Colbert's study of political science.'

'Oh, that sort of book.'

'Not one to your taste, I presume? Like every young lady in St. Petersburg, I expect you read only foreign novels full of fanciful notions.'

His opinion of popular literature was clear. Anna wasn't going to admit the bookcase in her bedroom was filled with romantic novels. His superior attitude nettled her and her chin came up.

'Alexander Pushkin's my favourite author. I recall he was staying with Madame Davydov for her birthday – along with yourself and Captain Dashkovy.' Her eyes held his gaze defiantly. 'You may consider novels a lesser form of literature, sir; but they're no more fanciful than matters you were discussing then.'

'I've no recollection of you participating in our conversations,' Nicholas Bulgarin remarked coolly. 'Be kind enough to remind me what we were talking about.'

'You were discussing the abolition of serfdom and curtailing the power of the tsar.'

'Please keep your voice down, Miss Brianski. Every house in St. Petersburg has a hundred pairs of ears.'

Stung by the reprimand, Anna walked over to the window. She drew back the heavy curtain and looked out. Lights flickered below as sleighs and carriages with bright torches galloped through the city that never slept. The huge silver disc of the moon hung above the Neva and the sky was filled with stars. All was just as it should be – except for Peter's absence. How could he be otherwise engaged? Did Bulgarin know his whereabouts this evening or was he just trying to provoke her? For a time, she stood staring into the night, then turned back into the room and gave a dismissive toss her head.

'I declare you exaggerate, sir. There are no eavesdroppers in this house.'

'And only one at Kamenka?'

So, he did remember! But what had he seen that night? Nothing that she wasn't prepared to deny outright. Anna was about to retaliate but checked herself. Sedition was dangerous in a city devoured by gossip, and she was silent.

'Those who listen to other people's conversations tend to pick up only what they want to hear,' Nicholas Bulgarin continued, brushing an invisible speck of dust from his waistcoat. 'Don't worry, Miss Brianski. Your secret is safe with me.'

Anna saw the muscles above his mouth twitch as if he were trying not to smile. He hoped to needle her but she wouldn't rise to his bait.

'I didn't know you were a friend of my brother's,' she said in a cold voice, deliberately turning the subject.

'We're only slightly acquainted. I was surprised and honoured to be asked.'

The insolence in his eyes was infuriating. Stifling an impulse to tell him to go to the devil, Anna collected herself and made a gesture towards the door. 'I will bid you goodnight, sir, and leave you to my father's books. You obviously find their company more entertaining than that of your fellow guests.'

'Why aren't you dancing? There must be a hundred partners waiting for you.'

'I'm not in the mood this evening.'

'Why ever not?'

Anna's hand moved to touch the silky pearls of her necklace. Nicholas Bulgarin asked too many questions and the conversation had gone on for long enough. A stony silence was her response as she began to walk away.

'Don't worry about Captain Dashkovy, Miss Brianski. I'll do my duty and dance with you instead.'

His offer stopped Anna in her tracks. She stood motionless a moment, then swung round, hands on hips. 'I'd rather dance with a baboon than with you, sir!'

There was a moment of deathly quiet. Anna felt mortification burn her cheeks and the swift, awkward beat of her heart. How could she have let her tongue betray her into a childish show of temper?

'Shall we agree to consider that remark unsaid?' Nicholas suggested softly.

Anna swallowed, then answered. 'I beg your pardon, sir.'

'So, may I engage you for the next waltz?'

'I've told you already I'm not dancing this evening.'

'Well, that is a pity. No doubt your guests will assume you're in a sulk because a certain gentleman failed to turn up.'

This, finally, was too much. Count Bulgarin was here at her family's invitation. His impudence was beyond forbearance and her voice broke with anger. 'You forget yourself, sir! I will not be insulted in my own home. Please will you leave this minute before I have you thrown out.'

'Anna! Where have you been all this time?'

Her mother's voice gave Anna such a fright she let out a small cry. How long had Mama been outside the door? How much had she heard? There was no time to think of an excuse before Valentina Brianski swept into the library, her eyebrows arching at finding them together.

'Good evening, Count Bulgarin. How kind of you to entertain my daughter. Sadly, I must now remove her from your company. Her father wishes her to partner him in the quadrille.'

Anna remembered afterwards that Nicholas Bulgarin made an exaggerated bow. She listened as he exchanged pleasantries with her mother, staring at her feet and wishing she were anywhere else on God's earth. When Valentina Brianski finally took her leave, Anna raised her head a fraction and saw amusement gleam in his eyes before she turned and stalked out of the room.

Chapter Seven

It was a beautiful day. The marsh birds that gathered in dark clouds last week had migrated south and the Neva River was frozen over. Pink and gold cupolas shimmered in the sunlight and the tall spire of the Admiralty shone in the distance. Despite the cold, there was incessant movement as people and sleighs skidded about on the ice. Young men pushed sledge chairs carrying ladies, and horse-drawn troikas crossed the river following tracks marked by fir branches that looked like clumps of white coral dusted with diamonds.

Close to the bank, great blocks of ice were being lifted out and piled on carts to be taken to cellars all over the city. Cab drivers and postilions were shouting for fares and near the English Quay a well-dressed crowd of people had gathered to skate. Some were expert, showing off their skill, while beginners clung to the backs of chairs fitted with runners. They passed each other, smiling and exchanging a few words, all of them enjoying the fine weather.

The sounds of sleigh bells and children's voices lifted Anna's spirits as she stepped onto the ice. She was relieved to be out of the house, but the memory of the reception weighed heavy. After dancing a quadrille with her father, she had stood on the landing watching as the first guests began to leave. Footmen held fur-lined capes for the ladies while gentlemen offered their shoulders for redingotes and cloaks. The party was still going when she went to her bedroom. Mazra helped her undress and Anna climbed into bed, blew out the candle and cried herself to sleep.

Peter had sent a note to her parents the next day, apologising that he had been waylaid. Waylaid? All Sasha's friends had been there except for him. She was sure he would come himself to say he was sorry. Whenever the doorbell rang or a carriage drew up outside, her hopes soared and then crashed with disappointment. Peter had stayed away but Major Renin had come to pay his respects. Anna rebuffed him as civilly as she could, until last week when he called twice. Irritated by his persistence, she told him straight out he was wasting his time.

'You may not appreciate my attentions now, but you will regret your coldness, ma'am.' The major stood up abruptly, his face reddening. 'Mark my words – there'll come a time when you and your family beg for my protection in this city.'

He had marched out of the room, leaving Anna perplexed. What on earth was he talking about? Boris Renin was a vain, prickly man – still, it was a strange thing to say. On Sofia's advice, she left instructions with the hall porter that, should Major Renin call again, he be told she was not at home.

Anna took deep breath and pushed off from the side. In her red jacket and fur-trimmed matching skirt, she made a graceful figure as she carved a line across the ice. A young man skated past, turning his head to smile at her, and lost his balance. He touched the ice with his hand before he pulled himself up, laughing as he skated away. When a boy in national dress, stooping low and swinging his arms, overtook her, she increased her speed. Cold air streamed over her face as she spun around, skating backwards until she reached the little wooden houses serving refreshments.

Anna slowed down and came to a halt. She had skated further than she realised, almost halfway across the river. There was a clanking of chains as sledges were pulled to the top of ice hills and a clattering and shouting as young men hurtled down them. They were laughing, cheering each other on, as they raced and she smiled at their daredevil antics. She would have stayed longer but Omelko, the coachman, was waiting and would be upset if he lost sight of her.

Seagulls swooped overhead as she began to skate back, her blades crossing fast and close until she could see Omelko. He was by the carriage, wearing a shaggy fur coat over his uniform and a cockade in his hat. He held a hand over his eyes to shield them from the sun and Anna executed a perfect figure of eight for his benefit.

As she came out of the final loop, she caught sight of Olga Bulgarin. She was standing apart from the crowd, dressed in a tailored green habit with a black fur hat and a muff hanging from her neck. A sable cape covered her shoulders, and she was looking towards the bank. The next moment, Peter Dashkovy came down the steps with a flying jump. He tried out his skates with a few quick turns and then glided across the ice towards her. She gave him her hand and they set off across the ice.

Olga and Peter skating together! Anna felt she had been struck in the face. She stared at them, then shut her eyes hoping to make the sight of them disappear. Dark spots fluttered before her eyelids and when she looked again Olga and Peter had passed the ice hills and were turning to come back. The quicker they went, the closer they leant towards each other, their bodies never losing contact. She forced herself to breathe, inhaling slowly until the first stab of shock passed and her mind steadied. They were skating fast and at any moment would catch sight of her. She must get away. She set off towards the bank, trying not to draw attention to herself, and waved to Omelko. As he raised his arm in acknowledgment, she heard a rasp of blades behind her.

'Wait for us, Anna Ivanova!' Peter Dashkovy shouted.

Anna dug her edges into the ice so that a plume of snow sheared up from beneath her skates. Turning around, she saw Peter with Olga close behind. Peter skated with long gliding strokes until he came to a halt beside her. He was hatless, his golden hair shining in the sun, and all she could think was how beautiful he was. She loved the lift of his head and the light in his blue eyes. He was so handsome her breath caught in her throat. If only they were alone, she would tell him she loved him right now! But Olga had caught up and was standing close by.

'What a lovely surprise to find you here,' Peter said. 'Are you on your own?'

'Omelko's with me.' Anna's arm felt stiff and awkward as she pointed towards the embankment. 'He's watching over me as usual.'

'Good day to you, Anna. It's an age since we last met.'

Olga's voice fractured the cold air and Anna turned her head, seeing the colour in the other girl's cheeks and the glow in her green eyes. 'I'm told you were the brightest star of last summer's season. I'm pleased to see you again.'

'My family were worried you might be unwell, Captain Dashkovy.' Anna poked the ice with the toe of her boot and looked at Peter. 'We were expecting you at Sasha and Sofia's wedding reception.'

'I'm sorry to have let them down. I've told Sasha we'll make up for it in some other way.' Peter's apology sounded vaguely half-hearted.

We? What did he mean, *we?* Intuition, fleeting and terrifying, made Anna's heartbeat quicken.

'It really wasn't Captain Dashkovy's fault,' Olga added. 'I'm entirely to blame for keeping him away. I hope it didn't ruin your evening.'

Olga flicked frost crystals off her muff with one hand and Anna flashed her a glance. 'Not in the slightest. It was a splendid occasion. It was only my parents who noticed Captain Dashkovy's absence.'

'I'm so glad you say so,' Olga answered with a glittering smile. 'I hear Maria and Sergei Volkonsky were there. Did Maria tell you she's leaving St. Petersburg with the baby to spend time with her family? Sergei will join them for Christmas and the Raevskys have asked us to stay for the New Year.'

The information filtered into Anna's brain. Olga always had to be the one who knew everything. She disliked that in her almost as much as the way she stood so close to Peter, her hand on his arm as if he belonged to her. There were people skating all around them, the sound of voices tumbling through her head, and she realised Peter was speaking.

'Olga hasn't seen Sasha or Sofia since we were all at Kamenka. She'd like to visit them and offer her congratulations.'

'Miss Bulgarin's been in St. Petersburg all season. She could have called on us at any time, had she wanted...'

The words came out of her mouth before Anna could stop them. She saw Olga frown with hurt in her expression. The atmosphere was so tense the air seemed to fissure as Peter put his arm around her shoulders.

'Are you suggesting Olga isn't welcome in your home?'

His voice was hard as his eyes narrowed, warning her off. Peter had never been angry with her before. A pulse began thudding in Anna's throat. How could he be so quick to defend Olga's feelings and careless of her own? Peter was behaving as if she meant nothing to him.

She curled her toes in her boots to control herself and struggled to find her voice. 'You misunderstand me, sir,' she said at last. 'My family will be pleased to receive Miss Bulgarin whenever is convenient. And now I must take my leave for I am already late. Good day to you both.'

If she stayed any longer, she felt she might collapse, and Anna was thankful they made no attempt to detain her. She tripped as she came off the ice and hobbled to a bench where she sat down to unstrap her skates from her boots. It was past two o'clock and the family were expecting her for lunch – but she couldn't go home yet. She needed to calm herself. She bent her head low, squeezing her eyes shut. Peter can't be in love with Olga, she thought desperately. Sasha or Sofia would have said something. Do they know? Why didn't they tell me? Nothing could be worse than finding out like this. Who else might be in on the secret? Nicholas Bulgarin was Olga's guardian. Was he aware that Peter was with his sister on the night of the reception?

A tear splashed onto her lap and she searched her pockets for a handkerchief. She found one with a monogram stitched in the corner. Peter had lent it to her at Sasha's wedding and she had kept it ever since. It was the last time she had seen him. Memories of the day flashed through her head – the way Peter caught her eye during the ceremony, and his strong arm under her hand as he led her out of the church. She thought of Olga's green eyes and her flirtatious glance. There was an alluring sense of mystery about her – had she bewitched Peter?

The sound of skates made Anna raise her head. The young man who had smiled at her earlier was approaching, dropping down and sliding across the ice on his knees. He had a bunch of red flowers in one hand and put the other to his heart as he offered them to her. Roses in November! Anna instinctively counted the stems. Thirteen not twelve! Good – a dozen was unlucky – but how much they must have cost! Who was he, this handsome boy with kind brown eyes? Had they met before? Before she could ask, he was on his feet and skating off, his green frock coat weaving between other skaters as he disappeared into the crowd.

The corner of a white envelope peeped from the bouquet. Anna took it out and withdrew a card from inside. There was a message written in a stylish, forward-sloping hand.

'I have prevailed upon my young friend to give these to you. Please accept them with my compliments in the hope they restore the bloom to your cheeks.'

What on earth? There was no signature. Anna looked around. A man in a greatcoat with a beaver collar was walking away. His hat was too low to see his face. She thought he was taller than Major Renin – but who else could it be? There was no one else in the crowd she recognised. It must be the major, damn him! Anna was possessed by a sudden urge to hurl the bouquet onto the river. She imagined the petals torn to shreds by blades, red as blood on the ice, and shuddered.

'Miss Anna, let me assist you.' Simeon Omelko leant down and gave her his hand to help her to her feet.

Omelko was a serf from her father's estate in the country and Anna had known him all her life. He rarely showed emotion but, beneath his bushy black eyebrows, she saw undisguised concern. Was her distress so obvious? Omelko was awaiting her instructions and Anna passed him the flowers.

'I was given these. Did you see Major Renin, by any chance?'

'I wouldn't know, ma'am. It was hard enough keeping my eye on you.'

It wasn't his place to chastise her, but Anna took no offence. Omelko had been the first person to lift her on a pony's back and the first to pick her up when she fell off. When she was old enough, he had taught her the difficult skill of driving a troika of three horses in the snow. She trusted him completely.

'I don't want them and they're too expensive to throw away. Do you know anyone who might have use of them?'

'There's a family over there. They could sell them to buy bread.'

Anna waited as Omelko walked over to the little group. The mother was crouched in a doorway with two ragged children clinging to her skirts. The younger one could be no more than five. Her face was pinched and blue with cold. The sight of them was pitiful and Anna felt ashamed. Never in her life had she wanted for anything. She and her family lived in luxurious comfort while children like these were starving on the streets. What was her heartache compared to their miserable existence? Omelko was leaning down, his head low as he talked to the mother. He was gentle for a big man and the pain in her heart subsided a little. As he handed over the flowers, she walked over, taking off her fur muff, and handed it to the woman.

'For the children...' She spoke in Russian and made a gesture towards the two wide-eyed figures staring up at her. 'Use it to buy them warm clothes. I have plenty of gloves.'

'Thank you, ma'am. *Bud zdorova*. God bless you.'

Anna let Omelko lead her away and help her into the open carriage. He tucked blankets around her, then climbed up onto the driving board and cracked the whip over the horses' heads. As they drove along the granite quays she looked back and saw the mother and children had gone.

The daily military parade was over and it was the fashionable hour of the promenade. Smartly dressed pedestrians jostled each other on the pavements as droshkies dashed about in every direction. They were driven by coachmen in belted caftans with furry hats and long beards who never used a whip, guiding their horses by voice alone. With their arms outstretched and a rein in each hand, they galloped from one end of the city to the other. Manoeuvring between the one-horse cabs and wagons piled high with hay and beetroot, the landau kept to a walk until they reached Anichkov Bridge. Here, cobbles gave way to blocks of wood and the horses broke into a trot.

This might be the last fine day for months. Soon the snow would arrive and, as winter set in, lamps on the bridges and in the streets would be lit all day and night. Anna heard the harsh craw of ravens and peered upwards, her eyes intent on the black shadows circling overhead. They were sinister birds and, as they turned past the great mass of the Winter Palace, she made the sign of the cross and began to pray.

'Dear Lord, give me a chance to talk to Peter. Men are weak as well as strong. I must save him from Olga's clutches. He'll forget her once he knows that I love him. I'll ask Sasha to arrange a meeting and tell him everything. There can be no more misunderstandings between us. Please God, don't let it be too late.'

Chapter Eight

'Sasha didn't come home again last night. It's the third time this week he's stayed in barracks.' Sofia picked at the cuffs of her sleeves as she looked out of the window.

'I'm sure there's nothing to worry about,' Valentina Brianski answered. 'The military are rehearsing for a celebration of the tsar's return to St. Petersburg.'

It was four days later and Anna was at home with her family. Ivan Brianski was standing with his back to the fire, his brow creased in deep furrows.

'The sooner the emperor returns from Taganrog the better. His Imperial Majesty's the only person who can knock some sense into these hotheads. When I was young, Russia had the finest army in all of Europe. Nowadays, the officers do nothing but lounge around, soaking up political drivel from France. Men like Pavel Pestel should be shot!'

Pavel Pestel ... the name momentarily distracted Anna from her own unhappiness. Major Renin had been disparaging, she recalled, while Maria Volkonsky had defended him. He was a friend of Pushkin. Her mind went back to Kamenka and the conversation with Count Bulgarin when Peter had spoken so passionately about justice and freedom. It was hard to imagine life without the armies of men and women who worked the land or were in domestic service and, with a hot glow akin to shame, Anna realised it had never occurred to her until then that serfdom was evil. She thought about their own household. Papa was a benevolent master. He rarely sold or punished his serfs. They seemed happy enough – but was that because she'd never truly thought about it before? Didn't everyone want to be free?

Anna picked up a bunch of silks and began separating the threads into different colours for Sofia's tapestry. The assumptions she had made about her home were shifting, unravelling and tangling like the silks in her hands. Everything she had believed in, Peter's love and a way of life she had taken for granted, seemed suddenly uncertain.

'The young are seduced by the new ideas of our age.' Count Brianski puffed out his cheeks and moved away from the hearth. 'They elevate them with fancy names, but they amount to nothing more than anarchy.'

'Don't work yourself up, Vanya. Sasha's not one of the radicals. He's far too sensible to be involved in their foolish pranks.'

Anna looked at her mother as she sat opposite dressed in a blue silk gown from Paris, a cornette cap with blue ribbons covering her hair. Valentina was the voice of reason in the family. Anna longed to lay her head on her lap and cry her heart out, but her mother wouldn't understand. She'll say I'm a hopeless romantic. Mama believes I don't see the world for what it really is, that I only dream about people in books, but it's not true.

Anna tried to still her mind, but the vision of Peter and Olga together tormented her. It might have been pure coincidence, she told herself. There were hundreds of people skating on the Neva that day. They could have met by chance – but she had seen the triumphant look in Olga's eyes and knew it was no accident. What was keeping Sasha away all this time? She desperately needed him to come home. Time was slipping past and she couldn't get to Peter without his help.

As anxious now as Sofia for her brother's return, Anna declined her parents' offer to visit Prince Gagarin and sat with her in the small salon upstairs. Sofia seemed outwardly calm, reading a book by the fire, but Anna was restless and fretful. Picking up a newspaper, she flicked through the pages without taking in a word. How could Sofia be so serene, not even looking up as the clock on the mantel chimed the hours? Anna sharpened her pencils and fiddled with an arrangement of dried flowers. She began a drawing but couldn't concentrate and put the sketch away. Taking a chair by the fire, she stared sightlessly into the flames until there came a knock at the door.

Anna and Sofia stood up as Maria Volkonsky was ushered in. She was dressed in a long green velvet coat, her black hair hidden under a bonnet trimmed with white fox. She took off her cloak, giving it to Josef, and held out her hands.

'I'm sorry to call in unannounced but I was passing by. I hoped you might be at home.'

'I'm so glad! It's a pleasure to see you, dear Maria.' Anna led her to a chair. 'I hear you're leaving St. Petersburg before Christmas.'

'Well, that's the plan, but nothing's decided for certain. I wondered if Sasha was at home? I wanted to talk to him about Sergei.'

'Is there something the matter?' Anna asked.

'I'm probably being stupid...' Maria paused and cast the two women a hesitant glance. 'It's just I've a feeling something's going on that I don't know about. Sergei's been so strange lately. He hardly ever comes home and, when he does, he's preoccupied. I asked what was the matter, and he brushed me off, telling me not to worry. I hoped Sasha might reassure me.'

'We're waiting for him now. He's been held up at the barracks,' Sofia responded.

'My brothers are being horrid,' Maria continued, ignoring Sofia's intervention. 'They say all Pushkin's friends are hotheads and revolutionaries—'

'But that's preposterous!' Sofia interrupted hotly. 'Our husbands aren't revolutionaries. Sasha's the most patriotic of men. And Sergei too. Why, the Volkonskys have fought and died for the tsars since the time of Peter the Great.'

With an unexpected pang, Anna thought of the book in Sasha's room. She had gone back later and retrieved it from the drawer. It was an illegal copy of Pushkin's poem 'Ode to Liberty', for which the poet had been banished from St. Petersburg. One verse in particular had stuck in her mind.

'You autocratic psychopath,
Your throne I do despise!
I watch your doom, your children's death
With hating, jubilating eyes.'

Anna had been brought up to fear and respect the tsar. She had been too young to realise the poem was about the Romanovs. Now she felt goose bumps rise on the back of her neck. Was Pushkin really a revolutionary? And did Sasha agree with him? The notion was inconceivable. Sasha was Pushkin's friend. He respected the poet's passion and talent. It didn't mean that he condoned everything he said.

'Pushkin uses words for their dramatic effect – not to incite insurrection,' she said quietly.

'I hope you're right.' Maria's gaze moved uncertainly from Sofia and Anna. 'The truth is I've been worried since the day of our marriage. There were bad omens at our wedding. An old woman crossed our path as we entered the church, then Sergei's witness dropped one of the rings. My mother says I am too superstitious...' Her words trailed off. Then Maria shook her head and managed a faint smile. 'The other reason I called is that I've a favour to ask of you, Anna. I wonder if you might find the time to paint a picture of me with little Nicolenka? I want to give it to Sergei as a Christmas present. He was very taken by your portraits of Sasha and Sofia.'

'I would be delighted to paint the portrait,' Anna answered.

'I'm longing for you to see him again. Nicolenka's utterly adorable – the single greatest joy of my life.'

There was such wistfulness in Maria's tone, Anna wondered if she was susceptible to the melancholy that afflicted so many. She thought of her at Kamenka. Beautiful Maria, always happy, always laughing. She had been the life and soul of the party. Was it possible that Sergei, whom she had liked so much, was unfaithful? Sensing her friend's distress, she kept her tone bright. 'When would you like me to start? The light's best in the morning and it shouldn't take more than a couple of sittings. Shall I come the day after tomorrow?'

'That would be perfect.' Maria stood up and Sofia pulled the bell rope for Josef. 'I'll expect you then. Thank you, dear Anna.'

Josef arrived with her cloak, and Anna and Sofia went with Maria to the door. She embraced them both and was halfway out when she stopped and looked back. 'Oh, I almost forgot! I received a note from Olga Bulgarin this morning. She's betrothed to Peter Dashkovy and they're to marry in the spring. Isn't it the most wonderful news? I'm so happy for them both.'

St. Petersburg. November 1825

Dearest Nicholas,

I am leaving you this letter to thank you. I understand being my guardian hasn't always been easy and there were times when I questioned your judgment. I know now that you have only desired what is for my good.

In giving your consent to my marriage with Peter Dashkovy, you have made me the happiest of women. Peter understands your reservations and we have spoken at length on the matter. He cannot abandon his principles but has given me his word that he is, and always will be, a loyal subject of Tsar Alexander.

Only since meeting Peter, dear Nicolay, have I understood how generous and wise you are. Aunt Varenka says you will never be married but I disagree! I pray one day you will find true love as I have done.

Your devoted sister,
Olga

Chapter Nine

It was still dark when Anna and Mazra left the house the next morning. Somehow Anna survived the evening and, as soon as dinner was over, asked to be excused. She tiptoed up the stairs in the silent hall and thought: there's been no official announcement. Olga's probably circulating the story to tighten her hold over Peter. I won't accept it as fact unless one of them tells me face to face.

Searching her bureau, she found Olga Bulgarin's address on a card under a pile of papers. On one side was printed a location in Moscow and on the other *12, Sadovaya Street, St. Petersburg*. If she couldn't speak to Peter, then there was no alternative but to confront Olga. Summoning Mazra, she asked her to arrange for Omelko to drive them to Sadovaya Street early the next morning.

A damp, chilly mist rose from the river as the carriage bumped over the snowy cobbles of Nevsky Prospekt. Labourers in sheepskin jackets were swinging their arms, stamping their feet to keep warm, and waiting for bakers' shops to open. Queues had already formed with beggars and injured soldiers lingering at the back, hoping for yesterday's crusts. Soon, *budnochiks* would emerge from their huts to police the streets, and labourers and vagrants would be replaced by an army of copyists and civil servants scurrying to their offices. Later in the morning, gentlemen and ladies in fur-lined cloaks would come to visit the coffee houses and shops on the most fashionable street in St. Petersburg.

Nevsky Prospekt was the face Russia chose to show to the world but behind the avenues and classical facades lay a very different city — a labyrinth of slums where the cold was so intense it cracked brick and stone. Poverty hung in the air like a miasma and disease was as rampant as the rats that infested the houses. Normally, it upset Anna as she stared down the alleys into this other world. But she was too miserable to notice any of this now. Maria's announcement had cut her to the core, and it was only Mazra who insisted she took trouble over her appearance. Her hair was tucked under a velvet bonnet trimmed with bands of narrow black ribbon and, beneath her fur-lined cape, she wore a blue coat with billowing sleeves, their cuffs gathered at her wrists.

Unseen carriages went past in the fog before they turned off the main avenue into Sadovaya Street and stopped outside a two-storey house. Night lamps glowed on the gateposts and a narrow footpath had been spread with sand and ashes. Anna asked Omelko to wait for them and walked across the forecourt with Mazra. Olga will still be asleep, she thought. She'll be annoyed at being disturbed so early and will make me wait. How shall I put it to her? I'll say Peter's a friend of the family and I've been sent to find out if the rumour is true. I don't care if she doesn't believe me. She has to give me an answer.

There was a closed carriage standing by the front door, its driver swaddled in rugs and smoking a clay pipe. The horse's breath rose in two streams from its nostrils and Anna glanced through the window as she walked past. The cab was empty. Who could be visiting at this hour of the morning? As she mounted the front steps, her nerve almost failed. How would she respond if Olga confirmed the engagement? She would have to congratulate her! I won't be able to get the words out of my mouth, she thought, as she stood shivering under the porch.

Mazra tugged the heavy bell pull. For a long time, nothing happened until at last they heard footsteps and bolts being drawn. A hall porter in livery opened the door. He had a thin face and eyes black as coal that looked at them suspiciously.

'I have an appointment with Miss Bulgarin,' Anna said.

'I'm afraid Miss Bulgarin's not at home.'

Anna could see a clutter of boots and canes in the porch. Beyond it, she glimpsed an elegant hall with marble statues and plants. A double staircase led to the upper floors and, before she could answer, a husky dog came bounding down the stairs. He ran across the tiled floor and leapt up at her, almost knocking her over. With a muttered expletive, the hall porter made a grab for its collar.

'Come in, both of you. And quick now! Follow me before Mosca eats you alive.'

Hanging onto the dog with one hand, he beckoned Anna and Mazra into a waiting room with a small fire. He left them, but was occupied with the dog and forgot to close the door. Above the hiss of damp wood, Anna heard low-pitched voices outside. She signalled to Mazra to stay quiet and squinted through the crack in the door.

Dressed in the long kaftan, Nicholas Bulgarin was accompanied by a woman in a flowing cape. When they reached the outer hall, he stopped and cupped her face in his hands. As he kissed her, the hood of her cape fell back, revealing ringlets of golden hair. Anna had dreamt so often of Peter kissing her like that! A sharp pain, like a metal band tightened round her chest as she watched him lead his companion down the steps to the waiting droshky. His guest must have stayed here all night. Who could she be? Was she one of those women everyone knew existed but never talked about? Like all innocent young women, Anna was fascinated by the idea of courtesans; only the golden-haired lady didn't look as if she belonged to the demi-monde. There was grace in her bearing and refinement in the delicate hand that reached out to touch Nicholas Bulgarin's cheek.

The cab moved off and Anna took a step backwards. She heard the dog snuffling at the threshold and a brief exchange of words outside. Then the door was thrown wide and Nicholas Bulgarin walked in with the husky at his heels.

His black eyebrows rose in surprise as he looked at her. 'How may I be of service to you, Miss Brianski?'

'I hoped... I mean... I expected to find your sister at home...' Anna stammered.

'Olga left for Moscow yesterday. She must have forgotten your appointment. I apologise on her behalf. '

'It's of no consequence. I'm sorry to have troubled you. We'll leave immediately.'

'You look frozen to death. Please warm yourself before you go.' Count Bulgarin ignored Anna's reluctance and turned to his manservant. 'Liev, please take Miss Brianski's cloak and accompany her maid to the kitchen. Then bring tea and brandy to my study.'

The doorman gestured to Mazra to follow him, and Nicholas guided Anna across the hall. Two high-backed chairs stood in front of a fire in the grate. He waited until Liev came to collect her cloak, and then went out.

Adjusting her bonnet, Anna looked around the study. The walls were wood-panelled and a stand-up desk stood in the centre. On every side were bookstands stacked with periodicals and journals. The room was well appointed in a masculine way and smelled of wax and leather polish. A serving girl appeared carrying a tray with cups and a samovar, which she placed on the table in front of the fire. Anna thanked her as Nicholas came through the door with the dog following him.

'I hope Mosca didn't alarm you. She is much too friendly for a guard dog. Do sit down, Miss Brianski.'

He poured out the tea, adding brandy, and gave Anna a cup. She stirred it slowly and watched the chunks of sugar dissolve before she took a sip. The fiery spirit burned her throat and all the way down to her stomach as she studied Nicholas Bulgarin over the rim of her cup. He wore a shirt and breeches under his kaftan; his shirt was unbuttoned at the neck, and she glimpsed dark hairs at the top of his chest.

'Forgive my disarrangement,' he remarked, noting the direction of her gaze. 'I don't usually receive visitors before noon.'

'I hoped to speak to Olga in private.'

'Is it important?'

Anna hesitated. Nicholas Bulgarin probably had a fair idea why she was here. However much she disliked him, it might be easier than having to ask Olga. She took a gulp of tea and passed her tongue over her lips.

'My family wish to know…' she began, her brow puckering in a frown. 'Is it true your sister and Captain Dashkovy are betrothed to be married?'

'The engagement has yet to be announced. However, I've given them my blessing.'

He might as well have told her Peter was dead. Anna's teacup rattled on its saucer as she returned it to the tray. A sense of blistering hurt stung her so she couldn't speak.

'I'm sorry you're upset, Miss Brianski.' Nicholas's tone was gentler. 'Has Captain Dashkovy broken his word to you? Will I be obliged to call him out?'

'Not in defence of *my* honour.'

'I was thinking of my sister. I can't possibly give permission for her to marry a man who's promised himself to another.'

One desperate lie and the wedding would be off! Anna's heart leapt with hope. She didn't need to denounce Peter or be too specific. She only had to hint that he had misled her. Could she do it? He was bound to find out. Peter will hate me for the rest of his life, she thought. And Sasha will be furious. I'll never hear the end of it.

She hesitated, searching for the right words. 'Captain Dashkovy has been very attentive. He gave the impression that he was fond of me.' Anna lowered her gaze and then added in a tight voice. 'Although he never made a formal declaration.'

'In that case, I must tell you Peter Dashkovy's been courting Olga for the last two years.'

The idea took Anna's breath away. Had Peter fallen in love with Olga when they met at Kamenka? Oh God … in all this time that she had loved him, his heart had belonged to Olga. Why hadn't he made it clear to her? At the very least, he should have been honest. Fresh anguish clawed at her heart and there was silence until the husky pushed her nose under Nicholas's hand. He stroked her and she lay down, curling at his feet with her chin on her paw.

'I'm sorry my flowers were of no use to you.'

What was he talking about? 'Your flowers?' she began and stopped, her eyes widening. Surely, he didn't mean the ones given to her by the young man that day on the Neva? 'So, it was you. You gave me the roses. But why on earth?'

'Because of something I saw long ago.'

Disconnected images flitted through her mind: Bulgarin watching her through the window at Kamenka, and their conversation in the library. Had he witnessed the scene with Peter and Olga on the ice? Did he feel sorry for her? Oh, the shame of it! She couldn't bear his pity.

'Why are you always spying on me? Do you think I'm some sort of fool?'

'I wasn't spying on you. I was chaperoning my sister. Please don't look daggers at me, Miss Brianski. I'm trying to pay you a compliment. Genuine feelings are rare in our world of artifice and intrigue.'

Anna could not bring herself to reply, and Nicholas Bulgarin leant forwards, resting his elbows on his knees. 'Will you vouch that Captain Dashkovy has behaved honourably towards you?'

There was no more to be said and Anna nodded mutely. She felt tears prick her eyes, but she wouldn't cry in front of him and the sooner she was out of here the better. Count Bulgarin presumed he knew everything about her. Well, she wouldn't mind asking him about his private life. It was on the tip of her tongue to enquire the name of his lady friend, but there was nothing to be gained by confrontation and she made as if to rise.

'I'm glad to have a chance to talk to you, Anna Ivanova.' Nicholas gestured with his hand for her to stay. 'I'm concerned about your brother.'

'About Sasha?'

'Sasha and Sergei Volkonsky are members of a secret society plotting a conspiracy against the tsar. Your brother must break all links with them immediately.'

For a moment, Anna wondered whether she had heard him right. How dare Nicholas denounce Sasha as a traitor? She should slap him and storm out of the room, but she was still half-paralysed by the shock of Peter's betrayal. She stared at him incredulously, not knowing what to say or how to react.

'The emperor has forgiven disloyalty once, but he won't do so again.'

'What do they hope to achieve?' When Anna finally spoke, her voice sounded far away, as if it belonged to someone else.

'A good question. To secure a constitution and put an end to serfdom. They believe the Russian people are unhappy because the tsars have stolen their freedom.'

Anna was silent. Since she'd first had cause to question the world she lived in, the trickle of doubt was gaining strength. A system that depended on bondage was reprehensible and no better than slavery. On that matter, she agreed with her brother. Serfdom had been abolished in other countries – in Prussia and Poland – so why not in Russia? She couldn't be sure of the arguments, but she knew enough, had lived enough, to recognise nothing was as straightforward as she wished.

She took a moment to compose herself before she responded. 'Sasha may have radical opinions, but he would never betray Tsar Alexander. He admires him.'

'He also admires men whose ideals are more powerful than their fear of death.' Nicholas answered sombrely. 'Two nights ago, I visited the Green Lamp Club and they were all there: your brother, Volkonsky, Muravyov-Apostol and others. The place was so thick with pipe and cigar smoke I couldn't see who raised the toast: "Death to the tsar". The whole company cheered until a light flashing on the quay sobered them up.'

Her hurt momentarily forgotten, Anna pictured the scene. She imagined officers in uniform sprawled on sofas, drinking and smoking as great white puffs of St. Petersburg fog swirled through the windows. She could almost hear the clink of spurs and popping of champagne corks. But Nicholas Bulgarin was mistaken. Sasha hadn't been there. Whatever his political views, he would never be involved in treason.

'A petition has been presented to the tsar, which he will consider on his return from the south,' Nicholas continued at last. 'In the meantime, please warn Sasha Ivanovich that the imperial spies are aware of his activities.'

'How do you know all this?'

'I have connections at court and keep my ear to the ground.' He reached for a poker and stirred the coals in the grate, then stretched his legs towards the heat. 'There are rumours—'

'Only a fool believes in rumours.'

'Then you'll have to take my word for it.' A harder tone had entered his voice and Anna knew she had annoyed him. 'Our friends dream of change, but most Russians are suspicious of progress. Deep in our hearts, we want to stay as we are — alone and different from other nations. It will take a century for revolution to succeed in this country.'

Nicholas Bulgarin was one of those intellectuals with an opinion on everything, Anna thought. No doubt he contributed to the various journals lying around. He might have reason to suspect others, but he was wrong about Sasha.

'My brother's no revolutionary, I can assure you, sir. Nevertheless, I'll pass on your message. I take it you've also warned Captain Dashkovy.'

Anna stood up, straightening her jacket, and Nicholas came to his feet. 'I believe Captain Dashkovy's finally come to his senses.'

Nicholas stood close enough to her for Anna to detect the scent of gardenia on his clothes. So, the golden-haired beauty was his mistress! And what did that mean precisely?

Unwilling to meet his eyes, she held out her hand. 'Thank you for the tea, Count Bulgarin. I will not trouble you again.'

'I'm glad we could speak, Anna Ivanova. Please don't be too disheartened. This disappointment will pass. Tolerance and compatibility are better companions in life than romantic passion. Forget about everlasting love. It doesn't exist.'

✿

He would say that, Anna thought as she walked to the carriage with Mazra. Pushkin wrote about people like Nicholas Bulgarin – libertines who drifted from woman to woman without loving any of them. Then again, she had believed Peter was a better man and had failed to see what was in front of her eyes.

She managed to hold herself together during the drive, but the strain broke as she arrived home. Without taking off her cloak and bonnet, Anna ran up three flights of stairs to her studio and slammed the door shut. Breathing hard, she leant against it. The sky was heavy with impending snow but the large window suffused the room with light. Her studio was as she had left it, the table covered with brushes and her easel set up and ready. A swathe of material draped the background of a chair where Peter would have sat for his portrait. It was in here she was going to offer him her heart – but he didn't love her. He loved Olga Bulgarin.

He's a coward, Anna thought with sudden anger. If he had a shred of honour, he would have told me. Peter only flirted with me because it's easy to captivate a girl of sixteen. Did he think I was too young to have feelings – too immature to fall in love?

She must do something, or she would scream. Her hand touched an empty vase and she picked it up and hurled it against the wall. The sound of smashing glass brought a sense of release and she sat down. She began opening drawers and pulling out her sketchbooks. There were drawings of Peter Dashkovy on almost every page. She had portrayed him as she believed him to be – beautiful and sincere. How could she have been so mistaken about him? Casting her mind back, Anna thought of his smile and the gentle pressure of his fingers when he gave her his hand. Peter had always been free with his compliments but had never gone beyond easy, teasing banter. Not once had he made amorous advances towards her. Had it all been an illusion? Had she only imagined that he loved her?

Anna rubbed her temples angrily. Peter might have loved her once, but he was going to marry Olga. She had lost him forever and hoped they would both be miserable for the rest of their lives. Picking up a knife, she began to cut out her drawings, not caring that she slashed whole pages and left serrated edges. She attacked her sketchbooks until every image of Peter was excised. When she came to the very last, she paused. She had sketched it from memory on the day after Sasha's wedding. Peter was smiling, and it was one of her best drawings, but she couldn't keep it. Gathering the pieces of paper, she threw them into the stove and waited until they caught fire before she shut the door. All traces of Peter had been destroyed. As heartbreak overwhelmed her, she bowed her head and wept.

November, St. Petersburg

My dear Olga,

Thank you for your letter and effusive compliments on my character which I hope are not entirely unmerited. I'm greatly reassured by Captain Dashkovy's promise. I believe him to be a man of his word and highly esteemed by his fellow officers. I trust they will follow his example.

Your friend, Miss Anna Brianski, came to call after you left us and was disappointed to miss you. She's an unusual young woman with an appealing lack of artifice, and a skilled artist. When Aunt Varenka next visits St. Petersburg, I suggest you recommend her to visit Miss Brianski. She will be interested and impressed by her talent.

We await the tsar's return to St. Petersburg at the end of the month and I look forward to seeing you next week.

Most affectionately yours,
Nicholas

Chapter Ten

Anna was preoccupied as she looked out of the window on her way to the Volkonsky palace the next day. For three years Peter had been the centre of her life and now he was gone. I loved him for so long, she thought, her heart swelling with misery. What do I do with all my love? How can I suddenly stop and not think about him? Somehow, I must or I won't be able to paint.

In an attempt to distract herself, Anna went over her conversation with Nicholas Bulgarin. He said government spies were watching Sasha and that he belonged to a secret society. Were these drinking clubs illegal? Until now, she'd had no knowledge of secret societies or anything like them. If only she understood more. Ladies were obliged to leave the room when men talked politics and she hated being ignorant. Had yesterday been different, there were many questions she would like to have asked Count Bulgarin. Had he read Pushkin's inflammatory poem? Who was the infamous Pavel Pestel? And what was it about the radicals that so upset her father?

As they drove beside the river, she saw fishermen crouched over lines dropped through the ice into the water below. The temperature was well below freezing and they would be lucky to get a catch. She would send Omelko home while she was painting, Anna decided. The first sitting usually took a morning and he could return to collect her later. Mazra had packed her mahogany box with everything needed: porcelain mixing pans, washbowls, trays for brushes and blocks of pigment, along with her travelling easel. It would be a half-size portrait of mother and child, as informal and intimate as she could make it.

Arriving at the front gates, they picked their way gingerly over the snow that had fallen since the path was last cleared. Two footmen were waiting at the door and Mazra was taken to the staff quarters while a page escorted Anna upstairs to Maria's apartments. He carried her equipment down the long gallery she remembered from her last visit. Her gaze passed over the portraits of the Volkonskys paraded along the walls. They looked an arrogant bunch, she thought, but Sergei was different from the rest of his family. He was courteous and kind. Maria had married the best of them.

The central chamber of the palace was a vast empty space with pillars of white marble and a mosaic floor. No fires had been lit and it was so cold that Anna could see her breath in front of her face. How anyone could live here in the winter was beyond comprehension and she kept on her furs until they came to Maria's rooms.

Maria embraced her and introduced her to her baby boy, who played with his nurse on the floor as Anna set up her easel. To prevent it from cockling, she stretched the woven paper and pinned it the edges of a drawing board, then asked Maria to sit sideways to the window so that the light fell on her face.

'Turn your head to look at me, as if I've just come into the room. Try not to move, if you can help it.'

Her friend looked happier than when they last met. Her eyes were bright, a smile touching her expression as Anna stood back to study her subject, absorbing the sweep of her eyelashes and lift of her cheekbones. Maria's beauty was cool not warm, with her clear complexion and black hair and, more than any other feature, her eyes expressed her character. They were unusually unblinking and, around the outside of each iris, a dark grey ring drew the gaze as imperiously as the pronounced corners of her mouth.

Many of her sitters were apprehensive at the start, but Maria's gaze was steady as Anna began by marking the connecting lines in pencil. It was crucial to get the proportions of the face correct – hairline to eyebrows, eyebrows to nose, nose to chin. Her practised eye took in the varying depths of colour, the contrast between glowing skin and the deep blue of the dress. Maria wore a gold bracelet at the cuff of her sleeve from which her thin, strong fingers emerged, adding emphasis to her hands.

Anna covered the marked paper with a pale wash and then went to pick up little Nicolenka.

'He's an angel. I hope I can do him justice,' she said, sitting him on his mother's lap. 'Can you stay like that? I'll do an outline first and add details and colour later.'

The little boy smiled obligingly, his plump hand reaching for the collar of his mother's dress as he looked up at her. This was how she wanted it. The best portraits conveyed relationships. Anna kept to a soft line of charcoal, using her thumb to smudge the edges. When Nicolay become restless, she handed him back to the nurse and returned to work on Maria.

'I saw Count Bulgarin yesterday.' Anna concentrated on mixing the pigments and spoke nonchalantly. 'I called at the house, hoping to catch Olga.'

'And did you find him alone?'

'Yes. Why?'

'There's talk of his liaison with a certain lady of the court. Nicholas had better be careful with that one. She's married to the tsar's cousin.' Maria spoke without moving her head. 'Oh, Anna I'm sorry about the other day. I don't know what got into me. I made up my mind Sergei no longer loved me – that he had someone else – and then he came home last night and told me everything. He's involved in a secret mission for the tsar. That's why he's been distracted and away so much. I'm ashamed of myself for doubting him.'

So, the woman at Count Bulgarin's home was a noblewoman. And she was his connection at court! If he was right, then Sergei had lied to his wife. Should she say something? But Nicholas Bulgarin might have been mistaken, in which case there was nothing to worry about.

The Volkonsky family had always been staunch supporters of the tsar and she didn't want to upset Maria. If Nicholas was unduly concerned, he could warn Sergei himself.

'Please can I have a rest now?'

Anna stopped and Maria stretched out her arms, wriggling her wrists. 'I must say, Olga's betrothal to Peter Dashkovy is a surprise. Why, only last summer I thought she was going to marry Prince George Dulov.'

Anna's stiffened, trying to keep her face a blank. She couldn't bear another humiliation. Never, never must Maria know of her feelings for Peter, and she answered in a flat voice, 'Apparently the captain's been courting Olga for over two years. Count Bulgarin was most specific on the matter.'

'Then her flirtation with the prince must have been a ruse to make Dashkovy jealous. Or maybe it was the other way around.' Maria resumed her pose on the sofa, her intelligent eyes on Anna's face. 'I love Olga, but we cannot forget the Bulgarins are Tatars. They're different from us. You never know what they're thinking.'

Anna was thrown by the remark, but this was a critical moment. The picture demanded her total concentration as she began filling in the contours of Maria's face, her thick black ringlets and the long line of her neck. Using a small sable brush, she painted her eyes below their distinctive black brows, her mouth and the oval line of her chin.

As she put down her brushes, Anna felt the fatigue she often experienced when starting a new work, and pressed her fingers to her forehead, trying to keep a headache at bay. She had been working for almost two hours, but the most difficult part was done. The composition was good, and the portrait should only take a couple more sittings. She would leave it for now and return tomorrow.

Maria took her through to her boudoir to tidy up and stood beside her as she washed her hands. As she took off her apron, Anna caught her reflection in the mirror. Her hair was drawn back in a net, but a few curls had escaped and straggled across her forehead. There was a smudge of blue paint on one cheek and dark shadows under her eyes.

'You're so talented, Anna,' Maria said, 'but too pretty be an artist all your life. Surely, some young man has captured your heart?'

'No. Not really.'

'What about Michael Pavel, Sofia's adorable brother? He's clever and charming. I'm convinced he has a crush on you.'

As they walked back to the nursery, Anna pondered Michael. She liked him but had never thought of him as a suitor. There were other young men whose company she enjoyed. If not for Peter, she might have chosen one of them. A ragged pain tore at her heart as she hugged Maria and then took her leave without delay. Wrapped in her furs, she walked behind the footman who escorted her downstairs. They returned the way they had come, through a series of salons, across the great hall and down the long gallery. As they came to the end, Anna heard footsteps on the flagstones behind her and glanced over her shoulder. She recognised Major Renin at once. He was wearing a full-length redingote, carrying a hat and cane, and, like her, was on his way out.

Boris Renin was the last person she expected to meet in the Volkonsky palace. Sergei and Maria had no time for him, yet he was without an escort and obviously familiar with the place. Anna expected him to stop and exchange a few words, but he walked past with no more than a curt nod of his head.

He must have been paying his respects to the dowager princess. Did Maria know that he came to visit her mother-in-law? There was something sinister about him being here. Could he be a government spy – one of those people Nicholas had spoken of? Boris Renin was an expert in flattery, but what could he hope to get out of Princess Volkonsky? Unless – the thought stopped Anna in her tracks – unless he had come to the palace for a specific purpose. If what Nicholas Bulgarin said was true, then Sergei Volkonsky was also under the surveillance of the secret police. Was Renin buttering up the old lady in order to extract information to use against her son?

Chapter Eleven

'Something must happen!' Anna said the words fervently as she knelt in front of the icon of Saint Anne. 'Olga doesn't love Peter. Please God, make something happen to prevent him marrying her.'

She looked into the saint's kindly, tranquil face and found no answer. It was heresy to doubt God's Will, but unquestioning obedience was not in Anna's nature. God was omniscient. He knew that she and Peter were meant to be together. If He doesn't help me now, she thought as she climbed into bed, why should I go on believing in Him?

She had finished the portrait today and decided against telling Maria about Major Renin. The dowager princess ruled supreme in her palace and permitted no interference from her daughter-in-law. She must be a nightmare to live with, but only once had Anna heard Maria be disloyal. 'I call her the sacred cow,' she had declared during the last sitting. 'Sacred to the tsar and a cow to the rest of us.' Her tone wasn't serious but there was an undercut to it that heartened Anna. Her friend had spirit and wouldn't be crushed by her mother-in-law.

Anna lay still, waiting for sleep to envelop her, until she heard the creak of footsteps on the floorboards outside her bedroom. Sasha was home at last. Sofia would be relieved, she thought, as his boots thumped crossed the landing. She sank back on the pillows, and had closed her eyes when a door slammed. Anna sat bolt upright, listening intently. It wasn't like Sasha to be clumsy. Was he drunk? She hoped not after Sofia had waited so long for his return.

All was quiet and she lay down again. Then, it seemed the very next moment, there was a loud crash. Anna relit her candle and got out of bed. Putting on a housecoat, she tiptoed across the landing and put her ear to the door of Sofia's bedroom. She could hear Sasha's voice, low and urgent, and the sound of muffled sobbing. Without stopping to knock, she turned the knob and walked in.

A chair lay on its side and a huge fire blazed in the hearth. Sasha was emptying the desk, turning drawers upside down so their contents fell to the floor. He was sorting through letters, reading them quickly, then throwing them onto the flames. Letters and documents were scattered all over the room.

She cried out, 'Mother of God, what are you doing?'

'Pavel Pestel's been arrested,' Sasha muttered without looking round. 'I must destroy all incriminating evidence. Do you have anything from Pushkin? If so, bring it here at once!'

Anna stared at her brother. His hair was dishevelled and there was a strange look in his eyes. On the mantelpiece, the flame of a candle wavered, wax dripping slowly down the edges into the copper holder, and behind her she heard Sofia's fast, shallow breathing.

'Go and fetch your Pushkin drawings! Anything to do with that man's dangerous. Do you have them? '

'But they're mine.' Anna's voice was hoarse.

'Damnation, Anna! Will you do as I say? Don't just stand there. Time is of the essence.'

'I won't let you have my drawings. They're the most precious thing in my portfolio.'

Her heart was pounding and her face burned from the roaring heat of the fire. At any moment, the leaping flames might set the chimney alight, but she would not hand over her Pushkin drawings. She had never seen Sasha like this. Silent and grim-faced, he went on tearing up manuscripts, scowling as they curled and blackened into ashes.

'Please tell me what's happening, Sasha. Let us help you.' Sofia knelt up on the bed, her arms outstretched as she pleaded with her husband.

'I don't have time now. I'll explain tomorrow. Promise not to say a word to anyone – nor you either, Anna. Everything will be fine. This is only a precaution.'

Sasha walked over and took Sofia in his arms. He held her to him, stroking her hair, before he took her face in his hands and kissed her. As Anna watched from the doorway, she heard the whinnying of horses and jingling harnesses in the street below. Sasha had a carriage waiting for him. It was snowing and past midnight. Where in the name of God was he going?

Sasha shrugged on his heavy military overcoat and gave the fire a final stir. She stood motionless as he bent down and touched her cheek with cold lips before he went out. 'Death to the tsar!' The words came into Anna's head, like water dropping onto stones, as his footsteps echoed down the stairs. Could she imagine her brother ever saying such a thing? She thought of Nicholas Bulgarian's description of the Green Lamp Club. He had insisted Sasha was among those toasting the assassination of the emperor and she'd refused to believe him. Even if he had been there, it was only as a sympathetic spectator, she had told herself. His actions tonight changed everything.

Sofia was trembling, her eyes like glass, and Anna sat down on the bed beside her. For a long time neither of them spoke. The fire burned down slowly until only small flames licked the grate. When Sofia seemed calmer, Anna stood up and kissed her goodnight.

'What does this mean, Anna?' Sofia asked tremulously, a look of strain returning to her face.

'I'm not sure, darling—'Anna began and then stopped. She must tell Sofia what Nicholas Bulgarin had said. If Sasha was in trouble, then his wife had a right to know. Between them, they could help him.

As she hesitated, uncertain how to begin, Sofia reached out and grasped her hand. 'There's something you must know, Anna. I wanted to tell Sasha, but he was too frantic to listen. I saw the doctor yesterday and I'm with child. We must pray it's a blessing.'

Chapter Twelve

St. Petersburg, 27th November 1825

It was Sunday and Anna was expecting her brother in the Sale d'Or. With its walls of patterned white and gold silk, it was the prettiest room in the house. Different kinds of wood made up the floor in a design as rich as an oriental rug and, at either end, sofas and chairs were arranged for conversation around gilded tables. It was an elegant, opulent room, always filled with flowers and used by the family on Sundays.

It was a clear, cold morning, the window frosted with ice, and Anna absently traced a pattern on the inside of the glass. When Sasha had returned the next afternoon, she had watched him like a hawk, but his air of artificial gaiety prevented her mentioning the events of the night before. With the news of Sofia's pregnancy, the drama had been swept aside, but she must pass on Nicholas Bulgarin's warning and had asked him to meet her alone before lunch. She hoped Sasha would take her seriously. How would he react? There was no time to wonder, for just then the door opened and Michael Pavel walked into the room.

'I overtook Sasha on the way up.' Michael bowed, then walked over and kissed her hand. 'I begged for two minutes alone with you.'

Michael was wearing a stylish double-breasted nankeen jacket and dark breeches. The high standing collar of his shirt reached the bottom of his ears and his silk cravat was immaculately tied. Anna had rarely seen him out of uniform and was impressed. She patted the seat next to her.

'I'm on leave for a week with nothing to do.' Michael leant back and crossed one booted leg over the other. 'I was wondering if you'd like to go for a sleigh drive this afternoon – with your parents' consent, of course.

'Are you sure it's not too cold?'

'I've enough bearskins to keep you warm. I'd like to spend more time with you, Anna Ivanova.'

The note in his voice brought Anna's head up. Michael was smiling and the good humour in his eyes made it impossible not to respond.

'Thank you. That would be lovely.' Anna hesitated. She wasn't ready to embark on a new love affair and didn't want to give the wrong impression. 'I know you only wish to be kind, but I'm hoping to establish myself as an artist and must devote myself to it.'

'A sleigh ride is hardly a lifetime commitment.' Michael rolled his eyes and put a hand to his brow in mock horror. 'I've no intention of compromising your burgeoning career.'

'I do love my work—' Anna began and stopped as Michael took hold of her hand. She had seen that look in men's eyes before, usually before a declaration, and caught her breath.

'I know I've no right to ask you, dear Anna, but is there someone else?'

'No one, upon my honour.'

'So, I may still hope?' Michael persisted.

'I don't know what you mean,' Anna answered vaguely. She searched her mind for a way to change the subject and thought of Boris Renin. 'I meant to ask you before. How well do you know Major Renin?'

'He's my senior officer. I wouldn't claim him as a friend. Why do you ask?'

'Because I ran into him at the Volkonsky palace. What do you think he was doing there? Could he be a government spy?' She'd spoken the question before realising how bold it sounded.

'Heavens, no! Was he wearing a cloak and carrying a dagger?' Michael laughed until tears came into his eyes. He released her hand to search for a handkerchief to wipe them away before he went on. 'I expect he was trying to gain favour with Princess Volkonsky. He's determined to be a lion of St. Petersburg society.'

'What do know about his background?'

'He never talks about his family, only his career in the army. I believe his father was a master at the Lyceum and he studied there for a time.'

Anna had heard of the Lyceum at Tsarskoye Selo. The school had been established by Tsar Alexander, and Pushkin had been a pupil there. She was silent, waiting for Michael to elaborate.

'I asked him once if he'd made friends among the other students. He implied they were all conceited, over-privileged young men. No doubt they made him feel inferior.' He paused and then added, 'Don't tell me you've taken a shine to him.'

'On the contrary. I have the impression he's the kind of man who uses people and then discards them.'

'Boris Renin has many faults., Michael frowned and gazed thoughtfully round the room. 'He's fiercely ambitious — but there's no harm in that. Why are you so wary of him?'

Before Anna had time to answer, there was a rustle of skirts and Count and Countess Brianski entered with Sasha and Sofia. Michael stood up and Sofia kissed her brother on both cheeks.

'Good morning, Mishka. And what brings you here today? Are you joining us for lunch?'

'Oh yes, do please stay,' Valentina interposed. 'Are your parents both well?'

'Indeed, they are, ma'am. And I'd be delighted to join you for lunch, thank you. If truth be told, I came to ask your permission to take Anna on a sleigh ride this afternoon.'

Sasha pulled a face of faint surprise. 'Don't get your hopes up, my friend. Anna's a veritable ice maiden.'

'Don't say a such thing, Sasha,' Sofia scolded her husband. 'Anna's right to take her time. Marry in haste, repent at leisure.'

'Is that your opinion of wedded bliss, my love?' Sasha teased.

'Of course not,' Sofia answered evenly. 'However, there should be no secrets between husband and wife.'

Sofia had her arm through husband's but there was the hint of steel in her voice. So, she hasn't forgotten the other night, Anna thought. How could she? She keeps Sasha on his toes; yet I must speak to him.

'Can you spare me a moment, dear brother?'

Sasha shrugged and smiled, detaching himself from Sofia. It was then that Anna became aware of the tolling of bells. They had been ringing all morning, calling people to Mass, their sound muted through the sealed windows. This was different. The slow, ominous peeling was unmistakable, and Anna glanced at her parents. Valentina's lips were pressed together while her father seemed unaware anything was amiss.

As Anna turned to Sasha, there was a clatter of footsteps outside the door and Monsieur Filot, normally the most polite and formal of men, burst into the room. Andre Filot had served her father for twenty years and never did anything in a rush. He was a tall, thin man with a head too small for his body and a receding hairline. His eyelids batted nervously as they all stared at him. His lips worked to form words, but no sound emerged.

'What is it, Filot?' Count Brianski asked brusquely. 'Come on! Out with it, man!'

'C'est absolument terrible...' Monsieur Filot began. His hands were shaking as he took a handkerchief from his pocket and wiped his brow. He swallowed and passed his tongue over his lips. 'Our beloved Tsar Alexander's dead. He passed away in Taganrog eight days ago.'

'Mon Dieu! How? Are you sure?' Ivan Brianski's knees seemed to give way and Michael caught him by the arm.

'He was taken by typhoid fever. Word reached Petersburg this morning. Grand Duke Nicholas was informed as he left the cathedral.'

'Dear Lord have mercy on his soul. God grant him eternal rest.' Valentina made the sign of the cross and fell to her knees. She clasped her hands in prayer and Anna and Sofia knelt down on either side of her. Her father sank onto a chair while Sasha and Michael remained standing. Ivan Brianski looked shocked, his mouth half-open and his eyes glazed.

'Holy Mary, mother of God,' Valentina whispered in a thin voice. 'Pray for us sinners. Now and at the hour of our death...'

Anna felt as if she had been hit by a thunderbolt as she murmured the response. Alexander had been on the throne since before she was born. He was the tsar who defeated Napoleon and was adored by his people. He wasn't yet fifty years old and had seemed in good health. How could he be dead? She kept her head bowed and peered through her fingers.

'Christ have mercy. Lord have mercy...'

Valentina and Sofia went on as Anna fell silent. She was looking at Michael as he clutched the back of the chair, gripping it so hard she thought it might break in his hands. Michael belonged to the Imperial Chevalier Guards, the tsar's regimental bodyguard. He was personally acquainted with Alexander. For him, it was like losing a member of his family. His face was drawn and his eyes wet with tears. She wanted to comfort him but dared not move. Sofia's chin was on her knuckles so she couldn't see her face, and her gaze went to her brother. The unholy glow in his eyes and tautness in the muscles of his cheeks sent an icy coldness down her spine.

In those few moments, Anna registered the visual details as vividly if she were working on a painting: Monsieur Filot leaning against the pillar of the doorway through which came the sound of weeping women, her mother and Sofia reciting the litany, and her father slumped in the chair with Michael standing rigidly behind him. It would stay in her mind forever. Her brother was alone by the window, his expression tense but not distraught. Anna knew him too well to be mistaken. Sasha had undergone a change — a flame had been ignited that could not be extinguished. She could feel it in her bones. Whatever it was he and his friends had in mind, news of Alexander's sudden death was not unwelcome.

Chapter Thirteen

14th December, St. Petersburg 1825

The winter solstice fell on the fourteenth of December. It was the lowest, darkest day of the year and Anna awoke with a sense of foreboding. Tsar Alexander was dead. Never again would he see his beloved capital in the north, and the city was in a state of mourning. No one went out and windows were swathed in black drapes. It seemed impossible that the tenor of life could change in so short a time. People spoke in low voices, moving quietly around their black-festooned homes and the streets were deserted.

St. Petersburg was riven by conflicting reports. Alexander had no legitimate children and no one knew who was the rightful heir. Was it Constantine, his next brother and governor of Poland? He had a reputation for courage and caring for his soldiers and was popular with the army. Anna believed Sasha would support him, but Constantine had not come back from Poland. It was even rumoured he had abdicated in favour of the youngest brother, Nicholas – a cold fish, if ever there was one. Others accused Nicholas of hatching a conspiracy to usurp the throne. It took five days for dispatches to travel between Warsaw and St. Petersburg. A fortnight had passed and still there came no announcement.

'We've become the laughing stock of Europe,' Count Brianski declared. 'Russia has no ruler, only two prospective tsars passing around the crown like a cup of tea.'

The Russian soldier held a mystical belief in the supremacy of the rightful tsar and the army was becoming restless. Sasha had been recalled to barracks and only allowed home twice to see Sofia. Anna had tried to talk to him but only succeeded on the last evening when he was on the way out. As they stood in the hall, she pleaded with him to break ties with all secret societies.

'You've been listening to gossip, dear Anna. Everything will be alright, I promise.'

'But Count Bulgarin insisted—'

'And what does Count Bulgarin know about anything? I love my family and am fully aware of my duties.' Sasha looked pale, even as the epaulettes on his jacket lifted in a shrug. 'Should anything untoward happen, I know you'll look after Sofia and our unborn son. I entrust them to your care.'

He spoke in a tone that alarmed Anna. What did he mean, 'should anything untoward happen'? Why couldn't he explain what was going on? Was he trying to protect his friends? She was his sister and would never betray him. Just when she needed reassurance, he had frightened her half to death. Thinking back to this last conversation, Anna let her head fall against the bedhead. Nicholas Bulgarin said a petition had been submitted to the tsar. Surely, once there was a new emperor, they could argue their case with him?

It was still dark, but Anna could hear doors opening and the careful tread of servants on the stairs. Soon Mazra would come with her breakfast and light the fire, then she would get dressed and go to see Sofia.

An hour later, wearing the same black outfit as the day before, she crossed the landing and tapped on her sister-in-law's door. She heard a faint 'Entre' and went in. Only one small candle was alight, and she opened the heavy damask curtains before she went to kneel beside the bed. Pale grey light filtered into the room. She rested her elbows on the counterpane with her chin on her hands so her face was the same level as Sofia's. Her sister-in-law's hair was spread like fine gossamer over the pillow and her eyes were open.

'Are you unwell? Is it the morning sickness?'

'I couldn't sleep last night. Every time I closed my eyes, I dreamt of demons and death.'

'I hope Sasha didn't say anything to upset you?'

'No, on the contrary. He was happier than I've seen him for weeks. He told me how much loved me – and that our son will be born at the dawn of a new Russia.'

'Try to sleep now. Mama will come and see you later.'

'The dawn of a new Russia.' The words echoed in her mind as Anna closed the door and made her way downstairs. Her mother was absent from the drawing room, and she searched the house until she found her in her private sitting room. Valentina was sitting on a chaise longue and staring out of a window.

'Sofia's staying in bed for now, Mama. She had a bad night.'

Silk and satins were too showy for mourning and Valentina wore a plain bombazine dress with a starched collar. Apart from two high spots of colour in her cheeks, her skin was white as marble as she sat with her hands clasped in her lap. Anna noticed how her fingers moved restlessly, hooking round each other, while the rest of her body was still. Her mother believed in self-restraint at all times and her fidgeting hands made Anna nervous.

'Your father received a message. Nicholas has declared himself Tsar,' Valentina murmured, almost as if she was speaking to herself. 'A group of officers have marched their regiments to Senate Square and are refusing to swear allegiance to Nicholas. They're protesting that Constantine is the rightful heir. Papa's gone to find out what's happening. I tried to stop him, but he wouldn't listen. He went by droshky so as not to be recognised.' For the first time, Valentina turned her gaze to her daughter's face. 'He's alone, Anna. I fear for his safety.'

'Papa's more than able to look after himself.'

'The message said three thousand men. God knows how this will turn out.' Valentina's face changed and the brittle smile left her lips. She gave a half-sob, then silenced herself. Lifting a crease in her skirt, she crushed the fold of material in her fist.

'Please don't worry. I'll go to find Papa and bring him home. I'll take the carriage and ask Omelko to drive.'

'It's too dangerous, darling—'

'Listen to me, Mama.' Anna cut her off and took Valentina's hand. It felt cold compared to her own and she squeezed hard. 'I'm no longer a child and Omelko's strong as a bear. He'll keep me out of harm's way. It's only a protest and will probably be over by the time I get there.'

Without waiting for an answer, Anna called to Mazra to bring her fur hat and cloak and then hurried downstairs. The clock was striking twelve as she went out and stood on the top step. A bitterly cold wind blew from the north as she waited impatiently until the closed carriage on its runners drew up under the portico. Omelko handed her in, then climbed onto the driving board and gathered up the reins.

The low, glancing light of the winter sun slid along the frozen banks of the Neva, streaking the snow with pink as they headed towards Senate Square. Small groups of people were gathered at corners, roasting chestnuts in braziers. A few solitary figures stood on the pavements, but the frozen streets and canals were mostly empty and wrapped in eerie silence. They passed a shop window with candles still burning. A man, wearing spectacles, sat scribbling at a desk. He was doing an ordinary job on an ordinary day and Anna tried to stay calm. *Sasha knows his responsibilities*, she thought. *No doubt the message sent to the house was greatly exaggerated. It won't be anything serious, just a few squabbling soldiers. I only have to find Papa and persuade him to come home.*

They were crossing St. Isaac's bridge when they were brought to a halt. The carriage windows had iced over, so she couldn't see and she tapped on the roof. Omelko climbed down and opened the door. Getting out, she stood on the top step so that she was high enough to get a clear view. The road ahead was jammed by a regiment of Finnish Dragoons. There was no way they could get past them. Gripping the top of the door to keep her balance, she looked over the soldiers' crested caps to the expanse of white between the Senate and the Winter Palace.

Snow that had fallen during the night was melting and the ground gleamed with a coating of ice. In front of the bridge stood the statue of Peter the Great on his horse. In its dark shadow, Anna saw lines of soldiers armed with bayonets in battle formation, standing in squares and stamping their feet to keep warm. There were officers walking up and down shouting orders as adjutants on horseback cantered from one end of the line to the other. She made out the high stiff-feathered caps of the Moscow Regiment and the bearskins of the Grenadiers. They were too far off to distinguish clearly but she couldn't see the uniform of Life Guards. This was far bigger than she had imagined. God willing, Sasha had stayed away.

St. Isaac's church was under reconstruction and the workmen on the scaffolding had downed tools and were tearing off planks and bricks. A dense, disorderly crowd had gathered below, and artisans and labourers were running from the building, carrying bricks and fragments of stones. There were so many people! Some were well-dressed in greatcoats and high hats; others wore tattered sheepskins and ragged cloaks. Women wrapped in shawls moved among them, handing out vodka and hunks of bread. It was meant to be a peaceful demonstration but there was an air of menace in the crowd that sent a quiver of fear through Anna. Papa could be anywhere. Even if Omelko could force a way through the soldiers on the bridge, how could he find him in such a throng?

Squinting against the glare, Anna turned to look towards the Winter Palace and glimpsed the Chevalier Horse Guards in their white and blue uniform with high red collars. With a rising sense of alarm, she realised the emperor's regiments massively outnumbered their opponents. If Constantine had refused the crown and the army remained loyal to Nicholas, the protestors would be crushed. And now the mounted guard seemed to be preparing for a charge. A bugle sounded. As the cavalry charged, galloping towards the rebels, they were met by a volley of bullets. There was a thumping sound of horses falling before the order to retreat rang out, followed by noise of receding hooves.

The tsar's troops immediately regrouped, soldiers dragging heavy artillery into position and, between lines of cavalry, Anna glimpsed the gaping mouths of cannons. Horror squeezed her heart. Never before had she witnessed any kind of violence, let alone bloodshed. How could this be happening?

She saw infantrymen bend a knee beside their guns and bow their heads in prayer. This was a battle within the army itself. Many of the protestors had fought with Alexander in the war against Napoleon. They were known personally to Tsar Nicholas. Surely, no Russian soldier would draw the blood of a fellow comrade? There was a moment of stillness and, with a dropping in her stomach, Anna realised the tsar's deadly purpose. This wasn't a show of brinkmanship. The emperor's men were armed with muskets and cannons while the rebels wielded only pistols and swords. Something terrible was about to happen and there was nothing she could do to stop it. She was powerless to save her father.

The hiatus was broken by occasional shooting in the air and ragged cheers from the insurgents. And then, from the imperial ranks, a single horseman rode out on a grey horse. As he came closer, she recognised General Miloradovich. He was a friend of Madame Davydov, a hero of the battle of Borodino and adored by the ranks. He began riding back and forth and Anna strained to hear what he was saying, He was urging the men to lay down their arms, promising if they returned to barracks they would not be punished. For a moment, the insurgents' line seemed to waver until an officer of the Dragoons rode up and ordered him to withdraw.

General Miloradovich ignored him, calling to the troops to listen, until he was drowned out by yells of 'Hurrah for Constantine!' Lifting an arm in a gesture of peace, he turned his horse's head towards the palace. He was riding away when a man in a long coat with a hat pulled down over his face dashed out of the crowd. He had a pistol in his hand with the barrel aimed at General Miloradovich's back. Two shots rang out and the general slumped in the saddle. Petrified, his horse reared up and he fell to the ground where he lay face down and motionless, his blood staining the snow with a pool of red.

Anna's brain swirled in confusion and panic. General Miloradovich had been murdered by one of the rebels! And now the crowd of people were surging forwards towards the Winter Palace. Builders were hurling bricks and stones, attacking regiments loyal to the tsar as they closed in on the square. Police with batons began moving among the crowd in an attempt to disperse the onlookers. And then, above the screaming and chaos, came the ear-splitting thunder of cannon fire.

Thick clouds of black vapour curled upwards, blotting out the sun, and the world became an inferno of noise and flame as one explosion followed another. The air was thick with acrid smoke and people were running in all directions, shouting and crying. Anna heard shattering glass as a window cracked. A riderless horse galloped past. Omelko was shouting at her to get down, but she could not move. She stood transfixed until his arms came round her waist and he lifted her off her feet and manoeuvred her into the carriage. There was a click as he locked the door and Anna retched violently. She opened the window, breathing in gulps of cold air, then shut it and sank back against the swabs.

The mob were on the rampage. At any moment, the door would be broken open and she would be dragged out! We'll all be killed, she thought frantically as men and women buffeted the carriage, screaming at soldiers who blocked their way. Clenching her chattering teeth, Anna forced herself to look out. The bumping and pushing came from people trying to escape beyond the vehicles stuck on the bridge. A soldier in the uniform of the Life Guards staggered past. A bullet had hit him in the throat and foam bubbled from his discoloured lips. Another man was being held up by two comrades with blood pouring through his sleeve. Dear God, these were men from Sasha's regiment! Had Sasha and Peter Dashkovy led them to this carnage?

At last, Omelko managed to turn the horses and they began to move forwards. Progress was slow against the tide of government troops marching in the opposite direction and the sky so dark it seemed dusk already. Figures with torches flitted past the window but, in her mind, Anna saw only blackened faces and wounded, dying men. As shock set in, her whole body began to shake, her only thought that, somewhere in Senate Square, her father was in mortal danger.

This was a nightmare from which there would be no awakening. She had seen Russians kill their own people, bodies trampled by horses and men bleeding to death. Innocence had been shattered and the memory would haunt her forever. She wanted to weep, but her eyes were burning as if there would never be tears in them again. She hung her head and the drive home seemed to last forever before they turned through the gates into the courtyard.

As Omelko lowered the steps and gave her a hand out, Anna collected herself enough to instruct him to go back and search for Count Brianski. James, the footman, opened the door and she gave him her cloak and hat without a word. Just holding herself erect required concentration as she started up the stairs. Passing a mirror, she caught sight of her reflection and stopped. Her face was white as a paper mask with two black holes for eyes. For a moment, she saw herself as a child terrified of the dark. Her heart had begun its awful thudding again. She bit her lips and pinched her cheeks to give them colour.

Her throat was so parched, she was afraid she wouldn't be able to speak. I can't break now, she thought desperately. I have to appear calm or I'll terrify them both. Mama must never know what happened today. If I frighten Sofia, she might lose her baby. Dear God, what shall I say?

Chapter Fourteen

Every step was an effort as Anna went on up. She stopped outside the small salon for a moment, then lifted her shoulders and opened the door. The room was warm and cheerful. Sofia was sitting with Valentina in front of the fire. Her mother was reading a book which she quickly put down. Both women turned to look at her, their faces taut with worry.

'Thank God you're home. We've had no news! Did you find Papa? Is he safe?' Valentina asked.

'Omelko thought it best that I came home. He's gone back to look for him. I'm sure he won't be long.'

'And Sasha?' Sofia's voice was a whisper.

'I didn't see him. There were so many people it was impossible to get beyond St. Isaac's bridge.'

Anna had left the door open and, as she spoke, voices rose from the hall below. A man was giving orders and Valentina came to her feet, brushing past her daughter as she walked out onto the landing.

'Thanks be to God!' she exclaimed. 'You're safe, Vanya. Are you hurt? Bring him up here, Josef. And someone help Count Bulgarin. Fetch me warm water, bandages and iodine.' Valentina was herself again, brisk and in charge as she came back into the room. 'Your father's been injured – I hope not too badly. Stay here and help me.'

Anna and Sofia stood motionless as a thumping sound came up the stairs and across the landing. The three men entered together. Nicholas's hand was at Count Brianski's elbow and Josef had his arm around his waist as they propelled him forwards and into an armchair.

Josef circled the room, lighting more lamps and Valentina knelt down beside her husband. There was a gash across his forehead. She rinsed a linen towel in warm water and wiped off the blood.

'Please tell us what happened?' she asked without turning her head from the task.

Nicholas took a cloth from Josef and wiped his hands. 'The tsar ordered his troops to cut off Senate Square and the mood of the crowd turned ugly. Count Brianski was caught in the middle of a riot. Fortunately, I was passing and managed to extricate him. No one was safe.'

Valentina applied iodine to the wound and the count winced. 'Count Bulgarin intervened at considerable risk to himself.' He spoke faintly. 'I'm most grateful to you, sir.'

'Please be so kind as to tell us everything?' Anna glanced at Nicholas. His hair was ruffled and there was a bruise on his cheek. 'Would you like to sit down?'

Nicholas shook his head and leant an arm on the mantelpiece with his legs crossed at the ankles. It was a moment before he spoke. 'The tsar spent the day vacillating. Only when he was sure the majority of the army supported him did he decide to take action. He ordered cannon trained on the insurgents. At first, the gunners were reluctant to obey and the protesters held their ground, but then the serious stuff began. The artillery was loaded with grapeshot and fired indiscriminately, killing soldiers and civilians alike.'

Sofia gasped, struggling to hold back tears. As if unaware of her presence before, Nicholas looked at her for the first time. 'Forgive me, Madame Brianski. I should have told you at once. Your husband's alive and unharmed. I believe he's being held at the Winter Palace with Sergei Volkonsky.'

His words were met with stunned silence. Anna could hardly believe what he was saying. Sasha and Sergei were men of integrity who wanted a better future for Russia. Was the tsar so afraid of the nobility that he was prepared to cut them down rather than consider their requests? She heard her father's rasping cough and Valentina's sharp intake of breath.

The mantel clock went on ticking, but time seemed to stand still until Sofia asked in a low voice, 'And officers of the Imperial Guard? Do you have news of my brother Michael Pavel?'

Her cheeks were drained of colour and Nicholas answered gently, 'As far as I know, apart from General Miloradovich, there were no casualties among government forces.'

'General Miloradovich – how can this be?' Ivan Brianski's eyes stared at Anna in disbelief. Twisting in his chair, he clutched her hand. 'What's he saying about Miloradovich, *Ivitsa*?'

'I don't know, Papa.' Overwrought nerves made Anna sharper than she intended. 'We must let Count Bulgarin explain everything to us.'

'You're aware Nicholas Romanov proclaimed himself tsar this morning?'

The three women nodded. Anna felt her father's grip tighten around her fingers until they hurt.

'The rebels believed their show of military strength would rally the regiments in support of Constantine.' Nicholas spoke clearly and steadily. 'When it was finally proven Constantine had sworn allegiance to Nicholas, the army turned against them. Their only route of escape was onto the Neva. As the defeated men broke ranks and fled to the river, the tsar moved his cannon onto the ice. They were mown down like animals. Those who survived were pushed into the water along with the wounded and dead.'

Anna heard a soft moan and saw Sofia's head fall forwards as she fainted in her chair. Nicholas moved swiftly, leaning over her and feeling for a pulse in her wrist. Freeing herself from her father's grasp, Anna ran to the dresser and poured water from a jug. She lifted the glass to Sofia's lips as she opened her eyes.

'I'm so sorry...'

'It's alright, dearest. Sasha's alive and unharmed. Count Bulgarin assures us he's safe.'

'Will he be released tonight?'

A sob caught in Anna's throat. She had no answer and raised her frightened eyes to Nicholas's face.

'The tsar holds your family in high esteem,' he said slowly. 'We must trust he will show mercy and compassion.'

The fire crackled and Sofia stiffened her spine. 'Thank you for your honesty, sir.'

'It pains me to bring you such distressing news.'

'You saved my husband, Nicholas Petrovich. Please accept our deepest gratitude.' Valentina tried to be dignified as Josef came in with a tray of cakes. 'I hope you will take some sustenance. Please will you join us for tea?'

'Thank you, but I must go home.'

Nicholas made a bow and left the room.

Ivan Brianski let go of Anna's hand. The veins on his cheeks were colourless, his mouth slack, as Valentina held a glass of brandy to his lips. Sofia seemed to have recovered and was nibbling on a cake as Anna slipped out of the room. She could see Nicholas going down, taking the stairs two at a time, and ran after him, her hand on the banister rail to stop herself falling. By the time she reached the hall, a page was helping him on with his greatcoat.

As she stood watching from the bottom of the stairs, her shuddering breaths turned to sobs and he looked round.

'They wanted to be martyrs for Russia.' His expression was grave. 'They were determined to succeed or to die in the attempt.'

Anna's chest was tight with tears and she fixed her gaze on the round table at the bottom of the stairs. 'Sasha promised me everything would be alright. Why was he there? He's always been so...'

'It was a point of honour for your brother to stand with his comrades. Pestel, Muravyov-Apostel and Ryleyev are some of the finest men of their generation.'

'But they didn't have a chance... You told them so!'

'My opinion was irrelevant. Their loyalty was to Alexander and Constantine, not to their brother. The tsar's death gave them an opportunity they couldn't resist.'

'And Peter Dashkovy?' At last, Anna asked the question burning in her mind.

Nicholas Bulgarin gave her a long look, then walked across the hall. 'I'm afraid Dashkovy was one of the leaders. Both he and your brother will be interrogated personally by the tsar. And now I must go and tell Olga.'

His words shattered the last vestiges of Anna's control. She swayed on her feet and Nicholas's hands dropped on her shoulders. Her face was pressed to the rough material of his coat and he held her against him until the weakness passed. Then she stood back and wiped her hand across her eyes. 'Yes, you must go immediately. It was kind of you to bring Papa home. Thank you.'

'We don't yet know how many died today. You must be brave, Anna Ivanova. Your family have need of your courage.'

As he opened the front door and went out, Anna put her back to the wall and slid slowly to the ground. Nicholas had known the revolution was doomed. He had tried to warn them and failed, just as she had failed Sasha. What would happen to them now?

The candles were burning low and hissing as wicks drowned in melted wax. Anna could hear no voices from staff quarters or from upstairs, and waves of guilt licked through her. She had prayed for something to happen. But not this! Never this! Dear God, let Peter marry Olga rather than face death!

I didn't try hard enough to convince Sasha. If I'd told Sofia, she might have made him change his mind. Why didn't I warn Mama and Papa? It would have made no difference, a voice in her head answered. Nothing on this earth could have stopped Sasha. He believes in freedom for all men. He risked his life to put an end to serfdom and you should be proud of him.

Anna was too distraught to feel proud. The first day of Tsar Nicholas's reign had been stained with blood and he would never forgive them. Cold terror seized her and she covered her face with her hands. 'Lord Almighty, protect our loved ones,' she prayed out loud. 'Spare them the tsar's retribution. Save Sasha, Peter and Sergei, and I swear I will never ask anything for myself again.'

Part Three

December, Boltyshka

Dearest Anna,

The news has broken my heart. It's not only Sergei's arrest that pains me but that he and Sasha could be lured into such danger. My sister, Ekaterina, tells me after the rebellion was put down, the tsar ordered the blood to be scraped off the ice and the ground covered with fresh snow so no one should know the extent of the massacre. I thank heaven that my beloved Sergei and your brother were not killed.

The tsarina has assured my mother-in-law she is to continue with her court duties. Indeed, she is to be honoured with the Order of St. Catherine. I am returning to St. Petersburg but refuse to lodge in the Volkonsky Palace and will stay with Olga Bulgarin.

My father and brothers blame Sergei for my misfortune and urge me to separate from him. I am tormented by their anger. Why can't they understand that I still love my husband? My father is trying to prevent me meeting with the wives of other prisoners but Count Bulgarin will help me. He is a good friend to Sergei.

I fear Sofia may face similar intimidation from her family. You are strong, dear Anna. Please don't let her return to Moscow until we have a chance to entreat the tsar for clemency. Sergei and Sasha have not sinned beyond forgiveness.

In haste, with love and sorrow,
Maria

POSTSCRIPT I have heard nothing from Olga concerning Captain Dashkovy —
no doubt all will be revealed when I see her next week.

Chapter Fifteen

One month later. January 1826

A small slit of light came through the curtains and crept across the room to the bed. Anna felt it on her face and opened her eyes, blinking at the brightness. Sleep had not come easily and it was morning already. Today was the day the fate of Sasha and Peter was to be announced. Michael had promised to come as soon as he received news. It was the day she feared most, the day that would demand her greatest strength.

Anna stepped gingerly onto the cold floor, shivering as she wrapped herself in a fur cloak and went to the window. She could see the low silhouette of the Peter and Paul Fortress on the far side of the Neva. Peter and Sasha were incarcerated in damp, cold cells beneath sea level. If only they could take them blankets and food – but the families were not allowed to visit. The fortress was notorious for outbreaks of small pox, pneumonia and typhoid. If Sasha fell ill, he could die.

There had been no word from him since the day of his arrest and the strain was unbearable. Anna saw it on her father and mother's faces. Papa, always so optimistic, could not bring himself to smile, while Valentina spent days locked in her bedroom. Sofia tried to be brave and kept her fears to herself, but Anna felt her despair. Christmas and New Year went by uncelebrated and days passed that she couldn't remember at all. She tried to bolster her parents' spirits but, when she thought of Sasha, her strength deserted her.

Their peaceful, leisured existence was gone forever. Every day, every hour brought fear and dread; yet outside the house, life continued as normal. Society was still in mourning, but sleighs and droshkies crossed the city as people went about their business. How could the world behave as if nothing had changed when her brother's life hung in the balance? Suspense, sorrow and diminishing hope frayed Anna's nerves to breaking point. To her parents, the cause of their agony seemed senseless. But Sasha had done what he believed to be right and she could not condemn him.

And then, yesterday they learned that five of the Decembrists, as the Decembrists were now called had been executed: the brilliant, charismatic Pavel Pestel, gentle Muravyov-Apostel, Ryleyev the poet, Bestuzhev-Ryumin and Kakhovsky. Despite pleas of mercy from the empress, there had been no last-minute reprieve. The whole of St. Petersburg was appalled. The hanged men came from some of the noblest families in Russia and been sent to the gallows like common criminals. The news terrified Anna. What would be the sentences for Sasha, Sergei and Peter? Only God could save them now. Was He listening? Did He hear her desperate prayers? She felt as if she was suspended in time, barely alive, waiting for a denouement she was too frightened to contemplate.

✿

'I hear Maria Volkonsky's returned to the city against her parents' wishes.' Count Brianski's voice broke the silence as they sat in the drawing room later that morning.

'Maria wants to be close to her husband. It's understandable,' Sofia answered.

'And how will it help him, if she's not allowed in the Fortress?' Ivan Brianski was dressed in a smoke-coloured tailcoat and white stockings. He had recovered from his injuries but looked haggard, his eyes sunken beneath their bushy brows. 'Mind you, the Raevsky family were never sure of Sergei Volkonsky and I don't blame them. His family has always supported the Romanovs yet he was one of the ring-leaders—'

'And what about Sasha? Do you judge him any differently?' Anna interrupted shortly.

'It's a comfort for Sasha that I'm nearby,' Sofia said mildly. 'I'm glad Maria's in St. Petersburg. It will help Sergei to know that she hasn't deserted him.'

'And then there's Olga Bulgarin.' Valentina was standing by a vase of flowers. She absently snapped the wilting head off a bloom, letting a haze of yellow pollen fall through her fingers. 'I suppose she'll put an end to her betrothal to Peter Dashkovy.'

Anna heart tightened, but she couldn't think about Peter now – only Sasha. She glanced nervously at the clock and saw it was past noon already. They had expected Michael earlier. Why was he so late? Did it mean bad news? It had been snowing all morning and large white flakes were piled high on the windowsills. Michael was delayed by the bad weather, she told herself, and began fiddling with her handkerchief. Her fingers worked agitatedly through the lace trim until the doorbell rang downstairs.

A few moments later, Josef ushered Michael into the room, followed by Nicholas and Olga Bulgarin with Maria Volkonsky. Anna was glad to see Maria, but why had the Bulgarins come? Maria was staying with them, she remembered. She must have asked them to accompany her – or else the verdict was so terrible that Michael hadn't the strength to speak to them on his own.

For a time, good manners demanded a measure of civility. Valentina sent Josef to the kitchen to fetch *zakuski* along with vodka for the men and cordial for the ladies. The footmen rearranged the furniture at one end of the room so they could all be together. Count and Countess Brianski sat on one sofa, Nicholas and Olga on the other, with Anna, Sofia and Michael in adjacent armchairs.

Nicholas acknowledged Anna with a nod and, as he leant over to speak to Maria, she studied Olga. She wore an elegant green coat with a high collar and sat on the edge of her seat, her expression tense. Despite her dislike of Olga, Anna felt an unexpected burst of sympathy. They both loved Peter and were suffering on his account. This was no time to feel anything as petty as jealousy. Olga glanced at her and gave a tight-lipped smile, but the green eyes revealed nothing. Beside her, Maria looked thin and pale but seemed calm.

Refreshments were passed around and, once the servants had withdrawn, Michael cleared his throat. 'I'm happy to say that our loved ones have been spared their lives.'

There was an audible release of breath but a chill, like the first wave of fever, made Anna shiver. Michael's stiff manner and expression signalled more and she waited for him to go on.

'Alexander Brianski, Peter Dashkovy and Sergei Volkonsky are sentenced to ten years' hard labour and lifetime exile in Siberia.'

Clearer than day. Blacker than night. Hard labour followed by a life of exile in Siberia! He would not hang, but Sasha was to be taken from them and sent to the ends of the earth. He would never return, never meet his unborn child. Hope vanished like mist before a breeze and Anna saw Sofia's face crumple. Her parents were clasping hands, Ivan Brianski weeping openly while Valentina's face was contorted with the effort of keeping her composure.

Michael started to speak again. 'The tsar has declared official mourning for his brother at an end this Friday—'

But his voice broke and Nicholas Bulgarin took over. 'A statement has been released to the effect that families of the criminals will suffer no ill consequences. The first convoy leaves for Siberia in two weeks' time. It's believed they will work in the silver mines of Nerchinsk.'

Like the moment before thunder, the air in the room seemed to vibrate and darken. Beside Nicholas, Olga was so still she might have been carved out of stone. Nicholas stood up and offered her his hand, but she declined and stayed where she was, staring ahead of her with her lower lip caught between her teeth. Only Maria appeared relatively collected.

After a long silence, she spoke first. 'I intend to appeal to His Majesty for permission to follow Sergei into exile. Whatever the future holds, I will share it with my beloved husband.'

'But what about little Nicolenka?' Anna asked. 'Are you allowed to take him with you?'

'I hope so. If not, then I'll return to collect him. I love my son, but my husband is the one who needs me now.'

'And I shall do the same!' Sofia spoke with unusual force. 'I will go with Sasha into exile. Maria and I will petition the tsar for permission to go to Siberia.'

'You don't know what you're saying!' Michael Pavel's arm dropped from Sofia's shoulders. 'You can't give up your life for—'

'We all need time to reflect,' Nicholas interposed coolly. 'Nothing should be decided on the spur of the moment.'

'This is no sudden impulse,' Maria responded. 'Sofia and I are married. We will act according to the law of God, not that of the tsar.'

Nothing will stop Maria from trying to follow Sergei, Anna thought, and Sofia seems equally determined. Is she really going leave us to be with Sasha? She must be mad! How will she ever manage in her condition? And what about Olga? Will she sacrifice her ambition for Peter's sake? Olga has another suitor. She won't give up her life for Peter Dashkovy. Lifting her head, she caught Nicholas's eye across the room. He had an unerring ability to read her mind, but the news was too shocking for her to care what he thought. Sasha and Peter were to be banished for life and she would never see them again.

Anna looked at her parents, clinging on to one another like seafarers in a storm. Michael was speaking quietly into Sofia's ear. She had her brother to console her, and Nicholas stood between Olga and Maria. He would take care of them, she thought, but there was no one she could turn to for comfort. She had grown up surrounded by love. Now suddenly she felt utterly desolate and alone.

Maria and Olga came over and kissed her cheek and Nicholas took her hand. The despair in her heart must have been palpable for he held it a moment, as if willing her courage. Anna was too stricken to speak or look him in the face. She was aware that the Bulgarins spoke briefly to Sofia and Michael, but when they approached her parents, Count Brianski waved them away and they left the room in silence.

Chapter Sixteen

It was ten o'clock in the morning and Anna's father was waiting for her in the library. 'Thank you, my dear. I wanted to talk to you before the others were up.'

Ivan Brianski was seated at his desk and Anna took a chair opposite. Mazra had brought his note with the breakfast tray and she had dressed hurriedly, barely taking the time to do her hair.

A large oriental rug covered the floor and the bureau was littered with papers. Through the half-open door, Anna heard the whisper of a brush as a maid cleaned the marble stairs. The household carried on with its normal routine, but darkness pervaded their home. The first shock had passed but anguish remained, a persistent feeling of doom that shrouded everything. If the prisoners withstood the hardships of the Fortress, they faced a journey of almost five thousand miles in terrible conditions. It would be a miracle if they survived.

Anna had never been afraid before. Now she was frightened all the time. She tried to comfort her mother, but Valentina was beyond consolation. The pain was locked inside and she could not cry. She stayed in her room and, when Anna slipped her arm round her, drew back and gazed at her through misty, vacant eyes. Sofia had been the strongest of them all. A petition had been submitted to the tsar and Maria believed the tsarina was sympathetic. Her Majesty would do everything in her power to persuade her husband to approve the wives' travel. She sounded confident but Anna wasn't convinced. Sofia and Maria came from prominent families in society. Their departure for Siberia was bound to attract exactly the attention the tsar hoped to avoid. Surely, he would never agree? And, if he did, would Olga follow Peter and go with them?

'You've always been a blessing to me, dear Anna…' Ivan Brianski placed his elbows on the desk, using them for support. He had been a vigorous man of fifty. Now, wearing a loose caftan over informal clothes, he looked ten years older. He was unshaven, his face puffy, and Anna felt a stab of pity. As far as she knew, he hadn't left the house in weeks. 'I've written to your aunt, Tanya, and asked her to come and stay. Your mother's always cheered by her company.'

'But I'm here, Papa! And Sofia, too.'

'Tanya is less involved in this tragic business.' Count Brianski leant forwards and studied his fingernails, unwilling to meet Anna's gaze. 'Please don't make this difficult for me, *Ivitsa*. I expect her to arrive tomorrow and trust you to make her feel at home.'

A hazy light fell on the bookshelves and Anna's gaze wandered around the room. Papa knew that Tanya and she didn't care for one another and she didn't understand her parents' fondness for her mother's younger sister. Tanya Vladimir was an unmarried busybody. Not so long ago, she tried to persuade them to stop Anna continuing with her art, saying it was an unladylike profession. Thank heavens, Papa had disagreed. *He can't cope anymore*, she thought. *He's clutching at straws in the hope that Tanya might lighten the burden that's crushing our family.*

'Of course, I'll make Aunt Tanya welcome, Papa. I pray she will help Mama to recover.'

'Good. Very good.' Ivan Brianski shuffled the papers on the desk in front of him. 'There's something else I must ask of you. I want you to dissuade your sister-in-law from following Maria Volkonsky's example. I received a letter from Sofia's parents yesterday. They blame Sasha for destroying her life—'

'If the tsar grants permission – which is unlikely – the visit to Siberia will only be temporary.' Anna cut across him before he could go further: 'Sofia will return before the baby's born.'

'But she can't possibly travel in her present state. Sasha must forbid it.'

'Then there's no need for my intervention,' Anna protested, tears springing to her eyes. 'You can't ignore Sofia's feelings, Papa. She's devoted to Sasha. She'd rather die than break her marriage vows.'

'But you will talk to her, won't you? Sofia listens to you. Do your best to persuade her to stay – for her own sake as well for our grandchild's.'

Ivan Brianski stood up and came round the side of the desk. He bent to kiss the top of her head, as he used to when she was a child. Anna did not answer. Papa has no right to ask this of me, she thought. I'm not going to tell Sofia what to do. It's between her and Sasha to decide. She was silent until there came a knock on the door.

'Yes, come in, James. What is it?'

'A communiqué from Prince Kochubey, sir.' The young page came forwards carrying an envelope. 'It was delivered just now.'

Prince Kochubey was a state councillor and a member of the tsar's inner circle. Anna had heard her parents speak of him but she couldn't recall him ever visiting their home. Ivan Brianski took the letter and dismissed James. He went slowly round the desk and sat down heavily on his chair. His hands were shaking.

Anna leant across the desk and took the thick vellum envelope from him. 'Let me open it for you, Papa.'

Inside was a stiff card. Anna drew out a gold-embossed invitation, glancing over it quickly before she read aloud.

"LE COMMANDANT DE LE MINISTRE D'INTERIOR, PRINCE KOCHUBEY prie l'honeur de la Comptesse et Compte Brianski avec leur fille, Madamoiselle Anna Brianksi, faire passer la soirée chez lui à partir de neuf heures, le douzième janvier, 1826."

'Why, that's wonderful news!' Ivan Brianski exclaimed, his face brightening as Anna handed him the invitation. 'The ball will be in honour of Tsar Nicholas. The fact we're invited proves our family is still in favour.'

'But Mama's not well enough. You can't make her to go. I'm sure the prince will understand.'

'Once Tanya arrives, your mother will rally. This sorrow will pass, you'll see. Valentina will never let down our family. We must do everything in our power to atone for Sasha's dishonour.'

Anna was startled by his words. Papa was behaving like the Raevskys with Sergei Volkonsky, but Sasha was his own son! Did pacifying the tsar mean more to him than his children?

She frowned and shook her head. 'I won't accept the invitation, Papa. Please send my apologies to Prince Kochubey.'

Her father's hand banged so hard on the table that Anna jumped. 'You will attend the ball and support your mother.'

'I will not.'

Ivan Brianski pulled back his shoulders and shouted at her, 'I command you, Anna! Your mother's right. I've been too lenient with you. It's time you thought less about yourself and acted as a responsible daughter. I will answer the prince immediately and accept on behalf of the three of us. I have no more to say on the matter.'

Anna bit her tongue to prevent a bitter retort. She stood up and walked out of the room. Closing the door behind her, she pressed her back against it. Her world had been shattered and the ground turned to quicksand beneath her feet. Her father had always been so proud of her. Now he accused her of being selfish and irresponsible. It's almost as if he blames me, she thought. Grief is a poison in your blood that destroys all sense of decency and humanity. How can we go to a reception in honour of the tsar when Sasha's about to be banished?

Anna was still holding the doorknob behind her back when James came up the stairs from the hall. 'Excuse me, ma'am. This has just arrived. They didn't leave a name.'

He gave Anna an envelope without a seal, only her name written in pencil on the front. Glancing at the handwriting, her heart began to race. James was still standing there and she thanked him, then bounded up the stairs to the privacy of her bedroom. She opened the envelope and unfolded a single piece of paper. The writing was faint and she went to the window to read it in the light.

Dearest Anna,

I hope you understand it was our patriotic duty to make a stand and that I willingly forfeit my freedom for the sake of our great nation. Please pray for me, sweet Anna, and forgive any pain I may have caused you. Give me your blessing and console me in my darkness.

You are forever in my heart,
Peter

Anna's finger traced the lines as she read, first in silence and then out loud. Every word seared into her mind. It didn't occur to her to wonder how the letter had been smuggled out of prison or to ask James who had delivered it. She had fallen in love, with a young girl's adoration for a man she admired. Here, finally, was proof that Peter was more noble than she realised. Her spirits soared from the jagged edges of despair. He still loves me, she thought. But why is he writing now? It can only mean one thing. It must be over between him and Olga.

An arrow of doubt pierced her happiness. Surely Peter would have made it clear, if that were the case? He wouldn't want his words to be misinterpreted. The delicacy of the script indicated that he was weak and hadn't the strength to write more. Anna pressed the letter to her breast. Closing her eyes, she thought of the last time they had met. The memory came with a hook of pain. If Peter truly loved her, she was prepared to forgive him anything, but she wouldn't run after a man who was engaged to another.

Coolness came back and her mind collected itself. How could she find out if the betrothal had ended? Nicholas Bulgarin was Olga's guardian. He must know and was bound to be at Prince Kochubey's reception. Anna had lost her fear of him betraying her secret, but he might suspect her motives. Suppose he refused to reveal Olga's intentions? Nicholas was a clever man with an uncanny knack of seeing through her. How to interrogate him without arousing suspicion? It wasn't going to be easy, but he was her only hope.

Chapter Seventeen

Anna sat opposite her parents in the damp chill of the closed carriage as street lamps flashed past the frozen window. Apart from an opportunity to speak to Nicholas Bulgarin, she dreaded the evening ahead. They had seen no one outside the family since the sentencing and the thought of being among so many people terrified her. Dropping her head, she glanced at her mother. Valentina was still pale, but she had rallied, just as Papa predicted. Now, with Aunt Tanya looking after her mother and running the household, Anna felt both relieved and superfluous.

Arriving at the Kochubey palace, they entered a courtyard large enough to accommodate a small army. It was illuminated by flares and high bonfires where coachmen stood warming their hands. A full moon shed its light on the nocturnal scene, turning the equipages into blue shadows on the snow as they neared the portico. Liveried attendants lowered the steps and Count Brianski alighted first, followed by his wife and daughter. Wrapped in fur-lined capes, they picked their way carefully over the red baize carpet into the hall, where footmen in powdered wigs took their cloaks and guided them towards a grand marble staircase garlanded with flowers.

At every landing stood Chevalier Guards with silver breastplates watching as a procession of guests went past them: soldiers in uniforms, their chests emblazoned with sashes and orders, and ladies decked out in floating ballgowns of silk and taffeta. Mirrors reflected diamonds and pearls cascading onto bosoms, and precious stones sparkling on every feminine head, neck and arm. All the opulence of St. Peterburg was on display, Anna thought. Once, it might have entertained her; now she knew the suffering it covered up, it seemed a hollow, glittering façade.

She was aware of people behind them speaking in low tones, and saw a couple in front glance back then quickly turn their heads away. These people used to be their friends, yet not one of them had called at the house in the last two weeks. Michael Pavel was the only person who came to visit Sofia. They're the lowest kind of hypocrites, Anna thought, fixing a brittle smile on her face. How many times have Mama and Papa offered them hospitality? Well, let them gawp and gossip! I'll show them that our family aren't ashamed of Sasha. We only have to get through the next few hours, then the ordeal will be over for now and we'll be on our way home.

Reaching the upper floor, they walked down a long, deep gallery where fragrant wood burned in stoves and the scent of sweet incense hung in the air. The queue moved slowly until they reached the end where Prince and Princess Kochubey stood greeting their guests. Anna had chosen a simple white dress with a high waist and flowing skirt embroidered with gold braid. Her only jewellery was the triple string of pearls around her neck.

She was aware of her hostess's cool appraisal as she curtsied and they passed through into the Salle Blanche, where a thousand candles gave an effect of dazzling daylight. There were flowers in full bloom everywhere she looked. The ballroom had been transformed into an exotic garden of lilies and orchids with branches of trees and ivy garlands adorning the walls. In front of Anna, the crowd seemed to sway and shimmer like a mirage as Circassian and Mongol officers in oriental uniform mixed with young Hussars who strutted about in elk-skin breeches and gleaming boots. There were Cossacks in scarlet, Lancers in blue, and a swell of voices and greetings rose and fell like the sea.

Ladies and gentlemen in court dress hovered near the doors at the far end, awaiting the arrival of the emperor, and Anna glimpsed the dowager, Princess Volkonsky. She was leaning on a cane and engaged in conversation with a man who stood with his back to her. She recognised the small head and short hair of Major Renin and noticed he was wearing a blue imperial sash. So, Boris Renin had been promoted for his services to the tsar. What part had he played in the calamity that had befallen them, she wondered?

Suddenly everyone stirred, pressed forwards, then back. As the doors opened, the Grand Marshall banged his ebony staff on the floor.

'His Imperial Majesty, Tsar Nicholas!'

Gentlemen bowed and hundreds of skirts rustled as ladies dropped a deep curtsy and Nicholas entered followed by his hosts. Everyone stood still as the orchestra played the National Anthem, then a young adjutant with a worried expression moved hurriedly from group to group asking them to move aside to make way for the tsar.

Tall and broad-shouldered, Nicholas Romanov wore a uniform encrusted with gold and medals that glittered in the candlelight. He walked rapidly, nodding his head to left and right as if keen to get this part of the evening over. Anna stood on tiptoes to get a better view. The tsar's height gave him presence. He might have been considered handsome, she thought, but it was a cold face with wintry eyes, lacking humour or compassion.

As the orchestra played the first notes of a polonaise, guests began forming themselves into two lines in the centre of the room, and Tsar Nicholas led Princess Kochubey onto the dance floor. Count Brianski offered his wife an arm and Anna was left alone. More than half the ladies had partners and were taking up positions for the polonaise. She stood where she was and shifted her weight from foot to foot. Never before had she been left with the minority of women uninvited to dance who crowded near the wall. Surely someone would come to her rescue? And then, as if from nowhere, Michael Pavel stood in front of her. He held out his hand and Anna smiled, manoeuvring her skirts with a flick of the heel as they joined the procession. They made a tour of the room, pausing at intervals as the gentlemen left their partners to bring in more couples.

'Have you heard Olga Bulgarin's the new favourite of the tsar?' Michael smiled mischievously as he returned to Anna. 'They say she's about to be offered an appointment at court.'

Anna's mouth opened with surprise, but the music quickened and they were separated. When he was with her again, she caught hold of his arm. 'What were you saying about Olga?'

'I'm saying the tsar has his eye on her.'

'But I don't understand. What does it mean?'

'It means she'll stay in St. Petersburg, and I hope Sofia will follow her example.'

Anna wanted to ask Michael more, but it was impossible to talk and dance at the same time. When the polonaise ended, he led her to where her parents were standing and set off in search of refreshments. The room was hot and she fanned herself as she looked around. There weren't many people she recognised but she caught sight of Anastasia Lenkov with her distinctive red hair. Anastasia had been married last summer and the man escorting her must be her husband. He was good-looking with an intelligent expression. She would like to have spoken to them, but the press of people made it impossible to move.

Michael returned with glasses of champagne and Anna sipped hers slowly. Letting her gaze wander over his shoulder, she caught sight of Nicholas Bulgarin on the opposite side of the dance floor. He was wearing a dark blue tailcoat with Olga beside him in a gown with long green sleeves and a turquoise train. Her luxurious hair was coiled under a traditional *kokoshnik* embedded with emeralds that complimented her eyes. Anna hoped Nicholas would notice her, but he was deep in conversation with an older gentleman. Could it be Olga's other suitor: the one Maria had spoken of? He was a stout man with fluffy hair whipped into a coif on top of his head – at least forty and not the least bit handsome, she noted with satisfaction.

From the orchestra came the first enticing strains of a waltz and all eyes turned to the tsar. He was looking around, his gaze passing over the company as he assessed the ladies present. Who would he honour with the second dance of the evening? A minute passed and everyone waited expectantly until he bent to speak in the ear of the young adjutant. The officer nodded and walked over to Olga Bulgarin. He gave her his arm and led her to the sovereign. She curtsied to the ground, then raised her head with a ravishing smile and placed her hand on his shoulder.

The entire assembly watched the pair as they circled the outside of the floor. The tsar grasped Olga round the waist and started smoothly, then at the corner caught her left hand and spun her around so her turquoise train spread out, flashing like a bird's plumage. Apart from the music, the only sound was the rhythmic click of his spurs and voices hushed in admiration. Other couples joined the dance, though Anna's gaze stayed on Olga. She was delighted by her success – Anna could tell from the radiance in her eyes and glow in her cheeks. Olga may have once cared for Peter, but she had replaced him soon enough and seemed indifferent to the fate of her friends.

'Will you do me the honour?'

Her train of thought was interrupted as Major Renin blocked her view. Anna glanced down at her programme, trying to think of an excuse.

'I'm afraid Miss Brianski promised me this waltz.'

She heard Nicholas's voice before she could alter her expression and was still frowning as he took the card and slipped it into his pocket. As Major Renin turned away abruptly, Nicholas gave her his arm and steered her through the crush onto the dance floor.

He placed one hand lightly in the centre of her back so the top of his gloved fingers touched her bare skin and Anna felt her heart beat faster. Nicholas Bulgarin danced well and knew it, guiding her fluently in time with the music. The pressure of his hand never altered as he took long, smooth steps and Anna followed his lead, her feet in their satin shoes moving lightly over the parquet. As he swung her round, she was carried away by the magic of the waltz – the brilliant, kaleidoscope of swirling dresses, diamonds in serpentine flashes and small white-gloved hands placed on the epaulettes of officers. Nicholas whirled her around the floor and she forgot Olga and the ominous presence of the tsar. Her supple figure matched his movements until she felt she was floating, her feet hardly touching the ground. From the freshness of her smile and luminous eyes, it might have been her very first ball. The tall, dark-haired man and the beautiful young woman caught the attention of onlookers and by the time the music stopped Anna was breathless.

'It was worth waiting for the pleasure,' Nicholas said in his languid voice as they left the floor. 'And only just in time. I leave for Moscow tomorrow.'

'Is Olga going with you?'

Anna hoped to sound casual but his eyes gleamed. 'She's staying in St. Petersburg, at least for now. Why? Do you wish to call on her in my absence?'

Despite his sarcastic tone, it was on the tip of Anna's tongue to ask about Olga's future plans but, as they approached her parents, Count Brianski stepped forwards.

'Good evening, Nicholas Petrovich,' he said with a formal bow before he turned to Anna, signalling his disapproval with a distracted wave of his hand. 'That's enough dancing, Anna. I don't want you making a spectacle of yourself this evening.'

Anna was about to protest but caught her mother's eye and kept quiet. Old Princess Volkonsky approached and accosted Nicholas, taking him by the arm to prevent him walking away. Was she asking him about Sergei? In any case, he was no longer paying attention. Following his gaze, Anna saw a woman in a blue dress rise from a table at the far end of the room. She walked with a smooth, swaying step, smiling as she inclined her head to the guests who separated to make way for her. Her bare shoulders glowed like marble and her golden hair was arranged in curls. Anna recognised her with a shock. She was the woman who had been with Nicholas in Sadovaya Street, and she was coming straight towards them.

'Princess Elizaveta's married to the tsar's cousin, Prince Dimitri Romanov,' Valentina whispered, curtsying and indicating to Anna to do the same.

Princess Elizaveta's eyes were dark and framed by long lashes under slender eyebrows. She wore a diamond badge of honour pinned to her sash, the insignia of lady-in-waiting to the tsarina. Anna watched in suspense as she held out her gloved hand to Nicholas. As he lifted it to his lips with graceful familiarity, she hastily cast her eyes down. How many people here tonight were aware that the princess was his mistress? Was it common knowledge or was she the only one?

'I really must have a chair.' Princess Volkonsky announced as Princess Elizaveta drew the small group into the conversation. Anna was mesmerised. She noticed how relaxed Princess Elizaveta was, addressing Nicholas as if he were no more than a casual acquaintance. They were both well practised in this charade, she thought as she turned her head to look at Nicholas. For an instant, his expression was unguarded and the devouring hunger in his eyes made her heart tighten. For the first time in her life, Anna felt the power of physical desire. A wave of heat travelled down her neck and shoulders, into her dress until every part of her burned. 'Nicholas and Olga are Tatars. They're different from us.' She blushed as Maria's words came back to her. Beneath their polished sophistication, the Bulgarins were as wild and savage as tigers – beautiful and dangerous in equal measure.

The heat was suddenly oppressive. Anna raised a hand in the air and caught the attention of a page carrying a tray of champagne flutes. She drank one too quickly, hiccupping as she replaced the glass on the tray. Princess Romanov and Nicholas had moved on, and guests were forming groups as they waited for the tsar to lead them into dinner. Prince Gagarin was talking to her parents before a gong sounded and the tsar strode forwards.

At almost exactly the same moment, there came shouts and the sound of jingling harnesses from the courtyard below. Anna was close enough to the window to get a clear view as four troikas swept in through the gates. They were escorted by a detachment of mounted Cossacks and came to a halt in front of the entrance. Huddled together between gendarmes were convicts with heads bowed and fettered in chains. Anna stifled a cry. She didn't need to see their faces. The two men she loved most in the world were in the front troika. The prisoners had been brought here to be paraded in front of all St. Petersburg society.

So, this was the reason they had been invited – to witness the disgrace of their loved ones as they set off on their journey into exile.

Now, other guests were moving to the windows, pushing and shoving to get past her. Anna felt Michael's hand on her wrist, trying to pull her away. She shook him off, freeing herself and twisted around. She must get to Sasha and Peter. Somehow, she would speak to them. Without a second thought, she forced her way through the melee, hastened across the deserted ballroom and ran down the long gallery. Afraid she might be followed, she kept glancing over her shoulder until she was in sight of the great staircase where the Chevaliers stood guard.

She slowed to a walk. She would have to go right past them and must appear composed. She collected herself, patting her hair and checking it was in place before tiptoeing cautiously forwards. As she came to the stairwell landing, Nicholas Bulgarin stepped out in front of her.

'Where the devil do you think you're going?' His voice was swift and rough.

Anna was too startled to answer. She gave him a blank stare and tried to walk past, but he caught hold of her arms, gripping them above her elbows.

'I want to see Sasha! Take your hands off me!' she hissed at him.

'Are you insane?'

'The prisoners are in the courtyard. I must speak to Sasha.'

'A public scene's the last thing your brother needs. Any display of loyalty is dangerous.'

'I will see him. I will!' Anna's voice rose.

'For God's sake, keep your voice down. Pull yourself together.'

The force of his command jarred Anna into silence. Nicholas let go and her arms dropped to her sides. She was trembling, her eyes full of tears.

He took a handkerchief from his pocket and gave it to her. 'Wipe your eyes and blow your nose. Then I'll escort you back to the reception.'

Anna blew her nose and looked at him imploringly.' I just want to say goodbye. Please come with me.'

If Nicholas escorted her downstairs, no one would stop them. She wouldn't cause a scene or embarrass him. She would get her cloak herself. He didn't even need to go outside. Anna waited for him to relent but there was no concession in his face. When he shook his head, she made a lunge to get past and his arm went round her waist. She struggled wildly, beating his chest with her fists, and his hand went over her mouth. Muffling her screams of rage and despair, he lifted her off her feet and carried her back to the gallery.

Nicholas sat down so Anna was pressed to his chest, writhing in his lap. She bent and twisted her body until she thought her lungs would burst, but he would not let go.

'Calm down. Your brother and Captain Dashkovy won't die. I've made sure of that.' He removed his hand from her mouth. 'Listen to me...'

He held her so tightly that dizziness swept her and she couldn't breathe. His voice was thin and faraway, his face swirling in a sickening mist until she no longer saw Nicholas or anything else. She had no strength to fight and was sinking into empty space. Was she dying? Was this how it felt when your time came? Lord, have mercy. Her last thought was a prayer before she fainted.

Chapter Eighteen

'It was very thoughtless of you to give your mother such a fright.' Tanya Vladimir straightened Anna's pillow, then went to stand at the end of the bed. 'Mazra tells me you ate nothing yesterday. No wonder you had a swooning fit.'

Anna was lying with her eyes half closed, trying not to listen. She remembered regaining consciousness, with Nicholas Bulgarin holding her, kneeling on the floor. Her memory of what followed was patchy. Her parents must have been summoned for they appeared, looking flustered.

'I told you to stay with us, Anna. What happened to you?'

'Miss Brianski was overcome by the heat,' Nicholas answered. 'She needed fresh air. Unfortunately, she collapsed before...'

Anna was terrified her parents would see Sasha and the others but, by the time the Brianski carriage arrived at the front door, the troikas had gone. Nicholas carried her to the carriage and Valentina held a sachet of vinegar salt beneath her nose all the way home. Thank God her mother had been spared the horror of seeing her son in chains. The cruelty of it was grotesque. What kind of man forced families to witness the degradation of their beloved sons and brothers the last time they would ever see them?

'It was selfish to cause your poor parents such concern — as if they don't have enough to put up with already.'

Tanya's remark made Anna sit up. Tanya wore her hair pulled back severely to reveal her widow's peak and sharp brown eyes. She normally preferred pastel colours but wore black today, as befitted her mood.

'Sasha's the one who caused them grief.' Anna met her eyes defiantly.

'That's not the point. I expect you to show them greater consideration in future.'

'We should never have gone to the ball.'

'Your father accepted in the best interests of the family.'

Tanya pulled her mouth into a disapproving knot, pursing her lips as she walked out of the room. How dare her aunt tell her how to behave – or interrogate poor Mazra for that matter? For a time, annoyance displaced anguish. Then Anna shook her head. Tanya was a minor irritant compared to the sorrow in her heart. Looking around the bedroom, she thought: Sasha will never come home. We'll never be together as a family again. How can we endure this heartbreak?

What was Nicholas Bulgarin doing in the gallery last night? His hands were icy cold, she remembered, so he must have been outside. Had he spoken to Sasha and Peter? She had only wanted to say goodbye. It was none of his business and she'd had enough of his interference. She tried to summon anger to her aid but she was too miserable. However much Nicholas annoyed her, she couldn't blame him for everything.

She was about to ring for Mazra when there was a gentle tap at the door. Sofia and Maria Volkonsky entered, Maria in an elegant dove-grey costume, her dark hair spilling out from beneath her bonnet.

'I was about to get up.' Anna pulled her wrapper around her shoulders.

'You should stay where you are and rest,' Sofia said as the two women sat down on either side of the bed.

'I'm perfectly alright now. It was only the heat and too many people...'

'The evening must have been terrible, darling.' Sofia's eyes shone as if she had been crying.

'I'm sure Aunt Tanya exaggerated. You know how she likes to make a drama out of everything.'

'She wouldn't let us come near you. We've been waiting ages for the coast to be clear.'

'We have wonderful news! We had to tell you first.' Maria opened her reticule and took out a large envelope. Anna saw the red, double-eagle seal of the emperor as Maria opened it and took out a folded piece of paper.

She handed it to Anna who pulled her knees up under the coverlet and spread the paper open. She glanced at the signature, then read in silence.

Dear Princess,

I have before me the letter you sent on 15th December. You are undoubtedly aware of the particular interest I have always taken in your personal welfare. It is because of this that it is my duty to warn you of the extreme dangers that await you and your friend once you travel beyond Irkutsk. Having said that, I leave the decision to travel to you and Madame Brianski.

I send you my affectionate greetings,
Nicholas

It was a strange sensation holding a letter written by the tsar himself. Some people regarded him as divinely appointed, but Anna thought of five young officers executed by his command and the terrible sentences meted out to the others. The emperor might be all-powerful but he was unworthy of respect. Her brow furrowed as she gave the letter back to Maria. Nothing would stop her friends from following their husbands now. They really were going to Siberia, and she would be left alone. How could she stay in St. Petersburg without them, and without Sasha and Peter?

'Oh Anna, our prayers have been answered,' Sofia said. 'We must be grateful the tsar has been merciful.'

'What does he mean by extreme dangers beyond Irkutsk?' Anna asked curtly. 'It's hardly a guarantee of your safety.'

'He's warning us of the harsh Siberian winter, so we're prepared. He should understand we're willing to endure any hardship to be with our beloved husbands.' Maria was elated, her eyes glowing with pride and eagerness.

Sofia's expression was softer and Anna touched her hand. 'I know what this means to you, but I still worry about you travelling so far, darling. Your family already blames Sasha for destroying your life. Should anything happen to the baby—'

'But without Sasha I have no life. I'll be careful, I promise, and I'll come home before my confinement in the summer.'

'Has the tsar promised you can come back?'

'Not in so many words, but I've made enquiries,' Maria answered. 'There may be a few bureaucratic problems but nothing insurmountable. I'll return with Sofia to St. Petersburg in the spring so she can have the baby here and I can collect Nicolenka.'

'How will you prepare for the journey?' Anna heard the flat tone in her own voice. She wanted to support them, but it was difficult.

'We've pawned our jewellery to pay for the travel costs and my sister, Ekaterina Orlov, has been very kind. Her husband was lucky to escape punishment. Between them, they'll provide for all our needs.'

'When do you intend to leave?'

'I'm going to visit my family at Boltyshka, then to Moscow to stay with Sergei's cousin, Princess Zinaida. I'll find out how many other wives are going to Siberia. We may be able to travel in convoy.'

Maria had everything planned, and talked about the journey as if it was a commonplace excursion, not an expedition to the other side of the world. Heaven knew what perils they would face travelling thousands of miles in the middle of winter.

'I know it's hard for you, Anna.' Sofia leant towards her and stroked her tumbled hair. 'I hope you can be happy for us.'

'I am happy.' Anna managed a tight smile. 'You've taken a courageous decision and I'm proud of you.' She realised she meant it as she said the words.

Sofia kissed Anna's cheek and Maria pressed her hand warmly. After they had gone, she slipped out of bed. She wasn't in the mood to sit with her mother and Tanya. Wrapping herself in the bed quilt, she curled up in a chair by the window. Until this morning, she had been sure the tsar would refuse them permission. Now he had agreed, she feared what lay ahead for Maria and Sofia but also she feared for herself. *I know how Sofia feels. My life has no meaning without the people I love.*

Nicholas said Olga was going to remain in St. Petersburg and Michael had intimated she was about to be given a position at court. Anna rushed to grasp what her heart wanted to believe. *If only Nicholas Bulgarin had confirmed the betrothal was definitely over! I should have asked him straight, but it's too late now. I must follow my instincts,* she thought, her fingers clenching and unclenching as her mind raced on. *What shall I do? Mama and Papa have Tanya to look after them and keep them company. They don't need me anymore.* An idea that had been forming unconsciously came to the fore and she stood up and threw off the quilt. *Peter loves me and wants me with him. Why else did he write? I'm not like Olga and I won't let him down. Somehow, I will find a way to travel with Sofia and Maria to Siberia.*

It wasn't going to be easy, but Anna experienced a lightness of spirit she hadn't felt in weeks. There were many obstacles to overcome, but her mind was made up and the thought of action brought strength and energy. She knew the risks, but she was no longer afraid. She would leave St. Petersburg with Sofia when the time came.

✵

Anna slept little in the nights that followed as she wrestled with practical problems. How could she get the necessary travel papers without her parents' knowledge? She might beg them to let her go with Sofia, at least as far as Moscow, but knew they would refuse. It was impossible to travel without documents. But the women weren't expected to travel alone. The wives were allowed to take one maid with them. Was it possible she could take the place of Lila, Sofia's maid?

It was an audacious idea that gradually evolved in her mind. Omelko would help her, she felt sure, and it was he who was to drive her sister-in-law to Moscow. On the first morning the Brianskis began receiving visitors, Anna went to find him. She walked quickly past the banya to the stable-yard where grooms were leading out her father's grey Orlovs. They were beautiful horses, with their proud carriage and flaring manes and tails. She recognised the two flankers, Flirt and Furious, and stopped to admire them before she made her way to the stable-master's office.

Omelko was sitting by the small grate, smoking a clay pipe and puffing out skeins of smoke. On the wall behind him, coiled like a snake, hung a rawhide whip with metal barbs. The knout was a barbaric instrument, symbolising the power of the master over his serfs. There was no reason for it here, Anna thought. Papa disapproved of corporal punishment, and she hated the sight of it.

Omelko's face set in deep grooves and his eyes looked doubtful as she outlined her plan. He was reluctant to act without her father's authority.

Anna tried to reassure him. 'It's a small diversion – hardly out of your way. Here's the address.' She handed him a piece of paper. 'You need only stop for a few minutes.'

Omelko put down his pipe. 'If the master doesn't know, then the master doesn't approve. I'm proud of your brother, Miss Anna, we all are, but if Count Brianski finds out about this he'll have me whipped.'

'He will not!' Anna felt mortification flood her cheeks. 'I'll tell him you're acting under my instructions and take full responsibility.'

Omelko shrugged his shoulders and raised one bushy eyebrow but said nothing.

'Please, Omelko! There's nothing wrong involved, I promise.' She flung out her hands in a gesture of supplication. 'There's no one else I can ask. Please help me!'

Tacitly and reluctantly, Omelko agreed, but there were further problems to resolve. She needed money and could not leave the house unseen to pawn her jewellery. She would have to take her pearls with her and raise the money in Moscow. Once there, she would buy suitable clothes for the journey. She could only take one small bag and must fit in everything she needed, including drawing materials.

The week passed in an agony of suspense. She longed to say something to Sofia but didn't dare and Tanya was constantly on her nerves. Her aunt walked quietly with short tripping steps, often appearing when she was least expected. Anna wondered if she was spying on her. She tried to seem calm and indifferent, but it was exhausting having to be on her guard all the time.

Then, on the day before Sofia's departure, Tanya walked into her studio as she was sorting through her paints. 'So, this is where you've been hiding. I've been searching for you.'

'And why should that be?' Anna did not look up.

'Because you have a visitor and your mother sent me to find you.'

Anna raised her head and glanced at Tanya. Her aunt had taken trouble over her appearance, she noted. The scent of vanilla and cinnamon clung to her clothes and her hair was curled in ringlets. It made her face rounder and she almost looked pretty.

'Who is it?'

'I'm not acquainted with him.'

'Then please tell Mama I'm sorry but I can't be disturbed.'

'She asked me to fetch you, no matter what you're doing.'

Tanya's lips thinned into a narrow line. She wasn't going to be put off and Anna sighed as she followed her downstairs to the drawing room. Her parents were seated on the sofa and, across from them with his back to the window, stood Boris Renin.

Anna stared at him as the major made a small bow.

'How nice to see you again, Miss Brianski.'

'Major Renin has come to give us news of Alexander.' Count Brianski's fingers worked at the ends of his moustache, twisting and curling them. It was a habit he had developed lately and seemed unable to control. 'He's in charge of transportation for the...'

'... criminals.' Boris Renin articulated the word for him. 'I'm glad to say they're in good health and halfway to their destination.'

'We're very grateful to hear it.' Valentina motioned to Anna to sit down. 'Major Renin's kindness is a ray of light in these dark times.'

Anna took a seat but did not answer. She noticed how Renin's eyes travelled around the room. *What does he want? He's not here to tell us about Sasha, that's for sure.*

'I'm sorry to hear you were taken ill at the ball.'

'Prince Kochubey's house was exceedingly hot.' Anna's tone was clipped.

'Major Renin is concerned for your well-being, Anna.' Count Brianski spoke reprovingly as he stood up. 'Now, sir. I will leave you in the company of the ladies. I hope you will do us the honour of calling again soon.'

He left the room and Anna tried to rally her forces, keeping her face blank as Valentina and Tanya made conversation. Her aunt used her fan a great deal, chattering inconsequentially as Renin listened with an expression of faint boredom. *He knows Sofia and Maria have received permission from the tsar,* she thought. *Is that why he's come – to make sure the rest of our family has closed ranks against Sasha?*

She waited for a lull in the conversation and then remarked casually, 'I gather anyone who travels beyond Irkutsk will face dangerous conditions...'

'We have fewer troops in eastern Siberia, but the convicts are well guarded. They've nothing to fear.'

Except what awaits them in the labour camps, Anna thought grimly in the brief silence before Renin continued. 'I was shown your portrait of Princess Volkonsky and the poor infant de malheur. It's very well executed. I find it despicable a mother should abandon her child.'

A smirk touched Tanya's lips, her hand fluttering demurely at her throat. Anna glared at her.

'Major Renin would like you to paint his portrait, Anna.' Valentina raised her voice. 'I've assured him you'll be delighted. It's the least we can do in return for his magnanimity.'

'But Mama,' she said flushing. 'I no longer do portraits. Besides, I haven't painted in weeks.'

'Well, I must say…' Valentina began, her nostrils flaring. 'Major Renin doesn't expect a masterpiece. If he can spare the time, then so can you. Besides, you'll need something to occupy you when Sofia cruelly deserts us.'

Anna felt a muscle tighten in her jaw. She hadn't expected this of Mama. How could she be so disparaging of Sofia? Surely, her mother realised Boris Renin wasn't to be trusted. He was an opportunist and a likely fortune hunter. He's cunning as a jackal, she thought. How can Mama and Papa be taken in by him? Is this a desperate attempt to regain their position in society?

'With your permission, Countess, I'd like a word in private with Anna Ivanova.' Boris Renin flashed Valentina an ingratiating grin. 'Perhaps she would take a turn with me about the room?'

'Of course.'

Valentina smiled and Anna was obliged to come to her feet. Without a word, she followed the major to the hearth at the far end, her pulse thumping with irritation.

'I want to offer my deepest sympathy for your loss. Indeed, it's been a terrible time for all of us.'

He held out his hand, but she ignored it and kept her gaze on the mantelpiece. She was aware of Boris Renin's eyes on her and wondered what he was going to say.

'You should understand I'm your friend, dear Anna – not your enemy.'

'I have friends enough already.' Anna was blunt to the point of rudeness.

'And, alas, most of them seem to be on the verge of abandoning you.'

Anna turned her head slowly. 'Michael Pavel's a good friend of mine and he's not leaving the city.'

'Not as yet… However, should your sister-in-law take advantage of His Majesty's generosity and travel further than Moscow, it may not bode well for Captain Pavel's prospects.'

'The tsar promised the families of Decembrists they would face no further persecution.' She used the word deliberately, then paused, taking care to modulate her voice. 'Are you saying he's not a man of his word?'

'His Imperial Majesty is a trustworthy and enlightened tsar.' The major leant so close that Anna could smell the mint sprigs he used to freshen his breath. 'He knows that, for the good of our nation, recent events must be confined to oblivion. Your friend, Olga Bulgarin, has taken a wise decision. Once her appointment is confirmed, an illustrious future awaits her.'

She wondered if Renin knew about Olga and Peter Dashkovy? He must do – but why mention her now? The man doesn't care about people, Anna thought. He wants a wife as an adornment to parade in front of the tsar – and the richer the better.

'I look forward to our first sitting,' Renin continued, letting the word linger like the hiss of a snake.

Anna drew her shawl closer to her chest. 'Forgive me but I have pressing matters to attend to. My Aunt Tanya will be delighted to entertain you.'

'I came to see *you*.' Renin's upper lip twitched beneath his moustache. 'I presume we may start the painting later this week?'

He took her hand, turning it over so the palm faced upwards, and lifted it to his mouth, letting his tongue slip between his lips. Anna tried to draw back but he held fast to her wrist. 'I'm a patient man, Anna Ivanova. I always get what I want in the end. It would be a mistake to try and escape.'

Did Boris Renin suspect what was in her head? Or was he hoping to frighten her? Intuition suggested the latter. As he pursed his lips in imitation of a kiss, Anna looked down at the tips of his polished boots and gave a shudder.

'You're hurting me, sir,' she muttered between gritted teeth. 'Release me at once!'

Renin let her go and stood rigidly as Anna dropped a curtsy and walked stiffly to the door, glancing at Valentina as she went past. Mama and Papa want me to marry Renin to wipe out the stain on our family name – but I can't help them anymore. I love them and can't bear them behaving like this. I will see this through, whatever the cost, she thought with a pang as she went out. Let Tanya be the bait for Boris Renin. I must have the courage to do what is right.

Chapter Nineteen

As the droshky galloped down the frozen road, Anna no longer felt brave. Dawn was breaking and a damp mist hung over the Neva making her bones ache. When she'd said goodbye to Sofia last night, her sister-in-law had cried, but Tanya was watching and Anna kept herself under control. She had retired early and waited until Mazra left the bedroom before she opened the desk. She found the letter she had written to her parents, read it over, then placed it in an envelope and scribbled a note to Mazra, asking her to give it to Count Brianski once Sofia had left. Finally, she packed her bag for the journey with a single change of clothes, a Kashmiri shawl and a pair of indoor shoes. Her precious jewellery was hidden in a leather folder next to her sketchbooks and paints at the bottom. In case of any unforeseen problems, she had the addresses of Maria's cousin, Princess Zinaida, and Nicholas Bulgarin in Moscow.

Anna had stayed awake until the church bells chimed five. The fire gave off little heat as she dressed by the light of a single candle. She had chosen carefully: a red woollen coat that reached her ankles, strong leather boots and her warmest fur-lined cape. The house was asleep as she went down to the vestibule and only the night porter on duty. She told him she was visiting a sick friend and asked him to find her a cab.

She was on her way to an inn near the city gates where she would wait for the carriage, then swap places with Lila and send her home in the droshky. The pony was fast and Anna pulled her hood low over her face, listening to the hum of runners on the icy snow as they flew through the streets of St. Petersburg. So far, everything had gone to plan. The last few days had been so nerve-wracking, there had been no time to consider the enormity of her decision. Now she thought: I'm running away and abandoning my parents. I pray they'll forgive me. It's not forever. I'll come home to them before the summer. I can't change my mind now.

The droshky slowed down as they approached the southern gates of the city. It was still early, but a few people were about and a wagon loaded with birch logs pulled up at a small square building with the painted sign of an inn. A woman with a basket of bread and salt approached the droshky. The driver waved her away. Anna twisted around and looked back up the road until the Brianski dormeuse finally came into view. The carriage was drawn by four black horses and swayed as it came to a halt. Omelko, his hat tight around the head with its brim turned up, gave the reins to his companion. Anna recognised Jacob, one of her father's grooms, as Omelko climbed down from the box seat and walked over to the droshky. The freezing wind had turned his eyebrows white and his voice gruff as he paid the driver.

'Wait here. There's a passenger to be taken back.'

With Anna hanging onto his arm, they crossed the short distance to the dormeuse. The horses snorted, tossing their heads and stamping their hooves, as Omelko passed up her bag to be stowed on the roof. Then he let down the steps and opened the carriage door. From the spacious interior two pale faces peered out of darkness.

'Heavens save us, what's this?' Sofia cried out.

'Don't be alarmed. It's only me. Anna! I'm going to take Lila's place. It's all arranged. There's a droshky waiting to take her home.'

Sofia seemed struck dumb as Lila's luggage was handed down. When Anna told the maid to go with Omelko, Sofia clasped the girl's hand. 'Goodbye, dear Lila. Take care of yourself. May God grant we meet again.'

Lila nodded, glancing suspiciously at Anna as she descended the narrow steps. The dormeuse was designed for long journeys with a well-sprung body and seats that could be converted into beds. Sofia sat facing forwards. Anna removed her cloak and settled down beside her. There was a creaking sound as Omelko mounted the driving board and her shoulders dropped with relief.

'I'm sorry I didn't tell you.'

'But why? I don't understand.' Sofia's grey eyes were concerned and bewildered. 'What are you doing here?'

'I promised Sasha to look after you. I couldn't let you make the journey alone.'

'But you didn't say anything. Oh Anna ... your poor parents!'

'Tanya will stay with them for as long as they want.'

'Even so...'

'It's alright, Sofia!'

She had expected her to be grateful, not make her feel guilty. The two women were silent for a while as the carriage picked up speed.

'I thought you'd be pleased,' Anna finally ventured.

'Oh, I am, darling. But where are you planning to stay in Moscow?'

'I hoped I might find accommodation at your home.'

'But that's impossible! My parents won't speak of your family. They refuse even to mention Sasha's name. They behave as if he's dead.'

Her words ended in a sob and the next minute Sofia was in Anna's arms, her body convulsed as they held each other close. Anna was crying too, her face pressed to Sofia's cheek as she gave way to the strain of the last few days. Sofia's been too brave, she thought. I understood her heartbreak for Sasha but not the pain of her parents' anger. Hot tears ran down her cheeks and Sofia's arms tightened about her neck.

'I'll never forget this, darling,' she whispered. 'My family are only allowing me home in the hope of preventing me from leaving Moscow. But where will you stay?'

'I have Princess Zinaida Volkonsky's address. Maria's staying with her, is she not?'

'Yes – only Maria doesn't arrive in Moscow for another ten days.' Sofia's forehead knitted before she broke into a tearful smile. 'But I'm sure the princess will be delighted to have you. Maria says she's the kindest person in all of Sergei's family.'

Dearest Mama and Papa

I write to you in the hope you will understand and forgive my sudden departure. Before the events of last month, I gave Sasha my word that I would take care of Sofia. I must fulfil my promise and therefore am going with her to Moscow. If all is well, we will then travel on together to Siberia.

Please be assured that neither Omelko nor anyone else is involved and this is entirely my own decision. Omelko was acting under my orders and had no prior knowledge of my intentions. He will return to St. Petersburg from Moscow and I will come home as soon as I am assured that Sofia is safe. You must not worry about me and I ask for your blessing.

I will pray for you every day, my dearest parents.

Your loving daughter,
Anna

Chapter Twenty

They had left St. Petersburg shrouded in fog and arrived in Moscow on a morning of frost and dazzling sunshine. For five days the sleigh had raced southwards, changing horses every six hours and stopping only at night. Omelko and Jacob stayed in post houses while Sofia and Anna slept in the dormeuse. When they finally came in sight of their destination, they saw a city dominated by the towering domes of the Kremlin. On the skyline were spires of churches, their gilded cupolas and golden crosses gleaming in the sunlight.

Anna had been five when Napoleon invaded Russia. She had grown up on stories of how Muscovites set fire to their beloved city so that Bonaparte was forced into retreat and his army decimated by the fierce Russian winter. It was still being rebuilt and piles of brick and mortar blocked the pavements. Many houses had been destroyed but the gilded roofs, brightly-coloured onion domes and fretted minarets were as beautiful as she had imagined.

The river Moskva wound sinuously through the streets and, in contrast to the vast scale of St. Petersburg, the old capital seemed like a rambling, overgrown village. The streets swarmed and jostled with people from every part of the world. Western dress was predominant but Anna saw bearded muzhiks in bast slippers and long kaftans, Russians in fur coats, Greeks in red fezzes and Persians in high conical hats. The variety of costumes gave an impression of flourishing commerce and beside the roads were stalls selling apples, herrings and lemons along with woollen clothes and artefacts. Boys carried wooden trays of meat on their heads and men with buckets of pickles and black bread provided food for peasants who came in from in the countryside to sell their wares. Moscow epitomised the colourful, chaotic heart of Russia, Anna thought. Here, where Europe met Asia, it was a city of the east and not the west.

As they crossed the river, church bells began to peel, then the chimes of a great clock over the Spassky Gate. They drove past the red and yellow brick walls of the Kremlin, down the Tversky Boulevard, and Sofia pointed out Princess Zinaida's home.

'Once he's dropped me off, Omelko will drive you here, then return to stable the horses with us and rest for a few days.'

Anna's heart sank. With its great portico and high walls, the palace was stern and imposing. Would Princess Zinaida want her to stay, if Maria wasn't in residence? The idea of turning up unexpectedly, unwashed with her hair undone, was inconceivable. Anna simply didn't have the nerve. Count Bulgarin's address was in her pocketbook and she determined she would try there first.

An hour later, having unloaded Sofia's luggage and said goodbye, the dormeuse lumbered in the direction of Vozdvizhenka Street. What kind of reception would she receive after their last meeting? It was crucial that Nicholas didn't suspect her motives. She must explain her situation shrewdly, not let him make assumptions, and speak only of Sofia and Sasha.

Residences away from the centre were set further apart with large snow-covered gardens and they came to a halt outside a white house with a green roof. Anna looked out as Omelko let down the steps, and saw a well-dressed man come out of the front door. It wasn't anyone she knew, but she flushed with embarrassment. What must she look like in her crumpled, travel-worn clothes? For a moment, she hesitated, then she squared her shoulders and walked with Omelko to the front porch.

'You will stay at Count Pavel's establishment. I'll send you a message in a few days. Thank you, Omelko. Thank you for being my good friend. Please don't wait.'

The coachman put down her bag and looked at her with doleful eyes. He's ashamed of me, Anna thought, and I don't blame him. Omelko returned to the carriage and she stood under the porch, a slim figure in her high-collared red coat with her cape over her shoulders. The Bulgarin house did not appear grand or ostentatious, but she was apprehensive. It was a relief when the door opened and she recognised the hall porter from St. Petersburg.

'Good afternoon, Liev. Please could you tell Count Bulgarin that Miss Anna Brianski is here?'

'Good afternoon. Shall I bring in your luggage?' If he was surprised, Liev gave no sign of it.

'Yes please. Is the count at home?'

'Not at the moment. We expect him back later this afternoon.'

'May I help you?' As Anna crossed the threshold into the hall, a tall woman came through curtains at the far end. 'I'm Varenka Bulgarin, Nicholas's aunt.'

Varenka Bulgarin was dressed in a house gown with an apron tied round her waist. She was a handsome woman, with blue eyes and wisps of grey hair slipping from beneath a turban. 'You must be Olga's friend, Anna Brianski! How lovely to meet you. When did you get here?'

'Only this morning. I'm sorry to arrive unannounced but my arrangements fell through.'

'Then you must stay here.' Taking in Anna's predicament at a glance, Varenka dispensed with polite formalities. 'Liev, please ask Gina to prepare the garden bedroom and take up Miss Brianski's bag. Come with me, my dear.'

Varenka Bulgarin had the same build and colouring as Nicholas but displayed none of his aloofness, and her welcome gave Anna confidence as she followed her into a sitting room. In the corner stood a square broad-wood piano and a line of unfinished canvasses were propped up against the skirting boards.

'I gather you're also an artist.' Varenka gestured towards them apologetically. 'Please forgive the mess. I work in a studio but bring my pictures in here to study them in a different light...'

This was her home, Varenka went on to explain, and Olga and Nicholas stayed with her when they were in Moscow. 'Olga's in St. Petersburg at the moment, so there's plenty of room.'

'Count Bulgarin is home early.' Liev appeared at the doorway. 'I suggested he wait in his study so that you could speak to him in private.'

'Very well. Please tell him I'll be there directly.' Varenka's gaze turned to Anna. 'Don't be concerned, Miss Brianski. I'll explain everything to my nephew. Take your time to refresh yourself. Liev will show you to your room.'

✽

There was no sign of Varenka when Anna came downstairs an hour later. Her bedroom was simple and comfortable, with a view of the garden. There was water to wash and Gina had unpacked her few possessions. Anna took off her coat and heavy boots, and checked her jewellery was safe. Her blue jacket was fitted to emphasise her small waist and she tied her hair back with a matching ribbon. Crossing the room, she checked her appearance in the glass. Her face was pale and pinched with exhaustion. Perhaps, her waif-like appearance would arouse sympathy in Count Bulgarin.

Liev was in the hall and showed her to Nicholas's study. He was standing at a writing desk with his dog lying at his feet and turned round as Anna entered.

'Thank you, Liev.' He drew up two chairs and beckoned to her. 'Good afternoon, Miss Brianski. Do sit down.'

Nicholas's took her hand briefly before he lounged back in a seat opposite her. 'I didn't expect to see again so soon after our last encounter. What's it this time? Have you run away from home?'

His acerbic tone made her bridle, but Anna kept her voice level. 'Is that what your aunt told you?'

'Varenka tells me you arrived in Moscow with nowhere to stay. I drew my own conclusions. I'm intrigued to know how you managed it.'

'I came with my sister-in-law, Sofia. She's staying with her family.'

'And they want nothing to do with the Brianskis. Why didn't you go to Maria Volkonsky?'

Nicholas wasn't going to make it easy and Anna hated being in a position where he had the advantage. She longed to snap at him but forced herself to smile instead. 'That was my original plan; only Princess Volkonsky hasn't yet arrived in Moscow.'

Nicholas flicked open an enamelled box on the desk and took a pinch of snuff, inhaling in one nostril and then the other. 'How did you obtain the necessary travel permits?'

'I took the place of Sofia's maid and used her papers.'

'So, you and Madame Brianski cooked up this adventure between you. Do your parents know where you are?'

'Yes...'

'And they gave you their blessing?'

'Not exactly...' Anna gripped her hands together, quelling an urge to tell a downright lie. 'They didn't know beforehand... I left a letter for them. We exchanged places on the way out of St. Petersburg.'

'Hence no luggage. Do you have any money?'

'I have my jewellery. It will raise enough to cover all my expenses.'

'I respect your resourcefulness, Anna Ivanova.' His voice mingled admiration with irony so she couldn't tell if he was laughing at her or serious. 'Do you intend to stay in Moscow for long?'

'Until we have everything ready for the journey. Sofia's with child and I'm going to accompany her to Siberia.'

Anna thought nothing could shock him, but his eyebrows went up and he seemed genuinely surprised.

'Surely, Madame Brianski can find herself another, more experienced companion —especially in her condition?'

'Sofia wants me with her.' Her mouth felt dry and Anna passed her tongue over her lips. 'I promised Sasha I would take care of her.'

Nicholas gave her long, penetrating look. Did he know what was in her mind? Anna looked down for fear of betrayal, but not swiftly enough, for his eyes narrowed.

'And your motive is purely one of sisterly charity?'

'I'm fulfilling my promise to my brother.' The old irritation flared up and she replied hotly, 'Is such an action beyond your understanding, sir?'

'Not in the slightest. Indeed, your loyalty does you credit. Please look at me, Anna Ivanova.' His voice was quiet and Anna raised her head. His expression was inscrutable but curiosity flickered in his eyes. 'Can you reassure me that you no longer harbour any thoughts of romance?'

'I came here because I need somewhere to stay, Count Bulgarin.' Anna's nails dug into her palms. 'I didn't expect to be faced with the Spanish Inquisition.'

'May I come in?' Varenka spoke from the door, her skirts rustling on the parquet floor. She took a seat beside Anna. 'Tea is almost ready. Poor Miss Brianski must be starving.'

'How very thoughtless of me,' Nicholas responded with exaggerated politeness. 'My aunt regards it our Christian duty to take you in, Miss Brianski, and I agree.'

'It's a terrible tragedy.' Varenka took out a handkerchief and twisted it into a knot. 'I weep for your family – and for poor Olga. I will travel north as soon as I can to be with her.'

'Why doesn't she come here?' Anna asked.

'Olga is presently in favour with the tsar,' Varenka answered candidly. 'She hopes her influence will persuade him to mitigate the sentences.'

'But surely the tsarina has greater influence.'

'The empress saved your brother and our friends from death,' Nicholas intervened. 'There's no more she can do. The tsar will never forgive the Decembrists. He's even gone so far as to declare their wives are widows and free to remarry.'

Anna stared at him in disbelief. 'But that's heresy! Sofia and Maria Volkonsky will never remarry. They hold God's law above any other.'

'And I respect their probity.' Nicholas stood up and his dog trotted over, wagging its tail. 'However, I advise you to think carefully before you travel further. Has the tsar given his word that any of you may return?'

'He promised not to punish the families of Decembrists.'

'Unless they take up their husbands' cause.'

Anna felt the cold shock of being struck without warning. Was he suggesting that the women who followed their husbands would also be exiled for life? The tsar wouldn't dare, she thought. Her fingers whitened as she gripped the arm of her chair and Varenka came hastily to her feet. 'Enough of this gloomy talk. Come along now, both of you. We shall have tea and speak of brighter matters.'

✿

'These are excellent. You've that elusive talent to express personality.'

Anna was with Varenka Bulgarin in her studio the next morning. She had shown her sketchbook and was pleased with the compliment.

'Now let me show you a drawing of mine. I trust you to be honest. I drew it a few years ago.'

Varenka handed Anna a silverpoint portrait of Olga and Nicholas. Olga looked no older than twelve. She was standing beside Nicholas who was in military uniform with a high crested cap. A smile played about his mouth and he looked relaxed. There was no trace of his usual arrogance and she searched for the right words. 'It's very good of them both. You portray them so naturally and silverpoint's an unforgiving medium.'

As Varenka set up her easel, Anna wandered round the studio, stopping to look at different paintings. One in particular caught her attention. It was an ink illustration of a bear in a spiked collar, and she picked it up. 'What's this?'

'I drew it for an article Nicholas submitted to the *Journal of Russian Studies*. He called it "An Empire in Chains". Sadly, they refused to publish it.'

Nicholas had gone out for dinner the night before and Anna hadn't spoken to him again. It was a provocative title and she was curious. 'Is your nephew a true reformer?' Varenka was mixing colours and, when she did not reply, Anna went on. 'I know he's very loyal to his friends. What I mean is, does he share their ideals?'

'Nicholas's sympathies are absolutely with those of your brother and the Decembrists.' Varenka put down her palette and looked at her with a straight, steady gaze. 'His writing has the power to inspire and ignite change. It's his contribution to the struggle against oppression. He believes serfdom will be abolished by influence rather than by revolution; that's the only difference between them.'

Olga had been betrothed to a Decembrist. Now she was a favourite of the tsar. Nicholas shared the ideals of the rebels, yet his mistress was married to a Romanov. It was a confusing picture and Anna wanted to know more.

'Nicholas Petrovich has a friend in St. Petersburg, Princess Elizaveta Romanov. Have you met her?'

'Not yet. There are many women in Nicholas's life – most of them married.'

'He told me he doesn't believe in romantic love.'

'I don't expect he does.' Varenka turned back to her easel and picked up a brush. 'Nicholas was fourteen when his parents died. It was an impressionable age. He rarely reveals his feelings. Olga, on the other hand, is an open, very loving person.'

Varenka was concentrating on her painting and Anna was glad she couldn't see her face. She looked out of the window to the branches of fir trees bowed down with snow and was uncertain how to answer.

'I was so happy when she found love with Peter Dashkovy,' Varenka continued. 'Did you know they were engaged to be married? The poor child is utterly heart-broken.'

Chapter Twenty-One

Olga's not heartbroken, Anna told herself. If only her aunt could have seen her dancing with the tsar at Prince Kochubey's reception! It was natural that Varenka should want to think well of her niece, but Olga wasn't languishing in St. Petersburg. She was having the time of her life.

The days that followed were so busy, Anna forgot about Olga Bulgarin. Compared to the stiff grandeur of St. Petersburg, the informality of Moscow society appealed to her. She liked the city's authenticity, the buzz of life and combination of old and new. Varenka took her to visit the great bazaar, a vast treasure-trove containing all the riches of the east. The shops could only be reached by individual ladder steps and sold everything from Siberian pelts to golden icons and precious stones. There were chests of tea from China, lacquered wood from India and Arabian horses for sale. Bukhara merchants with long beards and embroidered caps laid out colourful shawls and Anna bought one, along with boots, gloves and furs for the journey.

The church bells of Moscow rang from morning to night until Anna no longer noticed them. Other sounds stayed with her – the sharp cries of the fruit sellers, the gruff voices of horse dealers and smooth enticements of merchants. Varenka found her a pawnbroker where her zhemchuzhina fetched a good price. As she handed them over, she remembered the night her parents gave them to her and her eyes welled up. Mama and Papa want me to marry Boris Renin, she reminded herself. I can't go back. Not yet. One day I'll return to St. Petersburg and make my peace with them.

Anna's education had been similar to other girls of her milieu. She was fluent in French and spoke Italian and English better than Russian.

Her childhood had been happy; yet, looking back, it seemed cloying and claustrophobic. Our lives were too sheltered, she thought now; we were as unprepared for happiness as we were for disaster. I had so many dreams – my art and love for Peter – but knew nothing of the real world.

In Moscow, for the first time, Anna experienced a new sense of independence. Her only concern was for Sofia. Why was there no news? She couldn't visit the Pavels. Instead, she wrote to Omelko, enclosing money for the journey home and thanking him for his kindness. Varenka arranged for the letter to be taken by hand. Omelko was the last link with home and, when the letter had gone, Anna felt bereft.

'Do you miss St. Petersburg?' Varenka enquired astutely.

'I've never been away from home before but I'm happy here. You've been very kind.'

When asked, Anna evaded a definitive answer as to the duration of her visit. Sofia must write soon and surely Maria had arrived in Moscow by now? She would pay her a visit in the next few days, she decided as she slipped into the easy-going routine of the Bulgarin household.

The gates leading into the courtyard from the street were never locked so that visitors walked through the servants' quarters, up the stairs and into the hall to arrive unannounced. A constant stream of friends and acquaintances passed through the house and the humming of the samovar ceased only at mealtimes. Two young maids with trays and cups mingled with the guests until lunchtime, when it was whisked away and tables wheeled in, laden with caviar, smoked herring, lobster and cheese. Meals were accompanied by an assortment of vodkas and, when the last course finished and the table was cleared, the samovar returned as a signal for conversation to begin again.

Sometimes Nicholas joined them, sometimes not. Then, one morning, he offered to show Anna his library. Among a collection of Russian books, there were works by Voltaire and Madame de Stael and, in the lower shelves, the poetry of Byron, Keats and Shelley.

Nicholas told her to borrow whatever she liked and went to his desk while Anna sat reading in a chair. She loved books – the smell of leather and smooth vellum pages — but most of all she loved the work of Alexander Pushkin. Nicholas had the latest instalment of his verse novel *Eugene Onegin* — right up to the moment when Onegin shot the poet, Lensky, in a duel. Anna was so absorbed she didn't notice he had left his desk and was standing by her. A tear slid down her cheek as she came to the end, and he took the book out of her hands.

'Don't tell me Monsieur Pushkin's made you cry.'

'But the poet was Onegin's friend,' Anna mumbled, searching in her pocket for a handkerchief. 'He killed his best friend.'

'And you, my dear, are too sentimental.'

'Pushkin believes it better to have a thousand dreams than never dream at all.'

'Our great poet should stop making pronouncements and curb his addiction to duelling. If he fires his pistols over every woman he loves, he'll be dead before his time.'

'But he's a romantic. He can't help but feel passionately. How can he write poetry if his heart's closed?'

'Romantics use pretty words but they're blind to the inconsistencies of human nature.'

'Why are you so contemptuous of love?'

The question slipped out before Anna could censor it. She didn't mean to challenge him, but his attitude perplexed her. She fell silent and it was moment before he answered.

'I'm not contemptuous of love — but I pity those who fall under its spell. I've known too many people seduced by romantic illusion. They believe they're in love until one day they wake up and find boredom and bitterness have taken over their hearts.'

Just now, as she began to warm to him, he had to say something to annoy her. Nicholas was a cynic, Anna thought. Had he ever felt deeply about anything? Was his outward manner some kind of pretext — a defence against sentiments he refused to acknowledge? He wasn't coarse or ill-mannered, but nor was he a gentleman in the sense that she understood. He had a bold way of assessing women, his physical attraction at odds with his lack of emotion, adding to the confusion he aroused in her.

'I'm leaving for St. Petersburg at the end of the month.' His voice broke into her thoughts. 'You're welcome to accompany me, should you wish.'

'Thank you but I've no intention of returning north. I expect to hear of our departure for Siberia any day now.'

'I think that's unlikely. The doctors are bound to recommend that Madame Brianski waits until after the birth of her child.'

Sofia's pregnancy was not a subject to be discussed with a man, let alone a bachelor. In polite society, women only discussed such matters behind closed doors and Anna shifted uncomfortably in her chair. 'Let Sofia be the best judge of that. If wives are forced to choose between their husbands and their children, we've no right to interfere.'

'I'm not interfering, merely alerting you to the dangers of a miscarriage. Such a journey is perilous for a woman in her condition.'

It was shameful for a man to be so indelicate. If Nicholas had any decency, he would drop the subject. Anna was embarrassed by his directness and answered with as much dignity as she could. 'Sofia's determined to go to Siberia. She will make the journey, with or without me.'

'You carry a heavy burden of responsibility, Anna Ivanova. Madame Brianski is indeed blessed to have such a selfless sister-in-law. I'm only sorry you've made up your mind to abandon your family.'

'Sasha and Sofia are also my family.'

'Indeed, but they're not your parents.'

'My parents have their own ideas regarding my future. They want me to marry Boris Renin.'

Nicholas shook his head incredulously. 'That must be the strangest thing I ever heard.'

'Mama's even suggested I paint his portrait.'

'Hardly a contract of marriage! Has Major Renin kissed you?'

The question was so unexpected it brought Anna to her feet. 'Of course, not.'

'So, what makes you think he wants to marry you?' His eyes behind their blue gaze held a glint and Anna felt an inexplicable tremor in her hand. She didn't want Nicholas to think it was vanity that made her so certain of Renin and she met his gaze squarely.

'My family may be in disgrace but we're not poor. Major Renin seeks wealth and social position, I'm sure. Since my brother's exile, I'm the heir to my father's fortune. He's despicable and I dislike everything about him.'

'Have you ever been kissed, Anna Ivanova?'

His shift of mood threw Anna. She was aware of his gaze, lingering on her neck and throat. Was he mocking her or making advances? Surely, he wouldn't be so bold as to try anything when she was a guest in his home? Her thoughts showed in her eyes and he laughed softly as he returned the book to the casement.

'One day some lucky man will kiss you. I hope you won't be disappointed when the time comes.'

Anna refused to dignify the remark with an answer. Nicholas was outrageous, flirting with her one minute, then patronising her as if she were a child. What on earth would he say or do next? She was relieved when he changed the subject.

'Would you like to go for a drive after lunch? If so, I'll ask Varenka to accompany us.'

✡

As it turned out, Varenka was busy that afternoon and, by the time they left, the sun was setting. Anna sat alone in the back of the troika covered in bearskins as Nicholas mounted the driving board. The sleigh was pulled by three horses abreast, the shaft horse in the centre carrying the painted arc of the duga. The tracers on either side pranced with heads bent outwards, their harnesses strung with bells that made a jingling crescendo as they set off.

Omelko had taught her the art of driving a troika so Anna knew how difficult it was – how the driver must manipulate the horses through four sets of reins, all the while keeping the shaft horse at a different pace to the other two. They drove through the streets, and Nicholas guided them with his voice, keeping them at a steady canter. As they passed through the gates and reached open ground, the horses twitched their ears forwards, tugging at the traces, and he gave them their heads.

They were galloping fast and a fine spray of snow rushed past Anna's face. She loved the intoxicating pace of the sleigh, the plunging horses and whistle of runners. Le vertige de la vitesse was in her blood – a craving for speed born in every Russian. Exhilaration made the blood sprint through her body so she wanted to shout and wave her arms and, when Nicholas glanced back, she laughed aloud. She admired his strength and skill as he slowed the horses and turned their heads towards home.

The sky was dark with impending snow and, as they neared Vozdvizhenka Street, her elation faded and Anna thought of Peter and Sasha. Had they reached Siberia yet? Were they already at work in the silver mines? The idea made her shiver as Nicholas swung himself out of the driving seat and gave her his hand.

'Are you cold?'

Anna shook her head and asked, 'Were the Decembrists so very wrong?'

'They were right in what they hoped to achieve.'

'So why didn't you support them?'

'The strength of our nation lies in the hearts and minds of its people. Until serfdom is recognised as brutal slavery from the highest authorities to every peasant in the land, nothing will change. Our friends have made people question the tsar's unlimited power and the evil of our social system. It's a beginning...'

As always, he sounded plausible and Anna wanted to believe him. Nicholas was unlike any man she had ever met before and impervious to the opinion of others. He could be charming or sarcastic, depending on his mood, but there was no denying his intelligence. He could not walk into a room without the talk dying around him, or walk out without leaving a sense of absence. Anna noticed how everyone listened when he joined in a discussion with Varenka and her friends – how the company hung on his words and valued his opinion. Nicholas was seemingly at ease with women – although she doubted that he respected any of them very much, apart from his aunt. He was different with Varenka. There was never that derisive, slightly mocking look in his eyes, and a softer note came into his voice.

Anna marvelled at his ability to deal with so many discordant sides of his personality. She was more relaxed in his company, but never lost the uneasy feeling of danger lurking beneath the surface. Then, at the end of an evening they had spent together, Nicholas walked with her and Varenka to the bottom of the stairs. He gave his aunt a candle before she made her way up, and lit one for Anna also.

As she reached out for it, he took hold of her hand and turned it over. His mouth pressed the inside of her wrist and she was too startled to draw back. At the touch of his lips, something vital and electric leapt from him to her, caressing her whole body. Darkness hid her face but she knew he must feel the racing of her pulse. Suddenly, she was overtaken by a wild desire to throw her arms round his neck and feel his lips on her mouth. Appalled by her reaction, she blushed to the roots of her hair as Nicholas released her.

'Goodnight, Annushka. Sleep well.' There was a warm note in his voice as he gave her the candle.

Anna went up the stairs so fast she was out of breath when she reached the top. I love Peter Dashkovy, she told herself. How can I be attracted to a man for whom I have no feelings? Nothing, not even love, was as simple as she once believed. An image of Peter drifted across her mind. There had been a time when she could draw his face from memory; now, his features were hazy. What was happening to her? She had no illusions about Nicholas Bulgarin. He was a flirt who could make a woman feel like paper licked by fire, and she was shocked by her response to him. I won't let him manipulate me, she thought feverishly. From now on, my conduct must be more circumspect – no more sleigh rides or reading together in the library. Whatever his intentions, I'm strong enough to resist him.

January, Moscow

Dearest Anna

Forgive me for taking so long to write. The time I have spent with my family has been torture. Maman and Papa accuse me of causing them mortal grief and my beloved Sasha of being my assassin. I am shocked by their intransigence and the measures they have taken to delay our departure.

Thanks be to God, Michael arrived yesterday and is helping to make the arrangements. I pray we will be ready to leave by the end of next week. I heard from Maria this morning. She too has suffered greatly at the hands of her family but is now in Moscow and hopes to set off with Princess Trubetskoy within a few days.

Dearest Anna, I wouldn't have the strength to go on, were it not for your support. Michael tells me you are staying with the Bulgarins and he will bring this letter to their home. Mishka is the most steadfast and loyal of brothers and I look forward to hearing from him that you are well.

I embrace you, dearest sister. Until next week, adieu.
Sofia

Chapter Twenty-Two

Anna read Sofia's letter then folded it and put it back in the envelope. She was in the drawing room with Michael Pavel, waiting for Varenka to join them. He looked older, she thought, as he came in. The look in his eyes was unfamiliar – not anger or grief, but a bleakness that was new to her.

'Sofia told me everything.' Michael stood with his back to the window. 'I never thought I'd live to see this day, dear Anna. You, my beloved sister, and Maria, being punished for an act of madness that had nothing to do with you.'

Anna did not answer. Being with him made her think of the happier times – of children's parties and riding in the grounds of Tsarskoe Selo. Between them lay the bonds of family and friendship, memories of a childhood they had shared. It hurt to think of those beautiful days before the world had fallen apart. A few months ago, they had been young and full of hope. Now their lives were broken and they were like animals on the run, searching for somewhere safe to shelter. Nicholas said the revolution hadn't been in vain – but what had it achieved except sorrow and loss? Had the Decembrists' ideals been too lofty to consider what might happen to their loved ones?

Michael walked over to her and took her hands in his. 'Promise me you'll come back.' He smiled but his expression was urgent. 'I know Sofia will stay with Sasha once the baby's born, but I beg you to return home. Your parents are distraught, Anna. I'd like to offer them some comfort when I get back to St. Petersburg.'

Looking into his clear brown eyes, Anna's confidence was shaken. She had been so sure of her decision when she left St. Petersburg.

Now, she felt like a wavering needle on a compass, being pulled from one gravity to another. Not knowing how to answer, she put her arms around him. Michael held her close with her head pressed into his shoulder and she felt a lump rise in her throat. He's good man, she thought. In another life I might have loved him. I hope, whatever the future holds, he'll always be my friend.

For a long moment, Anna let his warmth comfort her until, without warning, Michael wrenched himself out of her embrace. Bewildered by the suddenness of his action, she stared at him.

A sardonic voice spoke from the doorway. 'Please forgive the interruption.'

Michael took a step backwards as Nicholas and Varenka walked into the room. Anna saw his hand go to his throat to straighten his cravat. He was mortified at being found with her, even as Varenka tried to put him at his ease.

'I'm very pleased to meet you, Captain Pavel. Welcome to our home.'

'How are you?' Nicholas shook his hand. 'Are you visiting Moscow with the tsar's entourage?'

'I came to see my sister and to say goodbye to Anna.' Michael's voice was compressed and he was obviously ill at ease. 'I promised to be home by lunchtime.'

'Do please stay a moment, Captain Pavel.' Varenka held up her hand. 'I'd like to offer Anna and Madame Brianski some advice.' She paused, her calm blue eyes moving from Michael to Anna. 'I'm worried about how you're going to manage in Siberia. Have you seriously considered the difficulties you'll face? Life will be completely different from anything you've experienced before. You'll need to do everything for yourselves in the most difficult of circumstances. I think you should be prepared.'

'I know how to cook,' Anna retorted. 'I spent my childhood in the kitchen.'

'In a city where food is plentiful. Our cook comes from the Urals. Together we can teach you some simple, local dishes. And one of you should be able to sew and mend clothes.'

'Sofia has been learning about medicine,' Michael replied. 'She's convinced there are no doctors in Siberia.'

'What about Maria Volkonsky?' Anna asked pointedly.

'From what I hear of Princess Volkonsky, she has the skill to negotiate with the devil – a most useful attribute in Siberia,' Nicholas commented.

What was he thinking? Anna wondered, seeing the inquisitive look in his eyes as his gaze rested on Michael. 'I'm acquainted with her cousin, Princess Zinaida Volkonsky. We've been invited to a soirée in her honour tomorrow evening. By all accounts Princess Maria is a remarkable lady and I look forward to meeting her.'

✿

The windows of the palace blazed with light as carriages dropped off their passengers at the door. The sound of music reached them as they entered the hall and Nicholas offered Varenka and Anna each an arm as they mounted the carpeted staircase to the first floor.

Varenka had persuaded Anna to borrow a ballgown belonging to Olga. The green velvet suited her auburn hair but the style was too bold for her taste. Sleeveless and with a plunging neckline, it made her feel immodestly exposed. I'm like a pale imitation of Olga, she thought. If only Sofia and Michael were going to be here, but she knew their parents had refused to let either of them accept.

The inside of the palace was lavish with white columns and carvings covered in gold leaf on every trim and scroll. Splendid pieces of French furniture lined the walls beside glass-fronted bookcases packed with leather-bound volumes. Anna glanced at the titles as they walked past and saw works by Walter Scott and Shakespeare at the front. Flowering orange trees and hothouse plants in tubs filled the air with their scent and, between fine silk hangings on the walls, hung landscapes and portraits – at least four them of the late tsar.

'Tsar Alexander was an intimate friend of Princess Zinaida's,' Varenka explained in a low voice as they approached the music room.

'She married Volkonsky to stem gossip, but they remained close until the end. She's one of the most cultured women in Russia and her salon the envy of every hostess in Moscow.'

Princess Zinaida stood by the door. She was a beautiful woman, with a long neck and soulful eyes, her face framed by curls and a feathered headdress.

'I'm honoured to make your acquaintance, Miss Brianski.' She gave Anna a warm smile, holding up her hand to stop her curtsying, and kissing her on both cheeks. 'We're privileged to have the company of such noble women with us this evening. Maria's dying to see you. She's waiting by the piano. Grigor, would you be so kind as to take Miss Brianski through?'

The princess's companion, a slim tall man with dark hair, led the way to an elegant salon filled with statues and palms. A small orchestra was playing and the grand salon was full of people talking at tables or occupying armchairs. Waiters in blue livery and red slippers moved silently among the guest with trays laden with food, champagne and glasses of vodka. The far end was dominated by a grand piano, the rallying point of the room. Beside it sat Maria. She looked unusually flushed, Anna noted as she rose to embrace her.

'I'm so glad you're here, darling Anna. How are you? Sofia wrote to me that you're staying with the Bulgarins.'

'I'm well, thank you. I gather it's been as hard on you as for Sofia. I'm so sorry.'

'It's over now.' Maria sneezed and blew her nose. 'I'm blessed to be here with Zinaida. Her tender care has warmed my heart. She shares my passion for music and has gathered the best talent in Moscow this evening. I hoped to take part but I have a touch of la grippe.'

Maria looked feverish. Her large, expressive eyes were bright and there was high colour in her cheeks. They spoke quietly and Anna held her hand until Maria was distracted by guests coming forwards to be presented. 'Promise to stay for supper after the recital. We can talk again then.'

A queue of people stood in line and Anna looked around for Varenka and Nicholas. They were still by the entrance and she noticed how close Nicholas leant to Princess Zinaida, who was smiling at him. Was she another of his past conquests? She didn't know why the idea piqued her as she began to make her way through the crush. She was halfway across the room, when someone called her name. As Anna stopped, a small gentleman with piercing blue eyes and dark curly hair stood right in front of her.

'My dear Miss Brianski!" Alexander Pushkin exclaimed. 'How wonderful to see you!'

Pushkin wore a frockcoat nipped in at the waist with a matching waistcoat and white silk cravat. His attention was like a spark of gunpowder. The intensity of his gaze seemed to make the air charge between them, and his magnetism left Anna speechless.

'When we last met, you were a child and now you're a beautiful woman.' His voice was as soft as a caress. 'I recall you had a precocious talent for drawing. So, what are you doing in Moscow?'

Anna swallowed and found her voice. 'I'm here on my way to Siberia with my sister-in-law Sofia Brianski. My brother's in exile, along with Sergei Volkonsky and Peter Dashkovy. I'm sure you remember them.'

A cloud passed across Pushkin's face as he pressed the back of his hand to his forehead. 'I have known the most prestigious youth of my time and your brother, Sasha Brianski, is one of the finest. I'm honoured to call him my friend. Volkonsky and Dashkovy are touched by arrogance. And yet they're all heroes.' He gave a long, meaningful sigh. 'An arctic winter has taken hold of Russia and they alone keep the flame of freedom alive. I exult in admiration for their courage and the heroism of their women. Are you staying here with Maria? Not a day passes when I don't think of her.'

'I'm lodging with Count Bulgarin and his aunt. They brought me this evening.'

Anna's gaze strayed over his shoulder to where Nicholas was still talking to Princess Zinaida. She was speaking in his ear and seemed to be asking him something. He hesitated, looking around the room, then catching sight of Anna, sauntered towards them.

'I hear Bulgarin received a challenge from Prince Romanov and high-tailed it out of St. Petersburg.' A querulous look came over Pushkin's face. 'An honourable man would have accepted.'

'Is Count Bulgarin not honourable?'

'I couldn't possibly say. But he'll be obliged to find himself a wife now. A fate that will come to us all one day.' Pushkin clicked his tongue, as if scolding himself, then shrugged. 'For all that, I respect Nicholas Bulgarin. He's a clever fellow. Thinks with his head and not his heart.'

'Good evening, Alexei Sergeyevich.' Nicholas held out his hand to the poet.' This is a fortunate coincidence. Anna Ivanova was moved to tears by your hero's misdeeds. Please can you reassure her Eugene Onegin's soul will be redeemed?'

'I've no concept of the outcome.' Pushkin's eyes flashed with petty annoyance. 'I'll send a copy of the next instalment to Miss Brianski once it's written. And now, I must attend to the reason I risk the tsar's displeasure to be here this evening.'

The crowd parted, heads turning, as Pushkin walked over to Maria. He took her hand as he sat down and Princess Zinaida joined them at the piano. The first notes from a violin were played and two singers began to sing from a Mozart opera as Nicholas led Anna and Varenka to a table. Anna felt tears start in her eyes as she listened and saw how Maria applauded.

'Again! Please sing that one once more. I may never hear it again!'

Her enthusiasm was plain for all to see and the aria was reprised, but the atmosphere was muted. Princess Zinaida tried to maintain an air of gaiety and singers performed songs from comic opera until most of the guests had departed. When only her closest friends remained, Maria played the piano and the Austrian ambassador sang from *Don Juan*. They tried to be cheerful but no one had the heart for merriment. Anna noticed how Pushkin stayed at Maria's side without speaking, his expression grave as he gazed sadly into her face.

His silence was unusual, and Nicholas remarked, 'Pushkin will always love the one woman he can't have.'

'Surely, that's the case with most men?' Anna retorted with flash of exasperation.

'Most men are content with whoever they can manage without too much difficulty.'

He was being deliberately irritating and Anna pulled a face as he turned to speak with Varenka. Supper was brought in and a young man drew up a chair on her other side. He was elegantly dressed, his hair carefully smoothed and he seemed somehow familiar.

'I'm John Lenkov. We used to play together as children.'

'Why, of course! 'Anna exclaimed as she recognised him.' Forgive me, there are so many people here. Of course I remember you.'

The shy young man had grown tall and was good-looking with copper-coloured hair and a fine moustache. He had a charming smile and Anna was flattered by the admiration in his eyes.

'How's your sister Anastasia? I always thought she was wonderful.'

'She's married and lives in the country, but she's as outrageous as ever! Her husband's a veritable saint. I believe your neighbour, Count Bulgarin, is acquainted with him. Could you be kind enough to introduce us?'

Nicholas was talking to Varenka and Anna waited until the conversation turned. 'John Lenkov is brother to Anastasia, who's married to Rubin Marinsky. I think you may know of them?'

'Indeed, they're my closest neighbours and good friends. Your sister's a remarkable lady and a first-class horsewoman. I'm travelling to Davinka tomorrow and hope to see them. Will they be at home?'

'I believe so. Please reassure Anastasia I'm attending to my duties and there's no need for her to worry.'

'What kind of duties?' Anna asked.

'We breed pedigree Orlovs. I bring them to Moscow for sale.'

John Lenkov was delightful and Anna felt relaxed in his company. If his family had come through all this unscathed, she was glad for them. It was strange that she should come across Alexander Pushkin and John

Lenkov here — two people she hadn't seen since Kamenka. The memory of that summer cast long shadows over this evening's sad gathering, she thought, as a bell rang and Pushkin came to his feet.

'Deep in the Siberian mines,
Keep your patience proud;
The bitter toil shall not be lost,
The rebel thought unbowed.'

Pushkin paused and sipped water from a glass. When he continued, his voice was on the point of breaking:

'Heavy-hanging chains will fall,
Walls crumble at a word;
May freedom greet you in the light,
And give you back the sword.'

As Pushkin words faded like the mournful chords of a lament, no one spoke or clapped. His audience was silent as he sat down and when dinner ended, chairs were pulled back by footmen and guests came to their feet. Varenka gathered her fan and reticule from the table and John Lenkov stood up and spoke to her.

'May I have your permission to call on Miss Brianski, ma'am? Where do you live?'

'We live on Vozdvizhenka Street. You're most welcome to visit us, sir — but don't leave it too long. Anna may not be with us beyond next week.'

Chapter Twenty-Three

It was after midnight when they arrived home and, as Varenka went straight upstairs, Nicholas took Anna's cloak and folded it on a chair.

'I'd like to talk to you, if you don't mind.'

He led the way to the sitting room and stood aside to let her pass through the door before him. A fire glowed in the hearth and the room was bright and warm, but Anna was tired.

'Can't it wait until the morning?'

'I'm afraid not. You'll still be asleep when I leave.'

Anna wasn't in the mood for talking and stood by the fire, tapping her foot impatiently until Nicholas joined her, bringing with him a decanter of wine. He poured out two glasses and handed one to her.

'I hear you're planning to leave for Siberia any day now and this is the last chance I may have to talk to you. I'd be grateful if you would be honest with me.'

'What do you wish to know?'

'The true reason you're embarking on this adventure.'

He was watching her carefully and Anna took a sip of claret, glad of its welcome warmth.

'I've given my reasons. There's no need to go over them again. I don't understand why you doubt me.'

'Because I believe you're still in love with Peter Dashkovy—'

'Really?' Anna interrupted. 'Well, I've no intention of discussing that with you.'

'I'm afraid you must. Captain Dashkovy and my sister remain betrothed. Olga may be in St. Petersburg for now but they still love each other.'

Nicholas was making it up, was Anna's first thought. She didn't know why he wanted to upset her, and she turned on him. 'You don't believe in love! You've told me so a hundred times. The only kind of love you understand is ... is ... whatever exists between you and your mistress!'

'You think I am only capable of carnal love, is that what you're saying?' There was a warning in his voice.

'I'm saying that you don't understand Peter Dashkovy—'

Anna broke off. She didn't need to explain – it was all there in the letter. Without another word she left the room and ran up the stairs. An oil lamp burned in the passage, but it was dark in the bedroom. She knelt down and reached inside the case, her fingers fumbling blindly to the bottom. She felt the ribbon first and then the paper. She pulled out Peter's letter and held it to her lips. Hurrying back, she arrived breathless and thrust the letter in front of his face.

'Read this!'

Nicholas took the letter, glanced over it and handed it back to her. A gust of wind rattled the windowpanes and Anna squeezed the piece of paper in her palm. There was an almost pitying look in his eyes. It reminded her of Sofia's expression when they had spoken of Peter at home. Then a mask came down over his face and his expression became blank.

'I visited Captain Dashkovy in prison and suggested he made his feelings for Olga clear to you.' Nicholas emptied his glass and put it down. 'It never occurred to me he'd write such nonsense. He's fond of you, Anna Ivanova, but he loves Olga.'

'You are forever in my heart.' In the first rush of joy as she read those words, she had let herself believe Peter loved her. Now doubt crept down her spine in icy waves. Despite the heat of the fire, Anna felt cold to the pit of her stomach.

'Please sit down, Anna. You look worn out.' Nicholas took her arm and led her to the sofa, collecting her glass and giving it to her. 'Drink your wine.'

Anna drank to the bottom. She was tired of Nicholas's pronouncements and of being reminded of Olga. If only she could tear off the green dress and throw it into the flames! I should never have come here, she thought. I should have kept away from the Bulgarins. Nicholas was determined to break down the last of her reserves and she wanted to get drunk – as intoxicated as her father and Sasha on New Year's Eve. She wanted to drink until her brain stopped working and her heart was numb. She didn't care what he thought and she held out her empty glass to be refilled.

'Not so fast... In a moment.' Nicholas took the glass away and sat down beside her. 'I'm not saying this to be cruel. You need to know the truth.'

'You're a stranger to matters of the heart, Nicholas Petrovich.' Anna went on the attack. 'Pushkin told me you ran away to avoid a duel with Prince Romanov.'

'Did he now?'

'He says an honourable man never refuses a challenge over a woman he loves.'

'Moral maxims are convenient when criticising someone else. However, we're not talking about me.'

'Well, it's time that we did! You despise weakness and emotion – so why are you determined to interfere in my life?'

'Do you mind if I smoke?'

Anna shook her head and Nicholas opened a silver cigar case. He extracted a cigar, flared a match and inhaled. An aroma of tobacco filled the room and Anna studied his profile from his forehead and aquiline nose to the strong line of his jaw. She noted the creases in his cheeks and laughter lines at the corners his eyes. There had been a time when he had been different, she thought, remembering Varenka's drawing. It was hard to imagine, but his eyes would always have been striking. Their colour changed with his moods and darkened now as he reached for an ashtray.

'Ten years ago, I knew a young woman. Her name was Natasha. The first time I saw you I was reminded of her. She was beautiful, warm-hearted and innocent.'

Anna kept her gaze on Nicholas's long fingers as he tipped a column of ash from his cigar. He took one more puff then threw it on the fire.

'She convinced herself that she was in love with me. One day she came and declared her love openly. I underestimated the extent of her passion.'

'What happened?'

'I told her I was fond of her but only as a brother. I broke her heart. She died six months later.'

'How? Why?' Anna asked, catching her breath.

'She drowned – whether by suicide or accident, no one knows. Love kills in a thousand ways.'

Despite her misery, Anna's heart wrenched for the poor girl. No wonder Nicholas held himself responsible. This had been on his conscience for a long time. She gave him a sideways glance, but the emotion that stirred him moments before had gone from his face.

'Worldly women understand the true nature of men. They take what they want from us and escape unharmed.' Nicholas was blunt. 'A man changes his woman according to his needs. I don't know if Dashkovy ever loved you, but it's Olga he needs now.'

Angry words rushed to her lips and Anna bit them back. It's not true, she thought, but she wasn't sure anymore. She couldn't go on like this, believing in Peter one moment and doubting him the next. It would send her mad. Why hadn't he had the courage to admit to her that he still loved Olga? He should have been honest. Her jaw trembled and she gritted her teeth to steady it. The letter was still clasped in her hand. She crumpled it into a ball and threw it on the flames. Her admiration and love had sustained her for so long. It had given her hope during the last dark weeks. But the brightness that shone around Peter was dimming, evaporating into thin air.

'One day someone will love you for your beauty and spirit, Anna Ivanova.'

Nicholas was trying to mollify her but she had heard enough. Between them, the Bulgarins had destroyed all that was precious in her life. The damage was done. She would never get back what she had lost this evening. But it would not change her direction. She would think only of Sofia and the baby. Sofia had never let her down and she would not abandon her. It was clear to her now and she stood up.

'Goodnight, Nicholas Petrovich'.

'You have many admirers,' Nicholas said, as though she hadn't signified the conversation was at an end. 'You're not tainted by association with the Decembrists and can marry anyone you want. Don't throw your life away for an empty dream.'

'You needn't concern yourself with my future anymore. I've made up my mind. I'm going to Siberia to take care of Sofia and the baby.'

'Then that's what you must do.' Nicholas came to his feet. 'If your mission is to look after your sister-in-law, I won't try to stop you. We should say goodbye tonight.'

Anna took a step back and he smiled. 'Don't run away, Annushka. I'd like us to part on good terms.'

He moved to stand closer and cupped her face in his hands. His lips touched her cheek lightly — a touch that shivered along her nerves. 'If you want me to stop, tell me now,' he whispered. The buttons of his coat pressed into her breast and Anna was too stunned to resist. He brushed her lips from side to side with his own, until the texture of his skin made her lips glow and burn. 'And now? Shall I go on?' The suggestion behind his words sent a quiver around her insides. His thumb traced the outline of her lips. Then his mouth came down on hers.

Anna's arms crept around his neck and Nicholas kissed her, softly at first, then more intensely. The ground seemed to shift beneath her feet as a shiver rippled over her scalp and down her spine until every inch of her body seemed to tingle. She felt her knees weaken as a hot rush of desire surged through her. His lips slid down her throat and he pressed them hard against the muslin over her breast, burning through the thin material to her skin. Anna was swept by passion she had never experienced before. She felt unknown parts of her stirring and the running swell of her blood. Her eyes closed as her tongue flickered against his mouth, tasting wine on his lips.

She wanted him to go on – to kiss her like this forever. And then a log broke in the grate, and the longing that had sprung up swiftly receded. As her mind cleared, humiliation clutched her heart. He's testing me. He wants to prove I never loved Peter, she thought, and began pushing against his chest. At once Nicholas lifted his head and looked down at her.

'To remind you of what you're leaving behind,' he said and smiled slightly.

In the depths of his eyes, a flame of light glimmered for a brief moment. Anna was tempted to slap him across the face. Shame and fury engulfed her, but she restrained herself.

'You presume too much, sir! I'm not susceptible to your advances, nor do I need your counsel. I pray God never to set eyes on you again.'

Part Four

January. Moscow

My dear Olga

I hope to be in St. Petersburg by the end of the month. Until then, please take care of yourself. It would be a grave mistake to underestimate the true nature of your patrons, but I trust you are aware of this already.

Here in Moscow, society is in full swing and Routs are the latest rage. They are gatherings that require neither wit, nor gaiety, nor talk of current affairs. One steps on people's feet, apologises and this passes for conversation. As you can imagine, I attend as few as possible.

Miss Brianski left with her sister-in-law ten days ago. Her self-imposed exile is a pity for she is an unusual and talented young woman. How she will fare in Siberia remains to be seen.

Your Aunt Varenka is well and hopes to accompany me north. She joins me in sending our love.

Nicholas

Chapter Twenty-Four

'*Poidi! Poidi!* Onwards! Forwards!' Ivan, their driver, shouted to his horses and Anna opened her eyes. She was tucked under a bearskin rug and Sofia was asleep beside her.

After weeks of lying horizontal in the interior of the *kibitka*, weariness and discomfort had taken their toll. They had begun their journey in good spirits, singing songs and reciting poems to pass the time. Now they slept as much as they could, dropping off to the sound of the runners on hard snow as they galloped across the frozen plains of Russia. Every fifteen miles they halted to change horses and one night they stayed at a *korchma*. The inn was dirty, with greasy tablecloths and huge tureens of cabbage soup, and crowded with merchants and soldiers drinking vodka and playing cards. The men ogled the women with blatant curiosity. Anna and Sofia took tea from the samovar and then retreated to the kibitka.

Hour after hour, the sleigh raced on towards an endless horizon and, as they headed further east, the landscape became bleak and monotonous. There were days when they saw no one, only sheets of white snow marked by the tracks of vehicles as they made their way over the steppe. They had crossed the Ural Mountains, leaving Christian Russia behind, and driven through pine forests as dark and endless as the sea, stopping at government post houses painted black and white with courtyards fenced in by sharp, pointed stakes. It was so cold, their breath turned to ice on the shawls covering their faces and the two women huddled together for warmth. One morning a crow, frozen in mid-flight, dropped like a stone from the sky beside the sleigh but no one said a word.

It felt as if they had been on the move forever but it had only been two weeks. Two weeks of being shaken and jolted until every bone in their bodies ached . To most Russians, the Urals represented the limits of civilisation. Ahead, lay the vast landmass of Siberia, an inhospitable wilderness where it was said human existence was intolerable.

They had left Moscow before dawn and Anna did not see Nicholas again. He was gone before she came down that morning and Varenka had helped with her final preparations. She showed her how to sew money and valuables into the hem of her clothes and gave her books, wool and knitting needles. She also advised her to wear a riding habit, rather than a dress, in case she had to walk in deep snow. It was pitch-dark when they departed. Varenka blessed Anna, then stood, watching from a window as the kibitka swept out through the gates.

Leaning back on her elbows, Anna touched the tips of her gloved fingers to her lips. She recalled Nicholas's kiss with a vividness that made goose bumps rise on her skin. She didn't want to think of him but he came into her mind whether she willed it or not, haunting her restless dreams. Whichever way she turned, he would be standing in front of her. Always too close, sometimes with a mocking smile, sometimes reaching out for her… When she thought of his dark, nonchalant face and how he had kissed her, something pinched deep in her belly. She had felt she was on fire, more alive at that moment than at any time before. What was it about him that attracted and disturbed her so much?

Anna had hoped to avoid talking about the Bulgarins, but Sofia was not to be put off. 'I don't understand why you're so mysterious about them. Didn't you enjoy your time in Moscow?'

'Their aunt, Varenka Bulgarin, was charming and generous. She's also an artist.'

'And Count Bulgarin?'

Anna waited a moment before she answered. 'He's difficult to get to know. I liked him, but…' Sofia was studying her inquisitively and she smiled. 'I'm not a complete goose, Sofia! Nicholas lives on a different planet from us. He's one of those intellectuals.'

'Never mind that, he's very good-looking.'

'Maybe to some people, I suppose...'

Anna did not miss Sofia's quick look, but refused to be drawn further. She was bewildered by her reaction to Nicholas. She didn't love him, she told herself, but everything was muddled in her head. The past was confused, the future opaque, and the present pressed more urgently.

She shifted herself into a more comfortable position. There were a few red streaks in the sky and she could see clouds banking above the mountain summits. It was the ominous sign of a *bourea*, the unpredictable steppe storm so perilous for travellers, but the horses were going well. If they kept up this pace, they would get to the next village before it reached them.

'Anna!' Sofia shouted in Anna's ear. 'Please ask Ivan to stop. My legs are so painful. I have to move...'

'We'll soon be there. Try to hold on. We need to find somewhere to stay the night.'

They both knew the danger of inflammation to the legs and Anna twisted her neck to look at Sofia. She was sitting up and grimacing with pain.

'There's a storm on its way!' Anna raised her voice. 'We can't stop now.'

'Please! Only for a few minutes.'

There was desperation in Sofia's face and Anna tugged the string of a bell attached to the driving box. The horses slowed down and came to a halt, steam pouring off their flanks as she helped Sofia to her feet. The women stood, bending their knees and swinging their arms until Ivan climbed down and lowered the leather roof over their heads.

'How long until we find shelter? Anna asked.

'There's a forest up ahead. Half an hour if we're lucky.'

'Then we must press on!'

The whip cracked and the horses set off at a canter, but they hadn't gone far before the *bourea* came racing down the valley. Snow began piling onto the roof and the horses stumbled so the sledge lurched forwards.

There was a sudden crack and Anna was afraid a runner had broken. She was relieved they didn't slow down, but the kibitka was off balance and tilting dangerously to one side. Suddenly it tipped over with a crash. The wooden panels cracked and Sofia cried out as splinters flew through the air. Anna tried to grab hold of her and heard a thud as Sofia's head slammed against something hard. She groaned then lay still.

Brushing dust out of her eyes, Anna took hold of her wrist and found her pulse. It was steady but Sofia was unconscious.

'Sofia, wake up!'

Under her eyelids, Sofia's eyes moved but stayed shut.

'Please, darling. You must wake up!'

The slits of Sofia's eyes widened a fraction. Anna placed her ear close her mouth and felt her breath.

'Are you in pain. Where does it hurt?'

'My baby...'

'It's alright, darling. We've had an accident. I'll send Ivan to get help.'

The door opened above her head and Ivan peered down at them.

'You must go to the village and find someone with a sledge. Madame Brianski's been injured.'

'But I can't leave the horses.'

'Of course you can! They'll be fine .'

'They're terrified of the storm, *devushka*. They'll take off with broken runners and—'

'My sister's hurt. I can control the horses. I've driven a troika before. You must get help, please!'

'I can't leave them. If they panic, they'll drag you to your death.'

A glimmer of light came through the opening and Anna looked at Sofia. Her skin was grey and her lips drawn into a tight line.

'How far are we from the forest?'

'I can see lights – but you can't go out in this!' Ivan shouted above the wind. 'We must dig in and wait to be rescued.'

Dear God, what shall I do? Anna cast about frantically. How could anyone find them in the storm? Sofia was hurt and Anna was terrified she might have a miscarriage. If they were forced stay here all night, she could bleed to death. Sasha had entrusted Sofia and the baby to her care. She couldn't let her die.

A soft moan escaped Sofia's lips and Anna leant over her. 'Where does it hurt?'

'In my head ... in my stomach.'

'The baby's well protected, darling. Promise to stay still until I come back.'

'But you can't go alone! Wait until the storm passes.'

Sofia's teeth were chattering and Anna pulled the bearskin rug up to her chin. She dared not touch her head, but found a warm brick and placed it under her feet.

'I won't be long. Here's the bell for Ivan. When the horses are calmer, he'll come and sit with you.'

Anna heard the tremor in her voice as she heaved on a greatcoat. It was old military issue Varenka had found, large enough to wear over layers of thick clothes, so heavy that it pulled her shoulders down. She already had on her fur-lined boots and she pulled her beaver bonnet down to cover her ears. As she climbed out of the upturned sleigh, a blast of freezing wind drove the air out of her lungs. This cold could freeze a man's soul, she thought. Ivan's a tough Cossack but no one can survive these conditions.

'Once the horses are quiet, get inside and stay with my sister. Do you understand?'

Ivan nodded and handed her a thick wooden staff, pointing towards a moving light at the edge of the forest. It wasn't so far, after all. The track was covered and the snow so deep it reached over her knees. Frost blasted down her throat as she lifted the staff and stabbed it into the snow. Holding fast, she moved slowly forwards until she had to stop and catch her breath.

Above the wind, she heard another sound – the eerie howling of wolves. There must be a pack of them, and they were close by! Anna fought to control her panic. There could be no scent in the freezing air.

The bitter cold might kill them all — but it wouldn't help predators. She took a step forwards, stumbled and lost her footing. As she put her arm out to save herself, Anna almost wrenched her shoulder from its socket. Wincing with pain, she picked herself up and floundered on.

Her heart was pumping with the effort, every step harder than the last, yet the light seemed no nearer. The cold was branching into her brain, telling her she should rest, rest until she was warm and could sleep. Snow devils began dancing and Anna imagined a fire glowing in the darkness. She longed to lie down — but she couldn't stop or she would freeze to death. She forced her brain to work by counting each step. Ten slow paces, then ten more before she saw a flare in the trees. Her eyelashes were spiked with ice so it hurt to blink, as she made out the figure of a man carrying a torch.

'Help! *Pomogi myne!* Help me!'

Her shouts were lost in the wind and the blizzard pushed her back, but Anna could see the dark outline of a cabin and a light in the window. The sight gave her renewed strength. She staggered on, climbing the steps in a dizzying series of lurches. As she fell against the door, it opened and she collapsed across the threshold. Someone lifted her up and she was blinded by light. She tried to speak but her lips wouldn't move and a croaking sound came from her throat. 'Accident. Please help us... I show you...'

'You stay here.' A woman spoke to her in Russian. 'Accident where?'

'Not far...' Anna indicated with her head. 'By the edge of the forest.'

There were two men and the woman, whose head shawl had fallen back on her shoulders. She had an oriental face and black hair braided in pigtails. Anna was so weak she thought she would drop at her feet, but the woman grasped her arm and helped her to a bench.

'Take the sledge and dogs.' The woman instructed the men. 'Go back towards the track.'

The room was lit by candles and heat from the stove made Anna's face burn. The woman removed her gloves and rolled back her cuffs to examine her hands. They were cold but soft, not hard with frostbite.

'You're just in time,' she said. 'We must take off your outer clothes.'

Anna's greatcoat was frozen with ice, melting into a pool of water on the floor. The woman took it off and hung it at the back of the room. She was small and sturdy with skin like beaten leather. She removed Anna's fur hat and then knelt down to pull off her boots.

'*Spasibo*, thank you... My sister is hurt...'

'Quiet now. Save your strength.'

Warmth seeped into Anna's body and tears of relief slipped down her cheeks. She looked around for an icon, to say a prayer, but the walls were bare. The inhabitants of the cabin must belong to one of the pagan tribes that roamed these parts., she thought. I don't care what their religion is, they're the kindest people on God's earth.

The woman brought her a mug and held it to her mouth. Anna pursed her lips, sipping the hot tea, and blessed warmth spread through her limbs.

'What's your name?' she asked.

'Lisanka.'

'I'm Anna... I must thank you...'

'Wait until your sister's safe. Is she badly hurt?'

Lisanka spread dry pine branches on the earthen floor and put rugs to warm on the stove.

'She's with child.'

There was the sound of dogs yelping and barking outside. Then the door opened and two men carried in a sledge. Sofia was hidden under the bearskin, not moving.

'Here – but not too close.' Lisanka gave instructions. 'Be careful.'

Sofia was carried in, laid down on the rug and branches, and the bearskin was lifted off. Her skin was waxy and her lips blue. She was so still that Anna's heart slowed as she stared at her. Sofia and the baby were dead. She had taken too long. Seized by terror, she stared around the hut. It was filling up and she could smell damp clothes. She heard men's voices and Lisanka asked for a curtain to be placed across the room before she turned her attention to Sofia.

'Her pulse is very weak.' Lisanka lifted her wrist and glanced over her shoulder. 'We must take off her clothes and warm her slowly.'

Relief flooded her. There was still a chance. With Lisanka on the other side, Anna knelt down beside Sofia. They unlaced her boots, then unbuttoned and removed her riding habit. Her underclothes were dry. Lisanka brought furs and rugs, and wrapped them around her. Her feet were frozen, and Anna began to massage them before Lisanka stopped her.

'Warm the centre of the body first.' Taking two bricks from beside the oven, she wrapped them in cloths, then placed one by Sofia's neck and one to the side of her stomach.

Lisanka leant over and breathed into her mouth. Then she straightened her back and used both hands to press down on her chest. She let go and repeated the action but still there was no response. Lisanka went on, pumping and letting go, and Anna watched, willing strength into Sofia. She cradled her hands in her own until, at last, she felt a slight movement of her fingers. Lifting her eyes, Anna saw the faint rise and fall of Sofia's shallow breathing. She was alive and her eyes were half open.

'Anna?' she mumbled.

'Yes, darling. I'm here.' Anna leant closer and kissed Sofia's forehead. She stroked her fingers until they were warm and then helped Lisanka massage her legs in long sweeping movements towards the heart.

'I'll get her some tea now. My brothers are helping your driver with the horses.'

Anna saw Sofia move her arm under the covers, feeling for her stomach.

'Does it still hurt?'

'No – only my head hurts. The baby is quiet...'

Anna's fingers searched gently through Sofia's matted curls. Above her left ear she touched a hard swelling and Sofia flinched. The curtain lifted as Lisanka brought tea and she glimpsed Ivan, his beard and hair glittering white, sitting by the fire. They were all safe, thank God. She barely had the strength to hold the cup for Sofia to drink.

When it was empty, she let it drop on the floor and lay down as close to her as she could get. Sofia whispered something to her, but Anna was already asleep.

She was woken by the honking of geese in flight. Sofia was snoring lightly and the yeasty smell of fresh nan bread in the oven made her stomach rumble. Her whole body was stiff and her shoulder hurt as she pulled aside the curtain. The log cabin was a single room with a bench, table and small window. There was no sign of the men. Lisanka was standing by the stove stirring a cauldron above the heat. She wore an apron made of rough homespun cloth with a kerchief tied about her head.

She looked like an old woman, Anna thought, as she rose unsteadily.

'You will stay until tomorrow,' Lisanka stated as Anna went to stand beside her. 'By then your sister will be better.'

'You saved our lives. How can we thank you?'

'Your ancestors saved you. They want you to live.'

Anna was silent for a time. She was appalled by the wretchedness of the place and the lines of weariness on Lisanka's face. She could see the bones of her hands, her fingers and knuckles bruised and scuffed with calluses.

'Do you live here all the time?'

'My brothers are woodcutters. We travel to find work but will stay here until spring. Our life is difficult – but who in Russia is happy?' Lisanka turned her head, her honest gaze on Anna's face. 'We are born crying and, when we've cried enough, we die. In the meantime, we do the best we can.'

Anna felt her cheeks grow hot. Until this moment, she had never experienced abject poverty. All her life there had been someone to care for her. She had grown up pampered, waited upon at every step, and she had taken her cosseted existence for granted. How complacent and spoiled she had been! Those days are gone forever, she thought. Never again will I lie down in comfort and not think of people like Lisanka, and the hardship they endure every day of their lives.

Lisanka removed the cauldron from its chain and ladled hot soup into an earthenware dish. Anna was famished and drank to the last drop, wiping the bowl clean with nan.

'The men slept with the horses. They'll be here soon. Go and check on your sister. She may be hungry.'

Anna took a bowl of soup and found Sofia awake and sitting up.

'How are you?'

'My head's sore but I just felt the baby move, thanks be to God. Anna, you were so brave.'

'We're fortunate to find these good people. It's still snowing so we'll stay here today. Ivan and the horses can have a break.'

There was faint colour in Sofia's cheeks as she dipped the bread in her soup, chewing it slowly. 'We must give them something for their kindness. Do you think they'll accept money?'

✿

The following day dawned bright and clear. The broken runner was replaced and the horses fed and rested. They offered to pay for their accommodation, but Lisanka and her brothers refused.

'Thank you,' Anna murmured as she embraced her. 'I'll never forget you.'

Ivan was keen to catch up lost time and the kibitka bounced over packed snow as they followed the Imperial Trakt with Asia closing in around them. The soldiers guarding the relay stations looked more Chinese than Russian, and they saw the Mongol and Buriat tribesmen dressed in reindeer skins, mounted on small shaggy ponies. As they drove across the Bratsky steppe, a chain of blue mountains was visible on the distant horizon. Beyond them lay the great inland sea of Lake Baikal and Nerchinsk where Sasha was imprisoned.

Days and nights blurred into one as they sped on. How much further? Anna wondered, every time she woke up. They were running low on provisions. How much more of this bitter cold and weariness could they bear? In just over three weeks they had crossed half a continent and entered a different world. Strange tales abounded of the people who inhabited the vast Siberia wilderness — of tribes who rode reindeer in deep, snowy forests and worshipped the storm spirits of Lake Baikal. Locked inside the kibitka, unfettered imagination and little food leant the journey a dreamlike, unreal quality, and Anna and Sofia retreated into their own thoughts as words gave way to exhaustion of mind and body.

And then, on the twenty-fourth morning of their journey, Ivan called to them and they looked out to see a skyline of cupolas skinned in turquoise, gold and green, and the turreted houses of Irkutsk. They had travelled four thousand miles and were within hours of Russia's most easterly capital. It was the first sign of civilisation they had seen since leaving Moscow and Anna was torn between relief and apprehension.

'Beware the extreme danger you will face if you travel beyond Irkutsk.'

The tsar's warning rang in her brain. The sight of Irkutsk was both welcoming and deceptive. Their destination was five hundred miles further east and, once they left the city, what perils lay in wait for them? There could be no turning back then, no bright domes or turrets on the horizon, only the dark vista of an unknown future.

Chapter Twenty-Five

Arriving in Irkutsk, they drove straight to the hotel where rooms had been reserved. The town had been built over the last forty years and most of the houses were plain wooden structures. The streets were unpaved and, apart from churches, the only significant building was the governor's white mansion. Their front room had a window which was piled high with snow, making the candlelight yellow in the dim interior; but it was clean, and Anna and Sofia enjoyed a bath and a good night's sleep for the first time in a month.

To their surprise, the governor was announced the next morning soon after they finished breakfast.

'I congratulate you on the speed of your journey.' General Zeidler's face was red with frost, and he spoke with a heavy German accent. 'You travelled almost as fast as our imperial couriers.'

His uniform was slightly dark in the creases with epaulettes showing signs of wear. He must be about fifty, Anna thought, and not far off a pension, no doubt the size of which depended on doing his job to the tsar's satisfaction. He walked with the heavy tread of a soldier and declined their offer of refreshment.

'Our beloved sovereign understands the emotions that prompted you to make this journey.' The general sat himself down on the far side of the table and took off his gloves. 'However, Irkutsk is the furthest outpost of the empire and I strongly advise you against travelling further. Beyond here is a harsh, inhospitable land where the summer is shorter than spring and winter lasts for eight months.'

Anna said nothing, observing Sofia who sat very still as she tried to control her frustration. 'We're aware of the climate in Siberia, sir.

To have come so far and not travel on to Nerchinsk would render our journey futile.'

'I expect you to act with common sense, Madame.' General Zeidler placed a leather folder on the desk and took out a handful of letters bound with red ribbon. 'I have here your correspondence to your husband. I will arrange for it to be sent to Nerchinsk and allow the convict Brianski to reply while you remain in Irkutsk. Once that is achieved, you should return to St. Petersburg.'

Anna heard Sofia's sharp intake of breath. The sight of the letters in Zeidler's fat hand struck fury and horror in her heart. No wonder they hadn't heard from Sasha! All their correspondence had been confiscated. Her brother must have thought they had disowned and abandoned him.

'I haven't travelled all this way to exchange letters,' Sofia said in a tremulous voice after a brief silence. 'I have the same right as any Russian woman to be with my husband.'

'That's true, but the emperor's keen I dissuade you from proceeding deeper into Siberia. He is against wives following their spouses into oblivion.'

It was the first time the tsar's censure had been stated so baldly. He had given Maria and Sofia permission to go to their husbands and they had taken it as approval. She glanced at Sofia and saw her cheeks go pale.

Zeidler was severe as he went on, 'For that reason, the traitors are not allowed to correspond with their relatives in the west. If you're determined to continue on your journey, you will be treated as little better than convicts yourselves.'

Anna felt coldness pass across her skin. Was the tsar afraid they might stir up public opinion at home? It was bad enough the Decembrists were cut off from their loved ones. Surely, he couldn't forbid their wives from maintaining contact with their families?

'It is my duty to make the situation clear to you.' The general made no attempt to soften his tone. 'Should you persist in your rash venture, you may only see your husband if the prison commandant gives permission and then under guard. For the rest, you will be confined to the prison village surrounded by felons who will treat you as their equal.'

Anna wanted to protest but could not get the words to her lips. She swallowed hard, too shocked to speak. Sasha had entrusted Sofia and their unborn child to her care. If she had known this before, she might have persuaded them to stay at home. Oh, Sasha... If only, you could have written to us! How could we know what was for the best?

She spoke at last, as loudly as the constriction in her throat would permit. 'This isn't what we were led to believe.'

Zeidler's pale eyes flicked over her and he did not reply.

'There must be someone in charge!' Sofia protested.

'The commandant can't protect you from the insults and attacks of depraved men.' The general's cold glance fell on Sofia. 'Criminals have no fear of retribution – not even if they assault the wife of a fellow prisoner.'

'Then God will protect me.' Sofia's chair scraped the floor as she stood up. Her voice changed, gathering strength as her gaze fixed on the governor's face. 'I will be with my husband, sir!'

General Zeidler puffed out his cheeks and placed a sheet of official paper on the table. It was embossed with the double-headed eagle and ran to several paragraphs.

'Here's everything I've tried to explain to you.' He stabbed a finger on the document. 'Before I allow you to proceed, you must agree to the conditions and sign this document. I advise you to read it with utmost care.'

'I take it there's nothing that implicates my companion,' Sofia said with a defiant lift of her chin.

'Your maid may travel with you to your destination, but no servants are allowed in Nerchinsk.'

Anna felt momentary relief that Zeidler had accepted her deception – but what were these conditions? Nicholas Bulgarin had intimated that wives who followed their husbands might be exiled for life. Surely, Maria Volkonsky had gone through this interrogation, too? The document could only be a bureaucratic formality, she told herself. It was inconceivable Maria would sign away the right to return and collect her little boy.

As if she had spoken aloud, Sofia said. 'My friends, Princess Volkonsky and Princess Trubetskoy, are expecting us to join them. I hope you will not detain us in Irkutsk for too long.'

Before Anna had a chance to stop her, she walked over to the table, leant an elbow on the desk and dipped a quill into the inkpot. Zeidler stood beside her as she glanced over the document and then wrote her name at the bottom.

The governor emitted a grunt as he signed his name alongside and picked up the paper. 'As the wife of a convict, you're in no position to expect any help from me.'

There was exasperation in his voice as he put on his gloves. Then, leaving a copy for them to read, he stalked out of the room. The document was spread out on the table and the two women sat down. Anna read quickly:

> '— A wife who follows her husband to Siberia must renounce all rights to her previous position. She will be considered the spouse of a state criminal and bear the consequences of her status, whatever they may be.
> — Any child born in Siberia out of such a woman's union with her criminal husband will be regarded as a serf and the property of the state.
> — She will never be permitted to return to western Russia, even on the death of her husband.'

There was more, but the these first three points sent a rush of blood to Anna's head. In a single stroke of her pen, Sofia had signed away her freedom. She would never be allowed home — not even if Sasha died. Why hadn't Maria been told the truth? She would never see her beloved Nicolenka again. How could she bear to be separated from her darling son? Sofia and Sasha's baby would be registered a serf and belong to the state. Never in their wildest dreams could they have imagined anything so monstrous. Anna's pulse was going at such a rate she felt dizzy. The Decembrists had wanted to end serfdom. Now their children would be in bondage and their families had officially ceased to exist. The tsar was too afraid of the church to separate husbands and wives, but he was determined to punish them, all the same.

Sofia must go to General Zeidler at once and retract before it was too late. Anna grasped her hand. 'You can't agree to this! Sasha will never allow it. You must go to the governor immediately and say you've changed your mind.'

'Thank God I didn't wait until after my baby was born.'

'But the baby will be a serf. He may be taken away from you!'

'I won't let that happen, Anna. My heart bleeds to think of poor Maria and her little boy...' Sofia faltered, then collected herself. 'This document only applies to me. You're free to return whenever you wish. I think the time has come for you to go home.'

Anna hardly heard what she was saying. Nicholas had suspected something like this. He had said the emperor would never forgive the Decembrists or those who stood by them. She thought of the tsar's cold face and hatred filled her heart. It was only when Sofia raised her voice, she realised that she was talking.

'My place is beside my beloved husband, Anna. But it's different for you. You've already gone beyond the call of duty. Nerchinsk is close to the border with China. It will be far more difficult to get home from there.'

Anna forced herself to think. This was the last point at which she had the chance to turn back. Now she understood the true nature of the Romanovs – their brutality and deceit – the idea of being alone in St. Petersburg made her feel sick. To return from Irkutsk would mean the tsar had won. She despised him and his court. How could she ever feel at home in a society where such cruelty existed just beneath the surface?

Only a long time later did Anna realise that Peter Dashkovy played no part in her decision. Her happiness no longer depended on him and he didn't cross her mind. She was here because of Sasha and Sofia, and she wouldn't let them down. The tsar's vengeful, savage actions made her bitterly aware of the sacrifice made by the Decembrists. They had wanted Russia to be free and had lost everything in their fight against tyranny. She believed in their cause and would do anything in her power to support them. I don't care about myself, she thought. I will stand by them to the end. Nothing else is of any consequence.

'I'm coming with you, Sofia. The next stage of the journey is the most dangerous. Besides, I want to see Sasha.' Sofia opened her mouth to interrupt but Anna held up her hand. 'Let's hope the governor doesn't delay us interminably. I'll go and find out if Ivan's managed to hire some fresh horses.'

Chapter Twenty-Six

The anteroom for the governor's office was crowded with petitioners. Having signed away her status, Sophia was required to join a long queue and waited for two days before he would see her. When she was finally admitted, his manner was barely civil. He did not ask her to sit down, and spoke to her in Russian. He could not issue travel orders in her name, he announced, because she had no legal rights.

Ivan had searched the town but there were no horses for hire. A team would only be available on General Zeidler's authorisation and all papers in the name of a local driver who would take them to Nerchinsk. They must obey his instructions at all times, however offensive, and Ivan must return to Moscow. As a final ignominy, Zeidler ordered a detailed examination of their luggage. The kibitka was unpacked and customs inspectors went through their personal belongings. They ransacked the bags of tea, flour and sugar they had brought from Moscow, helping themselves to whatever they wanted. Only the money Anna had sewn into the hems of her travelling outfit was safe, and she wore it every day she was in the city.

Sofia suffered it all patiently while Anna kept herself busy gathering fresh provisions for Nerchinsk. She went to the market, ignoring the stares of women with baskets as they talked together in their strange Siberian dialect. She bought cooked partridges and Siberian grouse, baked *pirozhki* and loaves of bread, and left them to freeze outside their window. Vegetables were scarce, apart from cabbage and potatoes, which she hoped would last the journey. When the inspection was over and the carriage repacked, they said a sad farewell to Ivan and left Irkutsk without delay.

Four days later, they reached Lake Baikal, the deepest lake in the world and the last major obstacle before Nerchinsk. Gliding along a narrow track cut through a forest of pines, Anna saw a ghostly whiteness with frozen waves like jagged rocks. The snow was so deep when they came to the crossing point they couldn't tell where the land ended and the ice began. The lake was famous for accidents, and it was impossible to stop once they were on the move. If the sleigh moved too fast and overtook the horses, they would run out of control and fall through crevices to their deaths.

A man was sent ahead with a boat hook to test the thickness of the ice before horses launched themselves onto the surface. Anna stood facing the wind with a blanket over her face as the Cossack guided his team with care. At times, the ice seemed to bend and crack beneath them like old leather, but the horses were surefooted and they reached the other side in less than three hours.

The lake was left behind and blizzards set in as they headed further east. The horses struggled through the deep snow, and they had to keep stopping so the driver could clear ice from their nostrils. The only food they could buy was raw meat and bitter tea that made Sofia sick. When the kibitka got stuck, they were forced to transfer to a telega, a lighter and more basic vehicle. Anna and Sofia were wedged between their possessions with only a piece of flimsy leather over their heads for protection. The cart had no springs, and every jerk and roll made them groan. The cold pierced through her clothes and Anna's eyes burned from staring into interminable whiteness. They had reached the end of the world and the landscape was as bleak as her heart. What would they find when they came to their destination?

Anna's first impression of Nerchinsk was of a derelict village. Grouped along the Ingoda river were Buriat cabins, a few buildings inhabited by mining officials and a high prison stockade with guard posts at each corner. It was a forbidding place and the two women held hands as they went past. Then, as they turned into the main street, a track of frozen mud lined by peasant houses, they heard someone shouting their names.

Anna pulled back the folds of her hood and saw Maria and Katyusha Trubetskoy striding towards them.

'Thank God, you've made it! We had almost lost hope.' Maria was in tears as they climbed out. 'It's a miracle you're here.'

Katyusha took charge. 'We rented you a cabin from a local man. Get your driver to follow us. We've prayed for you every day. I was afraid you would be stopped in Irkutsk and sent home.'

Anna and Sofia were too overcome to speak. With the telega following, they trudged their way towards a wooden hut and Maria opened the door. 'Wait until we're inside and then you must tell us everything.'

The log shack had two rooms and windows made of fish skin that let in little light. Anna glanced doubtfully around the cramped space. There was a wooden bed, a table and a tiled stove with a brick chimney that went up through the ceiling. She hadn't expected comfort, but the cabin was a quarter the size of her bedroom at home. How on earth were they going to manage once Sofia had the baby?

Anna tried not to show her misgivings and, once they were unpacked, the women sat together drinking tea. The two princesses were very different. Maria was tall and graceful, Katyusha small and vivacious. She was a pretty woman with light brown hair and round eyes. Brought up in Paris, she had married Prince Sergei Trubetskoy in France. Her husband was a leading Decembrist and lucky to escape the death penalty. Katyusha had a homely face and spontaneous manner. Anna liked her at once.

'Our husbands are working in the same mine as Sasha. He's in good health,' Maria informed them. 'You'll need to get your documents checked and present yourselves to the commandant. He's a ghastly fellow called Bernashev.'

'Maria has him eating out of her hand.' Katyusha smiled. 'Our black-eyed princess should have been in the diplomatic corps.'

They did not mention Captain Dashkovy. Was he with the others, Anna wondered? She did not enquire. It doesn't matter anymore, she thought dully. I'm not here for him.

'Bernashev insists that we speak Russian. No French is permitted. Katyusha explained. 'It's a nightmare because I don't understand a word.'

'We have to learn the language!' Maria exclaimed. 'Here we are, in Russia's oriental heart, trying to communicate in French. I'm determined to be fluent by Easter.'

'I can speak Russian...' Anna broke off as she looked at Maria. Her friend had lost none of her charm, but her face was riven by strain and sorrow. 'I'm so sorry about Nicolenka,' she said softly.

'If I'd known before Irkutsk, I'd never have had the strength to leave him.' Tears came into Maria's eyes and she bit her lip to stop them falling.

'When our families learn the truth, the tsar will be forced to give way.' Anna tried to sound more confident than she felt. 'He can't keep a child from his mother. You will see your son again.'

'I agree but it's best we don't talk about it.' Katyusha put her arm around Maria's shoulders.' Now you're both here, we're stronger already. I recommend you pay a call on the commandant before dark. You may be able to visit the mines tomorrow, but you'll need his permission. I'll show you the way to his house.'

✻

When they were ushered into Bernashev's office the commandant sat lounging in a greasy velvet chair behind his desk. He was a stout man with a sallow face, and obviously considered the arrival of the women a nuisance. Without a word of greeting, he pushed a sheaf of papers towards Sofia, ordering her to read them standing up. A heavy keyring dangled from his paunch and the room smelled of tobacco and stale alcohol. Anna leant her head against the wall, watching Sofia's slight figure bent over the desk. Her sister-in-law looked so pale she was afraid she might faint, but she signed every document.

'Had I balked at a single paper our journey would have been wasted,' she murmured as they left. 'It's worth the humiliation. We can visit

Sasha first thing tomorrow. I told him you're my companion and I have permission for you to stay until the baby's born.'

'But that's not true.'

'I don't care.' A weary smile touched Sofia's face. 'We're going to see Sasha at last. Thanks be to God.'

They were both exhausted but neither of them could sleep that night. The mattress was infested with fleas so they wrapped themselves in bearskins and lay on the floor, their heads propped against the wall and their feet touching the door. At the first crack of light, they were up, waiting for the guards.

They sat between the two soldiers as they jolted along the icy road to the foothills. The rock face was scarred by cavern-like openings and soldiers armed with halberds and steel pikes stood at the entrances. A woman passing by with a bundle of wood on her back pointed to a portcullis gate, muttering aloud, 'The secret ones go in there.'

The younger man gave Anna a hand to get down. He seemed polite and she acknowledged him with a smile. The guards accompanied them, their boots crunching in the snow as the gate was opened into a narrow shaft. It was total darkness inside and Anna was handed a burning torch. Fearful that Sofia might fall, she walked cautiously ahead, running her hand along a rough-hewn wall.

The tunnel was narrow and airless. They could see flickering lights in the distance. Then someone shouted from behind and Anna dropped the torch in fright. Clinging to each other in the darkness, they stumbled on, following the sound of picks splitting granite, until they came out into an open space illuminated by burning braziers.

It was so hot the men were stripped to the waist as they worked. Anna heard irons scraping the stone floor and saw bearded, skeletal prisoners in chains. One of them turned and wiped the sweat from his face. His mouth dropped open as he looked at them, and Sofia's small hand clutched at her throat. For a moment she was motionless, the veins in her neck throbbing beneath her pale skin as she stared at him. Then she darted forwards and fell on her knees. Taking his chains in her hands, she wept as she kissed them before she raised herself up to touch Sasha's face.

'My beloved darling,' she said in French. 'I'm with you now. I'll never leave you. Our son will be born here.'

A rough voice ordered them to talk Russian and Anna looked over Sasha's shoulder. There were other men in the small space and one figure was taller than the others. He had sunken cheeks, a filthy beard and hair white with dust. She thought he was a stranger until he uttered her name.

'Anna Ivanova.' Peter Dashkovy cleared his throat with a rasping cough. 'Are you really here? Do you bring news of Olga Bulgarin?

Slowly, recognition dawned. Anna hadn't seen Peter since the day they were skating on the Neva. For an instant, she couldn't believe it was the same man. She had travelled thousands of miles and his first words were of Olga. Her eyes hardened as he took a step towards her.

'You mustn't blame Olga.' Peter lowered his head and his swollen fingers dug into her shoulders. 'She wanted to come but I forbade her. I love her too much to let her perish in this hellhole.'

Chapter Twenty-Seven

Anna awoke to a silence so profound she put her ear to Sofia's mouth to make sure she was breathing. It was dark and the stove must have gone out. She should get up and fetch more logs but there would be no daylight for hours. It was warm under the bearskin and she let her mind run over the day before.

Peter had spoken from the heart and she had been unable to answer. Turning away, she had talked briefly to Sasha. He was so thin already, loose skin hung from the bones of his arms, and pity flooded her heart. She would give him all the news from home, she promised, as soon as they were allowed to visit the prison.

'Tell Maria poor Sergei's ill again,' Sasha whispered as they said goodbye.

Dust choked Anna's lungs as they made their way back. The lack of air in the mine was suffocating and she could hear the crackle of Sofia wheezing. How could men, especially those unused to manual labour, survive in such conditions? Her brother and Peter were fit and strong. They might get through the winter, but she feared for Volkonsky and Trubetskoy.

Peter hooked me like a fish, she thought, then threw me back in the water. What was I to him: an adoring younger sister, a foil for his vanity? She should be heartbroken but she was drained of all emotion. There was no anger or sorrow — not even surprise. Peter did not love her and she did not care. She didn't care because she no longer loved him. Perhaps she had never had... I knew when I burned the drawings. I knew then nothing he said or did could hurt me again. I went on hoping because I didn't want to let go of my dream.

Looking back over the years, she saw herself as a young, romantic girl who had fallen for the first handsome man who paid her any attention. Peter was the hero in a story she had invented to make herself happy. It was painful to realise how naive she had been. I made a picture of him and painted him the colours I wanted him to be. The person I loved was only in my imagination. I never knew him at all...

She was ashamed of her folly but was aware, too, of a weary sense of achievement that she had brought Sofia safely to Siberia. She might have died if I hadn't been with her, she thought. We've come through the worst and I will never fall in love again. As God is my witness, I won't be crushed by this.

The sky was lightening, and hunger pains sharpened in her stomach as Anna got up. She pulled on her boots and went to fetch firewood, keeping on her gloves as she went to the stove. There was a mound of red cinders and she knelt to fork the ash, then made a pile of paper and sticks and lit a flame. The oven was their only heating and must be kept going day and night. They would need more wood and she must ask Maria where to find it.

Anna fetched some frozen bread, putting it on the oven to thaw, and then set about sorting the house. She unpacked her belongings and hung the icon of Saint Anne in a corner opposite the door. When Sofia woke up, they dragged the infested mattress out of the house and Anna filled buckets with snow and brought them inside. She found two frozen partridges among the provisions and, once they were unfrozen, warmed them through. They were both starving and ate the meat to the bone before Anna boiled up the carcass for soup as Varenka had taught her.

That afternoon Katyusha Trubetskoy came to visit and her presence brought vitality and warmth.

'Maria's with the prison governor, trying to persuade him to give Sergei time off work. I hope she succeeds. Bernashev's an unscrupulous scoundrel.'

'I thought he was charmed by Maria?'

'Only when he's in a good mood — it usually depends on the size of bribe she offers. Everything here revolves around extortion. I take it you've both brought money?'

Anna and Sofia nodded. Katyusha put down her cup. 'Keep it safe and use resources carefully. The police in Irkutsk intercept letters, so it's not easy for our families to send more. The local people can provide most things — but you need to negotiate wisely.'

'Sasha says Sergei has a weak chest.' Sofia produced a phial from her medicine cabinet. 'I recommend hyssop honey with milk. Will Maria be able to give some to him?'

'It depends who's on duty. Most of the guards are brutes but a few are alright. There's a younger one we like called Anton.'

He was the one who had escorted them to the mine, Anna was sure. It would help to have him on her side.

'We need more wood for the stove. Where can I find some?'

'Either we have to forage for ourselves, which is difficult in these conditions — or else pay for it. Try to catch Anton's eye, Anna Ivanova. You're the only single lady among us. I'm sure he'll be happy to help you.'

✤

After Katyusha's visit, their days settled into a mundane routine. At first crack of dawn, Anna warmed two loaves of bread, leaving one for Sofia before she put on her furs, gloves and boots and set off for the prison stockade. An icy wind cut into her face like shredded glass and, as she made her way down the street, doors opened, letting out steamy air and then closed again. It was too cold to be outside, but their wood was running low and success depended on getting to the prison early. She must hurry.

Her first attempt had failed dismally. The guards told her she would have to offer something more enticing than bread if she wanted their favours. Anna returned home mortified, but yesterday the young Buriat had been on duty. He took her bread and promised to find wood. He would tell her today where to collect it.

'My cousin's agreed to sell you provisions at a good rate.' The guard spoke with his mouth full. 'She admires your devotion to your husbands.'

'I'm here for my brother, Alexander Brianski,' Anna explained, handing over a small bag of money. 'I believe we met the day I arrived. I'm Anna Brianski. What's your name?'

'They call me Anton. This is my friend, Igor.'

Both men wore bearskins over their uniforms, woollen papakha hats and heavy boots blackened with tar. Anton was good-looking, Anna thought, with his Siberian eyes, and eyebrows so thick they might have been drawn by charcoal.

'You're very kind. Will you be here tomorrow?'

'We're at the mine tomorrow,' Igor answered with a shy glance at Anna.

'Are you both conscripts?'

'Goodness no! God is too high and the tsar far away from Siberia,' Anton answered with pride. 'We're free people.' Then, as Anna's gaze wandered to the prison walls behind him, he dropped his voice. 'We've got your wood. It's hidden by a water trough in the old garrison stables. Do you know the place?'

'Thank you.' Anna nodded, lowering the shawl from her face and bestowed a winning smile on both men. 'I hope we may be friends. When you're off duty, please come and visit us.'

Later that afternoon, Anna found a pile of wood hidden under sackcloth. She loaded it onto the sledge and dragged it home through the dwindling light. There was enough to light a second stove, but nothing must be wasted. The money sewn into pockets and hems would not last forever.

By mutual agreement, Anna took charge of cooking and provisions. She bought oatmeal and mare's milk from Anton's cousin and made kasha, baking potatoes and bread in the hot oven. If they were lucky, Anton brought fish from Lake Baikal and pigeons from the forest, which she cleaned and plucked, burning off the feather-ends with a candle. One day he shot a deer and brought them a haunch of venison. He did what he could to help them, but there was never enough. The prisoners were malnourished and their basic fare must be shared with four men.

Only last summer, she had been a popular debutante, dancing at balls with a string of suitors in attendance. Now, her life was no different from any other peasant woman in Russia. From the moment she got up until night, Anna was occupied with manual chores. Hunger was a constant companion and she became obsessed with food. If only she had wheat flour to make dumplings! She remembered Varenka lowering them into the pan, watching as they sank to the bottom before swelling and rising to the surface. How profligate they had been in St. Petersburg! It had never occurred to her before to think of where meals came from or how much they cost. Now she thought of little else.

Instead of coffee, they drank tea infused with dried nettles. Sugar was rationed and Anna added salt drops when she felt weak. She was tormented by cravings and longed for cloudberry jam and sweet pancakes. Sometimes, when she was half-awake, she dreamt she could smell hot chocolate with cinnamon and croissants. She was hungry all the time but made sure her sister-in-law ate enough. The baby was beginning to show and, when Sofia wasn't looking, she slipped half her food onto her plate.

They washed their clothes in water heated in the oven and rinsed them in buckets of melted snow. Sofia tried to mend the prison linen, but the rough material broke her fine needles and she had to use fish bones that blistered her fingers. There was no smoothing iron, so their clothes were crumpled. Anna's hands became so raw the knife slipped when she was peeling vegetables, nicking the skin between thumb and finger. Nothing they had learned at home was of any use here. All her life she had had someone to help and do things for her. Anna thought of her mother, the way she moved with a swish of skirts and fragrance of lemon verbena, her pure white hands unmarked by labour. Mama had insisted on grace and modesty, but what good were pretty manners when you had to chop wood and risk the freezing cold to put food on the table? Every standard of behaviour went down before the need to survive. Only her courage and love for Sofia remained unchanged.

With Sofia's help, she brushed out the knots in her hair and pinned it into a chignon. The women tried to maintain a semblance of dignity, but Anna was losing weight. The softness went from her face and, above her prominent cheekbones, her tawny eyes took on the look of a hungry cat. Maria was gaunt and Katyusha's rounded features became sharp; only Sofia retained a healthy complexion.

Anna slept under a pile of blankets and furs but woke with a chill in her spine. She thought longingly of the *banya* — the steamy heat trickling down her thighs, sinking into the roots of her hair until every particle of dirt was washed from her pores. Over and over again she asked herself, what shall I do? I haven't the funds to pay for a sleigh and driver further than Irkutsk. I must wait until Sofia's confinement and then write to Mama and Papa. Surely, they'll find a way of getting money to me? But do I really want to go home? How can I live in St. Petersburg after what's happened? Do I have the strength to make the journey by myself? There were too many questions and no clear answers. I can only take every day as it comes, she decided. I mustn't lose heart. Once the weather gets better and the baby arrives, I'll know what to do then. I can't think about the future now.

Nicholas Bulgarin had been right about many things. If he hadn't been so sure of himself, she might have given him credit. Where was he now, Anna wondered — in Moscow or in St. Petersburg with Olga? However hard she tried to banish him, he was always there, a shadow lingering in the corners of her mind. She thought of his handsome face, long-limbed body and the warmth of his lips. She knew him from the outside, his form but not his substance. Who was he behind the facade he presented to the world? Nicholas despised sentimentality and tenderness. So, why had he tried so hard to persuade her to stay?

✿

'I may never see my darling boy again.' Maria's voice trembled. 'Thank God for your picture, dear Anna. I look at his angelic face and pray for him every night.'

They were in Maria and Katyusha's cabin with its tiny windows facing the prison walls and Anna felt her heart contract. Maria, Katyusha and Sofia are truly heroic, she thought. They've given up everything to live here and be close to their husbands. They never complain – how can Maria endure being separated from her only child?

Two weeks had gone by and, while Sofia visited Sasha regularly, Anna wasn't allowed in the prison. Sofia said Sergei was still unwell and Prince Trubetskoy had begun to spit blood.

'The tsar has ordered our husbands to work – but not to the detriment of their health.' A spark of anger flashed in Maria's eyes. 'What does His Imperial Majesty think they're doing – *crochet and needlework?*'

'He doesn't want martyrs on his hands.'

'Fortunately, Bernashev overestimates our importance. He'd shoot them all if he wasn't so afraid of our connections at court.' Maria fetched a jug of water, filled two glasses and gave one to Anna. 'Katyusha is learning how to cook, but it's your hard work, Anna, that keeps us alive. I don't know how you manage it all. Do you have any time for painting?'

'I haven't done any since I left St. Petersburg.'

'But it's your vocation. You mustn't waste your talent.'

'I brought my paints but it doesn't seem appropriate. I have no inspiration.'

'I felt the same about the piano. Zinaida sent a clavichord all the way from Moscow so I should have my music, but I couldn't bring myself to play it. It was only when Katyusha forced me to the keyboard that I started again. Now I can't live without it.'

'I can't imagine there's a queue of people wanting portraits.'

Anna gave Maria a doubtful look as her friend's dark eyes fixed on her face.

'Then paint or draw everything you see. Make a record of what's happening here.' Her cheeks turned pink as she warmed to the idea.

'You can help us, Anna. The tsar wants the Decembrists forgotten, erased from the history of our nation. We must keep their memory alive. Images are more powerful than words.'

Could she do it, Anna wondered? She had been trained to depict what was beautiful, not the subject of nightmares. Could she recreate the horrific scenes she had witnessed? Did she have the skill and courage to convey the suffering and misery of this place?

'I'll send them to Pushkin, and he'll have them printed and circulated.' Maria's voice was decisive. 'The world must be told the truth. It's in your power to make our sacrifice worthwhile.'

1st March. Nerchinsk

Dearest Mama and Papa,

I'm sorry not to have written before but it was impossible while we were travelling. You will be glad to know Sofia and I arrived safely in Nerchinsk and have seen Sasha. He is in good health and sends his love.

Maria Volkonsky and Katyusha Trubetskoy were here before us and other wives are on their way. Princess Volkonsky is able to negotiate with the authorities on the prisoners' behalf and it will comfort to you to know of the consolation we give to Sasha and the others. At first, they were anxious for our well-being but their happiness at being reunited has banished all doubts. However bad the weather, we stand by the prison gates every afternoon when they return from work. Our daily vigil gives them hope and stops the prison guards mistreating them.

I hope you are both in good health. I think of you often and trust God will bring me home to you once your grandchild is born.

Your loving daughter,
Anna

Chapter Twenty-Eight

Anna assembled her drawing materials and closed her eyes to test herself. The first picture would be of Sofia and Sasha's reunion. Could she remember it well enough to convey the poignancy of that moment? Yes, she could see every detail – the vertical line of Sasha's body broken by the arch of Sofia's back as she knelt to kiss his chains. It was all there, vivid in her memory.

She began a new sketchbook and prepared the first page with a grey wash. There could be no mistakes and the picture was strongly in her head. She worked with long, swift strokes using a wolf-hair brush tapered to a fine point. Obscure figures were visible in the background, but the emphasis was on Sofia and Sasha. Splintered dashes marked her brother's tall frame, and the scene was lit from the side so that half his face was in shadow and Sofia's hidden by the fall of her hood. Anna added black cross-hatching to the top and sides so that the walls seemed to lean inwards, creating a sense of claustrophobia. Sasha and Sofia stood in the light yet were locked in darkness.

She would do a drawing a day, Anna decided, each one taking up a single page of the book. Some would be from memory – Sasha and Sofia, the prisoners returning from work in an open cart and the small group of women waiting at the gates in the bitter cold. Others would be portraits of people whom she could observe. She drew Maria reading a book with a view of the prison through the window, and Sofia and Katyusha sewing. Her subjects were immobilised in poses that gave an impression of them being imprisoned in time and space. Anna had never worked like this before, using her emotions to create atmosphere rather than striving for a likeness. When she woke up in the night, she wrapped herself in blankets and drew by candlelight. Images came easily now, sharp on the surface of her mind. There was a feeling of dereliction in them — the prisoners' emaciated figures and bleak surroundings — as if they existed on the edge of oblivion.

When she finally blew out the candle and went to bed, Anna fell asleep at once, then rose with the daylight and carried on. Her drawing took on an urgent, feverish quality. If she never painted again, this would be her most important work. It didn't matter that her hands were clumsy and some of the images hurried. She would keep going until there was no more paper and, when the sketchbook was complete, Maria would somehow get it to Pushkin.

Anna was so occupied with the work, she forgot her household duties and failed to notice they were running short of wood. Late one afternoon, the stove went out and she found only a couple of logs left in the pile. The light in the room was fading and the sky dark with snow clouds as she carried them inside. Sofia lit a taper. A blue skim of flame raced across the paper and the wood caught light but there wasn't enough to keep them warm through the night.

'I must go to the stables and hope Anton's remembered.'

'But it's already dark. Is there nothing else we can burn?'

Anna shook her head. She warmed her gloves and foot cloths on the stove before putting them on, then pulled on her boots. Sofia made the sign of the cross over her before she went out. People were staying indoors and the streets were deserted. She shouldn't have left it so late. She pulled her scarf closer over her mouth and nose so only her eyes visible, but she couldn't walk fast enough to keep warm. When the sled runner stuck on a ridge, she jerked the rope so hard she slipped and almost fell.

Anna tasted ice flakes on her lips. 'Not far now,' she said under her breath. 'Don't let there be a blizzard or I'll never find my way back.' The temperature was dropping and silence gathered around her as she picked her way through snowdrifts. Cold numbness spread up her arms and she batted her hands together, her gloves making a muffled, ghostly sound. Straightening her spine, she lifted her head on her aching neck and forced herself on until she could see the old stable with its sunken roof. As she came closer, a figure came away from the wall. A man in a fur cap with a lantern slung over his arm stepped into her path. Anna stopped dead, her fist tightening around the rope. Then he lifted the lamp and she saw Anton's face.

'I waited for you yesterday.' Scarves muffled his voice.

'Spasibo ... thank you. We ran short of wood. I meant to come earlier.'

'Can I help you?'

'Do you have time? Are you off duty?'

'For an hour only.'

'Then please come home with me. We'll give you something to eat.'

Anton heaved the logs onto the sledge and tied them securely with ropes. Anna followed in his footsteps as he pulled their precious cargo. It was snowing hard as they approached the cabin and its windows were bright with light. Sofia must have lit at least ten candles. What was she thinking? They barely had enough to last out the month.

'It seems you have guests. Another time, perhaps.'

Anna wanted to thank him, but Anton turned away and disappeared into the blizzard. Panting with the weight of the laden sledge, she dragged it up the steps and left it in the porch. She pulled her scarf down from her face and stepped across the threshold, bolting the door behind her. When she turned round, her breath caught in her throat.

Maria and Katyusha were hovering near the stove and Sofia was kneeling beside a man lying on a stretcher on the floor.

'There was an accident in the mine.' Maria spoke first.' Captain Dashkovy's injured. I persuaded the commandant to have him brought here so that Sofia could attend to him.'

Anna stared first at her, then at Peter.

'What happened? How ... how badly is he hurt?' she stammered as she took off her coat and removed her boots.

'A shaft collapsed and he was crushed beneath it. He's broken his leg.'

Maria moved out of the way and Anna went over to Sofia who was looking down as she held a cup to Peter's lips.

'Take a small sip and swallow slowly. The sugar will restore you.'

Peter's beard was matted and his face ashen-white. He tried to speak and Sofia hushed him. 'Conserve your strength. We're going to set your leg.'

'A doctor should deal with it,' Anna protested, not bothering to lower her voice.

'The prison doctor's a butcher. If we leave it to him, he'll amputate the limb. Did you find any wood?'

'Yes. It's outside...'

'We must keep the room as warm as we can.' Sofia addressed Maria and Katyusha. 'I'll need two flat pieces of firewood for splints. Anna, please get me my scissors.'

Anna handed her the scissors and Sofia went on, 'I've looked it up in my medical dictionary. We have to manipulate the fractured bone into alignment and then splint the leg. I'll need your help.'

Sofia cut the trousers of Peter's right leg and rolled the material up above the knee. The break was obvious – halfway up his shin was an ugly-looking lump surrounded by bruised skin.

'The muscles have contracted, so we must straighten his leg. Katyusha, can you help Anna while Maria and I hold onto his thigh?'

Peter moaned and grimaced as they stretched knee ligaments, forcing his leg to its full length. Katyusha brought a bucket of ice and Sofia wrapped a handful of it in linen and pressed it to the fracture.

'Talk to him, Anna. Don't let him lose consciousness. It's imperative he stays awake.'

Anna moved to crouch by Peter's head. She dipped a square of linen into a bowl of water, wrung it out, and placed it on his forehead. After a moment, his eyes opened a fraction. 'Do you ... have brandy?'

'Does anyone have brandy?' Anna asked.

Katyusha produced a flask from her voluminous pocket. 'I always carry vodka for emergencies. Will that do?'

Sofia nodded. 'Vodka's fine – but not too much.'

This couldn't be happening, Anna thought, as Katyusha lifted Peter's head and held the flask to his lips. Peter had led her to make the greatest mistake of her life — and he was here in her home! Why hadn't they taken him to Maria and Katyusha's cabin? Sofia could have gone there.

The medical manual was open on the floor, and her eyes narrowed as she looked down at Sofia. 'Don't you think you might do more harm than good?'

'It's a straightforward procedure. Listen to this.' Sofia held up a diagram and read aloud. 'To achieve alignment, the lower part of the bone must be manipulated into the correct position.'

As Sofia spoke, Peter groaned and Anna saw his body spasm. She had only eaten one piece of bread all day and she was swept by a wave of nausea.

'Is this his only chance to walk again?' Katyusha asked.

'If we can manage it correctly.'

'Then we must do our best!' Maria was decisive.

'Let me see the splints. Do we have plenty of bandages?'

'I brought these from home.' Katyusha handed Sofia a bundle of rolled bandages. 'But firewood's no good. We'll have to use something else.'

Anna's gaze searched the room. One of the table legs might suffice. She could dismantle a travelling chest, but it may not be strong enough.

'What about a piece of wood from the bed?'

'That's a brilliant idea,' Sofia answered. 'Can you chop it up?'

Anna found a small saw and went with Katyusha to the bed. Once the end board was removed, they placed it on the ground and she cut the wood into lengths.

Maria brought a twisted cloth and put it between Peter's teeth. 'Bite hard on this, Captain Dashkovy. Princess Trubetskoy will hold your shoulders. Please try to keep still.'

'You're stronger than me, Anna. You'll need to use both hands to grip his leg just below the break. I'll tell you what to do.'

Sofia didn't ask if she felt up to the task. I can't do it, Anna thought. It's madness. Sofia's fragmentary medical knowledge did not qualify her as a bone-setter, but Anna saw determination in every line of her face.

There was no point arguing and Anna placed both hands around Peter's calf. She recoiled as she touched the coarse hairs on his leg, her palms so clammy she was afraid she would lose her grip.

'Maria and I have his knee. When I say so, pull down as hard as you can. Ready? Now!'

Anna closed her eyes and pulled. She heard Peter's stifled scream, and almost screamed herself but, when she looked again, the bone had hardly moved.

'Good – now push upwards! Feel with your hands until the bone's straight.'

Anna's hands ached with the effort. She felt sweat pooling in the pits of her arms and dripping down the back of her neck. She carefully ran her thumb down Peter's shin until she touched a jagged edge under the skin. Exerting as much pressure as she could, she manipulated the lower bone inwards and upwards.

'That's enough. Well done.' Sofia came to look over her shoulder. 'More ice, please, Katyusha. Then we'll bandage the limb and strap on splints.'

Maria and Sofia took her place and Anna staggered to the table. She sat down on the nearest chair and clasped her hands around her head. There was a scraping noise outside – feral dogs hunting for food. She should bang the door to chase them away, but she was too tired to move.

Katyusha came over and handed her the flask of vodka. 'You look as if you could do with some of this.'

Anna took the bottle, tilting the neck into her mouth. The spirit burned her throat and she took a second gulp, managing a faint smile. 'Thank you.'

'There's no more we can do for now.' Sofia fanned her face with her handkerchief as she stood up. 'Let's make some tea. We deserve it.'

Sofia looked exhausted, Anna thought. As soon as Maria and Katyusha left, they would eat something and go to bed. The samovar came to the boil and Katyusha was pouring out tea when there came a hard rapping at the door. The four women looked at each other. Who could possibly be calling so late? The knocking sounded again and Maria rose to her feet.

'I'll deal with it. You drink your tea. Who's there?' she shouted through the closed door.

'Colonel Bernashev sent us to collect the prisoner.'

Maria's strained face took on a new expression, one of irritation and disdain. 'Captain Dashkovy's extremely ill. Come and see for yourselves, if you must. Be quick about it. We don't want to freeze to death.'

As Maria opened the door, a blast of cold air came into the room that made the candles gutter and spit.

'The man's unconscious,' she continued in the same imperious tone as two guards entered and removed their hats. 'If you insist on moving him to the prison he will die. Colonel Bernashev won't thank you for a fatality.'

Peter lay so still Anna was sure he had fainted. The soldiers seemed at a loss, standing awkwardly by the door, and Maria pressed home her advantage. 'Well, now that you're here, make yourselves useful. We'll need to light a fire in the stove next door and carry Captain Dashkovy through. He can't share the ladies' quarters. You'll find plenty of wood outside.'

What in God's name was Maria doing? Anna wondered. They had enough wood to last a few days – but only for one stove.

Seeing her expression, Sofia said quietly, 'Don't worry. God will provide…'

And if He doesn't, what then? I'll have to go find more, Anna thought, resentment twisting in her gut. Anton won't always be there to help me. Don't they understand what a struggle it is? If he recovers, it will mean another mouth to feed – as if I don't have enough already! Exhaustion, combined with disquiet at Peter's presence, frayed her temper and she stood up.

'I'm going to lie down,' she announced to anyone who might be listening. 'There's soup, if you're hungry.'

Sofia nodded. Anna went through and stretched out on the hard bed. The sound of voices and the tread of boots drifted through the curtain as she pulled the blankets and bearskin up to her chin. Peter Dashkovy's not my responsibility, she thought, as she closed her eyes. I don't want to look after him. He was the one who led Sasha into danger. I wish he had never come into our lives.

✻

A hand nudged her shoulder and Anna opened her eyes to find Sofia with a candle in one hand and a cup in the other.

'I brought you some tea.'

'What time is it?'

'Past seven. I was worried about you.

Seven in the morning? How could she have slept so long? Anna was bemused. 'Have you been up all night?'

'I dozed by the fire... Maria and Katyusha went home after Captain Dashkovy was moved. They're coming back this morning. I've made porridge – you must be hungry.'

'How is he?'

'Captain Dashkovy's been asleep for as long as you have.'

There was no censure in her tone, but Anna regretted her mood the night before.

There was silence. Then she said, 'I'm sorry about last night. I should have had confidence in you.'

Sofia's face and fair curls were framed in a halo of candlelight and she smiled. 'I wasn't so confident myself. I think we did pretty well under the circumstances.'

'Well, it's your turn to rest. I'll take over now...'

Anna drank her tea and fetched a bowl of warm water. It was still dark as they took turns washing and brushing their hair. Anna's was so long it reached below her waist. She would ask Sofia to pin it up later, but they'd have breakfast first and check on the patient; then Sofia would go and lie down.

Anna tidied up and went through to the other room. Peter was asleep on the floor, so she stoked the fire and went to stand by the window. Ribbons of light crept over the horizon. In an hour, a pale sun would rise low above the hills, and it would be another bitingly cold day.

She felt sorry for Peter, without the bitterness she had felt the night before. There was a time when being in the same room with him would have made her tremble; now her heart was still. I never loved him, she thought. I know that now. Peter flirted with me, but it wasn't his fault. He didn't set out to capture my heart. He was careless and I was too young to understand.

'I'm sorry, Anna Ivanova.'

Peter's hoarse whisper made Anna start. Could he have guessed what she was thinking? She pushed her hair back off her face and sat down on a stool beside the stretcher. His cheekbones jutted out, the pain in his eyes unmasked. There was such sadness in them that her hand dropped on his arm.

'Don't be sorry, Peter Igorovich.' She spoke quietly. 'I'm glad I was able to bring Sofia here to be with Sasha. I wish I could have done the same for you...'

'I should have stayed in prison. What does it matter if I live or die?'

'Don't speak so, Captain Dashkovy!'

Sofia came through the door with a tray and Anna helped her lift Peter into a sitting position, supporting his back with cushions.

'Thank God Maria managed to get you to us. If you feel strong enough, we'll move you to a bed and you'll be more comfortable.' Sofia began feeding him small spoonfuls of kasha and warm milk.' A wash and shave will make you feel better. Anna will stay with you until the others arrive.'

At that moment, a distinctive sound caught Anna's attention. She moved to the wall, pressing her ear against it, listening intently. The sound was deadened by the sealed windows but grew louder as it approached until it was unmistakable – the jingle of troika bells. The others raised their heads, struck by her concentrated pose, and they too listened. No one came to Nerchinsk in a grand equipages and Anna caught Sofia's eye.

There was a whinny of horses and jangling harnesses right outside their door. The troika had come to a halt and someone shouted an order. For an instant, Anna thought she recognised the voice. She heard footsteps coming up the steps and stood frozen until a cane tapped at the door.

'I'd better open up and see who's there.' Anna gave Sofia a searching glance. 'It must be a person of some importance.'

If only she had done up her hair and made herself more presentable! The knocking came again and she drew the bolts. As she pulled the door inwards, all the breath went out of her lungs in a gasp of shock.

Nicholas Bulgarin was standing on the threshold.

He swept off his hat. 'The prison guards told us we might find Captain Dashkovy here. I hope we're not too early?'

Nicholas had a black beard that accentuated the piercing blue of his eyes. His fur collar was a mass of ice and Anna looked at him, thunderstruck. She couldn't move and stood speechless with her hand clasped over her mouth.

'What's all this?' Sofia came forwards, her brow furrowing before her face broke into a smile. 'Why, Count Bulgarin, this is an unexpected pleasure.'

Over Nicholas's shoulder, Anna saw the driver help a stylish young lady down from the troika. She was graceful and slim, wearing a fur bonnet of the finest quality and a cloak with ermine trimming. Never in a million years had she thought Olga would come to Siberia – yet here she was in flesh and blood, right in front of her and holding out her hands as she came up the steps.

Chapter Twenty-Nine

'When did you leave Moscow?' Maria held Olga's hand as if she would never let it go.

'Three weeks ago. My brother arranged for the best horses at every relay. He likes to travel at speed.'

Maria and Katyusha had appeared moments after the arrival of the Bulgarins. During the chaos that followed – the greetings, questions, serving of bread and salt – Anna had to pinch herself to be sure she wasn't dreaming. All at once, the small cabin was full to bursting. The warmth of Olga's embrace surprised her, but Nicholas's glance was cool as he bowed over her hand.

He was courteous to the other ladies but hardly spoke to her. He believes I'm still in love with Peter, Anna thought. No doubt he's convinced it was my idea to have him brought here so that I could look after him.

Nicholas accompanied Olga as they went through to the next room. He emerged alone a few moments later. His expression was grave as he took Sofia aside. They spoke in low voices and Anna couldn't hear what they were saying. Nicholas radiated a masculine vitality she thought would intimidate Sofia – but Sofia didn't appear intimidated. She looked him straight in the eye as she answered his questions, holding her darning in her lap and occasionally smiling.

Anna felt as if an unwanted ghost had invaded their home. Why was Nicholas paying so much attention to Sofia while blatantly ignoring her? His presence made her nervous, and she was relieved when he went off to find stabling for the horses. Now Sofia was resting, and the women gathered around the table.

'What happened in Irkutsk? Were you tormented by the dreadful General Zeidler?' Maria asked as she poured out tea.

'Nicholas dealt with him. There was no delay.' Olga paused and looked at Anna. 'Maria told me how you saved Peter's leg from amputation. God willing, he'll walk again.'

Her face was strained and Anna answered carefully, 'It was Sofia who managed it. The rest of us did as we were told.'

'When did you decide to come?' Katyusha dabbed at her eyes with her handkerchief as she gazed at Olga.

'I decided on the day we were in Anna's house. I hoped to persuade the tsar to show clemency—' Olga broke off, a frown gathering between her eyes as she collected herself. 'I misjudged the extent of my influence over him. The tsar made promises he never meant to keep. He had no intention of clemency. The truth is I made a fool of myself.'

There was a long silence. Olga sat opposite Anna in her blue riding habit. She had the same mannerisms as Nicholas, but her slanting green eyes with their black irises were even more striking. Her face had changed, Anna thought. There was a softness in her expression that she hadn't seen before.

'You mustn't blame yourself. You were trying to help us all.' Maria was reassuring.

'The tsar is obsessed by the Decembrists. Can you believe it— he's had depositions from the trial bound into volumes and reads them every evening! He particularly enjoys the confessions of the men he executed.'

A chill came into the room and Anna shivered. Despite what she knew already, revulsion and anger rose in her gullet. It was a moment before she could speak.

'How long does Count Bulgarin plan to stay in Nerchinsk?'

'A couple of days.' Olga's voice was subdued. 'Would it be a great imposition for me to stay here and look after Peter?'

'We would be delighted.'

'Thank you and—'

'And Nicholas must stay with us!' Katyusha clapped her hands. 'We can find lodgings for your driver in town.'

'Stepan will sleep with the horses. He never leaves them.'

'And what news of dear Monsieur Pushkin?' Maria enquired.

'He's back in St. Petersburg under the direct supervision of the tsar. Everything he writes is censored, poor man! Nicholas says he's become the cat's performing mouse.'

As Olga said his name, her brother returned. He brushed the snow off his boots and shook his cape before hanging it up. He had with him two bags, which he placed on the floor. Opening one of them, he took out a package.

'May I speak with you, Anna Ivanova?'

It was an instruction rather than a question and Anna gathered herself as she left the table and sat down in the chair Sofia had occupied before. She bent down and picked up the shirt her sister-in-law had been mending.

'I called on your parents while I was in St. Petersburg. They gave me a letter for you and money for your sister-in-law. They're worried how she will manage without you.'

His words brought Anna's head up, but Nicholas's expression was bland, telling her nothing.

'What do you mean?' she demanded, puzzled.

'They've asked me – indeed, begged me – to bring you home.'

'But how can that be? Surely, it's impossible!'

'There are mitigating factors.' Nicholas leant forwards, warming his hands near the stove, and caught her gaze so she could not look away. 'You travelled to Siberia to take care of your sister-in-law out of familial devotion. You're neither married or betrothed to a Decembrist and your actions were born of compassion, not political bias. This, I gather, is the basis of the petition submitted to the tsar – and to which he has agreed.'

Nicholas is my dark angel, Anna thought, and he's come to collect my soul. There was sarcasm in his tone, but she was shaken by his words. Uncertain how to answer, she stayed silent and felt his gaze on her face.

'Of course, you may not wish to accept my offer. Unless the situation has changed since my sister's arrival…'

'I'm glad Olga has come at last!' Anna countered hotly.

In an attempt to appear disinterested, she threaded a fish-bone needle with cotton, pricking her finger in the process. I can't travel all that way alone with Nicholas Bulgarin! He hasn't forgotten what happened in Moscow. He'll make my life a misery. What shall I say? This might be my only chance to get home. Oh, if only he and Olga had come later! I promised not to leave Sofia before the baby's born.

'I'm sure your parents have made everything clear.' The mocking light died out of his eyes as Nicholas handed Anna a bulging envelope. 'I'm here for three days. You can tell me tomorrow. It makes no difference to me what you decide to do. I'm merely delivering a message.'

He stood up, indicating their conversation was over, and Maria asked from the table, 'What are you two being so secretive about?'

Anna tugged nervously at her earlobe and Nicholas answered for her. 'Miss Brianski is considering her future. Whether to act according to the demands of love or duty – the usual dilemma of our human condition.'

But I don't love Peter Dashkovy! Anna wanted to cry out, but the three women were hanging on his words, so she smiled instead. 'Count Bulgarin brought me a letter from my family. I believe it contains some unexpected news. I'll tell you when I've read it.'

'Beloved Anna,

There is nothing we hold so dear as our children and since you left Papa and I have been in despair. We never meant to hurt you and beg your forgiveness for whatever it was that made you run away.' Here a sentence had been scratched out and the ink blotted. Her mother usually wrote in a clear hand, and her distress was palpable. Anna drew in a breath before she read on. 'We have worked tirelessly for your benefit and the tsar has finally acceded to our supplications. Count Bulgarin is leaving for Siberia next week and has agreed to make arrangements for your journey. Out of concern for Sofia and the baby, Papa sold his four best Orlovs to raise money for them.

I enclose 2,000 roubles for this purpose. Please give them to Sofia with our love and good wishes. Don't abandon us in our anguish, dearest Anna. We pray for you every day. May God in His Mercy bring you home to us safely.'

There was more in the same vein and Anna took the letter to Sofia to read. She was surprised and gladdened by her father's generosity. Six months ago, Mama's words would have made me cry, she thought with a qualm of conscience. I should have cared more for their welfare. Are they really so unhappy without me? Sofia will know. She has always guided me. I must put my faith in her. Sofia will tell me what to do for the best.

✶

'You must go home, Anna. This is your best chance to be with your parents again.'

'But who will look after you? I can go later. Papa can send money for the journey later once your baby's born.'

'Your parents have sent Count Bulgarin instead. Besides, Katyusha has attended births before, and Maria and Olga will help her. Your work is done, darling. You brought me safely to Sasha. It breaks my heart to lose you but there's nothing more for you here.'

'But all my dearest friends are here.'

'Michael's in St. Petersburg and you'll make new friends. Your parents have been so kind. Please tell them how grateful I am. When Captain Dashkovy goes back to the prison, Olga will move in with Maria and Katyusha will come and live with me. Count Bulgarin explained the situation and you mustn't worry.'

'But I don't want to leave you and Sasha.'

'You must go back, darling! You have a brilliant career ahead of you.' There was a glow of pride in Sofia's face. 'Count Bulgarin told me so – he greatly admires your art.'

'I don't trust Nicholas Bulgarin.'

'Why ever not?'

'He's without moral scruples.'

'Honestly, Anna! How can you say such a thing?' Sofia cheeks flushed. 'Count Bulgarin would be happy to be relieved of the responsibility. It's only because your parents are desperate that he feels obliged to help them – despite the inconvenience to himself.'

'You don't understand. He has a mistress—'

'I don't want to know any more!'

Anna looked into her trusting grey eyes with dismay. Sofia had a loyal heart. She wouldn't allow a word against the people she admired. However hard Anna tried, she would never convince her.

'I understand, darling.' Sofia's thin arm went round Anna's shoulders. 'If I didn't love you so much, I'd persuade you to stay. I'm happy to be close to Sasha. He and this baby are my life, but you have your whole life ahead of you elsewhere. You must live in the sunshine, not die here in the dark.'

✿

It was late when Anna collected her drawing book and went to sit with Olga and Peter. They were asleep. She wrapped two shawls around herself and sat on a hard stool, turning the pages of her sketchbook. The drawings of Nerchinsk were stark images, but her picture of Olga and Peter would be different.

She put on a pair of woollen mittens with the tips cut off and wrinkled her eyes to focus in the poor light. It was going to be a double portrait and she must work fast before the stove lost its heat. Using a willow charcoal stick, she sketched in the background and shadows on the walls, then the outline of Peter's body blurred by its pile of covers. Olga had Peter's head pressed to her chest and one hand outside the blankets, touching his cheek. Anna etched the downward sweep of her eyelids and curve of her lips. Her face was still beautiful, but there were lines of suffering around her mouth and on her forehead, Anna noted before she moved on to Peter. Rapidly, she marked the sharp silhouette of his nose and jaw, the sunken hollows under his eyes and angle of his neck, placing the top of Olga's head in a circle that held them both.

There was no time to stop and rework. It was so cold the charcoal ingrained itself in the paper as Anna filled in Olga's flowing black hair. The way she held Peter was so tender that her heart welled up. Olga truly loves him, she thought. And Peter loves her. It's as simple as that. She's his beautiful, brilliant woman. I hated her for taking him from me, but I knew nothing of love. It's utterly selfless – the giving of oneself to another without reservation. I can't ask for Olga's forgiveness. I can only make this small act of atonement.

The stove sighed as a lump of wood fell into the ash. Soon its heat would be gone and she hurried to finish Peter's hair, lightening his curls so they looked as golden as they had before. The picture wasn't perfect, but her fingers were stiff and there was no more she could do. Anna cut the last page out of the book. Standing up with a hand in the small of her back, she placed the drawing on the stool.

Tomorrow was to be an early start. She went through and climbed into bed beside Sofia, snuggling close. Sofia's my guiding light, she thought with an aching heart. She's my counterbalance, my friend and my beloved sister. I may never see her again. I've made so many mistakes. How can I face life without her?

Part Five

Chapter Thirty

The unexpected arrival of Count Bulgarin from St. Petersburg caused a stir in the small community. Having received no warning of the visit, Bernashev assumed he had been sent by the tsar to report back on the welfare of the prisoners. For what other reason would an eminent person travel so far? Hoping to make a favourable impression, he conceded to his every demand.

Within a day, it was agreed that Captain Dashkovy should not return to jail until he could walk with crutches, and Volkonsky and Trubetskoy would be given lighter duties. Nicholas Bulgarin also provided money to pay for better food for the prisoners and arranged for Anna to have a private meeting with her brother.

'I'm glad you're going home, darling Anna.' Sasha's wrists and ankles were manacled, but Nicholas had bribed the guards, and they were alone. 'How can I ever thank you for bringing Sofia to me? You have saved my life...'

Sasha sat on the edge of his iron bed and Anna took the only chair in the cramped prison cell. He was so thin his shoulders made sharp points through his rough linen shirt. He had always carried himself well. Now his spine was bent and his fair hair streaked with grey. Her mind ran back down the years to the handsome young soldier and adored older brother. For a moment, she felt a pain of longing in her heart for the happiness they had lost.

'Why are you frowning?'

Anna's unwanted tears dissolved in a smile, her head tilting to one side as she looked at him. 'I was thinking of when we were young and how proud I am of you. Do you have any regrets?'

'I'm sorry for our parents. I hope one day they'll accept that we had to make a stand. Perhaps you can try to persuade them?' Sasha looked down at his hands, turning them over slowly, inspecting the palms and then the backs, almost if he didn't recognise them. They were covered in bruises, the bones of his knuckles white beneath the skin. He let out a sigh before he went on. 'After Napoleon's defeat, we believed serfdom would be abolished and the tsar's powers curtailed. When the government refused a constitution, we had to take action.'

Sasha cleared his throat and Anna heard confidence strengthening his voice. 'The world is made up not only of good and evil but also of those who do nothing. Silence cannot not protect us. If we remain silent and let tyranny be forced down our throats, Russia will never be free. Take heart, dearest sister. Please don't lose faith.'

'I'll never lose faith, I promise. But what will happen to you and Sofia?'

'Now Sofia's here, I'll get through the prison sentence and then live with my little family in Siberia. There's so much we can do to bring education and advancement to this part of Russia. Sofia and I have no fears for the future as long as we're together.'

Tsar Nicholas hoped the Decembrists would be tormented by the suffering of their wives, Anna thought, stemming the pain in her heart. What does he know of love and loyalty? Sasha has no doubts and Sofia's devotion will sustain him. Let others say he was wrong. I know he was right. Somehow, I must make Mama and Papa understand.

✴

They left Nerchinsk two days later. Anna stayed awake all the night before and refused to allow Sofia to get up to see her off. She gave her honey and warm milk, feeding her vitamins for the baby, before they clung to each other. Her farewells to the others had been brief, too heartbreaking to prolong. There were no words or tears left as she packed her belongings into a valise and waited with Olga for the troika to collect her.

Nicholas had provided specific instructions and Olga insisted she took her wolf-skin cloak, fastened round the waist with a leather belt, and boots lined with fur. Anna was too hot and nervous to stay still. After sitting for a time, she stood up and wandered around the cabin looking for something she might have forgotten.

'You mustn't worry, Anna Ivanova.' Olga laid a hand on her arm. 'My brother will take care of you. He's a good man.'

As she spoke the door swung open and Nicholas came in. A fur *kolpac* covered his head and he wore a heavy bearskin coat and reindeer leather to protect his legs. Anna looked away as he embraced his sister. She heard him speaking to her and Olga crying quietly. Then he disengaged himself and turned to her.

'Is this all you have?'

She nodded and Olga came forwards holding an icon. She held up the painted image of the Virgin Mary and they bowed their heads. 'May God keep you safe on your journey. May He grant that we meet again...'

She faltered and Nicholas picked up the travelling bag. He went out and did not look back.

As she embraced Olga, Anna felt her cheeks wet with tears. 'I pray that you and Peter will be happy. God bless you both.'

'Thank you for everything, dear Anna. And especially for your picture. It will always remind us of you.'

It was the last goodbye before Anna stepped outside. The cold was intense. Nicholas gave her his hand and helped her into the sleigh. She lifted her head for an instant, encountered his gaze and looked away quickly. The roof was lowered as he climbed up to the driving board and then they were off. She turned her head to look back once, then let her chin fall on her chest and closed her eyes.

Her memory of the first part of the journey was clouded by sadness. Swaddled so that she could barely move, Anna tried to hold on to Sasha's confidence as she recalled her farewell to Anton. She had found him alone and given him a lacquered sandalwood box with a firebird on the lid that she had painted in St. Petersburg. As he stood with his head down, holding both her hands, she was lost for words. Anton was one of the kindest people she had met. If Nicholas hadn't taken her away, might their friendship have become something more, she wondered? The idea, unimaginable two months before, was somehow comforting. Perhaps, as Sasha said, happiness *could* be found in this harsh, far away land.

Anna drifted in and out of sleep as the hours and miles passed. She must have been unconscious when they traversed Lake Baikal, for she had no recollection of the crossing – only post houses that smelled of turnips and hard beds hidden by curtains. Nicholas and Stepan spent the nights in the main room by the stove while Anna was relegated to private quarters. She had her own bedclothes, but the post houses were rowdy and it was difficult to sleep.

Wearing thick coats with heads muffled, they climbed into the sleigh at first light, the troika bells ringing as the horses set off. When they stopped during the day, Anna walked about, swinging her arms and stamping her feet. The two men took turns driving and, when Stepan drove and Nicholas lay next to her, Anna could not rest. His superficial civility grated on her nerves. Was he still angry about what she had said in Moscow? There was no way of knowing, but Nicholas Bulgarin was not a man to trifle with and proximity was dangerous.

During hours of wakefulness, she studied his face, how his dark hair grew close to his temples, the strong line of his jaw and sensuous mouth. If she were to draw him, it would be a study in black and white with touches of chalk to bring out the lightness of his eyes. She was intrigued by his isolation and ability to suppress his feelings. What was he thinking behind that cool reserve in his eyes? Had Maria told him about the drawings? Did Nicholas approve? Might he persuade Pushkin to publish them? I must talk to him, she decided. If nothing else, I want him to understand I don't love Peter. That I know myself better than before. Surely, we'll spend a few nights in Irkutsk? There will be a chance to speak freely then.

On and on they went, the relentless motion of the sleigh cramping her muscles and rattling her bones, but Anna clenched her teeth and kept quiet. She could stand the physical discomfort. It was the shadowy pain of leaving her family and friends that hurt. *I can't think about them yet,* she murmured to herself. *I won't be able to bear it. Later, when I'm stronger, I'll be able to think about them then...* There was too much land and sky, too many trees marching towards a distant horizon. The sheer expanse of Siberia destroyed any sense of time or progress until, when Anna thought it would never end, she saw the lanterns of other sleighs and knew they must be nearing Irkutsk.

They stayed in the city's only hotel and Anna was given the same suite of rooms she had shared with Sofia – a bedroom and small salon. The upholstery was worn and the curtains musty, but it was a relief to shed the heavy layers of travelling clothes. The first evening, Anna bathed and washed her hair, drying it by the fire before she retired.

She was up early next morning. There was no one to help her so she twisted her hair in a scarf and put on the red coat she had brought from St. Petersburg. She sat by the window, looking down to the street below, and noticed the town was busier than on her last visit. There were children laughing and playing, and the snowy pavements were crowded with people. *It must be Maslenitsa, the day before Ash Wednesday.* The cheerful atmosphere brightened her spirits. Soon after breakfast, there came a knock at the door.

'Entrez,' Anna answered, coming to her feet.

Nicholas came in and glanced around. 'Is the accommodation to your satisfaction?'

'We stayed here before. It's old-fashioned but comfortable enough.'

'A cut above most hostelries in this part of Russia.' He paused.' You should ask me to sit down, you know.'

'Pray be seated,' Anna said stiffly, embarrassed by her lapse of manners.

She returned to her chair by the window and Nicholas sat down at the table. He was dressed in a dark frock coat and had shaved off his beard. His body was as lean and tough as his mind, she thought. He looked as if he hadn't a care in the world – so different from the anxious expressions of her companions over the last months. If only she could appear as calm and confident as he did!

'How long will we be here?'

'Zeidler's been called back to St. Petersburg. I'm meeting his deputy this afternoon but don't foresee any problems. The authorities believe you're Madame Brianski's maid and I'm taking you back to St. Petersburg out of the kindness of my heart.'

'Which is partly true…'

'Your outfit's rather too appealing for a servant girl.'

Encouraged by his more friendly tone, Anna answered with a smile, 'My mistress gave it to me as recompense for my services.'

'Did she now? It suits you well, Anna Ivanova. I'm glad you look a little more robust. You were thin as an urchin in Nerchinsk. We need to feed you up before your parents see you.'

'We ate enough when we could get food. Your aunt would be proud of my culinary skills.'

'So Maria told me. She sang your praises. She also said you'd been working on studies of the prison. May I be allowed to see them?'

'My sketchbook's still packed. I'm not sure you will approve…'

'I saw the one of Olga and Peter Dashkovy. It's a generous portrayal.'

Anna sensed the question behind his words. Should she tell him about Peter now?

She dithered and, taking her hesitation as a refusal, Nicholas spread out his hands. 'I would be honoured to be given sight of them.'

She might have declined, but Nicholas knew about art and she valued his opinion. Going through to the boudoir, she found the sketchbook in her valise and wiped the cover clean before she returned. Placing it in front of him, she stood watching as he turned the pages.

Nicholas said nothing, taking his time to study each one. When he came to the last, he twisted in his chair to look up at her. If she hadn't known better, she might have thought he was moved.

'I'm astonished, Anna Ivanova. How can you express such pain and depth of feeling?'

'When I'm working, it's as if I'm a channel for something over which I have no control.' It was difficult to explain but Nicholas was waiting on her words and Anna struggled on. 'I take what I see in the dark and bring it into the light. They don't always come out as I expect. Maria hopes Pushkin will circulate them. Do you think they're good enough?'

'I think they're extraordinary. You've captured every breath of suffering in that wretched place. My God, the courage of those women!'

She wasn't accustomed to hearing emotion in his voice. Nicholas's eyes met hers and then went back to the book. 'They're extremely good. However, I advise you not to sign them.'

'Why not?'

'Because they'll provoke fury and get you into trouble. The authorities will suspect they're by you. As long as they're unsigned, they have no proof.'

'What can they do — put me in prison for recording the truth? Besides, you put your name to articles critical of the government and it doesn't comprise your security.'

'My liberty's constantly at risk. The tsar's hands are tied only because of his late brother's affection for me — but it won't last forever. '

'I'm not afraid of the tsar.' Anna gave him a withering look.

'I'm sure you're not, but there's something you should know. Boris Renin is now an aide de camp to the emperor. It was on account of his good offices that permission was granted for your return.'

'But my father and mother—'

'They wrote to the tsar under Renin's supervision. He was the one who made sure they received a favourable response.'

Anna was dumbfounded. Why hadn't Nicholas told her this before? It wouldn't have made any difference, she thought. Sofia would still have told her to go home.

Suspicion began to throb in her breast. Renin wasn't a man to help without promise of a reward. What had her parents offered in return?

She hadn't thought of him in months but suddenly his face filled her vision. She saw his small eyes and bullet-shaped head, his furze of hair and the way he passed his tongue over his lips to moisten them before he spoke.

'I don't want to return to St. Petersburg,' she said, beginning to be angry. 'Please could you take me to Moscow instead? I'm sure Princess Zinaida will have me to stay.'

'Princess Zinaida has left Moscow. I'm told she's presently in Italy.'

'Then I'll stay in a hotel! I refuse to go home and be married off to that man.'

'If you love someone else, your parents can't force you to marry—.'

'I don't love anyone else,' Anna interrupted quickly. The room felt airless and she pulled at her collar to loosen it. When Nicholas made no reply, she turned on him. 'Boris Renin is evil. He's the one who betrayed our friends!'

'Of that you have no evidence.'

'I've the evidence of my eyes.' Anna gave a short, harsh laugh. 'I saw him with old Princess Volkonsky, wheedling information out of her to use against Sergei. Long before the revolution, he told me there'd come a time when my family would beg for his protection. He knew.'

'So why should he want to marry the sister of a traitor?' He came back harder and faster than she expected. Anna tried to think of a suitable retort but could find none and Nicholas continued, 'Your parents want you home and that's all there is to it. You're no more obliged to marry Boris Renin than to marry me.'

Nicholas Bulgarin has no idea, she thought. He's a rich, independent man. How can he understand my situation, what it's like to be the only daughter in a disgraced family?

'I'm never going to marry.'

Nicholas's eyebrows went up. 'Really? Are you determined to be a spinster for the rest of your life?'

'I intend to devote my life to my art. And why not? Your aunt seems happy enough.'

'Varenka's surrounded by family and friends. Do you have friends to support you?'

'All the people I love best are in Siberia.'

The road she had followed since December had come to an end and a breath of melancholy, cold as snow, touched Anna. Somewhere on that long road she had left youth and innocence behind. Hardship and disillusionment had changed her, and her dreams had vanished. She felt her throat constrict as she imagined returning alone to a life of empty comfort. The questions and recriminations. The disapproving superiority of her contemporaries. The sneers, slights and snubs. She dashed the back of her hand across her eyes and hoped Nicholas did not notice.

He stood up, took a turn about the room and went to look out of the window.

'I can arrange for you to be driven back to Nerchinsk,' he said without looking round. 'Is that what you want?'

He waited for an answer, but Anna didn't answer. She put her hand in her pocket and touched the *chotki* prayer beads Sofia had given her the evening before she left Nerchinsk. Her fingers curled around the cross at the end, clasping it briefly.

Nicholas broke the silence, his voice kinder. 'You've nothing to fear from Boris Renin. I assure you, when the drawings are circulated, he will withdraw his suit. He rids himself of friends as easily as other people discard yesterday's newspapers.'

Turning round, he took out his watch and glanced down at it before returning it to his pocket. 'Go home and make peace with your parents, Anna Ivanova. From then on, your life is your own.'

'I don't love Peter Dashkovy.' The words came from Anna in a sudden rush. 'I was mistaken in my feelings for him. You said there's no such thing as everlasting love and you're right. It's a beautiful idea — as beautiful and short-lived as a summer's day.'

'I referred to a general principle. It doesn't necessarily apply to you.'

'Oh, but it does! I'd rather be free than trapped in misery. How long will it take us to reach St. Petersburg?'

'No more than a few weeks, if the weather holds. I'd like to visit Davinka for a few days on the way.'

'Your estate in the country?' She looked at him sideways and was surprised by the unfamiliar warmth in his expression.

'I remember the first time I laid eyes on you, Anna Ivanova. You were an impudent child. It's a miracle you turned out alright.' Her mind went back and she blushed. Her reaction wasn't lost on Nicholas and he smiled, his eyes alight with amused memory. 'If it's any comfort to you, I remain Olga's guardian and intend to return to Siberia in two years' time. She's made up her mind to marry Peter Dashkovy. My sister still has influence with the tsar and no doubt will get her way. If you can face the journey again, you can come with me.'

'Without a chaperone?'

'I expect to be married by then and hope my wife will accompany me.'

Anna's mouth dropped open. 'To whom, may I ask?'

'I haven't yet decided...'

'But you said you'd never get married. Why have you changed your mind?'

Whether he heard the question or not, she did not know, for Nicholas smiled, made a slight bow and went out. As he left, the door swung slowly shut, leaving a crack of shadow in the passage behind him. Anna's forehead creased with annoyance. Nicholas was infuriating! He enjoyed provoking a reaction and it maddened her that she always came off worst. Why should she care what he did with the rest of his life?

Chapter Thirty-One

The sky flared briefly into sunset leaving a few red streaks in the sky as the day drew to a close. Birch trees stood out like white skeletons in the twilight and Nicholas was driving. The horses were cantering along the track, all around them eerily quiet and Anna let her thoughts drift back over the last two weeks.

Every day had been much the same. When they weren't on the move, they waited in post houses with merchants in kaftans and white-faced government officials on their way to the farthest parts of the empire. To make conversation, she asked Nicholas about Napoleon's invasion and retreat from Russia. He had been eighteen when he accompanied Tsar Alexander to Paris to sign the Treaty of Fontainebleau and experienced a world beyond Anna's imagination. Nicholas described the famous Louvre Museum, the sculptures and pictures by the great masters of European art, and she listened in rapt attention.

Anna noticed his concern for Stepan and that he took the reins more often than the driver. At every relay, it was he who inspected the new horses, running his hands down their legs and lifting their hooves. He handled animals as if he could feel their quality through the tips of his fingers and she was impressed.

The atmosphere between them had become less tense but Anna still had a feeling that his outward persona, polished manners and suave indifference, masked his true nature. Nicholas always kept himself in check and it occurred to her, if he ever let go, the detonation would be uncontainable. It will never happen, she thought. His self-discipline is unbreakable, but the memory of his kiss still lingered. Since that night in Moscow, he had made no advances that might be construed as in any way flirtatious. Was he truly intending to get married, she wondered with a prick of jealousy? He had obviously lost interest in her – so who did he have in mind?

One morning when he was asleep, she put her hand to his cheek. Nicholas hadn't shaved and she felt the stubble of his beard through her gloves. He stirred and she withdrew hastily, shocked by what she had done. What was the matter with her? Anna was bewildered by her strange compulsion to touch to him. It was unnatural for a man and woman to be together for so long, she decided. She must be suffering from some kind of travel sickness – emotional frailty brought on by constant movement. Only when she lay still, could she calm herself and quench the fire chasing through her veins.

A flock of birds burst from a tree as the sleigh passed beneath and Anna looked up at a deep blue sky with a scattering of stars. She felt the wind on her face and glimpsed a crescent moon.

'Derzhityes! Volki! Hold on! Wolves!' Nicholas shouted suddenly, and Anna grabbed the straps as the horses leapt forwards. At first, she couldn't see anything. Then, staring into the darkness, she made out the small green lights weaving through the trees. The wolves were running fast and in the same direction as the sleigh. Deep ridges of ice scraped the runners, making the troika bump and sway as the terrified horses broke into a gallop. She saw Nicholas hand Stepan the reins and lean down to reach for his musket before an explosion of gunfire shattered the night air.

The wolves scattered, but seconds later their shadowy silhouettes were back, the lights of their eyes closing in on either side of the sleigh. They were near enough to jump in and drag her out and she stuffed her gloved hand into her mouth to stop herself crying out. If the wolves cut them off between the wood and road, or the troika crashed, they would be torn to pieces. And then, in a dip in the road, the lights of houses came into view. Alerted by the gunshots and discordant ringing of bells, dogs came running out, yapping and barking as the troika rushed through open gates and galloped into a courtyard. Before Nicholas reined in, Stepan leapt down and shut the gates behind them.

'Have you fainted?' Nicholas swung himself to the ground and came to the back of the sleigh.

Anna shook her head, annoyed her legs were trembling as he gave her a hand down.

'Where are we?'

'I'm not sure. I'll go find out. Wait here.'

Anna leant against the side of the troika. The horses stood in clouds of steam, foam dripping from their muzzles as Stepan rubbed their wet flanks with straw. Instead of the usual government post house or inn, they were in the courtyard of a square stone house. Lanterns along the walls lit up the yard and there were lights in the windows. After a few moments, she heard the snow crunch as it compacted under boots and Nicholas returned.

'We're in luck — it's a private residence and the owners are away. The housekeeper says we're welcome to stay the night.'

Without a word, Anna followed Nicholas to the front door. A thin woman with grey hair and sharp black eyes led them down a stone passage to a kitchen. She took their heavy *shubas*, indicating for them to sit down.

On the table was the traditional offering of black bread and salt, along with shots of vodka. Anna lifted hers and swallowed the spirit neat as the housekeeper brought an earthenware pot from the stove. She ladled buckwheat porridge and milk into bowls.

Nicholas spoke between mouthfuls. 'Apparently she's allowed to take in travellers to supplement her income.'

As more vodka was poured, a slow trail of warmth spread through Anna's limbs and she was too busy shovelling food into her mouth to answer. Stepan had joined them, and they ate in silence. When they had finished, Stepan went out to the stables and the housekeeper showed them to a *gornitza*, the bedroom used for paying guests. There were a couple of tallow candles but no curtains so that moonlight flooded into the room with its open wood stove and high bed in the centre.

The vodka made her feel light-headed and, as Nicholas shut the door, his hand accidentally brushed her wrist. His touch was like a charge of electricity and Anna spun round. Putting her arms round his neck, she kissed him full on the mouth. For a fleeting, immeasurable instant, his body was pressed to hers. Then his muscles tensed and his hands unlocked her arms, returning them to her sides.

'What was that for?'

'We were nearly killed by the wolves. You saved my life.'

'You were never in any danger.' She saw the corners of his mouth lift at the tremor in her voice. 'Wolves are no match for gunpowder.'

'But they were starving. They'd have eaten us alive.'

'Well, you're safe now. Say your prayers and God will protect you.'

'Please stay! You can sleep by the fire. I don't mind.'

Nicholas was silent. He gave her a searching look and then shrugged. 'I must go and see if Stepan and the horses are alright.'

Was he coming back? Anna lowered her gaze to prevent him reading what was in her eyes. It wasn't that Nicholas lacked desire. She had felt the tension and confidence of his embrace. He knew what he was doing – so why the show of reluctance? Was it retaliation for her rejection before? She remembered how he had kissed her – the taste of his mouth – and felt thrillingly, dangerously alive. Her past was drawing away and she was on the brink of something from which there could be no return. I want to know, she thought. I don't care about my virtue. I've lost everything else. I want to know what it is to be loved by a man.

She took off her travelling habit and boots and poured warm water into a bowl to wash, then uncoiled her hair, leaving it in a long plait down her back. She slung a shawl over her shoulder and crouched by the stove in her petticoats, her emotions oscillating wildly between amazement at herself and excitement.

When the door opened and Nicholas came in, she did not move.

'I'd like to make one thing clear.' He sat down on the only chair. 'If you've transferred your affections from Captain Dashkovy to me, you've chosen the wrong man. I've no intention of being pursued to the ends of the earth for the rest of my life.'

'Have no fear of that, Nicolay Petrovich. I simply crave a little comfort.' Anna didn't even blush at the implication of her words.

'And you call this ... comfort?'

'I call this the culmination of what you started in Moscow.'

'Ah...' Nicholas sucked in his breath. 'I'm sorry about that. It won't happen again. Your parents entrusted me with your safety and I'm not about to betray them.'

'My father and mother are aware of your reputation, 'Anna replied curtly. 'They know what might happen.'

'Even so, I draw the line at maidens frightened out of their wits by wolves.'

His tone was deprecating, and Anna pressed her lips together as he placed another log in the stove. Flames crackled, throwing waves of heat across the room. She had hoped to break through his defences but one glance at his closed expression told her she had failed.

'You take the bed. I'll sleep on the floor.'

'What's wrong with you, Nicholas Petrovich? Are you incapable—'

Nicholas didn't give her time to finish. Before she knew what was happening, he stood up, swung her into his arms and dumped her unceremoniously on the bed.

'That's enough, or I'll spend the night with the old crone downstairs!'

For a time, Anna was too startled to react. She lay on the soft down mattress and stared at the ceiling. Nicholas pretended to be indifferent, but she had seen the flare in his eyes. He wanted her. Why he should hesitate, let alone refuse, was beyond her comprehension. Was he worried her parents might find out and make him propose? It was a ridiculous idea. Why, she had told him she would never marry!

The pelt of lynx was smooth against her skin as she listened to the sounds of the night, wind whispering in the eaves and dogs barking in the village. She could hear Nicholas moving about and mice scratching behind the wainscoting. The floorboards creaked as he took off his boots and stretched out on the floor, and gradually her mind stilled. She was thirsty but didn't dare get up for a glass of water. Apart from the occasional hiss of the stove, the room became quiet. Did Nicholas believe she was totally innocent of life? I bet he had no such qualms about Elizaveta Romanov, she thought. Well, let him sleep in the cold! It serves him right if he freezes to death. The idea soothed her and, with a sigh, she closed her eyes and fell asleep.

Chapter Thirty-Two

Daylight whitened the inside of her eyelids and Anna stirred. Lifting her head, she yawned, rubbing the sleep out of her eyes, and saw Nicholas standing by the window. He was dressed, his greatcoat lying on a chair, and the fire was alight.

'I hope you slept well? No nightmares of wolves?' Nicholas glanced over his shoulder. 'Stepan would like to set off within the hour. There's breakfast waiting in the kitchen.'

Anna stretched her arms and did not reply.

'Don't tell me you're in a huff? I endured the discomfort of a cold, hard floor at your bequest.'

'So, you're the perfect gentleman,' Anna answered.

'Come now, smooth your ruffled feathers. You should be grateful nothing happened. You're a very desirable woman and I'm flattered.'

He was smiling. Nicholas took everything in his stride, Anna thought. How could he be so calm with the memory of last night in his mind? Perhaps this kind of thing happened to him all the time. When he came over and sat down on the bed, she pushed herself back against the pillows and drew her knees up to her chest.

'Why did you change your mind about Peter Dashkovy? I thought he was the love of your life.'

'It was a childish infatuation, nothing more,' Anna said loftily, wishing she had never mentioned it. 'I hope he and Olga will be very happy.'

'Is he good enough for my sister?'

Anna did not answer, and he repeated, 'Is Captain Dashkovy good enough for Olga?'

'He's your friend. You should know. They love each other – that's all that matters—'

'Such love comes at a high cost. I'm glad you came to your senses.'

Anna was accustomed to his cynicism, but she bristled. She longed to speak tart words but held herself in check. 'Would you please leave now? I want to get dressed.'

'In a moment… And don't be angry. I have great respect for your resilience and honesty.'

His eyes flickered over her face as he took hold of her hand. It wasn't what she was expecting and she glanced up at him in surprise.

'It's what I like about you most – and the same with your art. You dispense with convention and reveal what's in your heart.'

They were double-edged compliments and Anna tried without success to pull her hand free. 'Don't be so presumptuous! You've no idea what's in my heart.'

Nicholas laughed and released her. 'You're as transparent as glass, my dear. It's both your strength and weakness.'

His tone was condescending, and Anna shot him a frowning glance. 'I don't care for personal observations,' she said coolly. 'How much longer before we reach your estate?'

'A couple of days. Tomorrow, we'll leave the imperial highway and head across country. It will be more dangerous and it's important we trust each other.'

'More dangerous than wolves?'

'Far more. We might come across deserters from the army, vagabonds, Cossack bandits. They're the most lethal horsemen on earth. We should be prepared for every eventuality.'

'I won't swoon or have hysterics, if that's what's worrying you?'

'I don't doubt your courage, Anna. You're an admirable woman – apart from your rash impetuosity–'

'And you're a *mudac!*'

She had had enough of his patronising remarks but, as the word came out, Anna's jaw dropped in embarrassment. It was an insult

Omelko threw at the stable boys when he was angry — a word never to cross a lady's lips. She could have bitten off her tongue, but Nicholas didn't seem shocked. Laughter danced in his eyes and he was trying not to smile.

'Thank you for proving my point. I'll meet you downstairs.'

With some difficulty, he assumed a serious look and moved away from the bed, picking up his greatcoat as he headed to the door. With his hand on the knob, he stopped and looked over his shoulder. 'Just one more thing. I advise you to be more discreet with your favours in future. I may not have the forbearance to refuse a second time.'

He went out, shutting the door as Anna swung her legs over the side of the bed. She had always been spontaneous. It didn't mean that she acted without thinking. All the years her mother had spent trying to make her a lady were superfluous in a world that had changed. The old rules were done away with, as surely as her old way of life. Despite all the bantering, Nicholas was attracted to her. That much she knew.

I want him, she thought simply. I want to be close to him and feel his strong arms around me. I don't want to be alone anymore. I don't care if Nicholas thinks I'm rash and impetuous. I won't give up on this bright ray of hope.

Chapter Thirty-Three

'Bayu-bayushki-bayu
Sleep my darling one
Tucked within your bed so tight
Or the old grey wolf will come. . .'

Anna was awake, dreaming of the lullaby her *nanya* used to sing to her. They usually spent the month of Easter in the country. Would her parents go to the dacha this year or remain in St. Petersburg? Spring was still buried under the snow but the thought of winter ending cheered her spirits.

In April, the ice on the Neva would begin to melt and lose its pristine whiteness. As the river became tinged pale lilac, a fast-flowing stream, like a dark ribbon, would appear in the middle, widening each day until the ice cracked with a sound of thunder. Large ice floes were carried by the churning current on their journey to the sea. They travelled at speed, rising high and crashing down, sending showers of splinters into the air, destroying every obstacle and carrying all with them. It was said the Neva swallowed her enemies in springtime and no one ventured on the river for fear of being swept away.

A white goshawk swooped past the sleigh, dropping down, then soaring high into the sky. All being well, they should get to Davinka by this evening. How long would they stay? Anna wondered. Nicholas wanted to reach the capital before the thaw and they had made good progress. The further west, the better the quality of horses and swifter the pace. Covering thirty miles a day, the troika skimmed over frozen lakes and rivers, passing villages and woods at a gallop. When they stopped, they rested for only a few hours and then drove on. At the last post house, Nicholas had hired three grey Orlovs. With their long stride and stamina, they were the finest carriage horses in Russia.

The journey had been hard and fast. If the days were bad, the nights were worse. The hostelries were full of men shouting, the door banging continually as people went in and out. Anna longed to rest in a proper bed, to wash and change her clothes. Now, Nicholas and Stepan were sitting up ahead, the breeze lifting the horses' manes. She was so tired that she was almost asleep when she was startled by a sudden crack of gunfire.

Her first thought was that one of the rifles had discharged by accident but, when she looked back, she saw a posse of horsemen on their tail. They were riding small ponies at the gallop and carrying muskets. What happened next happened so quickly there was no time to think. A bullet whistled over her head and, as she ducked, she saw Stepan slump forwards against the driving board. With a swift movement, Nicholas grabbed the reins. His muskets were in a box beside him, but beyond his reach, and he lifted the whip and laid it across the horses' backs. He was pulling their heads round so they were galloping uphill towards a wood. As they reached the shelter of trees, a flock of waterfowl rose shrieking from a pond and the troika slithered to a halt.

Nicholas hitched the reins to the bar before he sprang down and lifted Stepan out, carrying him to the back of the sleigh. He was unconscious, his face covered in blood. She had seen too much violence to be shocked, but the grim look on Nicholas's face frightened her. Was he dead? There was no time to ask as he grasped her arm and helped her up onto the driving box.

'Have you ever driven troika?'

'Once before – long ago.' Anna's voice was tight.

'I'll need to use both muskets. You'll have to drive. Can you do it?'

Anna nodded but her hands were clumsy as she separated the reins. 'One each for the flankers and two for the shaft horse,' she muttered, trying to remember Omelko's instructions. 'Never take your eyes off the middle horse. Keep him straight and the tracers will follow.'

Nicholas was attending to Stepan, bandaging his head and covering him with furs. Anna took long, deep breaths and gathered a measure of strength before he joined her. The leather creaked as he sat down and, incredibly, he smiled.

'It may be close but I'll wager we'll outrun them. Let's go!'

As he knelt up with a rifle in each hand, Anna clicked her tongue and loosened the reins. She had a glimpse of jagged black branches against an ashen sky before they broke cover. As soon as they were on open ground, she saw the bandits appear from the other side of the wood. They towered above their mounts, standing up in their stirrups and firing indiscriminately, bullets flying in all directions.

'Keep down, as low as you can!'

Anna bent down as Nicholas lifted the gun to his shoulder. He took aim and the explosion made the horses leap forwards. Clods of snow flew up, hitting her shoulders and knocking her fur hat down over her face. All she could see was a blur of hooves, flying horsetails and the brightly coloured duga. He reloaded and there was another loud bang. The outside horses shied violently, pulling in different directions so the troika veered from side to side. As they careered on, Anna thought her arms would be torn from their sockets. At any moment, she expected the reins to be jerked out of her control, but she clung on until Nicholas's hands closed over hers. He pulled hard until the horses slowed down and finally stopped.

'We've lost the bastards.' He was panting and breathless.

Anna opened her mouth to speak, but no words came and Nicholas's arms went round her. He held her until her heartbeat steadied and she stopped shaking.

'Well done! Stay here – in case we run into more trouble. I must check on Stepan.'

When he came back, he brought a bearskin, which he tucked over their knees.

'How is he?' Anna asked.

'He's alive and awake. He was lucky – the bullet only grazed his temple. I'm proud of you, Annushka.'

The spark in his eyes surprised Anna. Was it admiration? Surprise? Tenderness? Nicholas straightened her fur hat on her head and rubbed the ice from her cheeks with his thumbs. Then, taking her face in his hands, he kissed her, a firm, quick kiss on the lips. He picked up the reins and, as they moved forwards, Anna leant her head on his shoulder. She tried to stay awake but the effort was too much. Lulled by the smooth pace of the horses, exhaustion folded over her and she closed her eyes, dozing fitfully, until Nicholas nudged her elbow.

Chapter Thirty-Four

It was almost dark and, beyond a grove of trees, Anna made out a white manor house with a red roof. So, they had reached Davinka at last. As the horses trotted up the drive, a husky came bounding over the snow and leapt up onto Nicholas's lap, its front paws on his chest, trying to lick his face.

'Down now, Mosca! Get down, good girl...'

After the husky, more dogs came barking and jumping up as they drove under an archway. Lamps were being lit and doors opening as people rushed out of the house. Two grooms held the horses' heads and Nicholas gave orders for Stepan to be carried inside. Then he lifted Anna out and stood her on her feet. She felt snowflakes on her cheeks as he took her arm and led her into a warm, bright kitchen.

A large stove and wooden table with benches took up most of the space, and an old man with a flowing white beard was working a treadle. Another, with a brown, wrinkled face sat by the window mending boots. A woman in apron and cap came forwards and kissed her hand.

'Galina's our cook and chatelaine of Davinka. She's in charge of everything – including myself.' Nicholas made the introduction as a younger woman stepped forwards. 'And this is Ludmilla who'll look after you. She was Olga's maid.'

Ludmilla was a sweet-faced young woman with blue eyes and smiled as she bobbed a curtsy. Anna noticed how the men and women greeted Nicholas with either a handshake or a hug. They seemed relieved and happy to have the head of the family home. Stepan was lying in the corner, being fed broth from a spoon, and she recognised Liev as he helped Galina remove a heavy pot from the stove. On a corner ledge stood an icon of Saint Nicholas with row of small candles beneath it. According to Russian custom, everyone paused in front it and crossed themselves before they sat down to eat.

Nicholas said grace and earthenware bowls of steaming food were placed on the table. There were *pelmeni* dumplings filled with meat, roast chicken with turnips and potatoes and *babas* for pudding. Anna was starving. When the meal was finished and glasses refilled, Nicholas related the story of their encounter with the bandits.

'Miss Brianski saved the day,' he said as he came to the end and smiled at Anna. 'She handled the reins as if she'd driven a troika all her life. It's a shame poor Stepan was concussed. He might have learned a lesson or two!' There was laughter and he held up his hand' 'We have a great deal to talk about but it must wait until tomorrow. Ludmilla, would you be kind enough to fetch Miss Brianski's portmanteau and show her to Miss Olga's bedroom?'

Chairs scraped the stone floor and Anna came to her feet.

'Welcome to Davinka, Anna Ivanova.' Nicholas lifted her hand and kissed it lightly before he turned to the others. 'Goodnight, my friends. It's a great sadness that Miss Olga is not with us. Please remember her in your prayers tonight.'

As Nicholas left the kitchen and went out into the courtyard, Anna walked over to where Liev was sitting and Stepan lay on a straw pallet. The side of his head was bandaged, his eye black and swollen. She knelt down beside him.

'How do you feel — are you in great pain?'

'Nothing that can't be mended with rum and vodka,' Liev answered.

'You saved our lives,' Stepan murmured. 'God bless you, Miss Anna.

'Shall I take you up now?'

Ludmilla spoke at Anna' shoulder. She had her valise in her hand and led the way through a hall and up a flight of stairs. They went down a dark passage where the candle made flickering shadows on the walls. Anna glimpsed faded wallpaper and family portraits between closed doors.

'We always keep one room ready for guests.' Ludmilla explained as she opened the door into a bedroom illuminated by candles. 'I'll go and fetch hot water for you to wash.'

Olga's bedroom was pretty with red curtains and tiled stove. She had grown up at Davinka, Anna thought. Wreaths of dried corn-flowers, faded to sky blue, hung on the walls and it must have been her room since she was as a child. Ludmilla returned and helped her undress, unplaiting her hair and brushing it until it fell in a veil to her waist. As Anna washed, she searched the wardrobe and found a nightgown belonging to Olga.

'Count Nicolay says you're to borrow whatever you need...' The girl's eyes suddenly filled with tears. 'I'm frightened for Miss Olga, ma'am. How was she after the journey?'

'It's not easy for the women, but they're happy to be with their loved ones. Conditions will improve once winter is over...'

'Do you know Captain Dashkovy?'

'He's a friend of my brother, Sasha. He's in Siberia, too, along with my sister-in-law. She's expecting their first child this summer.'

'I'm so sorry... I can't bear to think of them so far away.' Ludmilla used the corner of her sleeve to wipe her eyes. 'We must thank God for bringing you and Count Nicolay safely home. Goodnight, Miss Anna. I hope you will be happy with us at Davinka.'

Chapter Thirty-Five

Would he come to her tonight? Anna put her hand to her mouth and felt Nicholas's kiss, his lips warm despite the cold. A shiver rippled over her scalp and down her spine. Surely, he would come to find her tonight? She could hear the servants going upstairs talking quietly as she sat on the bed in her night shift, waiting. A dozen times she tiptoed to the door listening, but heard nothing.

She had almost given up hope when there were footsteps in the passage. Nicholas stopped outside the door and she held her breath. He stood there a moment before he went on. She heard the door to his bedroom close and squeezed her eyes shut.

He doesn't want to disturb me, she thought. I must have courage! She found a wrapper, threw it about her gown and put on backless slippers. They were too big and made a clatter as she went down the unlit passage. Running her hand along the panelled walls, she crept forwards until she saw a sliver of light. For a moment she stared at the glow and flicker of candlelight in the crack beneath his door. Then her hand moved to the knob. Courage, echoed the voice in her head as she opened it and stepped inside.

Her eyes took a moment to adjust before she saw a long room divided by velvet curtains. Against one wall was a painted glass panel. Nicholas was standing by a water bowl in front of a mirror. He had his back to her and a towel in his hand, his hair curling as it dried. As the door closed with a click, he wheeled round.

'If you know what's good for you, you'll go back to your room right now.'

'I know what I'm doing, Nicolay Petrovich.'

Her voice was a whisper as she walked towards him. The wrapper slipped, falling to the ground, and Nicholas took her by the shoulders.

'I doubt that.' His eyes were keen and bright. 'You've no idea where this might lead. You're so young—'

'I'm almost nineteen. Most girls are married at my age. I won't hold you to anything...'

'And what will you tell your parents?'

'They'll never know. I've been living on the dark side of the world. Anything could have happened.'

He was silent so long that Anna thought he hadn't heard. Her mind was working everywhere at once. She looked round the room searching for words as if they might come from the panelled walls. Nicholas was too strong, too disciplined. Nothing, not even the longing in her eyes, would break his iron discipline. A lump rose in her throat. She must get back to her room before she burst into tears. As she made to turn away, his hands dropped from her shoulders and his arm went round her waist.

Anna's lips parted and he kissed her with a passion that made her weak. For a long moment, they stood locked together. Then her arms went round his neck and he lifted her across his body and laid her down on the bed.

Nicholas removed the rest of his clothes and lay down beside her. She expected him to snuff out the candle but he left it burning as he unfastened the hooks and buttons of her nightgown. Watching her face, he slid his hands over her ribs to the dip of her stomach and traced the line of her hips. His fingers made circles on her skin, moving upwards to her breasts, and Anna was filled with a sense of wonder.

When Nicholas extinguished the lamp and moved to lie over her, her hands ran over his back, exploring his body. She felt the ridges of his muscles and the long reach of his spine before her fingers went to his face. She was aware, without seeing them, of the colour of his eyes and shape of his lips.

'Be still, Annushka,' he whispered. 'I'll be gentle. Hold on to me.'

He spoke softly and encouragingly. A low moan came from her throat and he waited until her arms went around him, then raised himself up on his elbows.

'Is this what you've been wanting—'

Anna reached up, pulling him down so the rest of his words were lost against her mouth. She knotted her fingers in his hair and he gathered her to him. He began to move and heat streaked through her like summer lightning. Nicholas kissed her neck and throat, moving downwards over her bare flesh. His mouth seemed to sear into her, burning through her skin. He took her with a possessiveness that had lost all diffidence, showing, teaching her how to respond. He was a beautiful lover. If she had been blind, she would have known by his sensitivity and patience. He made love to her gently until her body was warm and yielding. Then his hands went beneath her, lifting her higher and closer, and she strained upwards, her arms stretching out to hold him as she was consumed by an explosion of dazzling sensation.

As she drifted back to hazy reality, Anna was trembling all over, from the tips of her fingers to her toes. A beam of moonlight came through the window and Nicholas looked down at her.

'Was that good enough for you?'

Anna wanted to cry and laugh at the same time. She wanted to tell him she was deliriously happy, but her heart was too full to speak. She kept her arms around him and he buried his head in her hair.

'You're beautiful, *lyubimaya*. More beautiful than I deserve.'

Chapter Thirty-Six

Anna tapped softly on the door. There was silence and she walked into a salon where tall windows at one end formed a bow flooding the room with light. Large rugs covered the floor between green-upholstered sofas and tables crowded with small objects. There was no sign of Nicholas so she sat down, going over in her mind what had happened the night before.

How wrong she had been to think Nicholas was cold and aloof. He had made love to her with a tenderness that touched her soul. Anna was stirred by the way he held her through the night, never letting her go. When he accompanied her back to her room, he had stoked the stove, then knelt beside the bed and cradled her in his arms. She had no idea it would be like this — the sense of peace he gave her and aching longing to be with him again. Last night had been a revelation. She felt she had been split open and Nicholas had seen the person she really was. He had knowledge of her — as they said in the Bible. Such intimacy could be mistaken for love, she thought. I vowed never to fall in love again. I must be careful.

Anna looked out to the garden where a blanket of snow lay over the flowerbeds and lawn. Branches of birch trees sparkled with a fine layer of ice, and red squirrels were scampering on the ground, scattering the powdery snow.

'Do you approve of my home?'

Anna jumped at the sound of Nicholas's voice. He had come in quietly, dressed in a frock coat, breeches and boots. He walked over with his long, easy stride and she blushed despite herself.

'From what I've seen, it's delightful...'

Anna stopped as Nicholas went down on one knee.

'Will you marry me, Anna Ivanova?'

He was joking! Anna stared at him. Had he gone mad? He didn't look mad. He looked calm and there was no mockery in his eyes.

'I'm honour-bound to propose to you after—'

'No, you're not!' she cut in quickly. 'I told you I'm never going to marry.'

'That was before. Not now...'

'It makes no difference.'

'What happens if you fall pregnant?'

Anna had pushed the thought to the back of her mind. The chances were slight. She shrugged. 'It's very unlikely... I'm sure we could come to an arrangement...'

'Such as?'

'I don't know. Whatever you do with your other women.'

As she said the words, Anna knew she had made a mistake. She was flustered by his proposal, but it was no excuse to be flippant. This was no slight matter. Nicholas had asked her to marry him, and she had refused without a moment's thought. He doesn't believe in love, she told herself. He only proposed out of a sense of duty.

Nicholas let her hand go and came to his feet, his expression stiffening. 'What happened to you, Anna? Did Dashkovy break your heart?'

'No! I never loved him!' She shook her head so hard that she heard hair pins fall and clatter onto the floor.

'So why have you changed?'

Anna didn't know what he meant. Nicholas put his hand under her chin so she was forced to look into his face. She felt he was peering into the corners of her mind, his gaze so intense that goose pimples pricked the back of her neck. Then, as if the sun had come out from behind a cloud, he gave a rueful smile and let her go.

'I accept your refusal, Anna Ivanova. And now, I would like to show you Davinka.'

'The visitors are here, sir.' Liev was standing at the door. 'Shall I take them to the study or the business room?'

'Take them to my business room, please. Can you find Ludmilla and ask her to give Miss Anna a tour of the house.' Nicholas frowned as he looked back to Anna. 'My guests have arrived early. I'm sorry – but you're in good hands with Ludmilla. She knows Davinka as well as I do.'

✻

Davinka was a pretty, three-storey house with the main rooms at the front. At one end, there was a ballroom with tall mirrors and a grand piano; at the other, a formal drawing room furnished in polished mahogany. The scent of birch and pine filtered through the house from logs burning inside the great stoves, and on the windowsills were jardinières filled with flowering bulbs. Parquet covered the floor, designed in different patterns for different rooms, dark for the dining-room and lighter in the library which was stocked with hundreds of books. Soft lights glowed on tables and in almost every room were divans that could be made up into beds as easily as a shakedown of straw.

'In the country, you never know when someone will arrive or how long they'll stay,' Ludmilla explained. 'They could be here for a night or a month.'

Anna liked the cosiness and informality at Davinka. Far away from the bustle of the city, time passed at a slower pace and at the heart of the house was a kitchen full of chattering life. On their way, they passed the open door of a sewing room where two girls were singing as their spindles whirled. Someone was strumming a balalaika. In the kitchen, Galina was busy cooking, her face was red from heat as she made pancakes on the range. A large crock of buckwheat batter sat at the side and she worked along a row of small, thick pans, moving deftly from one to the other, pouring in melted butter and then liquid. When she came to the last, she returned to the first and flipped the pancake over. There was already a pile of them on a plate, light and delicious, and Anna helped herself, eating as she drank coffee.

Ludmilla showed her storerooms with high poles hung with hams, sausages and cheese. The shelves that reached from floor to ceiling were packed with sacks of wheat and rye and below them stood barrels of salted apples, pears and cucumbers. There were dried vegetables and casks of salt, pots of honey, vats of butter, flour and sugar. Outside the back door, a courtyard was given over to pigs, chickens and a cow with a calf.

'Davinka has all we need to be self-sufficient throughout the winter,' Ludmilla declared proudly. 'When Count Nicolay freed his serfs, he wanted us to depend on no one but ourselves.'

'Yet you still work for him?' Anna asked.

'He gave us our homes and we take care of Davinka in return.'

Ludmilla found Anna an apron and gave her a knife to help peel potatoes.

'We believed we were born serfs because we'd sinned and God was angry with us. The count put us right about that. He told us that it's propaganda put about by rich men and God has nothing to do with it. The land belongs to him but he doesn't pay for our labour. We work the farms and keep most of the profit from the harvest. Some people round here don't like his new-fangled ideas – but Count Nicolay's a great man. He's changed our lives, God bless him.'

Chapter Thirty-Seven

Anna was walking through the hall that afternoon when the doorbell rang. Liev appeared and a gust of cold swept in as a courier handed him an envelope. Liev did not thank him and shut the door in the man's face, glowering as he placed the letter the table.

'I'll leave this here,' he muttered. 'Can I get you anything, ma'am?'

'No, thank you. Will Count Nicolay be long?'

'He should be finished soon. He's been interviewing all day...'

Who was Nicholas seeing? She might have asked Liev, but he probably didn't know. It wasn't her business, yet his abrupt dismissal of the courier was unlike him and she was curious. She stood by the table, feigning interest in a book of birds and studying the coloured prints, waiting until Liev had gone, before she inspected the large vellum envelope.

The address was inscribed in a flowery hand and she picked it up and turned it over. On the back was written 'Tsarskoe Selo' above a double-eagle red seal. It was the Romanov emblem and Anna's heart missed a beat. She had assumed Nicholas's affair with Princess Elizaveta was at an end. Was it possible he was still consorting with her? He'd been challenged to a dual and been obliged to leave St. Petersburg because of the scandal, she remembered. Pushkin had said Nicholas would have to find a wife. Was *that* why he had proposed to her – not out of a sense of duty but to put an end to rumours so he could carry on as before?

The idea made her furious. The old adage came into her head: a leopard never changes its spots. It was true, she thought. She knew what kind of man Nicholas was and it was stupid to think he would ever be any different. There were footsteps approaching and Anna quickly returned the envelope to the table. She sensed it was Nicholas as he came up behind her. His hand touched the back of her neck, lifting the heavy coil of her hair, and caressed her skin. When she turned towards him, he drew her close and kissed her. Her lips were soft but her eyes remained open.

Nicholas lifted his head, glanced at the letter and left it where it was.

'I've asked Liev to bring us supper in my study.' He took her arm and led her down the hallway. 'Did Ludmilla show you everything?'

Why is that woman writing to you? Anna wanted to ask but caught herself and gave a careless lift of her shoulders. 'She was an excellent guide. I learned things about you that I'd never imagined. She says you're a great man.'

'And you don't agree?'

'How would I know?'

'My dear, surely you've formed an opinion by now. You know me better than most people.'

I don't know you at all, Anna thought. You're as fickle as a sunny day. She stole a glance at him and saw he was smiling, a smile without a trace of shame that was hard to resist. He was so handsome, and she didn't want to think about Princess Elizaveta. The letter could be from anyone at court, she decided as he stood aside to let her pass through the door ahead of him.

The study was lined with bookshelves and they ate supper at a table in front of the fire. When they finished, Anna emptied her glass of wine and folded her napkin.

She waited as Nicholas took a pinch of snuff and then asked, 'Who were you talking to all today?'

'I was interviewing prospective teachers for our school. We're conducting a small revolution here at Davinka.'

Nicholas went on to describe in detail what Anna had gathered in part from Ludmilla.

'When the system was established, serfs weren't meant to be slaves – the landlord only owned the land they worked on – but the distinction became blurred. Now almost half the population of Russia is trapped in bondage. Serfs have no rights. They can't marry without their master's permission. If they try to escape, they're flogged or conscripted into the tsar's army. It's an evil as inhumane as slavery and must be brought to an end.'

As he was speaking, Anna realised what she had failed to perceive before. Nicholas was an intellectual, not a revolutionary, but his views were as radical as those of the Decembrists.

'Our friends wanted to end serfdom and they failed. What makes you think you can succeed?'

'Change requires patience and perseverance, but serfdom will be abolished in our lifetime. The government must be persuaded to grant compensation and force landowners to hand over enough land for the peasants to make a living. I can afford it and will give away my farms next year. In the meantime, it's crucial the people acquire a rudimentary knowledge of literacy and arithmetic.'

On the shelves were pictures as well as books and Nicholas stood up and took down a small portrait.

'The school here was Natasha Kulygin's idea.' He placed the drawing on the table in front of Anna. 'She believed education was the foundation on which everything else would be built. I want to name the school in her memory.'

Anna recognised Varenka's hand in the silverpoint portrait. Natasha? The name was familiar. She cast about in her mind. Natasha Kulygin? Why, she was the one Nicholas had spoken about in Moscow! This beautiful girl was the young woman who had died because of him.

'How sad... How desperately sad.' Anna spoke her thoughts out loud.

'I never had the chance to ask her forgiveness,' Nicholas said, as if it hurt to articulate the words. 'She was one of the best human beings I've ever known.'

Anna was startled by the look of remorse on his face as he returned the picture to the shelf. He was pensive, then his eyes came back to her and his voice changed. Now it was light and cool.

'Most of my neighbours are up in arms against me. They accuse me of undermining the tsar – but a few support my methods. They include Anastasia and Rubin Marinsky. You introduced me to her brother at Zinaida's reception. They have a large estate not far from Davinka. We should ask them to come over while you're here.'

Anna had glimpsed Anastasia with her husband at the ball in St. Petersburg. She smiled. She didn't know her well but had always admired her. Might John come with them?

'I would like that very much. I've never met her husband, but Anastasia was my heroine when I was growing up. She did precisely what she liked and was so charming no one minded.'

'I admire women who aren't afraid to get what they want.' Nicholas smiled as his gaze sought her lips, lingering a moment. 'It's been a long day, *lyubimaya*. Let's head upstairs.'

Nicholas carried the candle and went ahead to her bedroom. As they came to the door, he ran his hand up her back and touched the hollow at the nape of her neck, sending a shiver down her spine. Inside, the curtains were drawn and oil lamps alight. Anna expected to find Ludmilla and looked at him questioningly.

'I've given her the night off,' he said casually. 'I'll help you prepare for bed.'

'But—'

'If you think I don't understand the intricacies of a lady's toilette, you're wrong.'

He sat down on a chair and held out his arms. Nicholas knew only too well how to undress a woman, Anna thought, her mouth going dry.

'Don't be nervous, my love. Come here.'

Anna stood before him, looking at him through her thick eyelashes as he undid the buttons of her dress one by one. So much about him thrilled and surprised her. His hands were adept as he removed her gown, loosened the laces of her underclothes and lifted them over her head. Nicholas sat her down to take off her shoes and her stockings, then pressed the tips of her fingers to his mouth, kissing each one in turn. He held her face in his hands and studied her, the flare of her nose and tilt of her eyebrows, as if he had never seen them before. One finger ran down her cheek and lightly pressed against her mouth before he lifted her onto the bed.

'What will you do without me in St. Petersburg?' he whispered in the darkness. 'Will you take a lover?'

'I'll live a simple and chaste life.'

'Never, *lyubimaya!* You were born for this.'

Nicholas made love to her, by turn gentle then fierce, and Anna welcomed him with hunger and delight. She loved the feel of his body and smooth skin. Her hands slipped down his back and she felt the flexing of his muscles – then they moved up again to touch the long hair at his neck that curled against her fingers. Her head was crushed into his shoulder and she breathed in the smell of him. He was saying he loved her, telling her she was beautiful, and small incoherent sounds came from her lips as she instinctively matched the rhythm of his movements. She heard the cadence of his breathing increase and felt again the rushing warmth and thrill of abandonment, her heart pounding in her ears as he took her to forgetfulness, fulfilment and beyond.

Afterwards, he lay on his side, his tousled head on her shoulder, and drew her sleepily towards him. For a few seconds, he breathed against her body. Then he turned his head and looked up at her.

'For every man there's only one woman – one he'll never forget.'

He took a lock of her hair, curling it round his finger, and an image of Elizaveta Romanov drifted across Anna's mind. Nicholas couldn't have made love to her with such passion tonight unless it was over between them. *She* was his woman, the one he would never forget, and she pressed her lips to his cheek. As he lay beside her, naked and holding her close, she was almost afraid of the happiness she felt. She wouldn't think of the past or the future. Nicholas had brought her back to life and Davinka was a sanctuary whose walls kept the outside world at bay.

Davinka. 2nd April

Darling Sofia

I dreamt of you last night and miss you. By the time you receive this there will be less than two months until your confinement. I am desolate not to be with you for the birth of your child. Thank heavens Katyusha and the others are there to take care of you.

The journey passed without incident and we are presently staying at Davinka before travelling on to St. Petersburg. Please tell Olga her brother has been most solicitous and she is greatly missed at home. It is a charming house and I have been made to feel very welcome.

Count Bulgarin has agreed to speak to Monsieur P. as Maria requested. I will write again from St. Petersburg. God bless you, darling Sofia. May He give you strength and good health. The pain of separation will never leave me, but you were right to tell me to go home. Thank you. I pray for you, Sasha and the baby every night.

I love you, Anna

Chapter Thirty-Eight

There was much more Anna wanted to say that she dared not put in writing. The Imperial police opened letters and she must be discreet — especially about Pushkin and the drawings. Might Sofia guess that she and Nicholas had become close? What would she say? Sofia would tell me not to risk my heart, she thought, and she would be too late...

After months of numbing silence, the first sounds of spring could be heard — the slow, intermittent drip of water and, above her bedroom, creaking and crashing as sections of snow and ice slid off the roof to the ground. Icicles clinging to the eaves had begun to melt but it was still raw outside and the windows remained sealed.

In the five days they had been at Davinka, Anna learned many new things about Nicholas. He was clever and he made her laugh. Oh, it was joyous to laugh after the last bitter months. Nicholas encouraged her to be light-hearted as well as serious. His attention gave her confidence and made her feel secure. He urged her to speak her mind, to be daring in conversation even when she wasn't sure, yet she could talk to him about anything. At times, Anna felt such a powerful connection between them it took her breath away, before an uneasy memory came back her. 'Worldly women take what they want and escape unharmed...' Was that what their relationship meant him — a brief interlude in their lives before they both moved on?

Anna pondered the paradoxes of a man with so many conflicting shadows in his character. His physical warmth was so far removed from his cold rationality. He was affectionate and attentive yet, even in moments of passion, she sensed his restraint — as if he had bound his body in the same careful bonds he bound himself. She discovered unexpected sides to Nicholas but nothing of what he felt in his heart. Whenever she came close, he seemed to slip like water between her fingers. Who are you behind entanglements of your soul? she wondered as she lay close to him at night. Does anyone know you? Do you even know yourself?

When the weather was fine, Nicholas took her out in a pony sleigh. They drove from the old manor house through an estate of arable land, following a meandering frozen river to the village. The houses were made of wood and there was a small church surrounded by rowan trees. Anna could imagine it in summertime – the leaves of linden trees dripping with dew, and fields of green wheat. People came out to greet Nicholas and she watched how he spoke to them, noting the way he stood, his gestures and easy smile. Unlike the nonchalance he displayed in Moscow or St. Petersburg, there was a friendliness and warmth in his manner. Anna was conscious he was happy at Davinka – that it was here he felt most at home.

One evening they spoke of Olga.

'She was only four when our parents died. Olga's been searching ever since for someone who would never leave her again. That's why she can't give up on Peter Dashkovy.'

'And you?'

'I was old enough to begin cadet training. Varenka came to live here with Olga, and I returned as often as I could.'

'Tell me about your parents.'

'My father was an artist, my mother more of an academic. She wrote books on Russian history. They were good people who died too young.'

They were in sitting in the library after supper and Anna's gaze was drawn to two portraits that hung between the bookshelves. Nicholas's father had the same open expression as Varenka while his wife, with her black hair and sea-green eyes, was more enigmatic. She was the one whose grandfather was a Tatar and whom Nicholas resembled most. They could only have been in their thirties when they died. I've always taken my parents for granted, Anna thought. I can't imagine the loneliness of being an orphan. Was it then that Nicholas turned his back on love?

✿

It was their last day and Nicholas had invited Anastasia and her husband to visit. Ludmilla tried to persuade Anna to wear one of Olga's more fashionable outfits but she declined.

'I prefer my old dresses. They remind me of my friends. When I return to St. Petersburg, I shall wear them in their honour.'

Ludmilla helped her plait and pin up her hair and Anna studied herself in the glass. She was still thin, but the hungry, restless look had gone from her eyes and her face was softer. Nicholas has made me better, she thought as she went downstairs. He's shown me the person I want to be. I will always be grateful to him for that.

'We heard you were coming home. John will be distraught to have missed you.' Anastasia Marinsky stood up, greeting her with a kiss and speaking in a soft drawl. 'I declare you're the only woman he's ever truly loved!'

'And now I understand why.' Her husband's eyes twinkled as he bowed over Anna's hand.

'But we were only children. I was barely sixteen!' Anna protested.

'At that age, one loves more deeply than at any other time in life.'

Rubin Marinsky was no taller than his wife and good-looking with dark hair swept up at the sides. He had a lively expression and was as friendly as his wife was outspoken.

'It's uncommonly selfish of you to keep such a treasure to yourself, Nicolay,' Anastasia teased Nicholas. She wore a tight-fitting, blue riding habit, her hair arranged in a mass of copper curls under a hat trimmed with feathers that fluttered every time she moved her head. 'We'd have come to call before had we known Anna was here.'

'I'm sorry we're leaving tomorrow,' Nicholas replied. 'I want to arrive in St. Petersburg before the roads turn to mud and slush. I hope Anna might return to Davinka one day. I promise to give you more warning next time.'

'Nicolay's the best of friends, as long as you go along with what he wants.' Anastasia winked at Anna. 'Do you know we bought your father's beautiful Orlovs? They weren't cheap, I must say!'

'Nonsense. Take no notice of Anastasia.' Rubin's face relaxed into a smile as his gaze rested fondly on his wife. 'They're an excellent addition to our stud and we were fortunate to acquire them.'

Papa has been generous, Anna thought. The Orlovs were his pride and joy and he sold them to provide money for Sofia and the baby. I was wrong to judge him and Mama so harshly.

'Nicholas's going to explain everything that he's doing with his estate. We're keen to follow his example,' Anastasia said, drawing off her gloves and placing them on a table. 'But first you must tell us about Siberia.'

Anastasia and Anna sat down as Ludmilla poured tea and handed round sweet cakes. The sun was shining and broken rays of light came through the windows, dancing on the polished furniture.

'Siberia is primitive in many ways, but it's a land of freedom.' Nicholas spoke first. 'There are no serfs and little respect for the tsar. For all their poverty, the people are strong and self-reliant. They understand the dignity of man and value their rights. I admire them.'

Nicholas would have liked Anton, Anna thought. He represents everything that's best about Siberia. They come from different worlds but they're both strong, independent men.

'And how are your friends, Anna Ivanova?'

Anastasia's question interrupted her thoughts and Anna put down her cup.

'They're very brave, but their exile is cruel. The women bear hunger, illness and deprivation for the sake of their husbands. Instead of being rewarded for their loyalty, they're punished – degraded and stripped of their rights as citizens.' She paused, her fingers twisting in the cuff of her sleeve as she went on. 'The tsar wants to destroy all memory of the Decembrists. In the eyes of the law, their wives no longer exist.

My sister-in-law's baby will be born a serf and registered illegitimate. It's a travesty of justice and humanity.'

Anna was unaware of the effect to her words. When she finished, there was silence and she looked at Nicholas for reassurance. He said nothing but there was a glimmer of admiration in his eyes.

Ludmilla gave a stifled sob and Anna leant over and pressed her hand. 'We mustn't despair. Their sacrifice will not be forgotten. We'll fight for them until the tsar's persuaded to relent.'

'We haven't suffered as you have, but we'll help you.' Anastasia came to her feet. Her height gave her authority and all eyes turned to her. 'Please tell us what we can do. But take care, Anna Ivanova. The tsar's furious with Princess Zinaida for giving a farewell party for Maria Volkonsky. So much so, she's been obliged to leave Russia.' She gave an indignant toss of her head. 'John keeps us au courant with news from Moscow. He sells our horses to the nobility and hears all the gossip. Also, he's a friend of Michael Pavel.'

'Captain Pavel?' It was Anna's turn to be surprised. 'I didn't know. I must write and tell him I'm coming home.'

'There's no need. According to John, Captain Pavel has been informed by your parents and given leave from his regiment. He will be in St. Petersburg to welcome you home.'

'A distinguished reception committee awaits you, Anna Ivanova,' Nicholas remarked drily. 'So, what else has happened in my absence? Have they announced a date for the coronation?'

'The day is set for August. The tsar and tsarina arrived in Moscow for a preliminary visit last week.' Rubin handed his cup to Ludmilla to refill and remained standing as he sipped his tea.

He gazed thoughtfully around the room before he turned his head and looked directly at Nicholas. 'The court's a labyrinth of warring factions, and the imperial family's the worst of them all. I'm told the tsarina tries to keep the peace, but they're all at each other's throats. You know, of course, that Princess Elizaveta Romanov has separated from her husband...'

Chapter Thirty-Nine

Anna slept little that night, tossing and twisting the sheets into knots before she rose at first light. Her belongings were packed but it was too early to go downstairs and she sat by the window with her travel bag at her feet. Rubin Marinsky had meant no harm, but there was a feeling of dread in her stomach. When she looked at Nicholas, not a muscle in his face indicated that the news was of any interest to him. The conversation had moved on and he had been relaxed at dinner while she was desperate to ask about Elizaveta. The question burned on her tongue, but the opportunity never arose and she had gone to bed in a state of agitation.

The idea of Nicholas with another woman made her feel ill. Why did she mind so much? Because I love him, she thought, accepting the truth without surprise. I've loved him since we were in Moscow. I didn't let myself believe it because Peter stood in the way. I swore never to fall in love again, but Nicholas is different. He has always been there when I needed him – giving me flowers that day by the Neva, bringing Papa home from the revolution, stopping me at the ball in St. Petersburg. He didn't want me to go to Siberia because he was afraid that I'd be hurt. He's been the one watching over me. He wouldn't have gone to so much trouble unless he cared. Surely, he loves me?

For an instant Anna was so happy and her joy so intense, she felt light-headed. Then her heart fell. How many times had Nicholas told her not to trust in love – that it didn't exist? Her mind went back to the last evening she had spent with Olga and Peter in Siberia. It was then she had understood the meaning of unconditional love. To fear love is to fear life, she thought. Nicholas isn't a coward. How can I make him change his mind?

If only they could stay at Davinka longer! In five days' time, they would be in St. Petersburg. She had to find out about Elizaveta Romanov before they left. Better to hear the truth from Nicholas than be told by someone else. As Anna rallied her courage, she caught sight of herself in the glass. She looked pretty in her red coat, but the darkness in her eyes reflected the precipitous feeling inside. I promised not to hold on to him. What do I do if he doesn't want me in his life? What arguments can I use to convince him? Should I tell him I love him?

With an effort, she relaxed her face and smiled, a soft smile that spread to her eyes, driving away their shadows. I will make Nicholas love me, whether he wants to or not. There must be a way to penetrate his armour. I won't let that woman entice him back into her arms. The thought of it was unbearable. She couldn't – would not – let it happen. She tried to steady her nerves as she waited for Ludmilla before they went down for breakfast. She'd hoped Nicholas would there, but he had eaten already and was in his study.

She ate quickly, then went to find him. The door was open and she stood a moment observing his profile as he sat at his desk. Her eyes lingered on his black hair, his chiselled features and strong chin. It was a face she could see without looking and feel without touching. One day I'll paint him, and it will the best portrait I've ever done, she thought, lifting her shoulders as she walked in.

Her shadow darkened the window and Nicholas looked up. 'I'm just finishing some correspondence. I won't be long...'

Anna picked a book from the shelves and sat down. She listened to the nib of his quill scratching over paper and turned the pages slowly, waiting until he sprinkled sand over the ink and turned to look at her.

'Are you impatient to be off?'

'I'd like to talk to you, if I may.'

'So, tell me. What is it?'

Anna felt the atmosphere close in around them as Nicholas leant back in his chair. He was studying her as if knew what was coming, and she put down the book.

'Are you still close to Elizaveta Romanov?'

The collar of her jacket felt tight, scratching her neck. She wanted to loosen it but kept her hands folded on her lap.

'Elizaveta's my friend. I'm not in the habit of deserting friends when they're in trouble.'

'Is she still your mistress?'

'It would be indiscreet to answer that question.'

His unresponsive stare told Anna the conversation wasn't going to be easy. Did he have any idea how hard this was for her? Her heart tightened and her voice thinned. 'Why did she write to you?'

'She wanted my advice, which I gave her. There's no need to be jealous.'

'I'm not jealous. I'd like to have a clear understanding of the situation between us, that's all.'

'I asked you to marry me and you turned me down. There was nothing ambiguous about that.' Nicholas's tone was laconic. 'Are you saying you've changed your mind?'

A fly was buzzing against the window. Anna hadn't expected the question and was caught off guard. That she loved him wasn't enough reason for her to accept his proposal. She had to know if he loved her in return. If only he'd hold out his arms, she'd tell him what was in her heart, but Nicholas didn't move, and uncertainty formed in her mind, making her hesitant.

'Well, then?'

Nicholas was watching her with a penetrating, speculative look that made her nervous. Every word was important and she gave herself time before she answered. 'I refused your proposal because to marry without love is as base as a priest saying Mass without believing in God.'

His gaze stayed on her face but his eyelids dropped. 'You know my views on marriage. I've never pretended they're anything but pragmatic. Marriage is an accommodation that's best entered into with realistic expectations. It's a working partnership between two people who, if fortunate, are suited to one another. Nothing more.'

He was explaining why, as far as he was concerned, love didn't come into it, but Anna was only half-listening. She was thinking: I don't care what he says, he's not as detached as he pretends to be. I know from the way he holds me at night. I feel he loves me even if he can't admit it. She fumbled in her pocket for a handkerchief, crumpling it in her hand. Then she cleared her throat with a small cough. 'Surely, one should have the courage to change one's opinions sometimes?'

'It's not lack of love, but lack of friendship that makes unhappy marriages.' Nicholas spoke as if her words had no bearing on the subject. His eyebrows didn't lift and there was no mockery in his voice. His tone was as level and patient as if he were instructing a child. 'How can two people, under the influence of violent and transient passion, promise to remain in that condition until death do them part? It's an absurd idea.'

Nicholas was immovable – his strength and intellect, the qualities she admired in him, turned against her. He wasn't being stubborn for the sake of it but because he dismissed anything that had no rational explanation. There was something implacable at his core and, failing to find an answer, Anna changed tack.

'I want to know if...' She paused and felt a pulse jumping in her wrist as she clenched her fists. 'I want to know whether we'll meet in St. Petersburg or if you're still involved with someone else.'

For a moment he hesitated, as if debating whether to tell her the truth or a lie. Then he shrugged. 'We both have matters to settle in our lives, Annushka. Your family is waiting for you, and I must return to Moscow. You're welcome to come to Davinka whenever you wish.'

Whether he deliberately misinterpreted her meaning, Anna wasn't sure. Nicholas would neither admit nor deny his liaison with Elizaveta, and his evasion exasperated her. What was wrong with him? He was a generous and tender lover. Why couldn't he bring himself to say how he felt? She felt tears coming up in her throat and was afraid she might cry, but pride stiffened her and anger took over.

'You're a cold-hearted man, Nicolay Petrovitch. I don't expect you understand the meaning of fidelity—'

'Please!' Nicholas held up his hand in a gesture of restrained forbear-ance. 'Let's leave it there. There's nothing more to say on the subject.'

Did she hear regret in his voice? If so, it only served to emphasise the finality of the statement. She was aware of a clock striking the hour and came to her feet as Nicholas stood up. Her lips quivered as she tried to find some answering emotion in his eyes. She was desperate for him to say something – to give her a sign that she meant more to him than any other woman in his life. She searched his expression for the smallest hint, but there was none. She was powerless against his cool mind and locked heart.

'I'm not going to abandon you, Anna. Trust me...' He spoke slowly. 'And now we must get ready. The horses will be at the front door in an hour.'

✤

It was a tradition at Davinka to sit in silence before a journey, so they went to the kitchen and gathered at the table with heads bowed. Anna's nerves were strained to breaking point. She tried to pray but couldn't concentrate. The company rose and moved to the hall. The icon of St. Nicholas was carried through, and Galina held it over their heads, blessing them as they stood on the steps. They were all there: Stepan, looking pale, Liev and Ludmilla, farm workers, grooms and the old men from the kitchen gathered at the front door to see them off. The men wished her well and the women kissed her before Anna climbed into the sleigh and was covered with a mound of shawls and furs.

There was a second driver but Nicholas took up the reins. Accompanied by dogs and ringing bells, the graceful Orlovs trotted out through the gates and the troika headed downhill, running in a wide arc before it emerged from the trees. Then, as if sensing the freedom of the highway, the three horses fanned out in style and broke into a gallop, flashing away to the north.

Part Six

Chapter Forty

The day before had been wild and wet, but the sun was dipping in and out from behind clouds as they drove into St. Petersburg. Rivulets of water and churned up mud clogged the streets and Nicholas negotiated the troika with care. There was a rawness in the air after months of frost and Anna wrapped her fur cloak tightly around her as they made their way across the city.

How could she forget the poignancy and tumult of spring in the north? Even as the snow melted, pussy willow and apple buds were bursting into blossom. Soon it would be the turn of her favourite, the *cheryomukha* cherry, with its soft white flowers. The air smelled of the sea and, on every corner, stood women selling armfuls of bluebells, cowslips and sweet-smelling violets brought from the countryside.

Anna looked at the city as if seeing it for the first time. Suspended between sky and water, the capital gave an overwhelming sense of size and space with its long horizon and vast classical architecture. 'Peter –' she remembered how Pushkin always called the city by its first name '– we're always falling in love with Peter. It's the city of our dreams.'

Officers in full regalia crowded the streets: Chevalier Guards in white silver helmets, Cossacks in high sheepskin hats and infantrymen with bright stiff feathers in their caps. In front of the Winter Palace, the square was filled with soldiers preparing for the daily parade. The serene, beautiful city of her birth had become a military capital and the power of the tsar's army was on full display. Had St. Petersburg always been like this, she wondered as she stroked Mosca's head? The husky had come with them from Davinka, running beside the sleigh or resting inside, and she was glad of her company.

There had been no chance to talk to Nicholas during the journey. He had driven most of the way and had slept when he lay beside her. Anna felt comforted when he was close, but her heart was heavy with the weight of unspoken words. In a few hours we will go our separate ways, she thought with a drop in her stomach. How can we say goodbye, not knowing when we'll meet again?

The Neva was running fast as they crossed the Anichkov Bridge, blocks of ice breaking apart with a sound like gunfire. Anna remembered how dead and wounded men were pushed through the ice after the rebellion was crushed, and she shut her eyes with a shudder. When she opened them, figures of people moving along the quayside looked like shimmering pieces of silver dancing in the light reflected from the water. She could see the golden spire of the Admiralty; and then, they were on the Nevsky Prospekt with its colourful shop windows and bookstores, and she caught sight of her home. The gates to the courtyard were open, the front door swinging wide, as Nicholas drew rein.

Josef came out with James close behind and bowed his head. 'Welcome home, Miss Anna! Blessed be God that you've come back to us.'

He pressed the palms of his gloved hands together in prayerful gratitude and James helped Anna out. Nicholas swung himself to the ground as Mazra came running out of the house and fell on her knees.

'I'm happy to see you, Mazra – and all my dear friends.' Anna bent down, raising her maid up. 'Are the count and countess at home?'

'They're gone to watch the ceremony on the river.'

So, she had arrived home on the day that winter was officially declared over. There would be a gun salute from the fortress and fresh water from the Neva taken to the Winter Palace for the tsar to taste.

Surprised that her parents had gone to pay their respects, Anna glanced at Nicholas. 'I hope you'll come in and take refreshment. The count and countess will wish to thank you for your kindness.'

'I'd be delighted.' Nicholas unfastened his cape and gave it to James. 'May I introduce Mosca to your home?'

The rest of the household had gathered in the hall and Anna spoke to each one in turn before she went up the stairs. Nicholas, with Mosca at his heels, followed her into the drawing room and Josef brought coffee with oatmeal pasties and *pryaniki*, little cakes flavoured with honey and spices, and glasses of fresh water. '*Khristos Voskrese.* Christ is risen.' He gave the Easter greeting as he withdrew. Nicholas sat down next to Anna.

The inner frames of the windows had been removed and noises wafted in from outside – a broom sweeping snow from the balcony next door, and a boy whistling in the yard. There were flowers in vases and newspapers on the table. The house had returned to normal, but Anna felt like a stranger. This is no longer my home, she thought. I can't go back to the person I was before. I can only go forwards.

She looked at Nicholas. A dark stubble of beard emphasised the hollows of his face. A lock of his hair had fallen across his forehead and she longed to reach out and push it back. A helpless, silent sob welled up inside her.

He put down his cup. 'We must talk about your drawings. Are you sure you want me to persuade Pushkin to publish them?'

'I haven't changed my mind.'

'You know they will cause a furore. Everyone will know they're by you. No one else could have done them.'

Anna didn't want to think about the drawings now. She wanted to take hold of Nicholas's hand and cry, 'Please tell me you love me,' but the words crumbled in her throat. Instead, she heard herself say in a small voice, 'I understand the risks. No doubt I'll be ostracised by society – if not worse – but I gave Maria Volkonsky my word.'

'Then I'll visit Pushkin tomorrow.' His lips twisted in a slight smile. 'You're a woman of rare courage, Annushka.'

'Tell Monsieur Pushkin I'll bring them to him as soon as I can slip away unnoticed.'

'So, you don't intend to inform your parents?'

Before she could answer, there was a commotion in the hall below followed by the sound of footsteps coming slowly upstairs. Anna and Nicholas were on their feet before they reached the landing.

The door opened and Ivan and Valentina Brianski stood motionless under the arch. For a moment they stared at her. Then, walking stiffly and slowly, her mother came forwards and her arms locked around Anna in a tight embrace.

'My beloved daughter... Oh, my darling...' She stood back, reaching out and touching Anna's cheek. 'But you're so thin! Have you been ill?'

'I'm fine, Mama. It was a long journey, but Count Bulgarin took good care of me.'

Ivan Brianski's stooped figure shuffled towards her. There was an absent, anxious look in his eyes as he put out his hand and laid it on her shoulder in a weak grasp. 'Is it really you, *Ivitsa?*'

His head trembled a little and he blinked as he stared at her. What's happened to him? Anna wondered with a twist of fear. Has he lost his mind? Doesn't he recognise me? She saw how shrunken were the muscles that used to bulge in her father's arms, as Nicholas held out his hand. Her papa looked like an old man, gazing at him as if he were a stranger.

'I'm sorry it's taken so long to bring your daughter home to you, sir.' Nicholas's tone was relaxed despite the awkwardness of the moment. 'Anna Ivanova survived the hazards of the journey with steadfast resilience.'

'You're our saviour, Nicholas Petrovich.' Valentina spoke in a croaking, birdlike voice. 'How can we ever thank you?'

She raised a handkerchief to her eyes and fumbled in her pocket for smelling salts as she sank down on the sofa. Josef led Anna's father to a chair and helped him sit down. Her parents looked broken and far frailer than she remembered. They seemed to have lost all vitality and Anna was struck by guilt. I shouldn't have abandoned them without giving any warning. I should have written to them more often... Nicholas remained standing as she sat down and her eyes met his above her mother's head. This is why he brought me home, she thought. He knew

Mama and Papa needed me. Nicholas understands some things better than I do. Does he know I love him?

As the question formed in her mind, Josef came to the door and announced, 'Captain Michael Pavel.'

Anna stood up quickly as Michael walked in. Without pausing to speak to her parents, he strode over to her and kissed her on both cheeks. 'Thank God for this blessed day! I've been praying for your return.'

Michael's brown eyes shone, but Anna barely noticed him. She was aware Nicholas was taking leave of her parents. How could she make him stay – or at least promise to come back tomorrow? She thought of all the things she had forgotten to say – the answers she hoped to see in his eyes, even if he didn't speak the words – but suddenly there was no time.

Nicholas walked over and greeted Michael cordially. Then he took her hand and raised it to his lips. 'Goodbye, Anna Ivanova. Take good care of yourself.'

A flood of words rushed to Anna's lips. She opened her mouth to speak but there was a strangling pain in her throat and Michael Pavel answered. 'Thank you, Nicholas Petrovich. I'm very grateful for your kindness to my dearest friend.'

'The pleasure was all mine.' Nicholas smiled briefly at Michael before his gaze came back to Anna. 'Miss Brianski was an excellent travelling companion. I couldn't have asked for better.' He gave her a long searching look, as if memorising every detail of her face, then turned and sauntered towards the door. 'Come on, Mosca. It's time to go home.'

A silence fell over the room and Anna heard the sound of his boots dying away. Nicholas was walking out of her life and there was nothing she could do to stop him. He was going away from her, perhaps forever, without knowing her feelings for him. For one reckless, mad moment, she wanted to pick up her skirts and run after him. I can't just let him go, she thought frantically. I must know when he's coming back. But Michael had a hold of her arm, and she could only stand and stare blindly towards the window. Michael was speaking, but she never remembered what he said or how she responded - only the sound of bells on the troika's harness as it drove out of the gates.

'Thank God in His Mercy for bringing you back to us, darling.' Valentina signalled to Josef. 'You must be tired after your travels, Anna. Indeed, we're all quite worn out by so much happy excitement. Your papa and I will retire and meet with you later when we've had a chance to collect ourselves.'

Michael took his leave and, following her parents, Anna made her way up to her bedroom where Mazra was waiting.

'It's been terrible here without you – the house was like a morgue.'

'I'm so sorry, Mazra. I didn't realise—'

Anna stopped as her eye fell on a red jewellery box lying on the dressing table. She looked on in amazement as Mazra picked it up. She unfastened the clip and lifted out Anna's precious *zhemchuzhina* pearls. She had left them in the pawn shop in Moscow. How could they possibly be here? There was a rushing in her ears and Anna swayed on her feet as she stared at them.

'Count Bulgarin brought them with him when he visited.' She heard Mazra's voice as if from a great distance. 'I'm glad you decided to send them home. It meant we still had something of you with us. Will you wear them this evening to celebrate?'

Chapter Forty-One

Nicholas had redeemed her pearls in Moscow! He must have gone to the pawnbroker with Varenka and paid all the money. Why hadn't he told her? And why bring them here and not to Siberia? Had he been so sure of her, even then?

Anna's first days at home passed in a daze. She was disorientated and Nicholas was constantly in her thoughts. His face was the first thing she saw behind her waking eyelids, his name the last word she uttered before she went to sleep. She tried to move him to the edges of her mind, but Nicholas would not be shifted. She thought of his strong, lean body and dark head resting on her shoulder. Out of a welter of emotions – love, hurt and longing – one feeling never left her. She missed him. She missed his warmth and unusual way of looking at the world. I was too proud, she thought. I have no illusions about Nicholas. He is opinionated and uncompromising. But I love him. I should have told him.

Anna tried not to think about Elizaveta Romanov, but her pale shadow trailed across her mind. Was the princess in the south or staying at one of the royal residences at Tsarskoe Selo less than two hours' drive from St. Petersburg? Nicholas will never return to her, she told herself, but her moods fluctuated wildly. Some days she was buoyed up with hope, others cast down in despair. The house was full of ghosts, and she sensed her parents' suffering in every room. Sasha's exile was a wound that could never be healed, but Valentina tried so hard to be brave, Anna did her best to help her.

There was no mention of Colonel Renin, and Michael Pavel called almost every day. It was a relief to talk to Michael. Anna told him about Siberia and the treatment they received from General Zeidler in Irkutsk.

He didn't ask about Sofia, and she was aware of the way his gaze faltered when she mentioned her name. Something in Michael had changed, but everything was different these days. They were all haunted by sorrow and she was wise enough to tread carefully.

Most of her time was spent with her parents, reading or playing cards with her father and guiding him when he became confused. Every day after breakfast, Anna related the story of her arrival in Nerchinsk. She told them of their first meeting Sasha, playing down conditions in prison and the hardship endured by the women. She spoke of Maria's piano-playing, Katyusha learning to cook and Sofia's proficiency in medicine. Their first grandchild was due when the climate in Siberia was at its best and Anna described the countryside as she imagined it in summer. When she spoke of the friendship between the women and the consolation they gave to their husbands, the hint of a smile touched Ivan Brianski's face.

'It was good of you to go, *Ivitsa*. You made them happy. You have a gift for happiness.'

Her father appeared a little better, but time dragged in Nicholas's absence, and she was desperate to get her drawings to Alexander Pushkin. She sent him a message and received no reply. Pushkin's work was under the direct censorship of tsar. Had he accompanied the court to Moscow? It seemed unlikely but she couldn't enquire without arousing suspicion.

Anna went for excursions with her mother, sometimes shopping in the Nevsky Prospekt. The streets were crowded with people in Easter dress — women in black jackets with red sleeves and skirts. Older men had white linen bands wrapped around their legs and youths wore bright belts around their waists and shining top boots. Valentina offered to buy her new clothes, but Anna told her it wasn't necessary.

'You're not in Siberia now,' her mother protested.

Anna smiled but took no notice. They were upstairs and a blackbird was singing outside the window. It was the best of times to be in St. Petersburg: golden oriels were making their nests and the scent of lilac drifted up from the streets.

'When did Papa become ill?' she asked.

'He suffered a seizure shortly after he sold his horses. Omelko found him unconscious in the stables. Doctor Simeon hopes in time he'll recover his faculties – especially now that you're home.'

'Poor Papa. Does he understand how much the money will help when the baby's born?'

'I've told him, but he forgets everything. Tell him again, darling. It comforts us both to hear of Sasha and his family.'

Valentina's luxuriant hair was elegantly dressed, her delicate hands clasped in the lap of her lavender morning gown. A look of anguish crossed her face as she spoke of her son and Anna laid her hand on hers.

'I'd like to paint a picture of you and Papa together. I want it to be a portrait we can send to Sasha and Sofia. We could even start this afternoon...'

'How very kind, darling.' Valentina released a long, pent-up sigh. 'Only, Princess Galitzine's invited us to go for a drive with her today. It does your father good to get out of the house. Can we sit for you another day?'

✿

Anna waved her parents off and watched until the phaeton disappeared into the traffic. She had pencils and paper with her and went upstairs to the drawing room. She hadn't drawn in weeks and would make a start by sketching the Easter tree for Sofia. Moving the vase with its birch branches and painted eggs to a table by the window, she stood back to study the composition.

She was vaguely aware of carriage wheels on the gravel outside but took no notice. Whoever it was, she had left instructions not to be disturbed and went on drawing until she heard the door opening behind her. As Anna swung round, Boris Renin walked in, clicked his heels and made a stiff bow.

Her eyebrows drew together in a scowl as she stared at him, her pencil poised in mid-air.

'I saved your footman the trouble and showed myself up,' Renin said and closed the door. His was in uniform and his sabre made a slapping sound against his boots as he walked towards her.

'What on earth are you doing here?' Anna put down the pencil and folded her arms across her chest.

'I gather the count and countess have gone for a drive with Princess Galitzine.' Renin's lips smiled but his eyes did not. 'I hoped for an opportunity to speak with you on your own. May I sit down?'

Boris Renin obviously knew everything that went on in the city. He even had the audacity to keep her poor parents under surveillance. How dare he call upon on her uninvited and when she was alone? She was tempted to ring for Josef and ask him to show him out. But Mama will come to hear of it, she thought. I don't want to cause her further distress. With an irritated sigh, she gestured to a chair and sat down on the sofa as far away from him as she could.

Renin was dressed in a colonel's uniform and looked pleased with himself. He reminded Anna of a thin, sharp-faced rodent as his eyes slid around the room.

'My mother didn't say you were to visit today.'

'I came to bring a message from His Imperial Majesty. I'm here on behalf of the tsar to welcome you home to St. Petersburg.'

Did he really expect her to believe him? Boris Renin might be in favour with the tsar, but he was here on his own account, of that she was sure. What did he want? Momentary panic flashed through her. Had he found out about the drawings? Of course not! Her sketchbook was hidden in the wardrobe upstairs. No one knew of its existence except herself, Pushkin and Nicholas.

'I hope you've recovered from the journey.' Renin placed a monocle in his right eye and it caught the light in a disconcerting way. 'It must have been an arduous expedition.'

'I'm grateful to Count Bulgarin for escorting me home.'

'Indeed. He served our purpose well. So, tell me how his pretty sister's getting on in the land of oblivion.'

'Miss Bulgarin's in good health. She's happy to be with her friends,' Anna replied tersely.

'And the other princesses? Are they happy, too?' He wrinkled his nose as if he'd inhaled a bad smell. 'Does Nerchinsk offer the pleasures and comforts of St. Petersburg?'

When she did not answer, Renin raised his voice. 'Are they happy with their chosen lot?'

'They're good, brave women and are content enough. Their fidelity and sacrifice is to be admired for they've committed no crime.'

'Do you really think so?' Renin removed his monocle as he stood up and walked across the room. He took a seat next to her, leisurely removing his gloves and laying them on the sofa between them. 'His Imperial Majesty was disappointed in you running off and causing distress to your parents. It was for their sake, as much as for your own, that I pleaded your cause with the tsar.'

Did Renin want her to go down on her knees and grovel in gratitude? He was as conceited as he was repugnant and Anna sniffed, not deigning to reply.

'I gather you made a detour to the Bulgarin country estate on your way.'

How had he found out? Anna knew Renin ran a network of spies but she couldn't believe there were any at Davinka. Still, she was on the alert.

'We were attacked by bandits. The count's coachman needed medical attention.'

'I'm interested in your new friend Count Bulgarin.' Renin let the statement linger and his face took on an expression of absorbed interest. 'He was a protégé of Emperor Alexander yet fraternised with many of the traitors. There's no evidence he was involved in the revolution, but he's known to have expounded radical views in the past. Is Nicholas Bulgarin a true tsarist at heart?'

'I'm sure he's a loyal subject and respects the tsar – as we all do.' To Anna's relief, her words came out with more assurance than she felt.

'I'm glad to hear it, my dear. And now to the main purpose of my visit. I spoke to your father some time ago. We must decide upon a date for the announcement of our betrothal.'

'What are you talking about? We're not betrothed and never shall be!'

'Don't pretend to be naive, Anna Ivanova.' Boris Renin looked down and polished the nails of one hand on his cuff. 'You're aware that my intervention with the tsar was dependant on your accepting my proposal of marriage.'

'I'm aware no such thing,' Anna said with ice in her voice. 'Had I been, I would have remained in Siberia.'

Renin's lips tightened and the muscles of his neck bulged above his tight collar as he swallowed. Annoyance briefly furrowed his brow but was gone the next minute. Slowly, with his eyes on hers, he lifted her hand and pressed it to his lips. His white gloves lay on the seat like a spare hand and Anna stared at them, feeling the skin crawl at the back of her neck.

'But, my dear girl, I've already spoken to your father.'

'Have you indeed? And why not my mother?'

'It's customary to ask the father for his daughter's hand. Count Brianski will have told your mother of our conversation.'

Anna felt a squirm of nausea in her throat. She snatched her hand free and stood up. 'You know that my father's not well. He's in no state to agree to any kind of contract. How dare you bully an ill—'

'Control yourself, Anna.' Renin did not raise his voice but his words cracked like a whip. 'If Count Brianski's not well enough to give his consent, then I shall ask the countess.'

'You will be wasting your time. I'll tell her—' the words 'I detest you' were on her lips, but she bit them back.

'You may inform Countess Brianski I'll call again before the end of the week. I look forward to a more favourable reception then – that is if you want to protect your friends from further harm.'

As Renin came to his feet, Anna shuffled backwards, grinding her palms together as she struggled to hold her temper. 'Are you blackmailing me, sir?'

'I'm reminding you of the extent of my influence.' There was a sly look in Boris Renin's eyes. 'You should count your blessings, Anna Ivanova. Most young women would be honoured to receive a proposal from the rising star of the Imperial Court.'

But not many who stand to inherit a small fortune, Anna thought. You want my father's money, and the only way you can get it is by marrying me. She almost shouted these words aloud but forced herself to answer coolly. 'That may be so – however, you and I have nothing more to say to each other, Colonel Renin. I bid you good day.'

'I've not finished my business with you, Miss Brianski.' Boris Renin walked towards the door, following her step by step. 'And I expect you to keep a civilised tongue in your head in future. Petersburg society demands refinement and courtesy, not the vulgarities of a prison camp.'

'Get out!'

Anna tried to open the door with her hand behind her back. Her fingers were on the handle but slippery with sweat and she couldn't make it turn. Renin wasn't a tall man, but he seemed to tower over her. His face was so close she could see beads of perspiration on his forehead and saliva on his lips. He was going to try and kiss her, and she flinched, letting out a small cry as he took hold of her chin. The next moment the door opened, and James was at her side.

'Colonel Renin is leaving. Please would you show him out?'

She spoke coldly although she was hot with rage, and Boris Renin released her without a word. He strode over to the sofa, picked up his gloves, then turned on his heel and marched out of the room. His boots and spurs rattled on the stone stairs as he went down. She heard James offer to help him to his carriage but there was no answer. The front door shut, and he was gone.

Nerchinsk. April

Darling Anna

Your letter arrived yesterday and my joy on receiving it is indescribable. I am so happy the journey passed without mishap and that you found Count Bulgarin's company amenable. By now you will be in St. Petersburg and my relief is mixed with envy. How are your parents and how do you spend your days? Are you painting? I do hope so. Has the ice broken on the Neva?

Please tell me everything for I am starved of news. Maria has letters from her sisters, but I've heard nothing from my family. I wrote to Michael but received no reply. I expect he's with his regiment and I wonder if my letters ever reached him? When you see him, please scold him for his negligence and tell him to write at once! Sasha is well and Captain Dashkovy is walking with one stick, which is no less than a miracle. Thanks to the beneficial ministrations of our friends, I am blossoming. They treat me as if I'm the only woman alive who's ever been with child! Rest assured that I am safe in their kind and capable hands.

You are so very far away and I miss you, dearest Anna, but how delighted your dear father and mother must be to have you at home. Please send them my love and gratitude. I pray every day that you will find the happiness you deserve.

With deepest love, Sofia

Chapter Forty-Two

Just after eight o'clock the next morning, Anna alighted from a droshky near the Moika Embankment. She had left the house by the tradesmen's door, passing the stables where the air smelled of horses and hay. The grooms were in the tack room and she pulled her hood low over her face until she came to the street where she hailed a cab.

Whenever she thought of the meeting with Boris Renin, she was overcome by revulsion. She had been too outspoken and antagonised him. Heaven alone knew what he might do! The sooner her drawings were safely in Pushkin's hands the better. There had been no word from Nicholas so she had to find out for herself if the poet was in the city. The sketchbook in its leather folder was tucked under her arm and Pushkin's address in her pocket.

The Neva was as blue as the sea, and street vendors trading briskly in *pirozhki* and roasted chestnuts. There was still too much ice in the river for merchant ships to come upstream but the quayside was busy. Horse-drawn carts were being loaded with water casks as bleary-eyed soldiers headed back to barracks after a night of gambling.

Anna kept to the opposite side of the street, walking past dark-ended houses until she came to a canal leading off the embankment. Here she slowed down. It was quieter away from the river and, crossing a narrow bridge, she stopped beneath the arched entrance of a courtyard. Pushkin had rented lodgings in Moika Street. The numbers twelve and fourteen were painted above the doorway. His apartment was on the second floor and Anna looked up to see the shutters firmly closed. The poet was either asleep or not at home.

A woman pushing a cart of woven twigs went past and Anna heard the clatter of horseshoes behind her. Looking over her shoulder, she saw a curricle coming down the street. The driver wore a black hat with a low brim and was handling two frisky chestnuts. She couldn't see his face, but the man was the same build as Nicholas, and she stood staring after him until the curricle turned the corner.

Nicholas couldn't have gone to Moscow and returned already. Besides, he drove grey Orlovs, not Russian dons, Anna thought, wiping a hand across her eyes. Boris Renin's visit had frightened her and her mind was playing tricks. I must hold my nerve, she thought. The meeting with Pushkin is too important. Renin won't make a move yet. He'll bide his time and hope to persuade Mama to give her permission. I have to think of a way to protect Sasha and Sofia – all of them – before turning him down.

Anna clambered up the two flights of steps and was panting by the time she reached the second floor. She stood a moment outside the apartment to catch her breath. Then, pulling back the hood of her cloak, she lifted the brass knocker on the door. There was no response. A black cat jumped off the wall and ran down the stairs. She raised the knocker again. At last, there came a sound of heaving and grating on the inside as a heavy object was moved. The door opened and a sleepy-looking young man with fair hair stood before her.

'Please can you tell Monsieur Pushkin that Anna Brianski is here? He's expecting me.'

'Monsieur Pushkin's not up yet, ma'am. Come in, if you want to. But he'll not rouse himself.'

The chest used to block the door was manoeuvred to one side and Anna wiped the mud off her boots on an iron scraper before stepping into a dimly lit room.

'Sit yourself down, ma'am. I'm Pierre, his valet.'

Pierre opened the shutters to let daylight into a low-ceilinged apartment that smelled of sandalwood and sweet tobacco. The walls were faded gold, the curtains made of red velvet, and the room furnished with a couple of chairs and a table covered with sheets of manuscript. Every shelf overflowed with books. Pushkin was a fluent linguist and Anna saw titles in French, English, Italian, German and Russian. On one wall hung a heavy oak-framed mirror above two unopened crates marked *Chateau Lafite* and *Veuve Clicquot*.

Moving aside a tallow candle that was burned to the wick, she sat down at the table.

'He's been writing all night,' Pierre said to excuse the disarray as he tidied away ink-stained blotting paper and broken quills.

'What time does he usually get up?'

'Some days the master's at work before dawn – others he stays in bed until noon. I never know unless there's something urgent to attend to...'

'I have pressing business with Monsieur Pushkin. Please can you tell him that I'm here?'

Pierre shuffled his feet and Anna persisted. 'I'll take full responsibility for disturbing him. I can assure you he'll be pleased to see me.'

When Pierre went through to the second room, Anna opened her folder and took out her sketchbook, placing it on the table alongside Pushkin's scribbled verse. Unable to resist, she picked up a piece of paper lying beside the large ink pot. The poet wrote in a fast forward hand. There were whole lines scratched out in black ink, and in the margins were exquisite profile sketches of men and women. His skill as a draughtsman astonished her. There were silhouettes and caricatures on every page; even one of himself wearing a bolivar hat with his hero Onegin.

Anna was so absorbed that she lost track of time until a door opened and Alexander Pushkin swept into the room. Dressed in a long silk dressing gown, his dynamic, diminutive figure struck her with the same force as the first time she had set eyes on him. He was like an exotic bird – his expressive face, vitality and energy seemed to absorb all the air in the room.

'My dear Miss Brianski! I've been waiting for you.' His laughing blue eyes looked at her boldly. 'Young ladies rarely step outside without a chaperone in this city. Did you come alone?'

A smile hovered on his lips and Anna held out her hand. 'Quite alone. I believe Count Bulgarin explained the purpose of my visit.'

'Bulgarin and I discussed the matter at length.' Pushkin kissed her hand andhis expression became serious. 'He tells me the images are painful to behold. I am steeled in readiness.'

He stood at her shoulder as Anna began to turn the pages. The drawings were more powerful than she remembered. The dignity and suffering of her friends were so intense, it hurt her to look at them. How could she have drawn such tragic images of people she loved?

They came to the portrait of Maria, and Pushkin rested one hand on the page. 'My beautiful Maria. I pray for the day freedom warms her with its light. My heart, I believe, was once dear to her...'

'I made the drawings at Maria's behest. She was my inspiration.'

'Then we shall put her on the cover. I'm going to have them printed in book form and suggest the title should be *Visions of Hell*. Do you agree?'

Anna nodded. 'Who will publish them?'

'No editor in Russia will touch such material.' Pushkin' s fleeting glance moved from the drawings to Anna's face. 'We'll print and publish them ourselves. Your drawings are a powerful call to arms, Miss Brianski. We must be certain to leave no evidence of your identity.'

'But people will know... All the circumstances point to me.'

'Even so, both the drawings and the woodcuts from which we'll print must be destroyed. Count Bulgarin was most insistent. He paid for six hundred copies to be printed and distributed but refuses to endanger your reputation further.' Pushkin's gaze fixed on a point over Anna's shoulder and his foot began tapping on the wooden floor. 'The revolution was a pebble dropped into a pond – a few ripples and then silence. These pictures could create a tidal wave that will engulf our country. The fate of the Decembrists and their wives will become legendary throughout Russia.'

He stepped away and blew his nose, then turned on his heel and clapped his hands. 'Pierre, where are you? Forgive my inhospitality,

Miss Brianski. I was too distracted to offer you sustenance. Pierre, please bring us coffee and vodka immediately.'

Anna was familiar with his quicksilver moods and her eyes followed him as he began to pace the room, his lower lip jutting out and his hands clasped behind his back. She wondered what dark thoughts were on his mind. Finally, after a long silence, he spoke.

'I should have been with the rebels in Senate Square, but they refused to allow me into their ranks. They called me a gossip who couldn't be trusted with their secrets, yet my verses were found among the possessions of all those condemned.'

As he stopped pacing and stood still, Anna caught his reflection in the wall mirror. Pushkin wasn't handsome in a conventional way but possessed a powerful magnetic appeal. He could be witty and caustic, but his attraction came from the openness and depth of his feelings. He had been hurt by the Decembrists and their failure to trust him. So, *that* was the cause of the argument at Kamenka all those years ago, she thought. And the confrontation had been provoked by Peter Dashkovy.

'Strange are the ways of God.' Pushkin's expression lightened. 'While our friends languish in Siberia, I'm in [Petersburg], imprisoned in the tsar's pocket. I wasn't born to provide for his imperial amusement, yet can only write under his protection.'

Pierre came in and Anna cleared a space for the tray. The boy poured out coffee and glasses of vodka.

When he withdrew, the poet sat down opposite, studying her with a curious stare. 'So, are you going to marry Nicholas Bulgarin?'

Anna almost dropped her cup. She put it down and thought before she answered. 'He proposed to me and I refused. Nicholas Bulgarin doesn't believe in love.'

'Or so he says...' Pushkin chafed his hands together. 'Why else did he invest so much time and effort in bringing you home? Do you love him – or have I misjudged the situation?'

'You're not wrong...' Anna said, taking a breath as she forced the words out. She was embarrassed and yet it was a relief to speak openly at last. 'However, he's involved with someone else.'

Pushkin asked with a little yawn, 'The Romanov princess?'

Anna nodded and felt colour flood her cheeks. She might have said more, but Pushkin's hands began to move over the table, gathering up pieces of paper.

'Those kinds of liaisons are no more than a defence against boredom. Passion with its wayward tricks always brings pain, but to feel true love is what it means to be alive. Count Bulgarin may be guided by reason but he's not without sentiment.'

'How do you know?'

'Because I observe the vicissitudes of human nature. As we grow older, we come to understand that love has no boundaries. It's uncontrollable, a madness that never ceases to torment us until we acknowledge its existence in our souls.'

Pushkin broke off, staring at the window. He wasn't yet thirty, Anna thought, and so full of life and creativity, yet his brilliance was shot through with melancholy. Was he still in love with Maria? After a moment, he turned back and looked at her, drumming his fingers on the table as though keeping time with a tune in his head.

'But whom to love?
To trust and treasure?
Who won't betray us in the end?
And who'll be kind enough to measure
Our words and deeds as we intend?'

He smiled. 'You're young and beautiful, Anna Ivanova. Don't wait until it's too late. If you love Nicholas Bulgarin, then you must tell him so.'

✻

Pierre was sent to find a droshky and, as they drove home, Anna tried to fix in her mind everything that Pushkin had said. His words had cut into her heart, but the poet didn't know Nicholas as she did. He told me to trust him, she thought. I must believe he'll come back. If I let myself think otherwise, I will lose courage.

Arriving at the house, Anna ran upstairs to her room and changed from her walking habit into a house robe. Mazra told her she had visitors who were in the drawing room with the countess. As Josef opened the door and ushered her in, Anna saw her mother talking to Rubin and Anastasia Marinsky.

Rubin Marinsky came to his feet and his wife embraced her.

'I was telling the countess how we met again at Davinka.' Anastasia was dressed in a green coat with a tiny hat perched on top of her head.

'I didn't know you had visited Count Bulgarin's home...' Valentina sounded perplexed.

'We stayed for just a few days, Mama. Count Bulgarin wanted to rest his horses,' Anna replied calmly, turning to the guests. 'I'm so pleased to see you. What brings you to St. Petersburg?'

'The Marinskys have returned your father's beloved Orlovs!' Valentina put in before they could answer. 'They refuse to let us pay them back. I am overwhelmed by such generosity.'

'We're aware of your family's tragedy...' Rubin Marinsky began before Anastasia caught his eye and took over.

'Anna told us about your son and daughter-in-law. We wish to support them and the others in any way we can. It's the least we can do.'

'Those brave women deserve to be applauded,' her husband stated in his calm, sure way. 'How many wives would abandon security and comfort to live in exile with their husbands?'

'Well, it's the kindest thing I ever heard.' Anna smiled at him. 'Thank you from the depths of my heart. Papa will be delighted. I'll go and tell Omelko right away.'

'There's no need,' Valentina interposed. 'The horses are already in the stables. Your friends brought them here this morning. I'll take your father to see them later. How can we express our gratitude?'

'We'd be honoured if Anna could accompany us to the ballet next week,' Anastasia replied. 'Please allow her to come with us, Countess Brianski? I will act as her chaperone.'

Valentina gave her approval and Anna went to the door to say goodbye to the Marinskys. She longed to ask for news of Nicholas. Had they seen him in Moscow? Did they know when he might return to St. Petersburg? By a supreme effort of will, she stopped herself, turning her head away as they left.

Her mother was quiet after their departure, and she went to sit close by her.

'What are you thinking, Mama?'

'I'm worried about your father. He may not understand.'

'Oh, but he'll recognise his Orlovs, I'm sure of it! They'll make him happy.'

'But we only want Sasha and Sofia back...' Valentina gave a sob. Her face crumpled and Anna put her arm around her, feeling the bones of her shoulders.

'Darling Mama. I'm here...' she whispered, pressing herself to her and kissing her cheek. 'Papa will get better. We must have faith.'

'Yes ... have faith.' Valentina clung to her daughter's hand. She closed her eyes, then opened them. 'Anna, you do love me, don't you?' she said in a whisper. 'Tell me the truth. Will I ever see Sasha again? Will we die not knowing our grandchild?'

Anna looked at her, her eyes filling with tears. 'I love you, darling Mama. And God is merciful. I believe you will see your grandson and be reunited with Sasha. We must never give up hope.'

Chapter Forty-Three

In the days and nights that followed, an encroaching sense of dread preyed on Anna. As far as she knew, Boris Renin hadn't visited the house again. Could he have changed his mind and withdrawn his proposal? She wondered if Valentina had heard from him. Surely, her mother would have said something? She was burdened enough with worrying about Papa, so Anna refrained from asking her. It occurred to her Renin might have had her followed to Pushkin's apartment. She would have noticed, Anna told herself. But where was Nicholas, for heaven's sake?

The longer she waited, the tighter her nerves were stretched and, after a night of fretful sleep, Anna rose early. She was in the library, looking for a book, when James came to the door.

'Captain Pavel's here to see you, ma'am. I've taken him to the drawing room.'

Anna smiled as she followed James across the landing, a smile that left her face as she walked into the room.

Michael was standing with his back to the door and turned round as she came in. The grim look in his eyes stopped her on the threshold, stilling the words of welcome on her lips.

'I'm sure you know why I'm here.'

'I'm glad to see you, dear Michael—'

'I'm told *Visions of Hell* has been sent to every prominent household in the city!'

'I don't understand.' Anna advanced hesitantly towards him.

'Please don't feign ignorance. I know you did those drawings.'

'Have you seen them?'

'I don't need to see them! They're all everyone's talking about this morning. How could you be so cruel?'

Anna sat down abruptly, and Michael strode the length of the drawing room before he came back to stand in front of her. 'What gives you the right to portray my sister's humiliation to all the world?'

For an instant Anna wondered if she had heard him right. She pinched the bridge of her nose between forefinger and thumb, then took a deep breath. 'Sofia approved of the drawings. She agrees with Maria Volkonsky. The tsar must be held to account.'

'Princess Volkonsky doesn't know what's best for her husband.'

'That's not true!' Anna cried, stung by the attack. 'Maria understands perfectly well—'

Michael cut across her. 'Have you thought of the pain these images will cause the families of the traitors?'

A torrent of thoughts rushed through Anna's mind. Of course, Michael didn't support the Decembrists, but he had always been loyal to his sister. He couldn't abandon Sofia now! He had the gaunt, shadowed expression of a man gnawed by hidden pain. She wanted to take his hand and comfort him, but his voice kept her at a distance.

'The only way we can survive is by trying to forget. My parents can't bear to think of Sofia and the disgrace your brother inflicted on our family!'

'And you? Will you banish Sofia from your life, too?' Anna's lips whitened with anger. 'Sofia loves you. Besides, I thought Sasha was your friend.'

'Last December changed everything.' Michael's voice was dark and hollow. 'The Russian empire is held together by the tsar and his army. Those who seek to destroy the established order deserve to be punished. A Third Division's been set up in the military to eradicate all Decembrist sympathisers. The lines have been drawn. There's no going back now.'

'So why are you here?' Anna said sharply.

'To make sure that you denounce the drawings. The tsar will never forgive the Decembrists for bloodying the first day of his reign. Any exhibition of public support only serves to harden his resolve.'

For a time, she was silent. Then she squared her shoulders and lifted her chin.

'Thank you for telling me, Michael Yurievich. I'm sorry, but I can't help you. Please would you be kind enough to show yourself out?'

Michael's face was taut but he said nothing. Tipping his head to her, he stalked out of the room.

The moment the door closed, Anna went over to the bureau. Michael was Sofia's beloved brother. How could he turn against her? Her drawings had been published and Pushkin must have informed Nicholas. He knew the prints were in circulation. Surely, he had returned to the city by now?

With a shaking hand, she took out a piece of paper, dipped a quill in ink and wrote quickly.

Dear Nicholas,
I need to speak to you urgently.
Please come as soon as you receive this.

Anna

*

Anna paced the floor of the hall as she waited for the Marinskys to collect her for the ballet. It was warm for early May and she wore a dress of blue muslin with a gathered skirt and white sash. Mazra had pinned her hair high to show off the pearls gleaming around her neck, but the reflection of her face in the glass was pale and strained. She had sent Omelko with the note to Sadovaya Street and waited all afternoon for his return. When he came back with the news that Count Bulgarin had been in St. Petersburg the last two days, Anna almost exploded. Why hadn't he come to see her?

As the Marinsky barouche drew up at the Bolshoi Kamenny Theatre, she tried to put the conversation with Michael out of her mind. There had been no mention of anything untoward during the ride. She was strung tight as a wire but she wouldn't let her mood ruin the evening.

Rubin Marinsky alighted first and they passed through a foyer crowded with programme-sellers and theatre-goers before making their way upstairs to the circle. The sound of music could be heard as they approached the first tier, becoming louder as an attendant slipped before them and opened the door to their box. The orchestra was tuning up as they entered the brightly lit amphitheatre. Anna went to the front of the box with Anastasia, smoothing her skirts as she sat down and looked around.

The walls were decorated crimson and gold, the boxes luxurious and adorned with white and pink medallions. Dominating everything was the Imperial Box, two storeys high and surmounted by an enormous double eagle. It was empty, thank God. The tsar and his entourage had stayed away and Anna felt a glimmer of relief.

The theatre was packed with men in evening dress and ladies with bare shoulders, their heads coiffed and bejewelled. Below them in the stalls, soldiers stood about as dandies in swallow-tail coats wandered up and down the aisles scrutinising the beau monde; all of them waiting until the last minute to take their seats. As her gaze passed over the audience, Anna had the uncomfortable feeling of hundreds of eyes looking at her. She felt colour creep into her cheeks and opened her fan, holding it in front of her face.

'The young bucks are here to search for pretty girls and to be admired.' Anastasia remarked casually. 'They don't care two hoots about ballet.'

A door creaked and the steps of belated arrivals were heard as a woman and two gentlemen entered the adjoining box. Then the conductor came to his stand in the orchestra pit, lifted his baton and the overture began. Anna's arm, bare above the elbow, rested on the velvet rail, her hand opening and closing in time with the music, until the curtain rose and all eyes turned to the performance.

The stage consisted of smooth boards with a background of trees and the dancers moved in flowing arcs. Sometimes, the whole corps de ballet was on the stage; sometimes only one or two. The ballerinas wore loose skirts that reached just below the knee to show off their footwork on points. Their movements appeared effortless, but Anna heard ragged breaths and the soft thud of shoes as they strained to keep time with the music. The audience stayed silent until the music stopped and then burst into enthusiastic applause. Those in the stalls shouted and clapped, hurling bouquets of flowers on the stage and the prima ballerinas came out for curtain calls.

'I see our friend's here. He must have arrived late.' Anastasia hand touched Anna's elbow.

Anna looked to a box on the opposite side of the stage and saw Varenka Bulgarin sitting at the front. She was wearing a green headdress and next to her was a petite, red-haired lady. Anna caught sight of Nicholas's dark head sitting behind them. There was a woman beside him, partially obscured by the side of the box. Anna could see only her slender arms in long black gloves. She willed Nicholas to look at her but it was Varenka who noticed her first. She lifted her arm to wave and Nicholas leant forwards. When he saw Anna, he nodded and smiled. She inclined her head in acknowledgement as apprehension rippled through her. Who was his companion? Surely, it couldn't be Elizaveta Romanov? She might be a royal princess, but she wouldn't have the gall to appear in public – and certainly not with Nicholas!

The next scene was underway, but Anna could not keep her eyes on the stage. More than once, she stole a glance over the rows of pomaded heads to the Bulgarin box. Nicholas sat with one arm thrown casually across the back of a chair and seemed oblivious to anything else. A pain tightened in her chest and, when the curtain came down for the interval, she lowered her gaze to the stalls. It was then she caught sight of Boris Renin. He was wearing dress uniform with an imperial sash and walked down the aisle with a swagger to stand with his back to the orchestra pit. He was in full view of everyone and a group of young men thronged around him. They were joined by Michael Pavel and Anna saw him greet Boris Renin with a handshake. Were they now good friends? Would Michael betray her?

Despite the hum of conversation and the sounds of people enjoying themselves, Anna was so tense she began chewing the thumb of her glove. Boris Renin was surveying the audience through opera glasses and, when he looked up to the circle boxes, she quickly turned to speak to Anastasia. Friends of the Marinskys came to their box and champagne was served. A handsome young Hussar engaged Anastasia in conversation, obviously entranced, and Anna was introduced to a general and his wife. They were polite but it was an effort to exchange pleasantries and she was relieved when the interval came to an end.

'Duport's on next,' Rubin informed her as he studied the programme. 'He's the best dancer in the world – a Frenchman with the soul of a Russian.'

The maestro returned and people in the stalls took their seats for the second act. Deport was strong and young with finely toned muscles. He circled the floor in a series of thrilling leaps, splitting his legs wide and landing on one foot. There were yells of 'bravo!' from the galleries and he stopped, smiling and bowing to all sides. He waited until the audience quietened before he began again, spinning in circles and performing high jumps, his calves crossing like scissors in the air. The crowded theatre was spellbound. Looking towards the Bulgarin box, Anna noticed Nicholas had disappeared.

The violins were playing an entrée to the next scene when a draft of cool air came into the box. Anna knew it was Nicholas. She felt his closeness like heat and heard him speaking to Rubin in a low voice. Then his hand touched her shoulder and Rubin took her place as she went to stand out of sight of the audience.

It was too dark to see his face as he leant down and his lips brushed her forehead.

'I received your note. What's happened?'

'Why wasn't I informed the drawings had been published?'

'Pushkin and I decided the less you knew the better.'

'Well, you were wrong!' Anna answered in a fierce whisper. 'Michael Pavel believes I betrayed Sofia. He says they'll make everything worse.'

'Does he know they're by you?'

'Of course he does! Michael's no fool. And Boris Renin's the very devil! He tried to blackmail me to force me to accept his proposal of marriage. I told you he's dangerous. Where have you been all this time?'

'I was unavoidably delayed in Moscow.'

'And the last two days?'

'With Monsieur Pushkin, organising the distribution of the prints.'

'Damn you, Nicolay! You should have told me.'

Anna's voice rose in pitch and Nicholas's arm went round her, pulling her to him. She stood against him with her head down, longing for him to take her back under his protection and felt his hands on her shoulders.

'Don't let Michael Pavel make you lose confidence. I've told Rubin to wait here until I collect you. I'll come as soon as I've seen Varenka and her party off in the carriage.'

Nicholas tidied stray wisps of her hair into place and gave her hand a gentle squeeze before the door closed behind him. Anna hardly remembered the final act. She stayed where she was, fiddling with a programme, tearing it into shreds and dropping the pieces on the floor. Nicholas hoped to reassure her, but what if they had made a terrible mistake? Closing her eyes, she pictured Maria's face and resolute expression, and her mind changed pace. I won't let them down, she thought. St. Petersburg society may pretend nothing has changed, but my drawings will ruffle their complacency. They'll be all over the city by now and seen by hundreds of people. Everyone will know of the tsar's betrayal and cruelty.

The ballet ended and the curtain came down to a standing ovation. As the clapping died away, there was the sound of people talking and shuffling feet, and Anastasia demanded. 'Will one of you please tell me what's going on? What was Nicolay doing creeping into our box like that? Why didn't he come during the interval?'

'He wants us to wait here and leave with him,' Rubin responded. 'It's only a precaution. I'm sure there's nothing to worry about.'

He made a fuss of collecting their cloaks, but neither Anna nor Anastasia was convinced. Rubin tried to talk about the ballet but gave up against their silence. Anna nervously touched her pearls. She had meant to thank Nicholas for redeeming them but had forgotten in the suspense of the moment. She could hear seats being lifted and the musicians packing up their instruments in the orchestra pit. The theatre was almost deserted, but they seemed to wait forever until there was a soft tap on the door.

With his cloak thrown back over one shoulder, Nicholas escorted Anna, his arm steady beneath her hand, as they walked down the passage. A young attendant carrying empty champagne bottles came out of a box and shot her a suspicious glance, which she ignored. Nicholas said nothing and appeared calm until they came to the top of the staircase. There he stopped.

Below them, a crowd of people stood in the foyer as ushers called for their carriages. Michael was by the door and Boris Renin standing at the bottom the steps. He was blocking their way and there was a hush as all heads turned in her direction. By the time Anna realised what was going to happen, it was too late. Boris Renin raised his arm and pointed straight at her.

'Voilà, Mademoiselle Anna Brianski!' He delivered the line in a loud, theatrical tone. 'Here is the author of those scurrilous drawings, the Decembrist hussy who earns her keep by glorifying the enemies of our beloved tsar!'

Chapter Forty-Four

For a timeless moment the world stopped. No one moved or spoke. Anna glanced at Nicholas. He was frowning and his face had a hard steeliness about it. She wondered what he was going to do as he left her flanked by Anastasia and Rubin and loped down the steps until he was on the same level as Boris Renin.

'Withdraw your insult, Major Renin, or I shall demand satisfaction.'

'You're aware that duels are outlawed. I'm a loyal servant of the tsar and obey his laws.'

'I don't care whose servant you are,' Nicholas retorted in a biting drawl. 'You will apologise or we shall engage.'

He was a head taller than Boris Renin and held a glove in one hand. Anna felt her heart skittering in her chest. Nicholas regarded duelling as senseless – a medieval relic of barbarity that solved nothing – but, if he slapped Renin now, there could be no other outcome. The side of Renin's face twitched as Nicholas raised his hand. Then Michael Pavel shouldered his way between the two men, pushing them apart. Fellow officers followed and Anna saw Michael talking to Renin, speaking in his ear. Nicholas stood with his arms folded as people moved closer, trying to hear what was being said, until Renin shook off Michael's restraining hand and pulled himself up to his full height.

'I've nothing against you, Nicholas Petrovich. I refuse your challenge. If I have been misinformed, then I apologise.'

He clicked his heels with a bow and held out his hand to Nicholas who did not move.

'You will apologise to Miss Brianski for your malicious slander.'

Boris Renin hesitated, looking uncertainly first at Michael and then up at Anna. She glared at him, the hatred on her eyes so fierce he almost seemed to quail. Then his mouth twisted in a distorted smile. 'I beg your forgiveness, ma'am. It seems that I spoke out of turn.'

His tone was laced with sarcasm. He turned on his heel and Anna's breath came back with a shudder. Michael had persuaded Renin to back down. Had he lied in order to protect her? He'd been so angry this morning, she was bewildered by his turnabout. But a duel had been prevented. To her dazed mind, the crowd seemed to ebb away, voices fading as they went out into the night. Anastasia peered at her anxiously and Rubin gave them both an arm as they made their way down to Nicholas.

He took hold of her hand and Anna whispered,' 'Please stay with me.'

'I'm sorry but I must speak to Captain Pavel. Anastasia and Rubin will escort you home. The blackguard's apologised — that's all that matters. I'll call on you first thing in the morning.'

He could talk to Michael tomorrow, for heaven's sake! Anna stared at his face, waiting for him to yield, but his expression was rigid. Was this his way of telling her she was no longer his responsibility? If so, why not come out and say it? He promised he wouldn't abandon me, she thought bitterly. Now he thinks he's done his duty by challenging Renin and can hand me over to his friends. A final spark of outrage kindled inside her and she threw off his arm. Picking up the front of her dress she walked out of the theatre alone and settled herself in the dark interior of the carriage beside Anastasia.

Rubin Marinsky sat opposite with his back to the driver and Anna dug her fingers into the leather upholstery. Renin might have apologised, but the incident couldn't be hushed up. He had insulted her in public and all of St. Petersburg would hear of it by the morning. What must Rubin and Anastasia be thinking? She couldn't begin to explain. Nicholas should be here to tell them, she thought, dashing away a tear with her knuckle.

'Boris Renin's a toad,' Rubin announced emphatically. 'I'm almost sorry he retracted. I'd liked to have seen him shot.'

'Hush, darling! No one takes any notice of him. He's a second-rate troublemaker, not worth the cost of a bullet.'

The horses' shoes clip-clopped on the cobbles and the occupants of the carriage fell silent. It was a clear, bright night with a full moon and Anna stared sightlessly out of the window. They had crossed the river and were heading along the quays when the carriage stopped suddenly, the horses pulled up so violently that Rubin was thrown to the floor. The next moment the door was flung open and a man in a hood and mask pointed a gun at Anastasia's head. Another heavyweight stood behind him, also masked and armed.

'Keep still with your hands behind your back,' he ordered, using his boot to nudge Rubin onto his stomach. 'Don't try anything or you're dead. Which one of you is Miss Brianski?'

'I am,' Anastasia answered at once, her expression as cool as her voice. 'What's your business with me?'

'Your presence is requested by order of the Commandant of Third Division.'

For an instant Anna was too stunned to react. Then Rubin twisted his head and looked desperately at his wife. 'Anastasia! Don't be so foolish...'

'*I* am Miss Brianski, the person you want. This has nothing to do with them!' Anna raised her voice as she pushed past Anastasia. She glimpsed the ivory handle of a pistol in her friend's hand and hissed under her breath, 'Put it away.'

The gun disappeared into folds of Anastasia's cape and rough hands grasped hold of Anna, hauling her out. A rug was thrown over her head and she heard the command to the coachman to drive on. The carriage door slammed, and the wheels creaked as it moved off. Instinctively, she went limp as the men dragged her between them and she was bundled into another vehicle. She heard them talking among themselves and, when they stopped, she was lifted out, carried down a flight of steps and manhandled onto a chair.

The foul-smelling rug was removed and her eyes watered in the light. They were in a small cellar-like room with oil lamps burning in brackets on the walls. They must be close to the river for she could hear fast-running water. Apart from a table and two chairs, there was no other furniture.

What was it Michael said about the new Third Military Division? If only she had paid more attention this morning! Anna tried to gather her wits as she used her glove to wipe the grime off her face and mouth.

'You're to be interviewed by the boss.' The broad-shouldered man leered at her, whistling through missing front teeth. 'Been a naughty girl, have you?'

There was a sound of nailed boots on stone as two soldiers entered the room and he was dismissed. The older man wore a general's uniform and the younger, the red and green jacket of the Guards.

'I apologise for the unorthodox methods of your apprehension.' The general sat down opposite Anna. He spoke with a German accent, his voice slightly slurred as though he had been drinking, and Anna stared at him in shocked recognition.

'Rest assured your friends are unharmed,' the former governor of Irkutsk went on. 'I refrained from calling at your home so as not to alarm your parents. I've been transferred to the Third Military Division.'

Anna's eyes moved over him, taking in the new uniform and gold epaulettes. General Zeidler's moustache was waxed, his hair oiled and his pale blue eyes as hard as she remembered. He had tidied himself up, but there were broken blood vessels on his nose and his cheeks were sallow and flaccid. She felt a pricking of fear and concentrated on the details of his appearance to keep hold on reality. .

'I'm in charge of families related to the traitors,' the general continued. 'It's been brought to my attention that you remain close to the criminals and have recently been acting on their behalf.'

The young captain handed over a booklet, which Zeidler placed on the table in front of Anna. It was larger than she'd expected – foolscap size with the portrait of Maria on the front under the title *VISIONS FROM HELL*. The general licked his thumb to turn the pages and Anna saw each one was edged with a border of black. Pushkin had done well but she dared not think of him in case her face gave her away. An icy stillness descended over her manner, disguising the chaos inside.

'You're an artist, Miss Brianski, are you not?' The general leant forwards and she smelled brandy on his breath. 'I believe you're responsible for this pernicious work?'

Zeidler looked straight at her and Anna looked straight back. 'There are a great many artists in St. Petersburg. Do you suspect them all?'

'It can't be a coincidence such propaganda should appear within weeks of your return from Siberia.'

He paused, but Anna did not answer. Putting her elbows on the table, she rested her chin on her hands, her attitude conveying an impression of impatient irritation.

'Did you create these despicable images?' Zeidler voice was louder as he lifted the book and held it close to her.

'We're not in Irkutsk now, sir,' she answered coldly. 'I'm a free citizen of St. Petersburg and demand to be released immediately.'

'Who are your accomplices?' Zeidler ignored her statement. 'Someone must have helped you get them printed and circulated...'

Zeidler wanted a confession, but he had no proof and Anna met his gaze unwaveringly. 'I believe you've been misled, sir. I've never seen these drawings before.'

'You have a history of lying. I recall you travelled to Siberia under false papers.'

He paused, expecting an answer, but Anna shot him a look of disdain and was silent. He softened his voice as he altered tactics. 'It's late, Miss Brianski. You must be tired. The sooner you give me the names of your collaborators, the sooner you'll be allowed to go home.'

'As you know, enforced interrogation without evidence is against the law. I have influential friends in this city, sir. It would be a pity to lose your new position so soon.'

Anna's words left a void and there was silence, the change in the atmosphere like a drop in temperature. The captain stood to attention and Zeidler's eyes flickered briefly. She felt his body craning in tension, the younger man also, and heard the crackle of his breath. The general seemed to hesitate. Then he picked up the book and stood.

'We will make further enquiries and speak to you again. Captain Fedorov will escort you home where you will remain until you hear from us. Good evening, Miss Brianski.'

Chapter Forty-Five

Zeidler left the door open. Anna drew her cape about her and followed Captain Fedorov out of the room. She felt something brush against her ankle as a rat scuttled out of sight and they made their way up a narrow staircase to the street. They came out on an embankment and the captain hailed a passing droshky. He gave her a hand to get in and was about to join her when a figure stepped out of the shadows.

'You may leave us, captain. I'll escort Mademoiselle Brianski home, thank you.'

Boris Renin walked purposefully towards them and Anna felt her blood run cold.

'But General Zeidler asked me to take her home,' the young officer protested mildly.

Renin waved him away. 'I explained to him that Miss Brianski and I are betrothed. The general thought it more fitting that I should escort her.' Renin took his place in the droshky. 'Run along, old chap. You're off duty. Go and have a drink.'

'Don't listen to him, captain! We're not—'

She was silenced as Boris Renin grasped her wrist, twisting it painfully. Captain Fedorov touched his cap and strode off. His lanky figure disappeared into the night and Anna tried to control her fear. Boris Renin was a parasite who lived on the blood of others. He wouldn't dare do her any harm but she did not underestimate him. Panic sharpened her senses and she was as keen-witted as she had been in her life. All her instincts told her to play for time, but they had only been on the cab a few minutes when Renin ordered the driver to stop, gave him a tip, and insisted they alight.

The driver muttered a curse as the droshky trotted off. Renin's lips parted in a humourless smile. 'I'll walk you home from here. We need to talk, my dear.'

'I can't walk in these shoes...' Anna's voice died as Renin took her arm, forcing her to go with him.

On the other side of the street, lamps sent wavering shadows gliding along the walls. Windows were open and people awake but the sound of the river was too loud for anyone to hear them. She was alone with Boris Renin. God knew what he had in mind! Rubin and Anastasia would have gone to find help by now, she thought frantically. They would be searching for her. But how would they know where to begin? She could be anywhere in the city.

'You've miscalculated badly.' Renin raised his voice above the roar of water. 'Don't think you can make a fool of me and get away with it.'

'I'm shocked you think so badly of me.' Anna kept her voice as steady as she could. 'How dare you make such a terrible allegation?'

'Don't try to fool me, Anna Ivanova. Count Bulgarin's not here to defend you now.' For a moment Anna lost concentration and Renin sensed his advantage. 'Where did he go, I wonder – to spend the night with his Romanov mistress?'

They had stopped beneath a lamppost and Anna shut her mind to his words. She saw the rapid movement of his eyelids and drops of spittle at the corners of his mouth. His expression was cruel and agitated so that he almost looked unhinged.

'My mother's waiting for me, Boris.' For the first time, she called him by his given name. 'I should have been back hours ago.'

'I'll take you home when you've given me what I want.' With a sudden swift movement, his arm encircled her waist. 'You've ruined your chances of making a good marriage, but I won't be disappointed.'

She must get away from him! But where could she run? Her thoughts were in her eyes and Renin leant on her with a suddenness that made her shrink back. He was half-smothering her with the weight of his body, his face above hers, his eyes narrow and flinty.

'Once I'm through with you, I'll get the original drawings, even if my men have to tear your home apart.'

'It won't do you any good. They're all in my head! 'Anna shouted at him. 'I can recreate them whenever I want. You'll never destroy them.'

Renin's expression contorted in fury. His lips drew back, baring his gums, and Anna thought he meant to pick her up and throw her in the river. For an instant she imagined the flash of her blue dress vanishing in the current.

'Everyone heard you at the theatre. They'll know it was you who kidnapped me—'

'On the contrary, you're under the surveillance of the Third Division. General Zeidler's responsible for your welfare.'

Renin made a grab for her, and Anna lashed out with her fists with a force that made her knuckles wrench. She punched him in the face and saw blood spurt from his lip. She tried to hit him again, but he caught her arms, pushing her backwards until her spine was pressed against the embankment wall. Later, much later, she would remember the assault in terrifying flashes, distorted by its ferocity. Renin had one hand around her throat, half-strangling her, the other at the neckline of her dress. There was a ripping noise as the muslin was torn open from neck to waist. He was fumbling between her breasts, and horror made her scream, a high, unnatural scream that pierced the clear night air. As his hand went over her mouth, she bit his fingers savagely and screamed again.

'Damn you, filthy bitch!' he swore, using his knee between her thighs to force her legs apart. Maddened with fear, Anna clawed at his face and he slapped her hard across the cheek. 'It's time you learned—'

Whatever he was going to say was lost in an explosion of gunfire. There were more shots and Renin leapt back. He let her go, bending double and staggering as he began to walk away. After a few paces, Anna saw him stumble. The air was thick with gun smoke, but she sensed shadowy figures gathering to her right. Boris Renin was kneeling with his head bowed. Then, as if in slow motion, he pulled himself up and turned towards her.

'Stop!' Anna heard Nicholas shout as he hurled himself forwards. From the corner of her eye, she saw a belch of red flame seconds before the bullet smashed into her leg. White-hot pain tore through her flesh and she crumpled to the ground.

Nicholas was kneeling beside her, his hands under her arms and lifting her into a sitting position. With curiosity she noticed a large inky stain on her skirt and wondered if it was blood. Someone covered her with a cloak, and she thought she made out Michael's voice, then Nicholas's.

'Over here! Be quick about it!'

Something hard was pressed on her leg and a muffled scream came from her throat.

'We have to stop the bleeding, Anna. There's a carriage on its way. We'll get you to a doctor as soon as we can.'

She tried to protest but her jaws wouldn't open to speak. Darkness crept across her vision. There was a whirring in her ears. Her bones were dissolving. She closed her eyes and random thoughts filled her head ... dancers in the ballet ... beautiful music. Nicholas had been at the theatre. He had left her to be with Elizaveta. Her heart seemed to fold within her, the pain as intense as the pain in her leg. She was so tired ... so tired...

'Open your eyes, Anna! Don't lose consciousness.'

'Why?' Anna forced her lips to form the question, not knowing if she spoke or not.

She opened her eyes a fraction and saw Nicholas's tense face.

'If you fall asleep, you may never wake up...'

But she didn't want to wake up. She wanted to sleep and dream of the ballet. They were hurting her, strong arms lifting her up and carrying her, her head dropping over Nicholas's shoulder like a child. Why couldn't he leave her alone? She was pressed against him as the carriage rattled over the cobbles, every bump and lurch making her groan and whimper.

'Please, Annushka! You must stay awake.'

'Why?' she asked again. This time there was no sound.

'Concentrate on what I'm saying. You were right about Boris Renin.' Anna tried to turn her head towards the voice but her muscles refused to respond. Her body no longer belonged to her; only her ears functioned.

'I needed Michael Pavel's help to have him investigated. I was with Pavel when Rubin and Anastasia came. Thank God we found you.'

Anna's eyes moved beneath their lids, but they were too heavy to open.

'Hold on. Don't leave me...'

An invisible force was dragging her down and Anna heard him as if from under the water. She was floating on a warm, calm sea. This was how she had felt when she was a little girl. Nanya used to sing to her until she was almost asleep. Nanya was with her now and she was slipping into unconsciousness. In a moment, blessed sleep would envelope her. Then someone took Nanya's place. His voice was close to her – so close that she felt his breath moving over her face.

'I won't let you die, *lyubimaya*. Do you hear me? I'm not going to lose you...'

Chapter Forty-Six

Anna opened her eyes in a room she did not recognise. The curtains were half-drawn and, in the corner opposite the door, red candles illuminated an icon of the Virgin Mary. She could smell chamomile and burnt pastilles. She was lying on a high feather bed.

Where was she? Fever had swallowed memory and her mind was hazy. She recalled Nicholas talking to her, forcing her to stay awake and carrying her in his arms. There had been someone else with him — a man with a thin face and black coat. She remembered the bitter taste of laudanum on her tongue and Nicholas's hands holding her down. Then only darkness and pain.

She must have been delirious, for she dreamt that Nicholas had stayed with her. She had opened her eyes and seen him reading by the light of a candle beside the bed. She wanted him to hold her but, when her dry lips hoarsely whispered his name, it was Varenka who answered.

'I'm here with you, dear. Rest now...'

If she was thirsty, Varenka held a glass to her lips as she sipped iced water. It was Varenka's capable hands that changed dressings and held cold compresses to her burning head. Now the fever had gone at last, and Anna knew she was in the Bulgarin home.

Varenka came in and opened the curtains. 'Good morning. How are you feeling?'

'I'm better, thank you.' Anna winced at the pain in her thigh as she propped herself up. 'How long have I been here?'

'You came three nights ago and have been delirious ever since. The doctor says it's the shock of the injury. He assures me there's no infection.'

'What happened? I can't remember clearly.'

Varenka was matter-of-fact. 'You were shot by Colonel Renin.' She walked over to the bed and lifted Anna's wrist, checking her pulse. 'The bullet hit you in the leg. Nicholas brought you here.'

'Was Michael Pavel there, too?'

'Yes. But no one else was hurt.'

Anna sank back against the pillows as Varenka explained how Nicholas had brought her home while Michael Pavel scoured the city for a doctor. She had lost so much blood she was in danger of falling into a mortal coma. By the sheer effort of his will, Nicholas had forced her to stay awake. Somehow, he had kept her conscious until the doctor arrived.

'Doctor Saloman is the most eminent surgeon in Russia,' Varenka stated proudly. 'Fortunately, the bullet missed the main artery. He was able to extract it without too much difficulty.'

Anna learned that the Marinskys and Alexander Pushkin had called yesterday and her parents the day before. They had sat with her while she was asleep and would take her home as soon as she was well enough to be moved. She did not mention to Varenka that in her delirium she had been sure Nicholas was close to her. Where was he now that she was awake? She needed him — to hear his voice and feel the comfort of him close by.

Varenka removed the strips wrapped round her leg and examined the wound. 'It's healing well.' There was a large black bruise and a livid scar halfway up her thigh. The warm water and vinegar stung, and Anna gritted her teeth as Varenka soaked dressings in honey then rebandaged it.

'I'm afraid it will be very sore for a few days, but there's no permanent damage. Hopefully we can get you up and walking today. It's important to start moving.'

'You've been so good to me, dear Varenka. And Nicholas, too. I would like to thank him.'

'All in good time, my dear. Nicholas left St. Petersburg yesterday. He has important business to attend to in Tsarskoe Selo. We're expecting him home this evening or tomorrow.'

✻

Anna sat at a table in her bedroom, picking at the supper tray that Varenka sent up, before she set it aside. She was too weak to get dressed and wore a peignoir with a shawl around her shoulders. The door was ajar and she strained her ears for the sound of Nicholas's return, but the house was quiet. The clock on the mantelpiece struck eight. Why hadn't he come back? Was he was staying the night at Tsarskoe Selo with Elizaveta Romanov?

The warm glow of earlier went from Anna's heart. Love wasn't Nicholas's province; but for all his cynicism, she had let herself believe he cared for her. Useless to argue now that she had reason to do so. If she were stronger, she would ride out to the palace and confront him, but she was too weak. She could barely walk around the bedroom, let alone get on a horse.

'Plenty of rest and calm and you'll recover sooner,' Varenka instructed. 'I'll come up later and help you to bed.'

How could she stay calm when Nicholas was with Elizaveta? Anna remembered the ball and the expression on his face as he looked at his mistress. She remembered the first time she had seen them together. It was here, in this house. Dear God, he had brought Elizaveta to his home – possibly to this very bedroom! She had been a fool, a stupid silly fool, to imagine that he loved her. How could she be so conceited as to think he felt differently about her than any other woman he had taken to his bed? Anna felt a tear roll down her cheek. I can't stay here. I must get away before he comes back. I'll send a message to Mama tomorrow and beg her take me home.

She took a gulp of wine and gagged, splattering drops on the front of her chemise. Her head was throbbing and there were shooting pains

314

in her leg. If she wasn't careful, the fever would return. She rubbed at her temples and tried to think logically. The fact Nicholas had gone to Tsarskoe Selo wasn't conclusive. Princess Elizaveta might be in Moscow. It was possible he'd gone there for a different reason entirely.

It was still light outside and a warm breeze stirred the air. In an attempt to distract herself, she picked up a pack of cards and began to lay out a game of Patience Sofia had taught her in Siberia. She placed the four aces at the top, with seven cards beneath and began to turn over the cards on the deck. When she came to the knave of spades, she stopped. Nicholas had been the knave of spades at Kamenka. She had won him twice on that fateful evening. He had meant nothing to her then... I don't care if he saved my life, she thought hopelessly. He's selfish and unfeeling. I never want to see him again.

Misery and hurt filled her until the urge to do something violent was irresistible. She clenched her knuckles and, with a lunge of her arm, swept the cards and glass of wine onto the floor.

'Heavens above! Has the invalid gone berserk?'

Nicholas walked through the door and Anna flinched in surprise. She noticed he was wearing a clean shirt and trousers. He had taken time to wash and change out of his riding clothes. He looked tired but his eyes were alert.

'What's the matter, Annushka?'

'It was an accident...'

'Of course, it was. You wouldn't spill my best wine deliberately.' Nicholas bent down to retrieve the empty glass and gather up the cards. 'Varenka tells me you're better. You must be, if you're hurling glasses round the room.'

If he was going to taunt her, she wouldn't stand for it, but Nicholas looked serious. He wasn't teasing.

'Where have you been all day?' Anna heard the accusation in her tone.

'I went to Tsarskoe Selo to visit the Lyceum. I was meeting prospective candidates for Natasha's school. One or two were very promising.'

The Lyceum at Tsarskoe Selo was the most prestigious school in Russia and an obvious place to recruit teachers. If only she could be sure! She wanted to believe him, but doubt must have shown in her eyes.

'If you're wondering whether I've been with Elizaveta, the answer is no,' Nicholas said quietly and firmly. 'I haven't seen her in months. The last I heard, she was going to stay with Zinaida Volkonsky in Italy.'

Anna drew a short, sharp breath. Nicholas had always been able to read her mind. There were times he seemed to know what she was thinking even before she did. Hitherto, she had resented it. Now, despite her transparency, her heart rose.

'Is the pain very bad, *lyubimaya*?' Nicholas used the term of endearment as only he could, soothing and gentle. 'Can I do anything to help?'

Anna looked at him tentatively. 'Varenka told me Boris Renin's been arrested. I can't remember much after I was shot.'

'When you were kidnapped, the Marinskys had the presence of mind to drive straight to barracks. I was with Captain Pavel. He knew at once Renin was behind it.'

'But it was the Third Division who took me. General Zeidler, of all people—'

'General Zeidler was acting under instructions. He was meant to put the fear of God into you, so you'd be more amenable for Boris Renin.'

'Zeidler couldn't frighten a mouse.'

'I agree, but you were right about Renin, and I should have believed you.' Nicholas sat down in the chair next to her. 'It was only when the Marinskys arrived that we realised you were in serious danger.'

'How did you know where to find me?'

'Intuition or providence, I had a hunch he'd take you to the river. The Marinskys went down one side, Michael and I the other. It was my fault he assaulted you. I am more sorry than you will ever know.' Nicholas stopped for a moment, frowning. Then he asked, 'Do you want more wine?'

Anna shook her head and he poured a glass of water, which he placed in front of her.

'Renin's been charged with assault and attempted murder. There'll be a court-martial and Michael Pavel will testify against him. He'll be locked away for years. Whether we fall by ambition or violence, like diamonds we're all cut with our own dust. He'll never come near you again, I promise.'

'And Michael? Is he still angry with me?'

'I showed him your drawings and he's beginning to understand. He's promised to help us in any way he can.'

And Michael will be reconciled with his sister, Anna thought. Thank God. Sofia's sacrificed so much already. I couldn't bear for him to break her heart.

'Michael Pavel's a good man.' Nicholas paused. 'He loves you.'

'What makes you think that?'

'Because he was so distraught he wouldn't leave the house until the doctor assured him you were out of danger. I've never seen anyone so desperate.'

He spoke without mockery or sarcasm, but Anna didn't want to think about Michael. She changed the subject. 'Why were you delayed for so long in Moscow?'

'I had a letter from Olga to give to the tsar. It took a week before I was granted an audience. When he finally received me, he was preparing for a ball, drinking champagne with his valet in attendance. He leant me precisely ten minutes of his time.'

'Did he agree to her request. Can she marry Peter?'

'We'll have to wait and see... I told him, if he wants to prevent the Decembrists being turned into saints, he needs to appoint a decent commandant and get rid of Bernashev.'

'And why should he listen to you?'

Looking at Nicholas's handsome face, Anna saw none of the scepticism she knew so well. Behind their steady gaze, his eyes held an uncertainty and keenness that was unusual, before he looked down and ran his hands over his knees.

'Because he still loves my sister.'

'And what about you, Nicolay Petrovich? Do you love me?'

The question that had tormented her for so long came out of its own volition. If Nicholas refused to answer, she would know he didn't love her, and she would never ask him again. She hardly dared breathe as she waited. For a long time, he was silent.

Then he lifted his head. 'Since we left Davinka, there hasn't been a moment I haven't thought about you, not a night when you weren't in my dreams. If you knew the flames that burned and how hard I tried to beat them down with reason.'

Anna gazed at him, her eyes growing wider. His expression surprised her. Nicholas had the look of someone caught by an emotion he found almost incomprehensible. In that moment, she felt she could see right into him, deep into the depths he had always kept closed against her. There could be no going back from this moment, not for either of them.

Taking her hand, he began exploring the palm with the tip of his finger, his voice soft and vibrant. 'When I saw you at Kamenka, I knew you were different from anyone I'd ever met.' You were incapable of subterfuge or pretence, always true to yourself. I fell in love with your blazing honesty.'

'Is that why you kissed me in Moscow?'

'I kissed you because you're beautiful and I didn't want you to go to Siberia. You broke into my heart and infiltrated my soul, Annushka. I didn't think it was possible.'

Anna picked up the glass of water, emptying it to the bottom. Nicholas wasn't saying all this to make her feel better. He spoke lightly but he meant every word. Why hadn't he told her at Davinka?

'I had to wait until you were home and no longer under my protection. I didn't want you to love me out of gratitude and dependency.' He answered her unspoken question. 'When Michael Pavel arrived at your house, I could tell you were fond of him...'

'Michael is like my brother. I'm fond of him but I've never been in love with anyone except—'

'Except Peter Dashkovy?'

'No! I never loved him. That was just an illusion. I love you, Nicolay Petrovich. Only you! Why didn't you say something?'

'I offered you my hand in marriage and was too proud to be rejected more than once.' Nicholas slipped off his chair and knelt in front of her. 'But, when I thought you might die that night at the river, I knew I couldn't live without you. I can't forgive myself for letting that man hurt you...' His voice cracked.

Anna leant forwards and took his face in her hands. Nicholas was admitting feelings that had been long suppressed since boyhood, she could tell. He was only fourteen when his parents died, little more than a child when he became head of the family. Varenka had done her best, but he was the one who had cared for Olga. He had had to make himself strong and independent. She understood his aloofness and self-reliance, the discipline that held him back. To say he loved her was an act of faith, contradicting all that he professed to believe. She had thought his strength made him invincible and his pride callous, but she recognised now they were a defence against hurt. For the first time, she understood him completely – his determination that no one should pierce his armour, the barriers he put up and the struggle he must have gone through to resolve the conflict within himself.

An hour ago, she had thought she had lost him forever. Now, suddenly, she felt something she hadn't experienced for a long time – a rush of joy bubbling up inside her.

'Why don't you ask me again, Nicolay?'

'Do I stand a better chance this time?'

Anna smiled.

'Will you marry me, Anna Ivanova?'

'Do you promise you will always love me?'

'I promise.'

'And my parents? Will you help me take care of them?'

'We'll be close to them here. And we'll invite them to Davinka for the summer. It will do Count Brianski a world of good.'

The countryside and tranquillity of Davinka would make her father better, Anna thought. And Valentina would be happy there. She imagined her reading in the garden, her father riding out with Nicholas to visit the Marinsky stud, his unsolicited advice welcomed by Anastasia and Rubin. Her parents would be surrounded by people who understood their suffering and would find consolation in their company.

'Please make up your mind.' Nicholas took her hand and lifted it to his lips. 'Or are there more conditions?'

'No! I mean yes! Yes, I will marry you! I should have accepted the first time and saved us both a lot of trouble.'

'Maybe neither of us were ready. You needed to be with your family, and I had to make myself stop fighting so hard not to love you.'

'You only learn to love by being loved...'Anna had read that in some book, but she couldn't remember where. Nicholas loved her! He wanted her as his wife. He had loved her for longer than she knew. She felt as if a calm hand had touched and soothed her spirit. Nicholas would be with her for the rest of her life. He would never leave her.

'I'll visit your parents tomorrow and formally ask Count Brianski for your hand. Will he give his permission, do you think?' A smile creased the corners of his eyes as he came to his feet.

'You'd better ask Mama first. Goodness, what shall we say to Varenka?'

'I told her of my intentions when you were ill. Varenka wasn't sure you'd have me and will be delighted. I think she's enjoyed seeing me on the rack for love...' He glanced at the clock. 'She suggested I help you to bed this evening.'

Anna leant on Nicholas as she limped across the room. When she put her weight on her foot, pain lanced through her leg and he locked one arm around her waist and lifted her carefully onto the bed. He pulled up the coverlet, then fetched a basin with warm water and towels. As she washed, he unpinned her hair, lifting the heavy tresses, and kissed her bare shoulder. He gently stroked her back until the pain left her. She turned and lifted her lips to his. Her fingers combed through his thick hair, then circled his neck, holding his head down with his mouth on hers.

It was almost dark, the last of the light rippling over the bed as Nicholas lay down beside her. He held her close and kissed her, then drew back and laid his hand against her cheek.

There were seabirds flying over the Neva, their cries rising and falling before night set in, and Anna closed her eyes. There was no need for words. Nicholas knew what was in her heart and mind. He is my safety and my inspiration, she thought. I love him and he truly loves me. Once we are married, we'll make the journey to Siberia together to see Sofia and Sasha, Maria and Olga. With Nicholas by my side, I will go on fighting until they're allowed to come home. I will never give up. One day, they'll be free. One day, everyone shall be free. And we will be together again.

Historical Note

I first heard of the Decembrists on a delegation to Russia when I visited the Decembrist Museum and was given to hold the chains worn by the prisoners in Siberia. Some had been made into ornaments, worn as badges of honour by their wives; others left as they were. It was an unforgettable experience, and I knew from that moment I must write their story.

At the beginning of the nineteenth century, Russia was a vast empire ruled by the tsar with no political opposition or limits to his power. Almost half of the population were bonded serfs owned by the landowners. They had no rights and were treated little better than slaves. In the summer of 1812, Napoleon invaded, reaching Moscow to find the city set on fire by the Russians. He waited in vain for the tsar to sue for peace before finally setting out on his disastrous retreat in midwinter. Bonaparte's defeat and subsequent abdication were a triumph for Alexander I, but the last decade of the tsar's reign was overshadowed by growing disappointment among liberals at his failure to abolish serfdom and establish basic human rights.

The Decembrists were a group of charismatic, idealistic young officers who had accompanied the tsar to Paris after Napoleon's retreat. They had visited countries where serfdom had been swept away and monarchies had granted constitutions that acknowledged the rule of law. Influenced by western liberal ideas, they returned to Russia determined to change society, put an end to bondage and constrain the autocratic government of the tsar.

The rebel daughters came from the highest echelons of Russian society. They loved their families but had the courage and determinatio to go against them and share the fate of their exiled husbands in Siberia. Their actions were a triumph of love, bravery and humanity. It was they who ensured the ideals of the Decembrists were kept alive until serfdom was finally abolished in 1861. This book is dedicated to them in the bicentenary year of the revolution.

Author's Note and Acknowledgments

Although this is a work of fiction, I relied on contemporary accounts to imagine the world of the Decembrists two hundred years ago. The events described in the book are historically accurate but, for the sake of the narrative, I have shortened the timeline between the revolution and the departure of the Decembrists for Siberia. Of the many books I read for my research, I owe a great debt to Christine Sutherland for her biography of Maria Volkonsky, *The Princess of Siberia*, and to the writings of Alexander Pushkin, especially his lyric poem, *Eugene Onegin*.

I am immensely grateful to Genevieve Pegg, publisher at HarperNorth, for her brilliant editorial skill and suggestions, to Diana Beaumont, the best of literary agents; also, to my daughter Catherine who helped me with the final proof copy. And a huge thank you to all the team at HarperNorth for your contribution in preparing the book for publication.